TUMBLETICK & COMPANY

A Chronicle of Umiat and Kenai

by

Elliot Symonds

authorHOUSE®

AuthorHouse™ UK Ltd.
500 Avebury Boulevard
Central Milton Keynes, MK9 2BE
www.authorhouse.co.uk
Phone: 08001974150

First published by AuthorHouse 1/14/2008

ISBN: 978-1-4343-1500-7 (sc)

Printed in the United States of America
Bloomington, Indiana

This book is printed on acid-free paper.

For Edward and William,
may you have many excellent adventures together.

To my darling wife, maybe now you will read it.

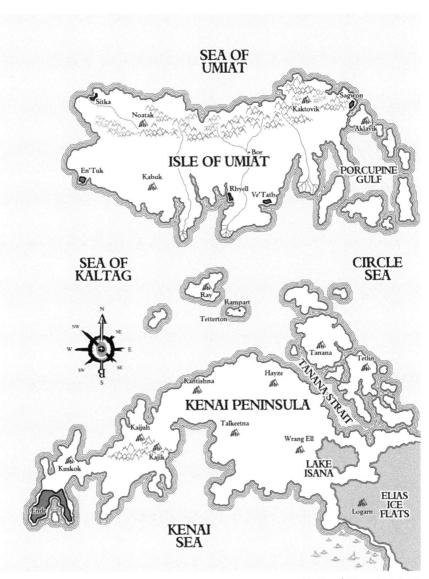

SEA OF
UMIAT

Sitka
Noatak
Kaktovik
Sagwon
Aklavik

Bor
ISLE OF UMIAT

En'Tuk
Kabuk
PORCUPINE
GULF

Rhyell
Ve'Tath

SEA OF
KALTAG

CIRCLE
SEA

Ray
Rampart
Tetterton

N
NW
NE
W
E
SW
SE
S

Tanana
Tetlin

Hayze
Kantishna
TANANA STRAIT

KENAI PENINSULA

Kaijuh
Talkeetna
Wrang Ell
Kajik
LAKE
ISANA

Kuskok
ELIAS
ICE
FLATS
Logarn

Ende

KENAI
SEA

BOOK ONE

TUMBLETICK WON

Chapter Zeroth

Tumbletick lived in the middle of an ancient copse, invisible to the Northfolk who dwelled around him.

His tiny wooden hut only had one room, no windows and barely a door, for it hung on one hinge and always let in a bullying draft. So he slept within a pile of leaves and bracken to keep warm.

It was for these reasons that Tumbletick found it difficult to keep up his appearance. He was an incredibly hairy, hunchbacked and deformed man of about five feet tall. His original hair colour was difficult to discern seeing as how he was now so dirty. His lopsided face, which was an unnatural, pasty white, was perpetually smudged and smeared with grime that covered his heavily lidded bulging eyes, protruding nose and permanently twisted, sneering lips.

The hut in which he resided had been built for him by his only two friends, Egremont the Lord Seau du Duvet and Is-Is. The reason the hut was so badly built was that neither Egremont or Is-Is had any skill whatsoever in building huts. Mainly because they had never even built as much as a shed before but secondarily because Egremont was a large wolfhound and Is-Is a huge hare. They were also trained warriors, not builders. The reason they had ramshackled Tumbletick's hut together and not hired some builders, whom they could easily have afforded, was that the location of Tumbletick's abode had to be kept secret.

Tumbletick was the ugliest and poorest man in the world and that suited him perfectly. He waited, quietly dozing, under the leaves and bracken of his bed for his friends Egremont and Is-Is to arrive.

Chorus Zeroth

An extract from 'A Geopolitical Treatise on Umiat and Kenai': by Hal Kearsley.

'The two great continents of Umiat and Kenai face each other across the imposing bodies of water known as The Sea of Kaltag and The Circle Sea. These natural frontiers have not only kept the two peoples apart but allowed jealousies to fester and grow on both sides.

Umiat, blessed by flatter lands, is rich in agriculture. Its clement weather and regular rainfall has allowed for a large population to develop and the arts to flourish. The land is fortunate to have eight types of cereal crop grow easily and in abundance. These crops provide vast amounts of calories for the human and animal populations to thrive on. The indigenous animal life is tame, pliant for working in the fields and produces mountains of meat and milk. How fortunate for the people of Umiat when they started to colonise the land that the animals they found bred easily, could be yoked and provided the food.

Kenai is mountainous, rough and rich in minerals and ore. Its weather matches the landscape. Torrid rain falls and ice fields dominate large sections of the land. The animal life is huge and fierce. Most are heavily toothed or tusked and hide out in the crags to ambush weary travellers. The people are hardened too and pursue trapping and mining as trades. The capital city of Ende imports most of the lands food and exports gems, metals, wood, furs and political dogma. It has however grown vast and powerful over the years with this trade and its port is the largest and busiest in the known world. The tip of Kenai is really the only area upon which building is easy on the peninsular so it is fortunate that a large natural harbour is also found there. From this port the natural commodities of the continent find their way to all corners of the world and the dogma into the minds of many.

The lands of Umiat and Kenai have regularly come into conflict over the eons, each avaricious for the benefits of the other. Geography has been cruel with her gifts. Tensions were inevitable between the peoples as soon as the Seas had settled and the lands were revealed.

Chapter One

It was early one morning when Is-Is and Egremont pushed their way through the overgrown copse to collect their friend Tumbletick. The skies above them churned with peculiar purply black clouds and great gobs of rain started to thwack through the trees. The leaves in the strong wind, sounded like a churning, breaking sea on a stony shore. As the two warriors, clanking in their assorted armours reached the broken door of Tumbletick's hut, they both thought simultaneously that they must get it fixed.

"Tumbletick!" barked Egremont in a mock gruff manner. "Are you in?"

"Of course I'm in, I'm never out," replied the voice of Tumbletick from beneath the pile of brown leaves and bracken. Warmth flooding within him at the sound of his friends he made the welcome effort and pushed his way to the surface of the foliage. He gazed upon them, framed by the doorway and surrounded by what little light had also managed to struggle through the canopy of the copse and the clouds from the impending storm.

Egremont the Lord Seau du Duvet was six foot dead. He held his visored helmet under his left arm to reveal his most noble canine face. Granite grey fur, tinged with silver, drooped into a great manicured moustache and neatly trimmed beard along his snout and lower jaw. When he spoke his long tongue danced around his fangs. His fur obviously covered the rest of his face, what with him being a wolfhound, and the back of his head too. His ears, atop of his head were quite small but still managed to flop neatly to the side to merge with the mass of his mane. Although the whole head looked quite shaggy, it was a visage that Egremont took a great deal of time to maintain. Especially his moustache and beard.

The Lord Seau du Duvet wore a tabard over his plate armour. The cloth of which was a rich vermillion red. Upon it was a yellow shield design displaying his family crest, a severed wolf head above two crossed swords and the family motto 'Fenris Est Mort' running underneath. At his side hung his weapon of choice, a rapier with an elaborate pommel and hand guard.

Is-Is was an entirely different kind of creature. Derived from a hare he stood eight feet tall to the top of his ears. Where Egremont was manicured grandeur, Is-Is was battle hardened chic. He had nicks and holes in his ears from numerous warlike encounters. Is-Is always complained that he was yet to meet the armourer who could devise a system to protect his over exposed and developed ears. So he had decided to turn the armourer's inability to provide a protecting garment for his ears into a fashion statement. In the holes that had been made by arrows, crossbow bolts, swords and teeth, he wore gold rings. Currently he sported twenty six as memoirs to his victories, fourteen in his left ear and twelve in his right.

When Is-Is talked in his very strong Northfolk accent, he revealed that he only had one of his buck teeth left but he still had both his eyes. His eyes were his pride and joy, on account of their perfect sight and dazzling blue twinkle, which was rare in hares he heard.

Is-Is' fur was a lustrous grey. Over his body he wore an expensive coat of chain mail armour. Is-Is preferred chain mail as it afforded him a lot of flexibility to move, run and leap in battle. Is-Is was exceptionally strong and his lithe muscles caused the armour to curve and bulge in all the right places. At his side he had a broadsword, across his back a long bow and a quiver full of barbed arrows. Secreted about the rest of his body, arms and legs were strapped daggers, knives and kukris, which he used for more delicate forms of warfare. Yet even without the accoutrements of butchery Is-Is was a lethal weapon. He was Grand Inventive Master of the 'Way of the Intercepting Paw', a martial art he had developed in the tough back streets of the port city of En'Tuk. He didn't just use his paws though; it could be his feet, elbows, knees, head or solitary buck tooth. He gave his art the nickname of Hare Kaido. To watch it in action it was not pretty but it was downright businesslike in its lethality and therefore valued by the hare. He loved it though in his own way and it meant that he really didn't need all the metal work attached to his body.

Is-Is considered himself two things above all others. He was a 'Bullybaiter' and Tumbletick's equal best friend.

Tumbletick broke into a huge grin and his otherwise permanent sneer disappeared. Is-Is and Egremont quickly picked up on the smile, despite the huge amount of muck on his face which tried to hide it, as they also knew he was smiling because of his eyes. Warmth for his friends flowed through his body and he broke free of his bed and bounced towards the two warriors and hugged them both in turn. All three then burst into a tirade of laughter and greetings that only true friends can share.

After a while Egremont said in a matter of fact way "It is time". The laughter ceased.

"Thought as much," replied Tumbletick in a sombre tone. "Let's go then. Never mind the rain. Might keep a few people away, hey?"

Chorus One

Tumbletick's world was one where more than one species had evolved at the same rate as the hominid which grew to become man. This was because of many reasons but primarily two. The peculiarity of the opposable thumb was also found in other species and the voice box had become usable when the larynx had descended and the hyoid bone developed. The entire Dog species had such adaptations and strangely, the hare. Tool making was rife and as a result so was war. While the world which wrapped itself around Tumbletick warred and wassailed, technology never really got beyond the stages of wooden engineering projects, building with stone and making weapons from steel. However the arts flourished, particularly theatre, so did customs such as building castles, subjugating peasants, bullying by barons and strangely enough the postal service and the collecting of stamps. The reason for the postal service explosion was uncertain but a direct result was that philately was almost a national obsession. There was always a two hour slot at the many open air theatres before the main evening show, auctioning off rare and wonderful stamps. Every theatre would employ their own tricks and tactics to ensure their auctions were full, such as free low denomination stamps for those that turned up early, or scantily clad female auctioneers. All of this was actively encouraged by the governments of the age as it was seen as a way for the masses to try and escape from the drudgery of the life they found themselves living. Trying to escape from being called up by their Baron to go to war, tilling the fields, attempting to stay clean, were all somehow easier to cope with if you owned a large leather bound stamp collection and had an evening at the theatre to look forward to.

Chapter Two

The trek from Tumbletick's copse to the capital city of Rhyell was quite long but not a particularly arduous one. They expected to be travelling for the rest of the day, rest overnight and arrive in Rhyell about midmorning. Tumbletick was glad of the rain and the ominous clouds because it would keep more people off the roads. Still the few they did pass had their heads down and covered trying to stay dry, which was futile. Egremont and Is-Is walked with their heads held high, aware of potential dangers and proud to be with Tumbletick. Strangely they got just as wet walking normally as those scurrying wretches who passed by. A couple of wet wanderers did catch the eye of Tumbletick and they immediately looked away as they realised the damp form on the road was a hideously ugly and hairy little man and not some strange pet of the noble looking wolfhound and militaristic hare. Although Tumbletick was shy to the point of insanity at times, he was grateful for his repulsiveness as it kept people away from him when they were on their own. However in pairs, and worse gangs, they would invariably bait and taunt him. This is why he stayed in his hut so often. With his friends, however, he felt both braver and happier, though to look at him now he still looked hunched and cowering as he scampered after his striding companions.

The journey eventually grew drier after a full day of sodden walking. Night smudged the grey light away into a pitch black under the heavy clouds now spent of rain. The distance from Tumbletick's copse to the Capital City meant one night of roughing it. Egremont, Is-Is and Tumbletick moved away from the road they had been following and found some shelter against a stone wall that marked the boundary of a farm enclosure. They clambered and hopped over the wall and lit a meagre fire hidden from any other nocturnal travellers still on the road by its small size and the wall. The ground was extremely wet from a full day of rain and the fire begrudgingly gave off a little heat. Even Is-Is had had trouble finding enough kindling and dry wood to light it. Yet Tumbletick found himself still filled with the happiness of the companionship afforded by being with Egremont and Is-Is.

As the night continued they found other bits of wood to feed the fire and it seemed to appreciate it and grow in both size and warmth. Their conversation turned to jokes and tales of their past together. They roasted rations of meat and drank some reasonable beer, from supplies brought by Is-Is.

Tumbletick could not remember falling asleep but knew he must have done so with a smile on his face because when he woke up again to rain lashing around him the smile instantly disappeared.

They were soon back on the road, stomping through puddles and sticky mud on the basic tracks of the backwaters of Umiat on their way to Rhyell. Egremont had suggested that a proper breakfast was in order as he knew a hostelry nearby that was renowned for excellent ham and eggs. He still planned to arrive at Rhyell at midmorning but a brief stop at 'The Ram' was to be enjoyed after a night sleeping rough. The tavern was still quite well used in these parts and smoke was ascending from the chimney into a peaceful blue sky after the previous day's rains. It was a large white building with many leaded windows and dark wooden beams. Pointed roofs in various places around the public house spoke of various extensions over the years it had been serving the travellers of Umiat. They entered by the main door and found themselves in a large common room with many tables and chairs and a fire burning well in the centre of the room. Several inhabitants had decided to take a table close to this central hearth that gave off warmth in all directions and Egremont, Is-Is and Tumbletick took one of the smaller tables close to it as well.

A young girl with pig tails and a brilliant white apron came over quickly and brushed away some crumbs that remained from a previous guest. She was about fifteen and spoke in a clear voice that reminded Tumbletick of birdsong. Clear and precise she asked them what they wanted and Egremont replied for them that three large mugs of small beer and a large plate of ham and eggs each would be a fine start. The trio settled themselves and placed cloaks and packs closer to the fire to dry out the damp. The serving girl returned swiftly with the small beers in large wooden tankards. Is-Is quickly took a long gulp and came up smiling with some foam clinging to the fur of his top lip.

"I think you'll enjoy the food here Tumbletick," said Egremont. "It has been a while since I've been to 'The Ram' but a place like this never really loses its panache."

They engaged in small talk for a couple of minutes before the girl returned again with the plates of food. Obviously this was a house special as Tumbletick noticed the thick cuts of meat and several eggs, poached and placed around it was also being enjoyed by other guests in the room.

The food was excellent, especially after the night against a wall and a begrudging fire and upon finishing Tumbletick leaned back and rubbed his belly in satisfaction. Egremont smiled to see his friend in such a condition and called the girl over again for another round of beers.

The door opened and a solitary man entered. He wore a weather stained long leather coat, a misshapen hat that spoke of many days on the road and he carried a peculiar looking case. It was rectangular, squared at the edges, with brass plates to protect the corners and brass studs that ran along each edge. Whether they were for decoration or for sealing up the case, Tumbletick was not sure. It was however a very obvious looking piece of luggage and made the man stand out. On his back he carried a small pack which probably contained his travelling essentials but Tumbletick found himself extremely curious about the case. He quickly realised that he should not really be staring as the stranger was heading straight towards them and a table which was nearby and would usually seat two. The stranger meandered his way through the tables and chairs lifting the large case above peoples seated heads as they ate and drank. He was heading straight for the table next to Tumbletick now and when he arrived the box like luggage was placed firmly on the table while his pack was removed from his shoulders and put beneath. The man took off his hat and rubbed his hands in front of the fire in the universal action of seeking warmth. He turned and nodded politely to Egremont, Is-Is and Tumbletick, who were the closet people to him and then looked enquiringly around for the serving girl. He was early middle age, slim in the face but defined and tinged with a purposeful look in his eyes. His hair was dark brown and neatly cut and when the girl came over he ordered hot tea instead of the more rurally requested beer with his breakfast.

"The ham and eggs are excellent," said Egremont in an effort of polite conversation.

"Yes, I often stop here on my travels," came the reply. "Although I rarely am allowed beer at this establishment."

"Really," said Egremont. "Rarely is a poor thing. This breakfast beer is excellent."

"I'm sure it is if the breakfasts are anything to go by but I'm not allowed to drink when I'm on official business."

"Official business?" Egremont probed.

"Yes," came the reply. "I am an Officer of the Court of Rhyell."

"Really," said Egremont. "We happen to be on our way to Court today."

"Oh are you going to the big event are you?" the man seemed to perk up a little. "Should be quite a thing. Of course usually I'd be there as well but duties must come first."

With that the man tapped the rectangular case with his hand in an affectionate manner. It was a light tan leather case, with a few areas of more weather beaten character which indicated it might be quite old and regularly used. Tumbletick found himself again staring at it wondering what would be inside, it seemed too large for official papers and if it was filled with gold it was bound to be far too heavy for one man to carry.

"The name is Longhurst, by the way," the man said.

"Pleased to meet you. My name is Egremont, this is Is-Is and Tumbletick," the wolfhound replied.

"Pleasure. Ah here comes my tea," Longhurst said as the girl came over with a large steaming mug. "Should warm me up a bit. I've got a very long way to go you know."

"Really, where are you off to?" asked Egremont.

"Well as far as you can really. I've got to get this to the far northwest. Past Noatak and up to the main city of the plains, Sitka," Longhurst said tapping the case again. "I do the journey pretty regularly. It can be quite lonely but at least I know I'm doing something important for the country."

"All the way to Sitka? I hope they give you a horse," Egremont laughed.

"Oh yes," Longhurst replied taking a sip of tea. "I get to stop at the staging houses on the way and swap horses at each one. That way I get to move pretty quickly. Well you've got to when you're on official business like this. It's a good job you know. Get to see the countryside, meet people, it's responsible but I'm just hoping for a promotion soon so I can take a smaller box and spend a bit more time with the family."

"Smaller box?" asked Egremont.

"Yeah. You know, the bigger boxes have to go to the four corners of Umiat and the smaller box gets to stay in Rhyell."

"Ah," said Egremont knowingly. "Have you been busy recently?"

"About one journey a month," Longhurst replied. "Ah here comes breakfast, I'm famished."

Longhurst attacked the ham immediately and ate quickly as if his conversation had taken up some of his precious time. He didn't speak again while he ate and Tumbletick looked inquisitively at Egremont as they all sipped on their beers. Egremont gave his friend a look which said 'I'll tell you later'.

Longhurst may well have been ravishing the breakfast but he never truly took his eyes off the case upon the table. He took further sips of the tea then bigger gulps as it cooled a little. Within a couple of minutes he was swiping up the last stains of egg yolk with the final piece of ham. He finished his tea and wiped his mouth with the back of his hand.

"Well nice to have met you," he said standing up, shouldering his pack and taking the handle of the case firmly in his left hand. "I hope your journey is a quiet one."

He left some coins on the table, more than enough to pay for the food and then he negotiated his way through the room again, careful with the case around other guests and was off out through the door.

"Interesting job," said Egremont. "Come to think of it I have never thought of it before as having to be done."

"What does he do?" asked Tumbletick.

"Well, he's essentially a courier. An employee of the State who transfers certain items to the farthest reach of the land," said Egremont. Is-Is was smiling broadly as he finished his second beer and waved the empty mug at the serving girl indicating desire for a third.

"So what was he transferring?" persisted Tumbletick.

"Well difficult to really be sure unless we head off to Sitka to find out what is delivered. But there will be three other similar shaped cases to the one he is carrying and three similar individuals heading off to three other far flung cities of Umiat," Egremont took a moment to finish his beer too. The serving girl had arrived with three more in anticipation that the table were all going to remain thirsty.

"Go on," said Tumbletick.

"Well my reclusive friend, there comes certain times when certain people find they are very much on the wrong side of the law. Sometimes, about once a month at the moment apparently, those people find themselves extremely punished. About the most extreme form of punishment actually. Hung, drawn and quartered in public. In the central square of Rhyell. Anyway, so that the other parts of the country can see that justice has been done and to act as a deterrent for other stealers of sheep, murderers, rapists and pick-pockets, the authorities send out the arms and legs to the four furthest parts of the land," Egremont picked at a piece of ham stuck between his canines with his knife. "It appears we have just met one of the fellows who has that rather important job. Never crossed my mind at all that someone had to actually transport the pieces but it must have been going on for years."

They finished their final quarts of small beer in silence. Egremont tipped the girl heavily for excellent service and they left 'The Ram' extremely full and very happy. Tumbletick felt a little strange to have met Longhurst who dealt with his macabre job in such an efficient manner and he wondered what other insights into the world lay ahead of him. However he felt very safe with Egremont and the imposing Is-Is with him.

The journey from 'The Ram' to Rhyell was not now a particularly far one. Longhurst probably was using the same horse as the one he arrived at the pub with. He must have just stopped off there because of the superb breakfast. The roads improved as they came closer to the capital and just before midday they saw the walls of the city in the distance. It took little less than the time they had spent on breakfast to make their way with increasing numbers of people heading in the same direction to the gates of the city which were flung open with only a couple of guards passing cursory glimpses at the varying merchants, peasants, farmers and the odd noble who were heading in and out of Rhyell.

Walking through the open city gates they trudged up the main cobbled street straight to the acropolis and the seat of power for the region. The castle had been built, destroyed and rebuilt many times during its warlike history but now filling the entire plain of the acropolis it was like a continuation of the living rock, looking squat because of its vast size but standing uniformly seven stories high, apart from the main keep which rose from within the outer walls to a height of twelve. Granite like its rock base it twinkled in the rain like only wet granite can. The climb up the path to the only portcullis twisted like a manic snake and Tumbletick's stomach twisted itself into knots as the nerves grew for he knew he was to be presented to Court and the Princess, Annabella Blaise.

The twisted ramp to the castle had been designed to slow down engines of war so they could be assaulted from the battlements, now Tumbletick felt as if he was being slowed down before the inevitable appearance and he almost wished it could come sooner.

They reached the gatehouse and walked under the raised portcullis; Tumbletick saw murder holes above him and to the side and swore he saw spying faces sneaking a glimpse at the small party. They emerged into a small courtyard where a line of assorted individuals queued upon the puddle laced flagstones. At the front of the line a bespectacled man, looking like a marmoset of ancient years, perused a large leather book. He was flanked by two huge bodyguards. One held an umbrella over the smaller monkey like man and book; the other held an ominous air and a large pole-axe. The marmoset impersonator, grey with age and authority, checked the names of the people in the queue against the approved names in his book before letting them proceed through an enormous double door in the centre of the courtyard wall and on into the guts of the castle. It looked as if court was going to be full today, despite the rain.

Egremont rose a hand to indicate that Is-Is and Tumbletick should halt in the centre of the courtyard and not join the queue. Other people came in, walked round them and joined the back of the line. Yet Egremont still indicated they should remain at the very heart of the courtyard. The desperate need to join a queue or the desire to get into the castle and out of the rain did not afflict or inspire him. He was waiting for the moment of highest dramatic tension and he knew the acoustics would be good here. So they waited as the administrator continued to let people enter the castle.

When the queue was past the point of the portcullis Egremont knew that the maximum amount of people were present that would be able to hear his pronouncement. He then barked out to the crowd in a voice so rich and so tactile that all felt roused by it.

"Citizens of Rhyell abate your waiting and hearken here. No doubt you brave the rain to attend court today for you know the seeker of the Umiat Stone is to be presented before Princess Annabella Blaise. That noble knight who quested for the greatest treasure the forces of light have ever held dear. You brave the storm which whips in from the Sea of Kaltag to appraise with your own eyes that wondrous man that searched for such a precious gift held by the forces of the Ahrioch Horde and the evil that was Ahriman."

Here Egremont paused, a flicker of a grin hidden beneath his moustache. He waited slightly longer than was internally comfortable aware that all eyes in this pre-performance crowd were on him. He wanted to create a buzz of anticipation in court which would grow to be electric. These voyeurs would be his voltage as they passed on the news.

"People of Rhyell," he paused again, his fist held in front of his chest. "I have met the most Honourable Knight of The Eagle and The Pelican." Egremont said with genuine pride.

"He is a man like no other and today you will all have revealed to you the protector of the Northlands. The warrior who sent Ahriman back to hell and damnation. The warrior who keeps this land safe. The warrior who holds the Umiat Stone. Today, you will meet Sir Bartle Rourke."

The queue, wide eyed was silent, then it turned this way and that as its component parts turned to each other with comments of "It's true" and "Today IS the day."

With the hubbub bubbling, Egremont led the way straight to the front of the line. Is-Is strode purposefully, with a stern gaze and fronted up to the poleaxe wielding gorilla. Egremont confronted the marmoset.

"I think you've been expecting us," he said in a conspiratorial, ominously tinged whisper. "Party of three. Egremont the Lord Seau du Duvet, Is-Is and Sir Bartle Rourke, Knight of The Eagle and The Pelican, Defeater of Ahriman, Protector of the Northlands, Fiancé to be of Princess Annabella Blaise."

"If you say so Eggers," replied the wizened little man looking over the top of his glasses at Egremont who leaned on the table, picking his teeth in a casual manner. "Lucky I schooled with your father otherwise

I wouldn't believe a word of it. This hairy bag of fluff cowering behind you is Sir Bartle Rourke, is he?" he continued.

"Appearances can be deceptive my dear Monty. Now just tick us off in your book and we will proceed to the ante-chamber which has no doubt been prepared for us in anticipation of today's festivities."

"Tick, tick, tick," said Monty, checking the names with a professional triple twitch of his quill. "You are in the Umiat Suite. To be honest we didn't actually think you were going to turn up."

Is-Is pushed open the monumental oak door with one hand, politely nodded to Egremont and Tumbletick to precede him into the castle, which they did.

Chorus Two

The lead article of The Rhyell Sentinel casts some light upon the occasion which had been the main focus of gossip and conversation in the Capital city of Umiat for months.

PRINCESS TO PROPOSE: ROURKE REVEALED

"Princess Annabella Blaise is to appear at court today and have presented to her the great hero Sir Bartle Rourke. Insiders at the castle have confirmed that on the tenth anniversary of the defeat of the Demonologist Ahriman and his Ahrioch Horde the legendary Sir Bartle Rourke is to be presented and the Princess is expected to propose. Sir Bartle Rourke, who has been on a sacred quest since the final battle of the Ahrioch Wars, has not been seen at court for the duration of the decade long departure. His whereabouts have been unknown but some insiders say he has been seeking the legendary Umiat Stone. The Umiat Stone has been missing since Ahriman stole it and began the Ahrioch Wars. The stone was believed to be hidden in Kenai and many believe that Sir Bartle will present it to the Princess today so completing the agreement signed by the late King Blaise, that anyone who returns the stone to Rhyell will receive the proposal of his daughter. The Umiat Stone has special powers to protect the Isle of Umiat so that no harm can come to the land while the stone is upon these shores. The Umiat Stone, as everyone knows, is set within a cathedral roof boss in the shape of a shield. The central spherical stone has been carved with a map of Umiat. Its rightful place is at the zenith of the nave of Rhyell Cathedral where a vacant space has been too long. The Umiat Stone, within its stone boss, shaped like a shield, should be protecting the inhabitants of Umiat again soon in full view of all worshippers at the Cathedral.

Court is expected to be packed today. For a full list of the great and the good invited turn to page six. If you can not get there, there will be a full report and commemorative pull out in Sundays Edition."

Chapter Three

The main hall of the castle was crowded, crammed full of figures. Throngs of people dressed in their finery stood shoulder to shoulder and moved in a group shuffling manner to gain better vantage of the dais at the end of the hall where soon, Princess Annabella Blaise would appear, take her throne and address the attending dignitaries. Then her Chamberlain would go through the boring and tedious legal matters of court before asking if Sir Bartle Rourke was present. Egremont's speech in the courtyard had had its desired effect and the whisperings it had caused were dynamite. Talk of two great warriors and a strange creature, probably acquired on Bartle Rourke's quest in Kenai, chattered alongside conversation of how the beautiful Princess would take a handsome prince in matrimony and there would be a King and Queen to rule over Umiat again.

Along with the dais the only space left in the hall was a narrow strip of red carpet, leading from the entrance straight to the dais. A row of resplendent armoured guards lined the processional route and kept the crowds back with long spears.

A gong sounded. The crowd hushed, eager, anticipated and gasped as Princess Annabella Blaise appeared in full bridal gown, dazzling white with a diamond tiara. Hand resting atop the hand of the Chamberlain who led her to her throne. He with the staff of office then proceeded to the front of the dais and unrolled a parchment scroll.

The Chamberlain, as predicted, proceeded to perform the duties of his office by reading out reams of legal matters pertaining to disputes over farm boundaries, notices of bankruptcy, lists of prisoners executed and those sentenced to death or banishment to Rampart. Several ears pricked up at the lists of prisoners who had been dispatched, either overseas or over the chopping block, they were always a popular part of the Chamberlains address. Then came the moment the multitude had been musing upon. The Chamberlain cleared his throat and announced.

"Today is the 17th of Frimaire. A decade ago, Sir Bartle Rourke defeated the Ahrioch Horde and banished their leader Ahriman from this world. As it was written by King Blaise now is the time for any suitor to the Princess to present the Umiat Stone and so claim her hand in marriage, upon her proposal to such a hero." The Chamberlain paused. He was quite pleased with the way that had gone. All eyes were upon him and he had a strong sense of being central to a pivotal point of history.

"Does anyone step forth with the Umiat Stone missing these ten years and so claim such a Royal reward?"

Absolute silence deafened the hall. All present looked to the huge oak panelled doors of the entrance, large black nails riveted into the ancient heavy wood. The assemblage strained to see the slightest movement of the door. Would they open? They all knew they must. The congregation was worshipping at the altar of antiquity. This was the moment of their lives, to say they were there at this seismic, epoch making, critical and fateful time. It did not get bigger than this. Nothing happened. Then the handle on the door squeaked a little, turned and a crack expanded into a gap and out stepped the most hideous, hairy little scrag of a creature any of them had ever seen.

Before the crowd had time to react to their shock the doors swung open at speed as Egremont threw back one and Is-Is the other. They stood at Tumbletick's side, flanking him, a guard of honour and in unison they walked up the red carpet to the dais. Silence is a funny thing sometimes and silence was also embarrassed by the event. It tried to smoother the trio as they marched to the platform, as if to hide them and pretend this was not happening. When Egremont, Is-Is and Tumbletick got to the platform, in a pre-arranged deployment, Tumbletick took a step onto the first tier of the dais and Is-Is and Egremont both fell to one knee.

Then in a voice resonant with all the palpability his dramatic yearnings could muster, Lord Seau du Duvet addressed the Princess, the Chamberlain and the crowd.

"My most Royal Highness, I, Egremont the Lord Seau du Duvet, have the most esteemed honour to present to you today Sir Bartle Rourke. As has been written he brings to you the great Umiat Stone." A gasp from the crowd, 'where was Bartle Rourke?'

Tumbletick took steps up the remaining tiers and pulled from within his great hairy mass a stone the shape of a small shield. It glowed a strange pale yellow as he handed it to the Chamberlain who had intercepted his path to the Princess. All assembled wondered why Sir

Bartle Rourke had sent his weird pet to present the stone. Perhaps he wanted to make the occasion more dramatic, perhaps he would appear on the back of some captured Centaur he had vanquished on his quest and subjugated to his mercy. Perhaps this ugly creature handing over the stone was some Lord himself of a missing link tribe he had befriended in the foothills of Mount Kantishna in Kenai. But hark; the wolfhound began to speak again.

"My Princess will you not keep the word of your father and propose to whoever brings you the Umiat Stone? It was clearly written and witnessed and it is well known that you are to do so!" Egremont's voice rose in volume and in steel.

The Princess remained silent, still and pale faced. Duty was one thing but what was this thing presenting the hope of a nation to her Chamberlain? Annabella remained silent, thinking. She did not speak, she could not speak. She was not going to marry this hairy creature.

Egremont spoke again, "Perhaps the Princess was expecting that Sir Bartle Rourke would present the stone himself? Well your highness.... he has. The most noble, brave and honourable man is before you now and has kept the stone safe these ten years." Egremont waited. "Will you not propose?"

"I knew Sir Bartle Rourke and he was a gentleman of infinite beauty, bearing and refinement. He stood fully six foot six and was the greatest warrior of his age. Lord Seau du Duvet, you play some cruel trick upon me with this creature, for what end I know not but I suspect treason in this act. Despite the return of the Umiat Stone."

Egremont shrugged and retorted with a smile. "Treason it can not be my Princess for the man you so insult is the same man you highly praise. Tumbletick, for he has another name, is Sir Bartle Rourke and I wish to tell all here now what an amazing sacrifice he has made to keep the Land of Umiat safe these past ten years."

The crowd, Chamberlain and Princess had not seen that coming even though it was clear to those of intelligence. Egremont cleared his throat. Is-Is took a seated position on the lower tier, choosing to relax in full knowledge of what was to come.

"It is true that Sir Bartle Rourke was the greatest warrior his age had ever seen. In all aspects he was the greatest soldier, the most educated scholar and the most courteous courtier at court. I wish to tell you now though of that day ten years ago when Sir Bartle Rourke, Is-Is and I fought with your father's army against the Ahrioch Horde that Ahriman led against this land. For the sake of posterity I have prepared a piece of prose which I hope will make the telling of the tale all the more…rewarding."

Egremont scratched behind an ear and then struck a theatrical pose adopted by all those players of the stage when one was relating a dramatic tale.

"Dear people, imagine this hall transported to the battle field. Your massed ranks facing each other over the red carpet are soldiers facing each other in pitched battle. You smell fear, see death, blood and sweat and hear the terrible noise of massed combat, groans of the dying, hacking of weapons on armour and on bone. A piteous and fearful sight. Then imagine Ahriman surrounded by his swarming hordes of mercenaries and vagabonds, his screaming demons and multitudinous imps of hell, gibbering, drooling and baying for the blood of your fearful Army. But all was too weak for brave Bartle Rourke, well he deserves that name, flaunting the fortunes of war, with his glinting sword he flashed the blade in bloody execution upon the hordes and carved a passage in the enemy's withering ranks, until he faced Ahriman alone. Bartle did not take time to shake his hand or say farewell but unzipped the traitor's innards from his groin unto his jaw, then took his head for your battlements. But the hordes of Hell seeing their master fall screamed to their Demon Lords to bring forth better warriors and new supplies of imps to begin a fresh assault."

The Chamberlain interjected, "Did this not dismay our knight Sir Bartle Rourke?"

Egremont continued, "Oh yes, as sparrows frighten eagles or lambs worry lions. I tell the truth when I tell you he was like a cannon firing at double time. He doubly doubled his strokes upon the foe. If he meant to bathe in reeking wounds I cannot tell but shortly after the death of Ahriman is when the curse took hold."

Egremont twirled his moustache and took a moment to look upon the crowd; all were wide eyed with gaping mouths. Some cheered and many of the palace guards shook their spears in delight. His theatrical bent was paying dividends. His voice rose to its very height as his speech continued.

"The Demon King himself climbed from a smoking pit at the bequest of his Hellish Lords. An entire bodyguard of the most obscene

Princes of the Underworld, gnarling and gnashing as he kept them chained, like attack dogs, on leashes around him. They were straining to attack, all horns and fangs, scales and claws. As the Demon King let them spring after us he called down a curse on Rourke that he should be smote for killing his servant Ahriman before he was ripped to pieces by the obscenities bounding towards us. So we saw the dashing Bartle Rourke wither and collapse before us as the curse took hold. The Demon King's voice echoed over the battlefield for all to hear 'You, Rourke, so vain and proud in your magnificence will die as the ugliest man ever to have existed, so weak as to be unable to even defend yourself'."

The crowd now was at a point of high excitement, surely this was the greatest regaling of a war story ever. Egremont now lowered his voice and slowed the pace.

"But sometimes the Forces of Good can weave their magic too. An Avatar from heaven descended to the ground in front of what was now Tumbletick and advanced upon the ravaging hordes, shining beams of purest light from its hands and eyes. They burnt like bugs unearthed from under a stone in the midday sun. Is-Is, valiant fellow, took Tumbletick under one arm and leapt from the battlefield. I decided to advance with the Avatar and dispatched those forces of Ahrioch back to Hell that had avoided the light. As the imps died and the unearthly bodyguard of Demon Princes melted under the rays, the King of Hell sunk back to the very depths of the pit, screaming in the agonies inflicted by his defeat and the scouring of his black soul by the phosphorescent beauty of Heaven." Egremont gave the slightest of smiles, never could he have hoped his classes in Rhetoric at school were so worth while, his audience was rapt.

"The Avatar and I were standing over the corpse of Ahriman, split asunder by Bartle Rourke and headless. I then heard a voice of such beauty emanate from the being of Good that I could have died in ecstasy at hearing what was the very music of Heaven. 'Victory goes today to the forces of Umiat, Egremont. Take the head of Ahriman that Sir Bartle Rourke claimed and place it on the castle walls in Rhyell as testimony to the forces of Good. But take this too; it almost went amiss in the carnage of war.' The Avatar made a gesture and the Umiat Stone rose from the centre of Ahriman's shield, a subtle click was heard as it broke free. 'Give this to the creature that was once Bartle Rourke. Keep him secret from the world. His very form will now keep him invisible to all but the kindliest soul. His future poverty will keep him safe from all thieves; he will be the ultimate keeper of the ultimate treasure'. The Avatar smiled and ascended back unto the sky. So I left that battlefield, head in one hand, stone in the other and fulfilled both of the Avatars orders."

Egremont stopped, expecting a huge rapturous applause but what he heard was the voice of the Princess cut through the silence.

"So Bartle Rourke did not leave upon a quest to regain the Umiat Stone, he has been in Umiat, in this form, keeping it away from all by dint of his hideousness and poverty?" Her clipped tones were astute and about to be cutting. "Well then my father's bequest has not been met for it quite clearly states that I should only propose to the man who returned the Umiat Stone to the lands of Umiat and now it seems as if the stone never left. So I will not propose to this 'Tumbletick'. No matter if the tale you tell was true and his heritage is nobler and more benign to look upon than this repulsiveness I see here and now. Chamberlain, dismiss the court and return the Umiat Stone to the vaults."

Tumbletick's heart did not sink. He felt quite happy really. He did not want the attention and publicity of a big royal wedding. Is-Is remained phlegmatic but Egremont was seething.

"My lady, before the Chamberlain performs his duty, I implore you to do yours. Semantics and equivocation may have a role in a court of law but in this court of honour they are misplaced."

"I have given you my decision," Annabella retorted. "The matter is over and I am now free to marry he who impresses and woos me best. Umiat shall have a King worthy of the title, not a Thing, no matter how glorious his supposed past." With that she left the Great Hall. The Chamberlain turned to face Tumbletick, Is-Is and Egremont and whispered apologetically, "I'm so sorry but to the letter of her fathers bequest she is technically correct. We could examine it together if you wish. The original document is kept in the same vault we will store the Umiat Stone in until we can get it safely to the roof of the cathedral. If you want to…" then the doors to the chamber exploded covering the crowd closest to them with great chunks of wood and lacerating them with huge splinters. About thirty men, dressed in black and covered with Wolf skins came bursting in after the explosion, swords drawn and started clearing a semicircle of space by cutting down those members of the crowd who still stood or who had made their way to help the injured. The rest of the court instinctively rushed towards the dais and became a great heap of humanity which trapped the guards that had lined the thin streak of red carpet as well as Tumbletick, Egremont, Is-Is and the Chamberlain. The doors at the back of the dais through which the Princess had entered and left only opened into the great hall, a design feature to add dramatic effect for royal entrances. Now they were pinned shut by the weight of the bodies of the terrified crowd.

A few guards and brave citizens who were closest to the wolves tried to engage them in combat but were shot down by a new group who had entered the room with loaded crossbows after the first sword wielding wolves. All in all there were now about forty men controlling a room of about seven hundred.

Had the Ahrioch Horde returned? All followers who wore the Wolf skin had been cleared of Umiat shortly after that last battle. Egremont and Is-Is tried to free themselves but could not. Tumbletick had disappeared from sight being so much shorter than most. Is-Is had the best view being so tall and saw a figure enter the room alone. It also was dressed in black but without the wolf skin. Is-Is' eyesight was superb and he saw that under the hood the man wore were distinctly Kenai features playing around a painfully thin face. Dark hair covered his chin in a crafted point and as the man smiled Is-Is saw that he had filed his teeth to points. Trying to look like Ahriman, thought Is-Is. As he was close enough to Egremont he quickly relayed the information of the number of wolves, their weapons, positions taken and the tall Ahriman impersonator all in a precise battle sign language developed for quick, exact soundless conversation in noisy environments like war. Egremont had his hand on his sword, just waiting to be able to free it from its sheath and get at the wolves.

The hooded man reached into the folds of his cloak to a pouch hanging from his belt and pulled out a handful of small white objects which Is-Is saw poking through the gaps of his clutching hand. Is-Is also just had time to see that his fingernails were manicured to points before the man shouted in a heavily Kenai accented voice.

"People of Umiat, I have returned for what is mine. I will show you fear in a handful of teeth! My servants know what is mine; they sense it and they will seek it!" With that he threw the handful of small white teeth to the floor of the Great Hall of the castle of Rhyell and unleashed simian carnage.

Chorus Three

Lead feature of The Rhyell Sentinel, Frimaire 18th.

HUNDREDS DEAD IN AHRIOCH
ATTACK AT COURT

The country of Umiat is today in mourning as many of the country's finest citizens were killed in the horrendous bloodbath at the capitals castle. Survivors tell of how the crowd was slaughtered by skeletons of monkeys which rose from the floor after a mysterious and evil man had thrown down teeth. These Undead creatures then proceeded to attack the terrified throng who had the choice of either being ripped to pieces by snarling fangs and claws, of what has been reported were Baboon skeletons, or trying to escape towards a band of Ahrioch Wolves with crossbows and swords. The Undead monkeys cut their way through the crowd directly towards the terrified Chamberlain, Lord Davenport, before dismembering him and stealing back the Umiat Stone. They then killed several more people as they made their way back to the mysterious man, who eye witnesses said was trying to look in every way like the deposed Demonologist, Ahriman. Although several members of court tried to put up some resistance the wolves and the Ahriman look-alike managed to escape the castle and proceed to the docks with their bodyguard of unearthly monkeys protecting them all the way to the wharfs of Rhyell. Dockers who witnessed this event say a black ship rowed at speed into the harbour and the band of murderers and thieves embarked upon it before it sped out of Rhyell, as if 'propelled by magic oars'.

Although no group has claimed responsibility, authorities suspect this is an Ahrioch attack due to the appearance of the wolves, the undead and no regard for life.

Chapter four

The top chamber of the tower of Rhyell castle could only be reached by a ladder lowered from within, through a trapdoor to the floor below. It had no windows and its only sources of light were a large fireplace, which was kept constantly lit and several candles and torches on the walls. Maps of the known world adorned the walls as well. The only furniture was a large rectangular, heavy wooded table built robustly from mahogany and the obligatory black iron rivets of the age. There were no chairs, everyone stood or leaned on the table or walls. There was always the floor to sit on though.

Present in the room were Egremont, Is-Is, Tumbletick, General Leach, Lord Jackson of En'Tuk, Percy Fenton and Raven Hill. The General was the present day commander of Umiat's Army. He was a large bear of a man, hairy and with a big head. Incredibly strong, warlike and not too intelligent.

Lord Jackson of En'Tuk was the noblest man in court. Most noble because he was the richest. A merchant from the port of En'Tuk who had made his money in all manner of trades, some of which he did not wish to speak about openly. His money bought him influence. By paying huge amounts of tax and voluntary donations to the Crown he reduced the amount the peasants had to pay and, as such, he was universally adored by the mob. This was where his true power lay. He was everything General Leach was not. Small, weak, pasty faced and immensely intelligent, quick witted and devious, in an honest businesslike way.

Percy Fenton was a pirate. Incredibly good looking, well dressed, witty and deadly. Mid-thirties and already a twenty year career keeping the coast of Umiat free from any Kenai vessels. Without a Navy, the powers that be in Umiat needed some coastal protection. As Percy Fenton was also captain of the Pirate League and provided such a service as part of his piratical interests he held massive influence within the realm.

Raven Hill was a foxy, beautiful red head, dressed in stitched black leather. Her devastating hair was long and luxurious and her lithe, sleek body moved in ways beneath the leather that drove most men to the brink of insanity. She was also the Head of the Secret Service, a sassy assassin and should have been in a position to know that the Ahrioch Horde was planning to strike at court the day before. Her code name was Vixen and little was beneath her, if it meant it would get her what she wanted.

The only other person who had been in the room was the servant who always kept the fire lit and could lower the ladder from within to let secret meetings take place. He had just left down the ladder so Is-Is pulled it back up and shut the trapdoor.

Raven Hill spoke first. "Gentlemen, I apologise on behalf of the Secret Service for their total lack of knowledge about this resurgence of the Ahrioch Horde. Our spies in Kenai knew nothing about any cult activities starting again which could lead to such an atrocity in the capital."

"Damn right you should be apologising," interjected General Leach slamming his heavy fist onto the solid table with a resounding thump. Aggressive and spitting phlegm he continued to rant, "Should be first to offer your resignation too! An absolute disgrace. I only had ceremonial guards on duty. Most of them are soft after ten years of peace. Where was the early warning from your pirate fleet Fenton?"

Lord Jackson brought the warlike attack to an end with softly cultured tones, "Leach, we are where we are. Many a good man lays awaiting burial and the Umiat Stone has been stolen. What we have to decide is what we can do about it, and quickly."

"We tried to have a couple of corsairs catch the clipper they escaped in, but it was too fast," crooned Fenton. "However before it got over the horizon we know it was heading dead southwest, which would indicate it was heading for the only port of Kenai, Ende." Percy Fenton busied himself cleaning under his nails with an exquisite dagger as he sat on the edge of the table. "You can check a chart if you wish but I am certain that is where they will have ended up, so to speak."

"Excellent deduction for one who seems so vacant," growled Leach. "But what are we going to do about it? We can't invade Kenai with an army. No resources. But we must get the stone back."

"Why do we need to get the stone back?" questioned Vixen. "We have been told for all these years that the Umiat Stone kept Umiat safe. And yet we have believed for the past ten years that actually it was in

Kenai with Rourke. It is a simple act of logic to therefore say that the land should have been susceptible to attack and yet no attack came until yesterday."

"Exactly," Egremont jumped in. "The stone actually was here being guarded in secrecy by Tumbletick. No attack came because the stone was here. No attack from any invasion force yet we were attacked by a small group. Perhaps the Umiat Stone could not protect us from that unless it was in its rightful place upon the ceiling in Rhyell Cathedral."

"Or, perhaps," piped up Tumbletick uncharacteristically. "Logic would suggest that we were not attacked by outside forces but by people who were not invaders but were always here."

"Tumbletick has got a point," said Jackson. "They may have been remnants of the last great battle here. Or more frightening, Citizens of Umiat who have decided to turn to the Ahrioch Horde." Jackson paused. "However, the evidence does suggest that we were not invaded by an army during the last decade. So who knows what the Umiat Stone set within a shield boss actually does at all?"

Leach joined the debate. "I do not have any interest in superstition but it is a well held belief by the People that the stone does indeed keep us safe. The morale of the land would be lifted if we could return it… we must return it. Maybe there is some truth in the myth after all."

"Then the decision is actually very easy," stated Egremont quite calmly. "A small party of highly trained and dedicated individuals will have to land on the Peninsular of Kenai and retrieve the stone from a ruthless and evil sect. This sect will stop at nothing to keep it for themselves. They seem to have a leader who is at the very least the equal to Ahriman in his control of the black arts of necromancy."

"There is also a wonderful parity at play here," Fenton observed. "They sent a small party to steal the Umiat Stone, well we will send one back to them!"

"Correct," said Lord Jackson. "Leach and his Armies would have been useless even if they were at full strength. The only place you can land with any degree of safety is in Ende. The rest of Kenai's Coast is fundamentally mountains rising out of the icy sea. Take a look at the contours of the maps!" The group did not need to, it was well known that the only way into Kenai was through Ende, which ironically was usually the end of most people from Umiat who tried. Lord Jackson of En'Tuk continued, "I will do my part and finance any such expedition.

I suspect we all have talents which can be applied to ensure a successful outcome."

"Indeed we do," said Egremont. "Naturally Is-Is and I will go and Tumbletick will come with us. Mostly for his own protection. I fear that whoever it was who stole the stone probably holds a grudge against Sir Bartle Rourke. And after my rather rhetorical rant the other day the known world will know who Tumbletick is now."

"I'll captain a ship and take you to Kenai," said Fenton with a wry smile and a confident tone. "Good to play my part in such an expedition and all that."

"I will come with you too," purred Vixen. "I have some peculiar talents which may well come in useful and I haven't been in the field for so long it would be beneficial for me to get back into the thick of things again. Rather that this desk job I have been landed with."

"Well you can count me out then," huffed General Leach. "I will remain in Umiat and begin retraining and restructuring the Army. In case the Ahrioch Horde has truly risen again."

Lord Jackson smiled and said, "A brave move General Leach. Your country needs you at this moment of crisis. General Headquarters would probably be the best place for you. As a major surprise, no doubt, I too would also like to offer my physical services above and beyond just the pecuniary ones. I have an itch I want to scratch and I suspect that my complexion and my general level of fitness derives from too much negotiation and not enough 'Time in the Field' as Vixen puts it. So if you'll have me?"

"Absolutely," replied Egremont with enthusiasm. Tumbletick felt a glow of happiness about Jackson volunteering. He suspected a kindred spirit resided within what appeared to be his small and weak physical frame.

Is-Is glanced at Egremont and raised an eyebrow slightly whilst clearing his throat in a knowing manner.

"Ah, yes, of course," remembered Egremont with a husky laugh. "We are forgetting someone who would be invaluable on such an adventure! We will have to take a little detour first and travel to the Isle of Rampart. To pick up a dear friend of ours, Campbell the Weasel."

"Campbell the Weasel," spluttered Vixen in surprise.

"Why he's the very worst level of scum notoriety has ever boasted about. An absolute legend in pirate circles too! I'd love to meet him," smiled Fenton in delight. "Thief, cut-throat, spy for hire, depraved lothario. The type of chap who could well be of use," he purred in continuance.

"Absolutely all true Fenton," agreed Egremont. "So, with this small and very elite expeditionary force assembled, will you lead us to the docks and take us to Rampart?"

"Too right! This looks like it could be some fun. A trip to Rampart to meet a legend like Campbell, then a brief cruise to the most dangerous port town in the World? I can not imagine how a pirate could have a better time."

"So it is decided then," concluded Jackson. "All of us, except General Leach, head off with the Pirate King to collect the most notorious thief of the age, in the great city of Rampart before heading to Ende, the only port in the country of Kenai. Where we will start our adventure to find out what has happened to the stone which keeps the whole of Umiat safe from attack?"

"That sums it up," said Egremont.

"Absolutely," continued Raven Hill.

"I'm genuinely aroused by it," smiled Percy Fenton.

"Then I suggest that rather than leaving immediately we leave at dawn tomorrow. I'll have my people get supplies for your Flagship Fenton. All the paraphernalia needed for a quest into the heartland of an ancient enemy. Not knowing how long you are going to be or what is generally needed!" said Jackson, a slight hint of nervousness encroaching now he was committed.

"If you could Lord Jackson," said Egremont in calming tones. " A back pack each with the best iron rations. Warm clothes for travel on cold days and a superb tent which is easily erected and sleeps six comfortably would be best. We all have our own favourite weapons and I suspect we will have to be truly adventurous types and eventually live off the land."

"Could we also have a map of Kenai, some rope, a compass, a couple of lanterns and a good supply of fire starting equipment?" said Tumbletick in a little voice.

"Certainly," replied Lord Jackson. "It will all be ready by dawn and delivered to the docks."

Chorus four

The City State of Rampart: by Decker Allemande
Rampart is a place of immense interest in the world as many places, which find themselves at a natural crossroads, so often are. The City State of Rampart lies between the Sea of Kaltag and the Circle Sea. It is a large island at the end of the Tanana Strait and is entirely fortified. Its militaristic history is mainly due to also being a fiercely proud democracy lying between the two continents of Umiat and Kenai. Rampart has always remained independent and neutral during the years of war and peace that have existed between the two large nations to the north and south.

On approaching Rampart by sea one notices its sheer cliff faces are topped by battlements, lined with weapons and engines of war. Indeed one is reminded of the castle of Rhyell atop the acropolis in the capital city of Umiat. Excepting that this is on a massive scale. The battlements top the entire perimeter of the island which is some thirty miles wide east to west and twenty miles north to south.

Rampart does have a natural harbour which lies protected within an astounding bay that was probably created by volcanic activity in the islands' prehistoric past. Entrance to the bay is between two spurs of rock, extending from the main land to form a portal roughly two hundred yards wide. Extending down the spurs are the obligatory battlements which have been built up to maintain a uniform height with the rest of the islands' defences. Then, bridging the spurs three hundred yards high, is one of the wonders of the modern world. A solitary stone block arch spans the divide in awesome elegance and atop that the battlements continue. Two hundred yards long and twenty wide the arch contains more weapons of war that can drop all manner of defensive and offensive items upon any fleet which wanted to invade Rampart.

Within the bay itself a marvellous harbour has been constructed with many quays and jetties to allow mooring to unload visitors and cargoes to the docks and the small town which clings to the reclaimed area of land at sea level. Even this is of a fortified nature as it would be the second line of defence to any attackers who had breached the portal.

Access to the plateau of Rampart is via extremely steep and twisting tracks at the back of this small town. Towers and turrets built of huge stone blocks stand robustly at each turn, overlooking the approaching gradient and this too is another awesome defending mechanism.

Once atop the plateau one is greatly relieved to see a break in the militaristic might of the isle and is greeted by lightly rolling farmland and olive groves. Rampart is largely self-sufficient in the production of crops and meat. This is another crucial factor behind the success of the isle. The one city of Rampart, named Rampart as well, lies in the very centre of the island. Although there are fortified farmsteads and the odd watch tower dotted around the countryside, the city is the only major conurbation. At the centre of this city is the main reason for the city states massive visitor levels of adventurous types who wish to seek their fortune.

The ancient city centre is behind a walled area which is patrolled by guards to keep the occupants from getting out. Ramshackle housing, decrepit monasteries, old merchant guilds and disused breweries make up some of the types of buildings which surround the old castle and its dungeon and catacombs, which eat deep into the heart of the island.

Within the old city there are treasures scattered about. You can see gold coins just lying in the street here and there. Great weapons of ancient heroes lie next to the bones of their former masters, still wearing decaying armour. The howls of monsters, imported from all over the world, rise up in anticipation over the walls of the next wave of warriors, thieves and mercenaries who wish to test their skill and cunning in the old city. The citizens of Rampart line the walls cheering on the wonderful array of such adventurers who enter through the two locked gates and courtyard every day. Most will try and make it to the castle where the greatest challenges and treasures are believed to lie. Indeed the Rampart Tourist Board regularly sends flyers back with all merchants who trade with the island showing pictures of the hordes of treasure and famous magic weapons which have been secreted around the old city.

A visit to Rampart is highly recommended, either for its natural beauty, the historical and monumental battlements or as a great place to test your prowess at treasure hunting. Fantastic hotels, bars and restaurants cater for the visitor in the main city although it is a little expensive.

Chapter Five

"It is always darkest before the dawn," thought Tumbletick to himself as he stood at the end of a stone jetty in Rhyell docks. Then he felt a pang of foolishness for coming up with such a cliché at such a magic moment. It was cold in Frimaire in the land of Umiat, but it was the darkness, which chilled Tumbletick more. You could not see anything out in the swelling sea. He turned around to look back towards the city and the docks, lights twinkled in the ships rigging and portholes. More lights were visible along the streets of the capital and closer still in the lanterns held by the small group of exceptional people who would travel with him to Rampart. Is-Is turned toward the lone figure of Tumbletick and lifted the lantern to his battle scarred face so Tumbletick could see the hare give him a broad grin and a chummy wink. Tumbletick ambled back to the group in time to hear Percy Fenton finishing a sentence.

"…might as well take the Flagship rather than a faster clipper or corsair. The crew are a good bunch and would probably enjoy some time in Rampart. Then we can buy a smaller, more secretive vessel. Hopefully purchase some discretion with it too, if you know what I mean?"

"A difficult commodity to acquire but a good idea," replied Vixen. "I trust funding will extend to that Lord Jackson?"

"Of course, do not even think about a budget on this enterprise my dear," the merchant answered. Jackson looked distinctly less pasty already with the thought of adventure flowing through his veins. "I have got offices all over the place. They will always be able to supply us with goods or coinage."

The small party had their backpacks with them now. Is-Is being the strongest would also carry the tent which folded neatly away into a separate pack just slightly smaller than Tumbletick.

They crossed the gangplank and embarked quietly aboard 'The Ardent Panda', Fenton's prize ship. Quickly he led them through a couple of doors to the stern of the ship and his quarters. A classic captain's room, with a large table in the centre used for navigation or feasting, plush benches with purple rectangular cushions running along the back of the room beneath a tightly latticed ornate window which took up three quarters of the wall. The rest of the walls were panelled in dark aged oak and the accoutrements of naval warfare and plotting charts at sea hung from them.

"There is only one other cabin for the first mate so we will all have to bunk down in here until we get to Rampart. Or you could sling a hammock with the crew down below decks should you prefer," laughed Fenton apologetically. "Still, I guess this might be one of the nicer forms of accommodation facing us before the quest is over!"

The group settled down around the cabin on ornate chairs surrounding the table and lounging on the cushions covering the benches. Fenton took his leave to rouse his drunken crew from their sleep into the world of hangovers and hard work. Before long the ship began to move on the exiting dawn tide and a light coastal breeze further eased the flagship on its way. The usual coarse cries of pirates were diminished in the early light of day as a slightly more surreptitious departure was required. It spoke volumes as to the professionalism of Fenton's hand picked crew despite their pirate status.

As 'The Ardent Panda' broke free of the confines of the harbour Tumbletick felt the swell increase and became very aware of the tilting, yawling, rolling, heaving mass of the ship and he decided very quickly that perhaps some fresh air might be best.

Tumbletick muttered something to the rest of the group about needing some space and knowing that he would not be missed, as they would be discussing more important things than the whereabouts of his small form, he exited the cabin and took the short corridor that led him to the main deck. On opening it he was greeted by the strong breeze of an open sea. He traversed the deck, dodging working pirates as he moved between feeling very light and very heavy with the pitching of the ship. He made his way to the bow and skipped up five short wooden steps to the starboard side and then made for the very limit of the bow where a little cover was formed by the bulwarks meeting. This afforded him some protection from the wind and spray. He hunched up, wrapped his arms around his knees and stared back towards the rest of the ship and started to replay some of the amazing things that had happened to him in the past two days.

Today was the 19th of Frimaire, yesterday they had had the meeting in the secret chamber, two days before that he had woken up in his pile of leaves and bracken and headed to court with Egremont and Is-Is. There he had been subjected to so many assaults of theatricality, lies and carnage that only now did the shock set in. Tumbletick's little heart began beating fast, he felt hot and the emotions of his body rose and forced their way through to his face as he began to cry, sniff and release some of the confusion through little moans and whimpers that he prayed the pirates would not hear or see. He turned his back to the deck of the ship now and attempted to tuck his way further into the nook at the bow to start asking himself some questions that had to be asked. The biggest was quite a simple one. Why had Egremont told so many people that he was the illustrious Sir Bartle Rourke? It was meant to be kept a secret for ever. No one was ever supposed to know and he cast his mind back a decade and a day, Frimaire 18th, the day after the pivotal battle that had seen Ahriman killed by Bartle Rourke. Is-Is and Egremont had arrived at Tumbletick's hut that day. Is-Is carried the body of a fallen warrior. Tumbletick remembered how scared he had felt seeing his two friends covered in the gore of battle, now dried upon their armour. Their faces were grim and desperately sad. Is-Is so strong and noble held a full grown man in his arms as if holding a sleeping infant. Even though the burden was obviously great Is-Is would not put the body down out of immense respect. The man was dead. Tumbletick could see no wounds but surely his friends would tell him why they had brought this corpse to his copse. How clearly Tumbletick remembered that day, how Egremont had knelt before him and took a hand into his and said how they begged a favour of Tumbletick which would make him nobler than he could ever hope or dream. Tumbletick was so rapt in his thoughts and memories that he was now completely unaware of the dipping and rising of the prow on the stomach loosening sea. He could no longer hear the screeching of the wet straining ropes and creaking flexing of the planks of the hull. What he heard was the voice of Egremont in his head saying how he wanted Tumbletick to protect two things, the unmarked grave of the dead knight and a stone. Egremont said that this guardianship would last for ten years and then Tumbletick would be rewarded for his service and sacrifice with gifts and treasure, love and respect which was unimaginable to him now. Then Tumbletick fast forwarded his life to the day in court. He knew he was going there but had not been prepared for Egremonts speeches. He had been told how he was to approach the Princess on the dais and present her with the stone and that in doing so he would no longer be an invisible and ignored abomination but a venerated and revered Lord himself. Yet Egremont had given his fancy dramatic speech, playing to the crowd, enjoying their complete attention, relishing how they gazed upon him. Yet he had won all of this rapture with lies. Lies. Lies that made Tumbletick out to be the great warrior Sir Bartle Rourke, Knight of The Eagle and The Pelican, whose bones Egremont and Is-Is had laid to rest under a solitary slab of stone without inscription. They had knelt in prayer and silence before the grave for a whole night from sunset to sunrise, while Tumbletick had watched them from within his hut. Tumbletick had kept an eye on the grave for ten years but let it become overgrown and untended so as to hide it from anyone who might have come to his copse. He kept the stone on his person always, looking at it, protecting it, knowing that no-one would ever try and rob someone as poor and as desolate as him in his dilapidated hut. His friends would come and visit with him quite often, sometimes together, sometimes alone. They would bring him food and news of the goings on in Umiat. How peace reigned and people were happy and that this was because Tumbletick was keeping the grave secret and the stone safe. Is-Is would come most often and would bring beers with him, his pipe and a desire to sit by an open fire outside the hut, dug deep into the ground so the light could not be seen through the trees of the copse. They would talk late into the night of the quality of the beer and the pipe tobacco and take comfort from the flames and each others company. Egremont on his visits always asked about the stone first, the grave second and Tumbletick's health third before talking about the most recent play he had seen. When all three were together, talk seemed to turn to food or they gossiped about the goings on in Umiat. Tumbletick was always hungry for news and always ravished the voluptuous joints of meat they brought with them to roast on a simple stake they would thrust beside the fire. Happy times, thought Tumbletick. Now he felt sick again as he realised what had been said at court two days earlier and how everyone thought he was the remnants of a curse placed upon the glorious Sir Bartle Rourke by a vicious Demon King. Anonymity is lonely but also ignored and Tumbletick thought that perhaps that was best.

"Tumbletick. I'm sorry," Egremont's voice was calm behind him and it bought him sharply back to his cowering position in reality. He shuffled around to face the wolfhound and managed a smile.

"It was to be your reward for your dedication my friend. To have you married to a princess, venerated and adored for your glorious past. What you have done deserved that level of recompense."

"I never wanted it though Eggers, "Tumbletick said shyly, stopping the smile but managing eye contact. "I liked my hut and my two friends visiting. Why would I want to be married to a Princess?"

"Well it's everyone's dream, isn't it?"

"Not mine. I'm surprised you didn't really know."

"I thought I was doing something great for you. Now I know I have cursed you, exactly as in my dramatic rant Bartle Rourke was cursed. Now every supporter of evil is going to think you are the man who killed Ahriman. I fear I have made you a target. I should have also venerated the memory of Bartle rather than attempting to create a myth that he still lived on in you. I miss him Tumbletick. I'm sorry for what I have done to you. We won't leave you alone now. We will be with you always, Is-Is and I. Come back to the cabin, we miss you."

They navigated their way back across the deck with the gait of those unused to the pitch and yaw. In the corridor outside Fenton's cabin Tumbletick felt Egremont's paw land on his shoulder, he turned around to look at his friend.

"I really am sorry for the theatrics. My penchant for affectations does make me a fool too often I fear."

"But it is who you are Eggers and as such you should not apologise for it. Remember when you wanted to wear a monocle so that when you were in conversation with people who really were fools you could stare in shock and the monocle would fall with sensational aplomb and swing on its chain at your side? Then you would be able to make a cutting witticism which would highlight your own brilliance over their dull existence. That is what you are and I am honoured to be your friend. So do not for one second regret what, or the way, you said things at court. I am happy that because of it we are about to spend a lot of time together. Please do not change."

Egremont looked long into Tumbletick's hairy face and deep into his eyes, his own face a picture of sincerity and thoughtful perusal. Then he said in a voice as rich in character that he could muster, "Well said Sir! But the honour of friendship is mine!"

Egremont gave Tumbletick a brief nod and a smile then opened the door to the captain's cabin. Fenton and Lord Jackson of En'Tuk were looking at a chart together on the table. Vixen lounged on the cushioned bench in a languid manner and Is-Is sat cross legged on the floor, leaning against a wall and sharpening a kukri.

"Feeling okay?" asked Fenton of Tumbletick.

"Feeling fine," replied the honourable little abomination.

Lord Jackson looked up from the chart. It was a map of the main city of Rampart. "We were just highlighting some of Campbell the Weasels known haunts. It appears to me that he is well known to the hostelries of the isle."

"We should be able to find him quite quickly though," said Fenton. "From what I understand of the cad, if we see a wailing wench running in the street we just need to head in the direction she came from and he's bound to be in the nearest inn."

Tumbletick let out a little giggle. He liked the pirate captain with his smart clothes and easy going wit. He also thought that Campbell the Weasel sounded interesting. Tumbletick himself had only ever met two women and had never spoken directly to either of them, the Princess or Vixen. What would a character like Campbell be like who frequented taverns making maidens moan?

Chorus Five

aken from "Sea Sense: A Pilots Guide." By Phineas Bunch.

Sea travel in the coastal regions of Umiat is notably a rough affair which grows rougher as you approach the islands to the north of the Kenai Peninsula and the Tanana Straight. The reasons for this are quite simple and are due to four main causes.

Firstly the prevailing winds of the region are northerly and as such the fetch developed causes the main swell and currents of the waters to flow south.

This combined with the second reason, quite a shallow sea around the islands and Kenai coast, means that the waves produced cannot form their full and natural rolling rhythm. The deepest part of the Sea of Kaltag, around the mountainous islands and Kenai Peninsula is thirty fathoms, however mostly it is around ten fathoms deep.

The third reason is that there are no known beaches in the region onto which waves can easily break and dissipate their energy. As such they smash with huge ferocity upon sheer cliffs causing shock waves to rebound which create extremely steep and choppy waters.

The fourth reason is the Tanana Straight itself which acts like a funnel emptying water from the Sea of Kaltag. Riptides here move faster than any wind or rower can propel a ship as such navigation becomes a chaotic and chance affair.

Chapter Six

'The Ardent Panda' had been at sea for four days and the group had remained pretty much in the cabin the entire time. Jackson and Fenton had been looking at charts a lot during this time, often joined by Egremont. Vixen had lounged for the most part in a luxurious way which made it quite clear she was doing so deliberately in an effort to store up energy. Is-Is had taken the opportunity to care for his arsenal of blades and had often gone on deck with Tumbletick to scan the horizon for sight of land. They wouldn't stay on deck for long though, the seas were harsh and the strong winds brought lacerating shards of spray into their faces, feeling like they had frozen into tiny daggers of ice. Tumbletick had enjoyed these moments, facing the elements and had really hoped to catch sight of some forbidding sea monster, arching through the waves, its head coming up on a serpentine neck to scan for prey in the sea. He knew that monsters must exist in these waters, for in the odd moments when he could push his way amongst the others in the cabin and take a look at the maps they had spread out on the table, there was always the etching of a terrifying creature in the corners.

It was around midday of the fourth day when they heard the cry of 'Land Ho' from a crew member quizzing the horizon from the crow's nest. Naturally each person sprang up keen to see the first signs of Rampart, the famously fortified island. They quickly made their way out to the deck and the bow of the ship, even those who had been to Rampart before were still excited as the entrance to the harbour was such an amazing sight.

A line of light grey grew thicker and rose from the horizon, out of the sea as the battlements could first be seen. Only rough geometric shapes could be made out, from this distance, by most on board the ship. Is-Is, however, could already see the warriors and engines of war upon the bastion. Then the mighty cliffs, scarred, ravaged and made rugged by the sea started to climb towards the sky. Tumbletick was amazed by the scale of the island; it suddenly seemed a very long way back home to the hut and his protective copse.

"They certainly will have spotted us by now. Time to send a rather strong message while we are still technically outside Rampart's territorial waters," said Fenton in an unusually serious manner. He called over to the first mate, who was busy tightening some rigging amidships. "Mr. Battfin, fetch the prisoner! The scurrilous excretion of a whore!" Tumbletick was shocked. Fenton sounded completely vicious as he spat out the order. The astute pirate sensed Tumbletick's anxiety and put his arm round him as he said in a completely camp pirate brogue.

"Ah ha, me' lad. When dealin' with pirates you got to sound like a pirate. Do you know the pirate alphabet me' lad?" He finished the question with a more comforting and usual smile and a wink.

"No, I don't think I do Percy," Tumbletick replied.

"Aaay, Eeee, Arrrghh, Ohhh, Yooouu," Fenton retorted in a complete pantomime pirate fashion. He gave no sign of any embarrassment at the terrible joke but changed to his normal voice and stated, "What you are about to see is not going to be pleasant but it is absolutely necessary. Stay up here and please do not get involved." With that he took a piece of rigging that was nearby, cut a knot with a swiftly drawn cutlass and swung on the released rope in a wide arc, after a short run, out over the side of the ship, above the tempestuous sea and gracefully came to land back in the centre of the ship by the mast.

"Ships company to attend punishment of the prisoner," he shouted with complete authority and the crew quickly assembled behind Fenton forming a tight huddle of pirates. "Mr. Battfin, bring forth the prisoner!"

Mr. Battfin, a huge, heavily scarred, bald, black pirate with a variety of ear rings, dragged a smaller, fatter man out from below decks. His arms were tied behind his back, with painful looking ropes around his scrawny biceps, elbows, forearms and wrists. He was very securely fastened. He had no clothes on above the waist and no shoes. Barefoot and with only a pair of ripped and ragged trousers on he was covered in all manner of filth. Tumbletick dreaded to think what level of the ship he had been kept prisoner on. He was whimpering like a child who had cried himself hoarse in a darkened room. His moustache was covered in mucus from his streaming nose and his tears had cut little tracks of cleanliness into his feculent face.

Mr. Battfin pushed the wretch the last couple of yards with a single shove of his right arm and the scrag of a man collapsed before the imperious Fenton, now so obviously the captain of the ship.

"Whispering Bob, you have been found guilty of breaking the Pirate's Code. As such your punishment is to be pronounced now. I have decided to give you a choice in the matter," Fenton turned to his men and, raising his voice a little louder with his arms open said, "For never let it be said that I am not a fair captain." Fenton received the agreeing cheers from his men standing on the deck. "You can choose either one hundred licks of the cat to be performed by the immensely strong Mr Battfin. Or you can select to walk the plank. Usually I would have given you the option of being marooned with a bottle of rum and a pistol with a single shot. But it appears we are in colder climes today and there are no desert islands available."

A decent amount of laughter bubbled up in the crew at this point. Witnessing punishment was not a difficult chore when the captain was as fair as Fenton and the prisoner had, known to all, genuinely broken the Pirate's Code. Mr. Battfin bent forward, grabbed the snivelling little man by the back of the head and pulled it so as to raise Whispering Bob's face from the deck.

"Yur Cap'n desires an answer post haste Bob," he growled in thickly accented buccaneer tones, his teeth flashed with a hint of gold at the back.

"P-P plank," was just about audible through the streams of dribble that emanated and fell from his mouth.

"Wah Hey!" the pirate crew yelled in appreciation. Plank walking was extremely rare. In fact none on board had ever seen the most romantic and stylised of all pirate punishments performed before.

"Thought you would take the easy option," Fenton said coldly and quietly to Whispering Bob. "Fix the plank!" he yelled. A group of the crew moved quickly and lashed a plank about eight feet long so that it protruded over the port side of 'The Ardent Panda'.

Mr. Battfin hoisted the miscreant up in a rough fashion and placed him standing on the plank. Whispering Bob took a few steps toward the end, jeers and catcalls of the crew screeching in his ears. He got to the end of the plank but could not take the final falling stride. The pirates starting shouting all manner of insults about his lack of courage. Fenton gracefully skipped onto the plank in a single bound and swaggered behind the condemned.

"Last chance to show some honour and bravery Bob," he whispered into an ear. Then when no step was taken, Fenton swung round to face his crew and shouted, "Let us find out if Bob can live up to his name!" Fenton turned again and in one fluid and continuous motion lifted his left leg and firmly pushed with the tip of his boot into the back of the timorous prisoner, setting him into an unstoppable totter. Whispering Bob fell into the sea and immediately was swallowed into the depths by a voluminous swell, the ship raced on leaving the sinking body of Bob behind.

Fenton put his hand to his brow as if searching for some sign of resurfacing and said, "That looks like a 'No' then."

Tumbletick turned to Egremont, bewildered by what he had just seen. Egremont looked back, no sign of shock on his face and said, "Fenton will explain back at the cabin, I'm sure. Look, the crew have all gone back to their duties now. It's all over. Let's head back and get the answer to the question we must all be asking."

Back at the cabin, Fenton was the last to enter and shut the door behind him. Jackson, Is-Is, Tumbletick and Vixen were all sitting down on the bench. Egremont was standing at the table, "Well?" he said.

"Yes. An absolutely necessary part of pirate life I am afraid. Reason One. Bob had broken the Pirate Code. The part of it which states, quite clearly, that all pirates share any booty in equal shares. I am the captain and I get the same share in any treasure as even the lowliest deck-swabber. It has always been that way. I get to be captain by virtue of the fact that I am voted to be captain. We are actually a totally democratic lot, us pirates. Bob had kept two hundred and fifty nuggets of gold for himself and had not shared it. Simple decision once we found out. Reason Two. If it did not happen then the crew would think I had gone soft and would probably vote me out. Reason Three. I wanted to do it. Reason Four. It will have been seen by the watchers on the battlements and they will now know that we are honest pirates who follow the codes that have been laid down for centuries. Now that that has been answered let us get back out on deck and marvel as we enter Rampart Harbour. It really is quite a sight going through the Portal."

"Do you really think that such an elaborate execution was really necessary for taking two hundred and fifty nuggets for himself?" quizzed Vixen.

Fenton turned immediately towards Vixen and fixed her with a flinty stare. He slammed a fist down onto the immense table causing cutlery to jump momentarily due to the violence of the strike.

"Did I not make myself clear? I thought I had made it very plain indeed. I would not question you on matters of State Intelligence and spying. Bob was a wretch who betrayed his colleagues. He will sit in the very lowest levels of Hell for that crime. I have honour and my honour has been upheld. While the two hundred and fifty can not now be equitably distributed, the crew have had their equivalent share paid by the Pirate Code being upheld. Whispering Bob would have been less of a miscreant had he murdered another member of the ship's company."

Fenton then looked at each in the room in turn. "I asked you not to get involved and that it was absolutely necessary. Now I trust the matter is closed and we will not have my authority questioned while I am captain aboard this ship."

A smile then removed the frowning stare from Fenton's face. He went to the cabin door, opened it and gestured for all to make their way outside.

Back on deck the island pretty much filled the entire view ahead of them. Mr. Battfin was at the wheel towards the stern of 'The Ardent Panda' and while the group decided to take various vantage points around the ship to sensationalise at the sights with outpourings of superlatives. Tumbletick was engrossed by the fortifications of the island. Such a manmade labour must have taken eons he thought.

"Egremont, what are the bits called on top of the battlements that look like teeth?" Tumbletick asked the wolfhound who was standing nearby.

"A good question Tumbletick," he replied. "The raised areas that you so eloquently describe as teeth are called merlons. The areas in between that allow defenders to shoot through are called embrasures or crenelles. You can take your pick of names for them."

Lord Jackson ambled over to Tumbletick and suggested that the two of them go and stand with Mr. Battfin.

"I've been through the Portal several times on business and it still impresses me Tumbletick but I think being beside the helmsman adds certain significance as he takes us through."

Mr. Battfin gave no indication of welcome or showed any sign that he wished they would depart. He kept a true line towards the western tip of the island and Tumbletick kept a close eye on the wonderful Portal opening up before them. The line of battlements which spanned the gap across the two spurs of rock yearning towards them looked like a row of grey teeth just waiting to chomp down on the tiny ship and unprotected crew. Tumbletick's sense of fear began to grow even stronger as he picked out a half ring of white crested waves extending from the bottom of the Portal and forming what he was now convinced was the bottom jaw of a mouth, the sharply spiking waves completing the image. He broke free of the hallucination and summoned the courage to ask Mr. Battfin directly what he felt sure was a stupid question.

"Mr. Battfin, why is there such a pronounced 'U' shape of waves like that before we reach the Portal?"

Mr. Battfin looked down quickly to his left and into the upturned face of Tumbletick.

"An observant question Mr. Tumbletick. Lots of those landlubber types don't usually notice the shape of differing waves at sea," he said reasonably loquaciously but still with his buccaneer brogue. Tumbletick felt a shock of pride in the fact that he was now no longer scared at having asked the question.

"Those waves are caused by what lies beneath 'em."

"And what lies beneath 'em?" retorted Tumbletick, a little flush now in what he felt was a burgeoning friendship.

"There lies a man made reef of sunken ships and barges. What is there to give habitat to creatures of the sea. In return they give us sailors, cutthroats and pirates a calmer harbour on the other side," replied Mr. Battfin, now looking ahead again. "They break up the waves that are heading on into the harbour or across the front of the Portal. Then the waters are very well behaved on the other side. All I have to do is find a safe passage through. Otherwise we become part of the reef by sinking on it. A good question Mr. Tumbletick, make no mistake." Mr. Battfin reached out a strong arm and slapped Tumbletick on the back. Tumbletick, in spite of the stagger forward, felt he had found his sea legs with the confidence of Mr. Battfin's conversation. Lord Jackson of En'Tuk gave a secret smile as he saw Tumbletick stand a little taller.

"Mr. Battfin," said Jackson. "Do you think that Mr. Tumbletick could navigate 'The Ardent Panda' through the reef and then under the battlements into the harbour?"

"Why Mr. Jackson, I'm positive that he could," the huge bald pirate replied.

So it was that Tumbletick stood behind the large spoked wheel, Mr. Battfin behind him and steered 'The Ardent Panda' safely through the reef. The wheel was so big that Tumbletick had to stand very close so that his arms could reach either side. Although he had never even so much as sailed a model boat before he felt quite confident, especially as he knew Mr. Battfin kept readjusting the course by moving the wheel occasionally above his head with little taps to port or to starboard.

Chorus Six

Diary entry of Raven Hill, 23ʳᵈ Frimaire.

"I had a very boring day until witnessing the execution of a pirate called Whispering Bob, who had broken the Pirate Code. Percy Fenton sure knows how to combine kangaroo court tactics with style and flair. Then it was down to the important business of major sight seeing as we were to go through the Rampart Harbour Portal. I positioned myself at the extreme bow of the ship. The guide books are correct about it being immensely impressive. The engineering and construction of such a span is truly awesome. Particularly interesting is the defensive array of weaponry built into the very structure itself. Every two or so yards both in width and depth of the span there is placed a metal cage, cylindrical in fashion which, to my estimate, contains ten cannon balls stacked on top of each other. Although I can not be certain I would suggest that these projectiles can be released on the simple press of a trigger, either dropping one at a time or all at once in a devastating volley. A dropping weight of iron from that height would be fantastically destructive to any ship beneath. Upon the battlements themselves I saw trebuchets, catapults, balisters and mangonels, all of which would be able to hurl rocks and bolts at any approaching fleet. I suspect that Greek Fire could also be dropped upon any shipping. What is clear is that any naval attack would be futile if it was to approach the Portal during war.

Docked safely and spent the night in an adequate tavern in the harbour town of Tetterton. Ascend to the plateau tomorrow."

Chapter Seven

The 23rd of Frimaire was another day that Tumbletick would always remember too. Upon entering the harbour one was greeted by the majestic rising cliffs of the spurs to the north and south and the wonderful dock complex built beneath the eastern cliff. Tumbletick saw many solid stone quays and jetties jutting out from a fortified town at the waters edge. The town was quite small, being constructed into a space about a thousand yards north to south, slightly curving like an unstrung bow. At its widest point this strip of reclaimed land was perhaps two hundred yards. As space was therefore at such a premium, the warehouses and offices of merchants who traded in such a restricted area had been built out on the jetties. Using space better but also it afforded an efficient way of getting goods under cover and lock and key quickly. Tumbletick noticed how the buildings of the town were all built of stone, were all square or rectangular and all had flat roofs with mini battlements running around the perimeters. They were also built around a rigid grid system and Tumbletick could see parallel roads running between the buildings. These roads were busy with all sorts of people hurrying along on business. Lots of them were pulling or pushing various carts and trolleys some loaded, some not. There were many ships and vessels moored up in the docks being laden or unladen by stevedores, wooden cranes lifting nets filled with boxes directly into the warehouses. It was a busy place filled with movement. Then Tumbletick began to hear the sounds of the port. It enthralled him with the colourful language and noises of industry merging into an opera of commerce. Tumbletick was still with Mr. Battfin and Jackson and asked of the famous merchant, "What is the name of the town?"

"That is Tetterton Market. One of the greatest trading centres of the known world. A completely free market protected by the city state of Rampart. The officials of Rampart charge absolutely no taxes to trade here and as such it becomes very busy. The people of Rampart benefit hugely though as most that come to the island stay a while and spend money. Also the island gets nearly all of its supplies brought to its doorstep for free." Lord Jackson suddenly realised he was going on a bit in his enthusiasm.

"Mr. Battfin, if we could head for Jetty Seven I have some offices there," Lord Jackson of En'Tuk changed his tone to one of official command.

"Aye aye," replied the first mate and he started shouting orders for a pilot ship to be lowered with a rowing party to act as a tug to bring 'The Ardent Panda' into dock while the sails were furled and stowed.

After docking they grabbed their gear and walked up the same plank Whispering Bob had graced so briefly a little earlier. They found themselves, however, walking onto a solid dockside. Mr. Battfin was to join them the following day after ensuring everything was ship shape aboard Fenton's Flagship. Fenton had encouraged Egremont to let his first mate join their group as it turned out he was an extremely capable fellow with a resourcefulness and a swordarm that was bound to come to good use.

"Seeing as it is getting on a bit why don't we head for a cosy tavern I know with a suite of rooms. We can bed down for the night and ascend the eastern cliff tomorrow morning," suggested Fenton. The others agreed quickly and they traipsed towards the alleys of Tetterton. Tumbletick found himself walking at the rear of the group next to Lord Jackson as they passed rows of merchant's shops on the harbour front. He noticed a sign above one shop which said 'Watchmaker and Merchant'. Tumbletick thought to himself how he had so few possessions and really did not want that much but he had always wanted a really nice pocket watch. A gold one on a chain that he could bring out on occasions where he needed to know the time, press a little button and the protective case would spring open revealing a clean white face with precise black numerals and beautifully crafted hands. He gave a little sigh realising that he was the poorest man in the world walking beside the richest and yet they were now close friends on an adventure together and the gulf in wealth meant little when compared to the closeness in admiration.

'The Grobbling Smith' was a large squat building, stone like all the others in Tetterton. It filled an entire city block and was three stories tall, topped by the compulsory battlements. Fenton led them to one of the doors to gain entrance to 'The Grobbling Smith'. Each of the four sides of the tavern had a door in the exact centre, strong and sturdy. Tumbletick glanced in through leaded windows upon scenes of merriment within, people eating and drinking around large wooden tables. Within there was all manner of people showing all manners, but mostly happiness and comradeship. The door that Fenton took them to gained access to the hotel part of the inn. He opened it and they entered a pleasant lobby area. Doors led off to evocative sounding rooms such as 'snug' and 'tap room'. An elaborate desk for reception was beside a wide staircase leading upwards in a graceful arc to the next floor, it then swept further above their heads to the top floor. Fenton rang a gold hand bell on the reception desk with a familiar flick of his fist and a stunning, buxom, lithe young lady with blonde hair in bunches and a classic 'serving wench' white bustier and long flowing black skirt emerged from a curtained arch with a sign above it stating 'office'. Fenton flashed her his most winning smile and she instantly burst into a peeling giggle as delightful as the bell and could not once manage to look Percy in the eye as she proceeded to book the group into a suite of rooms which she strangely referred to as 'your usual apartment Mr Percy sir!' Tumbletick noticed she was grinning inanely the whole time and he wondered if she may be a little mad.

The apartment was on the top floor and was situated in a corner of the hotel. Three bedrooms, a bathing room with a large iron tub and a lit brazier providing hot water. There was also a water closet and a separate dining room for private functions. The rooms all led off from the sumptuously appointed lounge. Wonderfully comfortable chairs and couches sat upon luxuriant rugs. Paintings of naval battles and famous seamen adorned the walls with tapestries of hunt scenes of mythical beasts. They quickly made themselves comfortable and selected bedrooms. Tumbletick, Is-Is and Egremont were to share one. Fenton and Jackson another and Vixen was to have the smallest bedroom to herself, to enjoy a little privacy after sharing a cabin at sea with a group of men. They relaxed and chatted for a couple of hours before it was decided that they would have dinner and a good drink of ale in the taproom whilst Vixen would have a bath and eat alone in the apartment. As the men made their way down for a decent evening of food and beer, Tumbletick found himself trotting down the stairs beside Lord Jackson.

"Lord Jackson?" enquired Tumbletick.

"Yes my good man," replied Jackson.

"You know you said we only had to ask if we wanted any supplies for the mission."

"Yes."

"Well it's not exactly supplies, but you see. Erm. I mean. Well if I had the money I would not ask, naturally."

"Naturally. You only have to ask," Lord Jackson goaded nicely.

"Well. I've always wanted a nice pocket watch but my financial situation denies me that opportunity of ownership," spluttered Tumbletick more eloquently than he was used to.

"I thought I saw you glance over at Giger's the Watchmaker when we were walking through that part of town," Jackson smiled. "He is a fine craftsman. Tell you what. Tomorrow before we leave, what say you and I go and do a little shopping. You've already learned how to pilot a ship from Mr. Battfin. Now let me have the honour of teaching you the art of negotiation."

Tumbletick nodded his agreement enthusiastically as they continued their descent to the Taproom. The main drinking part of 'The Grobbling Smith' was moderately busy now. A hubbub arose with the smoke from many pipes and candles. The candlelight was transformed into various colours by the protective glass vases the candles sat in. The conversation lowered in volume a little as they entered. Not in any ominous way, a few heads were turned and a couple of eyebrows raised but the confident and extremely competent aura of the warriors Is-Is and Egremont, the knowing charm of Fenton and the extreme presence of a man as wealthy as Lord Jackson, soon meant that all the denizens of the drinking den turned once again to their smoking, chatting or dice games that had been previously in motion. Very few of the bars customers even noticed the small, ugly hairy creature that was accompanying the group.

"Only bar food is available in the Taproom but there is a wide variety of ale," said Fenton in a strangely servile manner. "I have often found that the Landlord keeps and excellent barrel of Three Wyches. I'll get a range of sandwiches in and a round of beers. Take the empty table in the corner."

Tumbletick wondered whether Fenton was trying hard to change his tone after the extremely forceful one he had shown aboard his ship. He did not wonder for long though as he found he had rarely felt happier with his new friends around him and a beer in front of him. He got increasingly euphoric as the pints kept coming and the sandwiches were found to be superb. Many fillings in many types of bread. They drank till just before midnight and all laughed their way up the stairs back to the apartment and into a deep sleep.

Chorus Seven

A 'Negotiation Diatribe' by Lord Jackson of En'Tuk. 24th Frimaire, given over a hearty breakfast in the Taproom of 'The Grobbling Smith'. Some suspicion that Lord Jackson of En'Tuk was still slightly tipsy from the previous night's bout of ale.

"The First Law of any business conversation is to never underestimate anyone that you talk to. Always remember that everyone you meet is better than you at something. No matter what. Everyone has a skill, some knowledge or an ability with which you could not compete or compare. Knowledge of the First Law has seen me become what I am today.

The Second Law is to ensure that you are always better prepared than everyone you ever enter into a business conversation with. Knowledge of the Second Law has seen me become what I am today.

The Third Law is to never give anything away without getting something back of equal or greater value. Knowledge of the Third Law has seen me become what I am today.

The Fourth Law is to always ensure that you know what your competitive advantages are and to exploit them to the utmost limit at every opportunity. My competitive advantages are that I know the four laws and that I have more money than anyone I enter into a business conversation with. Your competitive advantages, Tumbletick, are that you now know the three rules and everyone you meet thinks that they are better than you due to the fact that you must be an imbecile because of the way you look. As such you will make a perfect negotiator. Knowledge of the Fourth Law has seen me become what I am today.

Now there are also a range of tactics you must employ from your arsenal of tactic tricks that will make negotiation more fun and more successful.

Tactic One is to always throw in some personal feelings, as your adversary can never deny them.

Tactic Two is to always have a range of options you can negotiate around. You must always have an end plan as per the planning indicated in the second law but it is a tactic to have planned in further depth than your opponent.

Tactic Three is to have the odd irrational outburst to throw your enemy off kilter at crucial points of the battle of words you are engaged in.

Tactic Four is to ask lots of questions that have real value and worth to make your conversational assailant peruse deeply.

Tactic Five is to occasionally act stupid so that your adversary will slip into the error of ignoring the first law.

With this knowledge you will always win."

Chapter Eight

Tumbletick and Jackson made their way to Giger's so they could be there after the merchant had been open about an hour. The group had decided they would begin the ascent to the plateau of Rampart at about midday, so Tumbletick and Jackson had some time to make their purchase. Jackson was wearing a hooded cloak to cover his face in case anyone might recognise him and spread the word that Tumbletick was associated with the legendary trader. It was a very basic disguise and several people had also been enjoying breakfast at 'The Grobbling Smith' so it was more in hope that none of the other residents were on their way to the watchmakers with a warning.

"Now Tumbletick we could, of course, just send you in to buy whichever watch you want but where's the fun in that?" said Jackson handing Tumbletick a large leather bag. "Remember what we planned over breakfast and enjoy yourself in there. Select the watch you want and get it but on your terms, your negotiation."

Tumbletick grinned at Jackson; he felt surprisingly confident with the quick fire training he had received as he turned away and reached for the handle of the heavily reinforced door to the shop. He pushed the door open and a bell rang, knocked into life by a metal spur at the top of the frame.

Giger's was essentially a square room with large counters running around three sides. Thick ornate panels ran around the bottom of these counters. Made of dark wood and heavily carved with clocks through the ages. On top, glass allowed potential buyers to peruse the differing items for sale. Tumbletick desperately want to pounce over to a counter containing the pocket watches but he remembered that Lord Jackson had said that most people would think he was an imbecile and underestimate him so he thought it best not to demonstrate any buying signals whatsoever so he stood in the very centre of the room and tried to strike as strong a pose of an uninterested consumer as he could whilst he waited for an assistant to show themselves.

A svelte, youngish gentleman, clean-shaven with light brown straight hair, long on top, shaved at the sides in some foppish attempt to look stylish, glided into the room on very light feet. He was dressed all in black, his hands clasped in front of him. He looked with disdain at Tumbletick, sneered an only slightly perceptible sneer and managed to utter from behind clenched teeth the immortal shop assistant line of, "Can I help you…sir?"

Tumbletick looked him straight in the eye, held the gaze for a pause too long for it to be a comfortable glance and retorted in a steady tone, almost purring.

"I don't know, can you help me? Do you have an extensive knowledge of pocket watches which is going to impress me enough that I might want to purchase one off of you?"

The young man spluttered. He had not expected such an insolent reply from the obvious vagrant standing before him.

"Well sire. Our cheapest pocket watches cost a mere two hundred gold pieces, which I would suggest by looking at you is more than you probably wanted to spend. May I suggest that a stall on the market in the beggar's quarter is where you start and end your shopping excursion today? Giger's is an establishment that counts among its patrons members of the aristocracy and the wealthier merchants of the region." Condescension, condensed and in liquid form amassed at the corners of his mouth and began to drip from the side of his slimy jaw.

"Ah," said Tumbletick. "And pray tell, how much is your most expensive pocket watch?"

"Well it's two thousand gold pieces but why would you need to know that?" snorted the assistant.

"I might want to buy that one. Can you show me what sort of line you do for about five hundred? I'd probably want to get about six of them!"

"Listen, I think I have been patient enough. Now do I have to call for security? They are very big, hugely muscled and would have no problem in kicking you out of here very quickly indeed." The assistant's voice began to raise in both pitch and volume.

"Why would you want to throw the gentleman out, Sven?" interjected a man entering onto the shop floor. "He's just enquiring about the prices of our pocket watches. Why don't you let me deal with him?" The man was about six foot tall, also dressed in black, with a closely cropped grey beard and hair. His skin was leathery and heavily lined and he had light blue eyes which were laughing and obviously incredibly perceptive.

"Mr. Giger, I'm sorry but he's a piece of scum who has drifted in on the tide," whispered Sven sidling up to the master watchmaker.

"No, Sven, I do not believe that he is. I believe that he is a customer," Giger turned towards Tumbletick and in hearty tones and a big embracing smile said, "Good day to you sir! I am Giger, owner of this humble emporium and I sincerely hope to be able to provide you with a pocket watch which you will love and cherish always!"

"Excellent," retorted Tumbletick. "I am looking to buy a pocket watch and you can provide me with one. Let us embark upon an exploration of your 'humble emporium'," Tumbletick was surprised by the loquaciousness he had just expounded and thought to himself that he must have spent too much time in the company of Egremont recently.

Giger was an attentive salesman and his enthusiasm as the creator of the watches was obvious and infectious. Tumbletick attempted to feign some lack of interest but found it difficult. Although he did not actually like the overly ornate expensive items, Giger could sense the rapture, thinly veiled, when he presented a simple gold watch with a plain white face and clear black lettering and numerals.

"Is this more complimentary to your needs sir?" he asked in a calm voice.

"Why yes Mr. Giger, I think that you have actually complimented my dreams with this piece!"

"Well then we only have to discuss price now and for a gentleman as discerning and pleasant as you I am willing to offer this to you at my very best price. This is a favoured design of mine and I will let you have it for one thousand two hundred and fifty gold pieces. Would you like it boxed?"

Tumbletick was aware of the closing technique and was also conscious that he did not want to haggle but to negotiate with Mr. Giger. Haggling was crass and uncouth.

"I am sure Mr. Giger that you must have factored in the cost of the box into that offer. Tell me what the price would be for the watch with no box plus no commission for Sven who very nearly lost my custom with his lack of customer care?"

"I think those are fair points and well made. My boxes do indeed have a value attached and Sven will not be surprised that this sale will pay him nothing. So I can let you buy this from me at a reduced one thousand two hundred."

"I am stunned by two things Mr. Giger!" exclaimed Tumbletick. "The cheapness of your boxes and the desultory commission structure you must operate! No wonder Sven is so ill mannered, he must be permanently light headed and grumpy from the starvation wages you enforce upon him!" Tumbletick chuckled to himself at engaging tactic three so humorously.

"Sir," replied Giger. "Believe me that the box is more expensive than you guess and the wages lower than you could imagine. However that response of yours was worth a further fifty gold pieces itself as it has lightened up my day with its wit and wit is always worth paying for. One thousand one hundred and fifty to you, Mister...?"

"Tumbletick, Mr. Giger, but no Mister to me please."

"Tumbletick. It is a pleasure to meet you. Now, I can offer wrapping paper for free at one thousand one hundred and fifty. How would you like to pay?"

"I would like to pay with a promissory note but I only have a one thousand gold piece note left. For this watch to therefore leave your establishment today I am going to have to see a further discount for cash."

"I am afraid then we are not going to be able to conduct what looked like was going to be a very pleasant transaction. The absolute lowest I could offer would be one thousand one hundred and then I am making nothing from the watch and my thousand hours of loving creation was a gift to you for free from me." Giger looked genuinely sad at this.

"Is one thousand one hundred a firm offer then Mr. Giger?"

"Reluctantly it is indeed Tumbletick but you only have a thousand gold piece promissory note so we can not conclude."

"Mr. Giger, I said I only have a one thousand gold piece note left for this watch." With that Tumbletick opened the leather bag Jackson had given him and pulled out from a secured inside pocket a one thousand note and a couple of two thousand notes as well.

"I have five thousand I am willing to spend in your shop today," he passed the notes onto the counter and Giger checked for authenticity and seeing that all the correct stamps and signatures were in place he smiled broadly.

"I think that perhaps 'Sir, Tumbletick Sir' would be a more befitting name than just Tumbletick," enthused the watchmaker.

"Hmm, maybe. Now this is my offer to you. My earlier boast to Sven is correct, I do want to buy six other watches as well and I want to pay five hundred for each of them and one thousand for mine. A total I think you will find of four thousand."

"That would be the correct maths. What is your proposal then Tumbletick?"

"The little platinum watches with the bright gold face and jade numerals you have marked up at five hundred and fifty. Therefore I want six of them and mine for a total of four thousand."

"Done," said Giger and instantly held out his hand to shake.

"Damn," said Tumbletick shaking it. "You would have gone lower wouldn't you?"

"Maybe Tumbletick, maybe. However you still got a saving over list price of five hundred and fifty gold pieces. Which, fundamentally is one of the little platinum watches for free, or the price you wanted to pay for yours and a substantial discount for the bulk order. Plus you have got some very nice watches as well. Tell you what seeing as it was so much fun I will give you boxes for each as a gesture and you can tell Lord Jackson you did even better with wily old Giger!"

"How did you know I know Lord Jackson?" spluttered Tumbletick in admiration.

"I recognise his combative negotiation style and your bag has got his monogram stitched on the inside of the lining. I saw it when you opened it. Amazing eyesight and attention to detail some of us watchmakers have got eh?"

Chorus Eight

The party of extraordinary people decided to have lunch at 'The Grobbling Smith' before making the long and arduous ascent to the plateau of Rampart. Mr. Battfin had joined them now after giving the crew of 'The Ardent Panda' strict instructions to remain in the town of Tetterton and await their return.

At lunch Tumbletick decided that he would continue with his new found confidence and hit his fork on the side of his empty wooden tankard which he had just drained of Three Wyches. The hollow drumming sound attracted their attention and Tumbletick stood up.

"Lord Jackson and I went on a little trip this morning and I am very happy to say that I bought you all a present because you have all been so pleasant and accepting of me in your company."

Several cries of pleasure, surprise and of gratitude rose over the half eaten meal as Tumbletick handed out the boxes containing the watches to his friends. New cries of shock, gasps of amazement and comments of 'you shouldn't have' now mixed over the table.

"They are all the same and a symbol of the time we have spent together and the time we will spend together. If ever, or when, we are apart, hopefully you will look at them and think of me and when we may have the time to meet again."

"Well said Tumbletick," applauded Egremont rising to his feet.

"A well thought out gift and well thought out speech," nodded Fenton.

Vixen gave Tumbletick a blown kiss across the table and Is-Is just clicked open the cover of his watch and smiled broadly, unable to speak. Mr. Battfin fought back a solitary tear unbelieving that a friendship formed in such a short amount of time could warrant such a rich gift.

As Tumbletick gave the watch to Lord Jackson he explained the peculiarities of the deal. He was particularly clear in how he had decided to break down the final finances to suggest how the watch he handed to Jackson, the master merchant, was fundamentally gratis and for free.

Lord Jackson smiled and held Tumbletick's little hand in his with a strong clasping shake and said, "You did extremely well Tumbletick for a first attempt. Giger is a wily old foe." He then drained his own tankard of ale and he too struck it three times with a fork.

"Lady and Gentlemen. This watch shall be with me always as a true token of friendship, meaning and negotiation ability. I have decided that I shall have it engraved with a message which will add to its charm. That message will be:

'With a bellicose wit,
Tumbletick pocketed it,
in Tetterton Market.'
Well done Tumbletick!"

A chorus of laughter ran through the group followed by many questions as to how Tumbletick had managed to get so many expensive watches in lovely boxes!

Chapter Nine

The ascent to the plateau was physically the hardest thing Tumbletick could ever remember or have imagined. Only Is-Is looked unbothered by the constant climbing. The others were all fit and relatively unencumbered with only a backpack but still all of them felt pain during the climb. The decision not to use donkeys, which were available for hire at special paddocks at the bottom or to be lifted up in counter-weighted baskets that could carry several people at once, now seemed absurd. However they had decided to walk up the constantly damaging gradient in an effort to look like normal adventurers short of cash on their way to the old city of Rampart to seek their fortunes. After only three turns of the relentless upward zigzag Tumbletick was remonstrating that they had all been seen living in the finest apartment of 'The Grobbling Smith' and he had publicly given out extremely expensive watches in the main bar. Others started moaning that surely they could have afforded the money to take the baskets up the cliff face instead. Fenton replied that he had been spreading it about that they were spending the remainder of what little money they had in some tiny luxuries before facing almost certain death on treasure hunting in the challenges of the old city. It was not as if they had been as conspicuous as perhaps they would have liked to have been. Fenton did eventually acknowledge that, staying at a favoured suite of apartments might have meant news of him being in town would have spread quickly through the ranks of a certain type of young lady.

Tumbletick felt his usually white face redden a little as his imagination conjured up what 'type' that possibly could mean. His memory of the girl from 'The Grobbling Smith', who had booked them into the suite, was certainly a positive one.

Soon his thoughts turned very directly to the climb. Eventually every step felt like a sharpened pole was impaling the body in mind numbing pain. The group had to stop regularly to attempt to regain both fitness and breath.

"Can't see any army ever invading by this route!" gasped Vixen out loud during one of the frequent stops.

As they had earlier seen the path was carved steeply into the almost sheer face of rock of the eastern escarpment to the rear of Tetterton. The path turned tightly back on its self at measured intervals during the three hundred-yard ascent. Three hundred yards might not seem very far on a flat walk but straight up slopes of almost thirty degrees it seemed an amazing distance. At each turn a stone turret was built with half of the structure carved into the face of the rock where secure storerooms and guardhouses held supplies and soldiers in case anyone ever did try to assault the Isle of Rampart. With the news from Umiat arriving at around the same time as Tumbletick and company the guards were slightly more aware than in recent times and helmeted heads peered down from between the battlements. However, people still needed refreshments and vendors had stalls set up around the turrets at each turn to provide food and drink for travellers. The group stopped several times at these stalls purchasing energy giving nuts and pieces of cake which were drizzled in hot treacle from clay pots suspended over candles, protected from the rapidly increasing winds by wire gauze.

Even through the pain of the ascent Tumbletick found himself feeling happy still. He was protected by his friends and he was basking in his new found confidence. Yet a nagging doubt began to gnaw away at the deepest part of his stomach, a slight tickle of teeth bringing fear to Tumbletick that he was heading towards darker and more worrying times.

Chorus Nine

Diary entry of Raven Hill, 24th Frimaire.

"I do not think I will EVER forget the pain of the climb to the plateau of Rampart. The decision not to use donkeys to do the donkey work will remain in my thighs for a month I'm sure! Any attacking force would lose perhaps half its remaining strength trying to climb that path of potential death from exhaustion alone never mind the weapons of the turrets. The turrets that protect each turn are well embedded and covering fire would come from the turret directly above as well as the one at the end of the next leg of the trail. There are thirty legs in total to climb the face of the cliff so twenty nine turrets would have to be nullified. At the end of the last leg the path turns abruptly to the right and arrives on the plateau by heading into the face of the rock with a huge gatehouse built either side of the path and arching over the last twenty yards. I believe this would only ever be taken by elite shock troops, sabotage or extremely strong magic.

We found a nice spot on the plateau about a mile away from that final gatehouse. It was in the middle of a small copse of trees just off the main path where we finally pitched our tent. Tumbletick seemed particularly happy with the location. A campfire was lit and we relaxed our aching legs and bodies by the warmth of the fire and with swigs of strong liquor. Interesting insects flittered towards the light of the flames only to come too close and drop and die and crackle in the embers of the inferno."

Chapter Ten

Even though the group was in relative safety upon the top of the Isle of Rampart they still kept watch in pairs during the night. With Mr. Battfin with them now, the tent which was designed to sleep six would have been a bit crowded. So with two keeping watch a little more space was afforded in the canvas dwelling. Tumbletick was very pleased that, when his two hour watch came around, it was to be held with Percy Fenton. They sat by the fire, frequently feeding it faggots of wood, collected as they made camp and piled in a little heap by the bonfire. Fenton had a wonderfully ornate hipflask which contained a pint of an interesting whiskey from a distillery found on the slopes of Noatak in the northwest of Umiat.

"You will find," winked Fenton passing the silver flask to Tumbletick. "That because of the altitude of Rinkabar on the northern slope of Noatak, that this whiskey is particularly light and honeyish, with definite hints of heather kissed by bumble bees with feet that dip in a delicately perfumed peat."

"Umm, I like it a lot," said Tumbletick smacking his lips and shuddering as the warmth of the whiskey coursed down to the nagging little doubt in his stomach, dulling it and eventually lulling it to sleep for a while.

Tumbletick also liked the pirate Fenton a lot. He always seemed so full of joy, confidence and an affectation of bravado which never caused offence as blatant arrogance would. He was also marvellously lovely to look at and this made Tumbletick feel warm and satisfied like the whiskey. Tumbletick remembered well the complete ruthlessness Fenton portrayed, or displayed, in the execution of the snivelling wretch of a pirate Whispering Bob. However, he now certainly believed that the 'true' Percy Fenton was sitting beside the spitting wood fire of the campsite. His features made all the more pleasing by the chiaroscuro effects of the night behind and the flames before him.

"Tell me about your life Percy. As a pirate and before," said Tumbletick intently. "I've seen so little of the world. Living in my shack, guarding the treasures that Egremont and Is-Is entrusted to me."

64

"Well it is an easy tale to tell Tumbletick. I grew up on a farm about twenty miles northeast of En'Tuk. By the age of sixteen I had quickly realised that mucking out pigs and pulling potatoes wasn't really for me. I had won the charms of all the local dairymaids, knew where all the most comfortable haystacks containing all the juiciest farmers daughters were and found that actually running off to En'Tuk to seek fame and fortune was preferable to being chased off by a bunch of irate farmer's daughter's fathers. So I got to En'Tuk, got drunk rather too easily far too early one evening and found myself waking one morning with a throbbing head due to a hangover and a crack to the base of the skull. I was on board a pirate ship about twenty miles southwest of En'Tuk." Fenton laughed and took a big swig on the hipflask. "Mmmm, happy days they were. I quickly found out a few things. That the strength I had built up from all that mucking out, mucking about and harvesting, all the charm from years of convincing dairymaids to perform other duties than the ones they were employed to do and all the dexterity developed from jumping out of haystacks at midnight avoiding farmer's daughter search parties actually made me into the perfect candidate to become a very good pirate indeed."

Tumbletick found himself blushing a bit. "What about your parents, didn't you miss them?"

"Never knew them old chap, an orphan I! I was purchased from the orphanage to become a bonded farmhand. Old Farmer Greystock was supposed to have had me in service until eighteen but I stole two years from him. I should really send him some money in honour of my debt or compensation actually."

"We have something major in common then," blurted out Tumbletick. "I never knew my parents either! Egremont and Is-Is are really the only two I have ever known. I remember living with Egremont in his castle. Well, in a tower that was part of his castle, when I was young. Then one day they both came and took me to my shack and said I had to live there for a while. Quite a while actually, I've been there for years," he stopped to give a little laugh at what he thought was quite a funny twist on living there 'a while', to find that Percy was staring at him with deadly serious eyes and parted lips in an expression which was creeping towards shock but was very much at a stage of sudden realisation and awareness. Then just as suddenly Percy Fenton broke the silence, smiled and began to speak.

"Hmmm. Lucky you told me that Tumbletick. You are supposed to be the still living embodiment of the cursed form of Sir Bartle Rourke." He leaned in closer to Tumbletick so that his breath was upon his face. Quick as a scorpion stinging a mouse he drew a dagger from inside a fold of his jerkin and started twisting the handle so that the light danced from the flames and caught Tumbletick's eyes. Fenton's face constructed itself into a new look, one as set as the steel of the blade.

"Never ever tell anyone else what you have just told me. It was extremely foolish and weak. If a little whiskey and a sob story about some parentage issues gets you to blurt out information like that we could all be doomed. Egremont did not brief you well enough. It is imperative that the cover story of you being Bartle Rourke in a disfigured and cursed form sticks, Tumbletick. Do you understand?" Fenton's voice was now quiet but laced with intent and tinged with threat. "Do you understand?" he asked again.

"Not really," came the stuttered reply. "Not really."

"I see I am going to have to have quite an important conversation with Lord Egremont in the morning. Now give me your hand!"

Fenton took Tumbletick's left hand and very quickly drew the dagger sharply in a cut about an inch along the muscled base of the thumb. Tumbletick's eyes instantly bulged and then filled with water at the pain and the shock. Blood began to drip onto the leaves of the copse floor. Purple pools of thick sticky blood in the dark, shining by the fire. Insects and hard black shelled beetles crawled and writhed in to them and feasted. Fenton let go, then still holding Tumbletick's gaze cut into his own left hand at the same place and let blood fall into the same pools. Then he threw the dagger down so it embedded in the ground, clasped his bleeding hand to Tumbletick's and said.

"You need to know Tumbletick how very important you are in all this nonsense. Never, ever, tell anybody anything about your past again. It was merely luck that it was I. Know also that I will always be your friend, your companion and your brother. For now we are sanguine brothers of blood. Only twice before have I performed that rather basic but significant ceremony. Once with Egremont and once with Is-Is." Still holding onto Tumbletick's hand he swigged deeply on the hipflask with his free right hand then proffered the whiskey to the small deformed man in front of him. Tumbletick took the flask and drank as well. What little was left by the time Tumbletick had imbibed, Fenton poured onto both their wounds. Pain flashed through their bodies as the alcohol cleansed their cuts. Then Fenton took some bandages from his backpack nearby and gently dressed Tumbletick's hand first and then his own.

Tumbletick and Fenton sat next to each other for the rest of the watch in silence until Is-Is and Jackson came to relieve them just as the very slightest hint of dawn began to tinge the night with a lighter blue. Is-Is noticing the bandages said nothing but gave a big grin and promptly put a couple of faggots on the fire, scratching an inch long scar on his left paw as he was doing so.

Chorus Ten

The private thoughts of the group on approaching the City of Rampart, on the 25th Frimaire, just before noon, were varied.

Egremont found himself turning to his ward: "Got to brief Tumbletick on the role he is to play better. Lots of eyes and ears about in a place like Rampart. Campbell, yes Campbell, he'll know what to do."

Vixen continued to look at the military aspects of the isle: "Just look at that city! The plain around it is so flat and wide you'd be able to see anyone approaching miles in advance. Still easy to camp out here. Not many trees to build engines of war from."

Tumbletick was a little remorseful from the previous evening: "My goodness that whiskey was strong. I shouldn't have been a blabbermouth. I quite like being a blood brother with Fenton."

Mr. Battfin was drifting into a negative frame of mind: "I miss being at sea. If there's going to be any trouble in this city I bet we find it. This track is in pretty poor condition, very straight though."

Percy Fenton was attracted to the architecture: "Lovely city walls to Rampart. I can just see the higher walls inside surrounding the Old City. That's an odd looking steeple from a monastery or something sticking out over there!"

Jackson was thinking of his stomach, which felt more ravenous more often with the ravages of travel: "I wonder if we'll be able to find a good spot for luncheon before we try and find Campbell the Weasel. He probably won't be out of bed by the time we arrive anyway."

Chapter Eleven

The party of seven approaching the main city gate of Rampart made no effort to conceal their many weapons. They now looked like one of the copious groups that came classically seeking fame and fortune in the trials of the Old City. The news of the atrocities at the court of Rhyell had now reached Rampart but the gates were still wide open. The sentinels in full armour gave polite nods to everyone allowing the slightest of cursory checks.

The main gatehouse broadly slumped in confident strength in the wall that surrounded the city. The blocks of granite were finely polished so as to allow no footholds for any attackers and the joins were almost invisible. Unseen within, the ancient craftsmen of Rampart had cut interlocking fists and sockets of rock to add extra robustness. Also they had ingeniously left further cavities into which molten iron was poured and set to add further reinforcement still to the defences. Masonic knowledge such as this would be hard to emulate in the majority of the workforce of the current age. Inside the walls, passageways six foot wide would allow troops and quartermaster's servants to move unseen to the battlements and the regularly spaced turrets around the fortifications. Tunnels that could be blocked at a moments notice by the pulling of a lever, dropping a megalithic block of granite at strategic locations should any attacking force ever gain entry and hope to control the conduits.

The city itself, as they entered, was busy. They were in a commercial district that one would find at the main entry point of most cities. Taverns and hostelries jostled for attention with shops selling clothes, foods, weapons and medicines. The buildings themselves were all of the obligatory stone but were not as strictly planned as the grid system lanes of Tetterton. There was a more organic feel to the place and the further they traipsed in, the more random the buildings' planning became. There was also a steady but slight rise towards the centre and the Old City. Here and there Tumbletick kept gaining glances of that old and wicked heart. He noticed circling above the very centre many large and dark looking birds. Gliding around in lazy arcs, their hooded heads arched down so their beaks touched their breasts.

"Carrion," whispered Vixen into Tumbletick's ear. "They are looking for fresh meat in the heart of the Old City. Meat that will not fight back any more." She gave a hoarse chuckle and sidled up to Fenton who was further ahead and looked genuinely pleased at her slinky approach.

Tumbletick stopped. He suddenly felt oppressed by all the people around him. Jostling, occasionally bumping into each other, curses and cries speckled the air with insolence or fear. He saw city guards and hooded, cloaked figures. Strange faces, ugliness, brutality all around him. He caught sight of people looking at him briefly and then speedily turning their heads away in disgust at his ugly form. He felt light headed, hot, angry, then dizzy, claustrophobic and the nagging doubt suddenly surged in his stomach and he felt like he was going to vomit. His mouth wetted in preparation and he kept swallowing to quash the feelings. He felt hot and wet around the shoulders and base of his neck, he felt as if he was back in the packed panicked throng of people being butchered in the courtroom of Rhyell.

He felt a large hand come down on his shoulder. No not a hand, a big paw with a scar near the thumb. Tumbletick looked up into the perfectly clear blue eyes of Is-Is, with his big ears lolling with the weight of gold rings, the familiar face of his friend brought him suddenly back again to the relative safety of the present.

Tumbletick saw the other five about thirty yards ahead, looking back at him and Is-Is. Egremont broke away and moved with some urgency towards the strange pairing of a huge warrior hare and the world's ugliest man. Joined by a noble wolfhound in plate-mail breast plate with a distinctive tabard they made a conspicuous trio.

"Are you okay Tumbletick?" Egremont asked intently. "We sort of lost you for a while there!"

"I'm fine. I just felt a little ill and panicky. Thought I was caught back at Court in a mass of people. I'm okay now though. Is-Is brought me back."

"Look, we are nearly at the hotel we are going to stay at. Jackson convinced me that we should try and gain lodging at a fine old establishment called 'The Swan'. It's nearer the centre, very shabby chic and priced to keep the riff-raff away but it's not an unreasonable place for some well heeled adventurous types to reside at. Are you okay to carry on? It's about another fifteen minutes?" Egremont had his left paw on Tumbletick's other shoulder and he felt a little oppressed by the two warriors strength pushing down on him.

"Yeah, I'll make it there. If you two could just walk with me I may feel even better. I'm getting some funny looks from people so with you two with me I will be fine."

They ambled up to the rest of the group and after some brief enquiries about the state of Tumbletick's health they all moved on through the streets of Rampart until they reached 'The Swan'.

'The Swan' was old. As old as the old centre and it was obviously a coaching house that had once been placed outside of the original city of Rampart, as a better place to keep horses and travelling types. Huge bay-fronted windows at ground level afforded plenty of light into the common rooms and bars situated there. As you went up the outside of the four story building the windows got smaller and smaller until quite tiny windows could be seen in the roof which had once been dormers for the dormitories of the servants who had lodgings there. The stone walls had been painted cream for the bottom two stories and then a sage green for the top two. The roof had old black tiles but speckled with newer red ones where repairs had been made. Impressive chimney stacks, ornately decorated in an effort to make their girth look daintier were at both ends and in the centre of the building. Many chimney pots indicated that many fireplaces offered warmth within from Frimaire nights atop a plateau that found itself in the middle of the Sea of Kaltag and the Circle Sea.

There were no doors to gain entry to the pub from the outside walls. One had to enter though a wide arch slightly to the left of centre of the facade that led onto a central courtyard. 'The Swan' was not busy and Lord Jackson negotiated a rate for a suite of rooms on the second floor in a quiet corner of the hotel. The rooms were large and well appointed but when one examined the detail one could find areas of peeled plaster or decaying paint but the fires were well stacked with charcoal and the tapestries were interesting.

They took a hearty repast in their private common room served by the staff of the hotel. The Landlord busied himself around the bar area. He was a man of extreme experience who grumbled about his customers and wore a wide brimmed hat. Tumbletick found him to have a dry wit and an ability to know what everyone wanted to drink, he found himself immensely drawn to the man and wondered if they would be able to spend some time here and get to know the landlord and his beers a bit better. Percy was outrageously flirtatious with the serving wenches and Tumbletick found that he blushed less now observing such behaviour and thought more about who the real Percy was. He decided that the flirty Percy was a front to build his swaggering legend and that the serious side he had encountered at the campfire and before the execution of the traitorous Whispering Bob aboard 'The Ardent Panda' was more his true self. The violently aggressive and forceful Percy was another front that could be employed at will, if the situation demanded it. Tumbletick hoped he would not have to see that Percy again for some time to come.

The discussion over luncheon centred on the hunt for Campbell the Weasel. It was generally agreed that they would be likely to find him in some drinking establishment. More likely still where card games based on chance and a little skill were played. Even more likely where painted ladies of dubious character often congregated in the hope that some drunken, lucky gambler could be waylaid of his winnings by exercising some blatant charms and false promises.

It turned up during the conversation that Mr. Battfin knew Campbell the Weasel personally as well as Egremont and Is-Is. Jackson, Fenton and Vixen only knew of his reputation. Mr. Battfin didn't elaborate too much but said he owed his life to Campbell. Fenton raised an eyebrow and asked if it was to do with the 'marooning incident'. Mr. Battfin gave a conciliatory nod of his head and said that Campbell would probably enjoy telling the story as soon as they met again and would not elaborate further. Fenton merely smiled and whispered to Tumbletick that Campbell could obviously add pirate to his list of achievements or bad habits, depending on your own particular point of view.

It was decided that they would split into two groups to look for the elusive thief. Egremont, Is-Is and Tumbletick would form one, Fenton, Jackson and Mr. Battfin the other. Vixen was to stay back at 'The Swan' as it was not totally befitting for a lady to go out on what was likely to be a lot of trawling and then likely crawling around Rampart's inns and taverns. It was thought that Campbell would probably be out and about by four and that they should return by midnight to their suite whether they had found him or not.

So it was that the two groups strode out into the already darkening afternoon after their leisurely lunch. The prospect of a few pints was perfectly acceptable in their quest for Campbell. After all there is little that is ruder than to walk into a drinking establishment, wander around looking for someone and then leave without at least investigating how the Landlord maintains his cellar.

Chorus Eleven

Campbell the Weasel was as flash as a rat with a gold tooth but everyone loved him. He was a lithe and energetic man with facial features which easily lent him the nickname that stuck for life. He had dark, almost black hair, a pointy nose and the inability to grow a full beard, even though he was in his early thirties. When he did attempt some facial hair it was very sparse but somehow added to his weasel like qualities. He was extremely agile, fit, fast and wriggly, both of body and mind. On many occasions he had been bested by bullies with beatings but would always have a sarcastic line to throw in before his own knockout punch. This would usually confuse his assailants just before he managed to sprint away or stick a spike up through the bottom of their jaw and into their brain in a fluid upward motion from the ground where he had been grovelling and spurting sarcasm or sycophancy seconds before. He was everything that people expected of him. He could hold a crowd's attention and he could beat you at any game you cared to play, be it card, board or mind. He held the heart of many ladies and the admiration of most men. Yet to look at him you were never quite sure why. He was also the finest thief the world had ever, or would ever, know.

Chapter Twelve

Egremont, Is-Is and Tumbletick had only been in a couple of pubs before a kindly Landlord told them he was quite certain that Campbell would be in 'The Lillith Arms' playing poker. 'The Lillith Arms' was a grotty little dive smelling of spilt fluids from cracked glasses and wracked bodies. It was a single room establishment, single door for an entrance and a single bar on the back wall. There were a few round tables where the denizens would dump themselves in alcoholic hazes and ignore those around them. However, recently it had become favoured by certain rich youngsters as a fashionable place to slum it and mix with the colourful locals. This was a fashion that had mostly been contrived by Campbell as a way of getting the vacuous rich to hand over their money to him by playing poker.

'The Lillith Arms' was in an unkempt quarter of the city which backed right up to the Old City walls. Buildings here were mostly made of wood and it lent them a rough and rotten look compared to the ubiquitous stone found almost everywhere else.

As they were about to enter the pub a church clock called out the chords to say it was a quarter past six. It was dark as Tumbletick checked his watch to find that the church was fast and that his expensive pocket watch had a luminescence built into it to allow easy night reading.

The pub would be able to hold about a hundred on a busy night. There were ten tables too tightly packed to allow easy movement to the bar. One would have to push by the backs of people sitting at them whether they were too drunk or too rude to move for you or not. Tonight the pub was not full. Regulars slumped at the majority of the tables nursing their beers however about twenty customers were gathered on two sides of a table in a corner by the bar. Eight people sat around the table playing cards. Seven were in fine clothing and wearing hats with too many feathers. The eighth was a dishevelled and unkempt bleary blue eyed man with dark matted hair and a grin on his face like he knew something. The rest of the crowd were mostly finely dressed young scamps of the wealthy families of Rampart although there were trampy types intermingling as well. Swaying a little more under the influence of cheap beer but enjoying the game equally. The flop was out, eight of clubs, eight of spades and the six of diamonds. The second round of bidding was just about to commence.

Campbell had of course noticed Egremont, Is-Is and the small ugly form like a hairy monkey with them. He was hugely shocked to see the two warriors in such a pub as 'The Lillith Arms' but he did not let it show at all on his fixed grin. He had positioned himself in the chair with its back to the end of the bar where it met the wall of the pub. Here he knew it was impossible for anyone to get into a position where he could be compromised from behind but also he could keep an eye on the crowd, his fellow players and notice when people entered the pub.

Five players had been encouraged by their hole cards to pay to see the flop. Campbell the Weasel was one of them. With a pair of eights out already it was interesting but not enough for any huge amount of chips to come in. A couple of players checked, Campbell raised by eighty, the next player folded then the following put down eighty to stay in the game and the original two who had checked also paid the eighty to stay in the game and see the fourth turn card. A five of hearts. So potential straights and full houses raised themselves. The crowd perked up as the betting went wild building the pot to a healthy sum but by the end of the round it was down to three players, one of which was Campbell. The river card was dealt and it was the three of spades. The first player checked, the next checked too and Campbell announced the immortal words of "I'm all in!" and stood up, winking at everyone and giving the briefest eye contact and recognition stares to Egremont and Is-Is. The player to his left folded, thinking that Campbell must have hit a full house or straight, he was also a little annoyed that the Weasel like man had broken etiquette by standing while two other players remained. The last player who was also chip leader was holding in his hand a pair of Kings. He was an extremely rich young man, courtesy of a father who made his fortune in the fur trade. He was mainly here to be seen playing poker with local rough types and so matched Campbell's 'All In' to see the hand.

Campbell flipped over his cards, Ace of Spades, Ace of Clubs. That made only two pairs. Not the great Straight or better Full House that might have been expected or suspected with the posturing of standing up. However it was enough to beat a pair of Kings and the rich young man simply smiled, tilted his head so the feathers in his hat swayed a bit like a purple plant touched by a summer breeze and threw his cards to the dealer face down. He still had plenty of winnings left and it had been worth matching the bet to find out what was in his opponents hand.

Campbell laughed a little impolitely and leaning so his stomach lay on the table embraced the pile of chips he had just won and scooped them towards himself.

Is-Is, Egremont and Tumbletick made their way to the bar after the entertainment of the round of poker and did not pay much attention while Campbell was still playing. The Landlord was a hugely fat man with a bald head, shaved at the sides, shiny and sweaty on top. He made a lot of noise as he breathed and moved about. He wore a massively stained apron that once was white but was now all sorts of tans and browns, yet he wore it like a proud badge of office. He was probably a miserable sort at heart but with the newly found popularity of his pub he had a wide eyed look of welcome for the new patrons propping up his bar.

"Three pints of your finest ale, stout yeoman!" ordered Egremont rolling a gold coin over his knuckles in a cascading affair, back and forth with utter dexterity. Three pints of 'Bruin Bear' came their way. Tumbletick sat on a stool so he could more easily reach the bar and the pewter tankard that was handed to him. Is-Is leaned with his back on the edge of the saloon counter, his arms spread wide resting on it too. He was looking out to the rest of the room, oozing the confidence of the capable and keeping any talkative drunks at bay with the slightest of menacing airs.

Egremont engaged the Landlord in conversation in between his serving of customers. It was mostly small talk about the quality of the beer and the present popularity of poker.

So they waited and drank and glanced over at the game and enjoyed themselves. The beer was of a good quality despite the outward appearance of the pub and the Landlord, the cellar was probably very well maintained.

The trio had just finished their third pint when the game had reached the 'heads up' stage of the final pair. Campbell and the purple feathered fop had become the remaining adversaries. After only a few hands the young buck was well in the lead with piles of chips in front of him and Campbell started risking silly 'all ins' which eventually caught him out when his Jack of Hearts and Six of Spades were easily beaten by his opponents Queen of Diamonds and Ten of Diamonds and the flop of pool cards revealed two other Queens and another ten. A Full House. The crowd applauded and the final two players shook hands with rousing comments of "Good game" and "Well played" echoing from the watching fans. A new game quickly started up but Campbell announced that he would be sitting this one out as some old associates of his had been waiting for him at the bar for some time.

Campbell ran with unnerving speed and somehow managed to gather both Egremont and Is-Is into an enveloping bear hug. Laughter from all three and opening salvos of chat merged with fond looks and shaking of hands for several minutes before Egremont finally introduced Campbell to the quietly smiling Tumbletick.

"Tumbletick," announced Egremont in his deepest and silkiest tones. "I have the very great honour of introducing you to the indomitable Campbell the Weasel. A man of a dubious past but a glorious future in our company. Campbell, there is little other to say than this is Tumbletick. You will have heard us mention him before."

Campbell ceased his smiling and adopted a very genuine demeanour. Even though his small eyes, positioned above a long nose and thin lipped mouth, surrounded by a bitty goatee meant most men read him as deceitful and disingenuous, Tumbletick at that moment saw through to the truth of his soul and that Campbell, ultimately, was honest, good, loyal and true.

"Tumbletick," Campbell's voice had lost all of its earlier banter. "It is my pleasure to finally meet you. I have often heard Egremont speak of you as a man of utmost trust. A gentleman of modest wit and a caring heart. Though Egremont never described your appearance to me, I can tell he had painted your character perfectly with his words."

"Pleased to meet you too but I only really heard of you about a week ago and some people were pretty scathing in their description of you which seems a little unfair now that I have met you. But I can't really say 'a pleasure to finally meet you', so a pleasure to meet you too," gabbled Tumbletick. He was slightly upset with himself for being too nervous in his opening statement with Campbell. Tumbletick instantly decided to blame it on the beer instead.

"Ah refreshments!" declared Egremont as the Landlord set down four more tankards of 'Bruin Bear'. Tumbletick quickly set his face to the rim and drank deeply. Is-Is, Egremont and Campbell clashed their three together in the universal act of comradeship. "Cheers". They drank together until just before eleven and regaled in stories of past adventures before Egremont announced it was time to head to 'The Swan', where he could more safely explain what the glorious future was for Campbell in their company which now made up the very nice number of eight.

Chorus Twelve

Rules for entry to the Old City of Rampart are extremely simple. Anyone can enter. Who is allowed back out is a different matter. Nearly every day from noon, new groups enter. The Old City, clustered in various states of ramshackle and ruin around the old castle, is a huge draw to all types of people. Adventurers, fortune seekers, misfits wanting to see if they can disappear there. Mostly it attracts those who think themselves capable in a fight and who are drawn by treasure and the spoils of combat. It is well known that the city is regularly stocked with monsters, animals and prisoners sentenced to life. Indeed Rampart does a good trade with other cities of the wider continental region who wish to reduce their prison population. One hundred gold pieces per prisoner to Rampart to dispose of a few convicts is much more efficient in most budget plans of penal centres as a one off payment rather than twenty gold pieces a year for the term of a sentence.

Food is not thought to be common in the Old City. Occasionally a flock of sheep is driven in to enhance the diet of the denizens but it is thought that cannibalism is probably rife.

Once any set of adventurers has decided they want to exit they have to make their way to the only gatehouse in the huge walls surrounding the Old City. There they would have to recite passwords they had been given upon entry in order to get back out as well as show distinguishing features which will have to be cross referenced against the approved password and adventurer's name. More than once before passwords had been extracted using the brutal act of torture by inhabitants looking for a way back out into society.

Chapter Thirteen

The reunion back at 'The Swan' had been an exciting one. Mr. Battfin and Campbell the Weasel seemed to have an enduring bond which caused the huge pirate first mate to cry with happiness at seeing the charismatic Campbell again. Exactly as Mr. Battfin had predicted before the groups had set off in search of the little thief, Campbell was soon embarking on the glorious tale of how he knew Mr. Battfin.

"Now, Battfin and I were once pirates together aboard a wonderful little clipper called 'The Bucking Groom'. He was just a lowly swab then and I was the first mate. Many swashbuckling tales we have but my favourite is how I saved his life after he got caught by another rival group of pirates and they marooned him on one of the thousands of little islands around Porcupine Gulf." Campbell was a natural raconteur and he was pleased how everyone was looking at him in the private common room of their suite.

"Being a loyal first mate and true to the Pirate Code I impressed upon our captain, a man by the name of Bridge, that even though we had only lost one of our number to a rival gang during a skirmish in a little port in the shadow of Mount Aklavik, it was our duty to endeavour a rescue mission despite the odds of ever catching them as they had made off in their ship faster than us because they were less drunk at the time." Campbell paused for breath after his monumental opening sentence to the main body of his tale. "Now if we could track them down and be sober when we caught them I was extremely confident that our skill at arms would out-match them. A simple case of grappling hooks, heave their barge next to our clipper, board 'em, dispatch 'em and rescue old Battfin and steal their loot into the bargain. However there was also the chance that they might just as easily slit his throat or do the honourable thing and maroon him with full pirate honour. A bottle of brandy or rum and a pistol with a single shot. So we began what was likely to be a futile expedition around the islands, shoals and sandbanks of the Porcupine Gulf. I figured that they had about a four hour head start on us and a stiff north westerly breeze would probably have taken them about thirty nautical miles. In rescue missions like this we would usually give a good whole day searching for one of our lads but seeing as it was Mr. Battfin, three whole days were to be allocated. If he was marooned on one of the numerous sandbanks that flooded under the tide or thrown overboard then there was little chance of success. If he was placed on a larger island then there was some hope." Campbell paused and looked at his eager audience who stared back and made little gestures of hope that he would continue.

"On the second day the lookout spotted smoke on the horizon. A thick column rising then bending in the breeze and streaking the sky away from us. We approached a reasonably large island, wooded around a little peak. Probably an ancient extinct volcano. As we got closer we noticed a flashing light, the sun being reflected towards us in a regular pattern of quick then slow deliberate signals. As we got closer still we could see a large bonfire and still closer a large, completely naked Mr. Battfin, wearing nothing but a smile and eating a large leg of roasted goat. Needless to say, seeing as he is sitting in the room now we did decide to rescue him. His signalling had guided us easily to him but how had he managed to guide us to his location with such signals, lit a bonfire, butchered and roasted a goat when he had no clothes and no tools I hear you ask. There is where the genius of Mr. Battfin lays and why such a resourceful fellow is so useful a companion." Campbell took some pride in the fact that more than one of audience's jaws was unhinged revealing gaping mouths.

"Mr. Battfin, would you care to regale us in how you achieved such a feat?" urged Campbell.

"Nah, you do it better than I," came the curt reply, based also on the knowledge that the raconteur secretly desired to tell the story again.

"As I have already stated, if the captors of Mr. Battfin had marooned him upon a sandbank then he was as good as dead. Their big mistake was to show a little sympathy and they chose a wooded isle which, as it turned out, also harboured a small population of goats. They were probably the last survivors of an earlier shipwreck and they had managed to do quite well on their little island. His captor's slightly smaller mistake was to have listened to the silver tongue of Mr. Battfin who upon being offered a bottle of rum and a pistol with a single shot asked heartily and good naturedly if his final drink upon this earth could be the finer liquor of brandy. This they allowed him. Mr. Battfin was and still is a pirate of some repute in the trade and they swapped the bottle of cheap rum with an expensive brandy to many cheers and congratulations on deciding to get drunk as a gentleman now his pirate career was over. They then rowed him ashore, allowed him to undress himself and departed with his clothes and cheery waves. Now Mr. Battfin waited until the marooning party had boarded their ship and slipped away over the horizon before he put the pistol and brandy bottle down and started to collect fallen branches from the tree line and driftwood from the beach to build a large beacon. He had already noted that there were several goat tracks on the beach so knew if he could capture one and light the fire then food was going to be quite pleasant and as goats lived on the island then there must be water too.

Mr. Battfin opened the bottle of brandy, poured it over the bonfire then waited for a goat to arrive on the beach, which he was sure one would do soon as goats are notorious alcoholics and would be attracted by the aroma of fine brandy. As soon as one did he placed the bottle in between himself and the goat, crouched near to the alcohol drenched wood and fired his flintlock, gun held on its side. The spark from the flint lighting the charge of gunpowder which caused an explosion in the air and brandy fumes. The goat startled by the light of the flames was even more startled by the bottle which suddenly shattered as the single shot sheared through it and then thumped into the chest of the goat killing it instantly. Mr. Battfin took one of the sharper shards of glass, cut up the goat and impaling fine fillets of meats on stakes stuck in the sand let the roaring bonfire slow roast his dinner."

Tumbletick found himself applauding with a childlike enthusiasm and grinning inanely at the end of the tale of pirate resourcefulness. The rest of the group were also looking impressed.

"Is that what really happened then Mr. Battfin?" probed Fenton.

"Well, pretty much captain, excepting the embellishments by Campbell of shooting the goat through the bottle of brandy."

"A mere trifling licence of the imagination," barked Egremont. "It is still a rip roaring tale and proves Mr. Battfin's worth to continue our quest with us. Resourcefulness is a rare and valuable commodity in a man. Sometimes it is completely vacant in those who appear successful by other means."

Lord Jackson of En'Tuk stood up and cleared his throat, fist in front of his mouth, a staccato of coughs bringing all eyes upon him.

"Now that we have Campbell with us our party is complete and we must now turn our attention to getting to Kenai. Time is, as always, a pressing master and we must be aware that we may be watched as we depart."

"Then," interjected Campbell, "May I suggest that we travel by a route by which none would see us leave and most would suspect that we are dead?"

"Ah, an intrigue!" laughed Fenton, "Tell us more."

"Well, it is my understanding from my brief brief from Eggers that secrecy in this mission would be a benefit."

"Correct," chipped in Egremont.

"I have a plan then which is also blessed by being extremely dangerous, potentially rewarding and would guarantee that no-one would see us leaving the island."

Chorus Thirteen

*V*ixen's Diary. Entry of 25th Frimaire.

The plan of Campbell the Weasel is as follows. Percy Fenton would return to the docks of Tetterton and purchase a small skiff or schooner with funds to be provided by Lord Jackson's office at the harbour. Jackson had quickly written out a coded message to his staff there which would mean funds would be handed over even to a famous pirate captain. The rest of the party would enter the Old City as fame and fortune seeking adventurers. Then they will need to fight, sneak, run and hack their way to the very heart of the city, the old castle itself. Here, they will then make their way to the dungeons of what is likely to be the power base of any outlaw King who has made it as chief of the anarchy which must be found within the Old City walls. For under the dungeons are the catacombs where citizens of the ancient past of Rampart have buried their dead. Under the catacombs are caves and passages cut by lava and then moulded by centuries of water finding its way to the sea. Beneath the caves is a larger vaulted sea cave which can only be entered at low tide by a vessel no larger than a ship's launch, usually used to ferry passengers to docks or between ships or pirates about to be marooned on deserted desert islands. This cave, lit by light diffused through the sea and into veins of quartz stretched across its walls and ceiling is a secret of the Thieves Guild. Revealing it to us means Campbell is now a man marked for execution, should anyone find out, by the Guild and its affiliates worldwide. They have been using it for years as a way of getting goods and services to people within the Old City who have the money and the influence to pay for what is a very difficult route to market.

Chapter Fourteen

Any group of adventurers who wish to enter the Old City have to first register themselves at a small stone hut near to the double gated gatehouse which acts as controlling mechanism into the city. The stone hut has two doors on its walls facing the square, one to the extreme left, one to the extreme right. The left door has 'ENTRANCE' painted in neat white letters about six inches high, the door to the right has 'EXIT' in the same style of lettering and can only be opened from the inside. There are no windows to the small stone hut so what goes on inside is even more secretive and alluring. Crowds gather each day and stand around or sit at one of the many public houses who have chairs and tables outside so one can peruse the comings and goings over a pint. Each day at half past eleven a small wizened man opens up the entrance door to the hut. He is escorted by a group of four city guards in full ceremonial dress and carrying dangerous looking halberds. For this man is the 'Executor of Entrants'. As he enters the hut the soldiers take up their duteous posts, two to the sides of the entrance and two to the sides of the exit. They cross their halberds so they bar both doors for half an hour whilst the 'Executor of Entrants' gets his papers in order and makes his first mug of tea of the day on a small stone stove in a corner a little way a way from his rather large desk. At noon precisely, by the chimes of Rampart Cathedral, the guards snap to attention and raise their pikes indicating that the hut is now open for business and will remain so during the hours of daylight that remain. Sometimes a queue may have already formed of young gallants, professional mercenaries, cut-throats seeking more honest work or exotic warriors from around the world. Sometimes you might see a group leave a pub like 'The Black Bull' or 'The Hangman's Noose' and trot along to the hut, full of drunken bravado, like they were buying tickets to a show at a box office. The plaza where the hut, the gatehouse and the inns all stood was always popular but the city walls near to the gatehouse were always crammed with people who had paid the entrance fee to get fantastic views from atop the battlements. The crowds thinned out the further you walked around the walls but parties perambulating the perimeter were always present, gazing down upon the Old City from different angles hoping to see some monster or encounter between an adventurer and a famous prisoner who had been incarcerated. Genteel ladies escorted by their beaus, holding parasols and nosegays perfumed to guard against the smell of the city and giggling at the horrific howls that occasionally jolted out to them and then squealing in pleasure as they were then grasped a little tighter by their brave attendant. It really was the social scene of outdoor life of Rampart. Although the 26ᵗʰ of Frimaire was early in the year the day had dawned bright and clear and there were plenty of people about as Is-Is, Lord Egremont Seau du Duvet, Mr. Battfin, Vixen, Campbell the Weasel, Lord Jackson of En'Tuk and a small, hairy, ugly little creature called Tumbletick made their way to the flagstone square. They joined a small queue of about a dozen outside the hut at a little after two o'clock, after a fine luncheon and only a couple of beers at 'The Swan.'

Tumbletick felt really quite nervous now. It felt really real. Like something genuinely huge was happening. This was it. Several adventures and big things had occurred but now they were going to put themselves right in the midst of it. The queue suddenly lunged forward as a group of six, black ninja robed, individuals went into the hut together. Tumbletick decided to try and gauge the remaining six who stood in front of him and his friends. They were obviously a party as well as they stood too close together and chatted too easily to be new acquaintances. Tumbletick had learned a little about squads of adventurers from his friends Egremont and Is-Is during their fireside chats back at his hut. Tumbletick examined the six in front, they had a fully plate mail armoured knight with a broadsword and shield and a barbarian who was hugely muscled and in furs. They were obviously the warriors. There was also a small, quick moving, fidgety man who looked like he might be useful with locks and traps. A kindly looking man with religious robes looked as if he might understand medicine and the staunching of wounds. He also carried a heavy looking iron mace as well as a benign smile. Then there was a slim, tall person who carried a bow and a long hunting knife. They were also insanely beautiful and Tumbletick couldn't make out if it was male or female but was entirely sure it must be an elf from the forested lands miles and miles across the sea to the west. The sixth man was in robes of a deep, inky blue. He had flowing white hair and a long beard. Tumbletick was sure that he must be 'useful' too, but for what he could not guess but the others behaved in a deeply reverential manner towards him. Perhaps if people were looking at his own group as they were taking a spot of lunch at 'The Black Bull' they might think the same thing about Lord Jackson. What could he do in a tight spot? Or maybe watchers in the crowd would have negative thoughts regarding Tumbletick. 'What kind of creature is that? What use could it possibly be? Perhaps it is good at climbing trees, or for testing unknown foodstuffs on, which might be poisonous.' Tumbletick shook his head in an effort to clear it of such negativity and listened to the other party's conversation in an effort to learn their names. Within a couple of minutes he had. The barbarian was called Seton Rax, he was easiest to identify as he kept talking about himself in the third person, only using his own name rather than the more customary 'I'. The paladin, for the knight was referred to as a holy warrior, was named Beran. The little thief was known as Lambert. The priest with the evil looking iron club was Nazar Grant, the elf Vigor and the old man was called Garraday.

Tumbletick found himself immersed in their hopes for treasure, their bravado and their plans. He thought they seemed like good people, not an evil bunch that would wait near the entrance of the Old City and then ambush his own group as they started out on their quest for the Sea Cave.

A short time after he had learned all their names, the exit door opened and revealed the other group of six depart for the gatehouse. Almost immediately Seton Rax brazenly pushed open the entrance but then held the door for his companions to enter before him. Proof positive of manners and respect which must mean he was a gentleman at heart and unfairly labelled a barbarian thought Tumbletick.

Chorus Fourteen

" **R**ules of entry to the Old City of Rampart are extremely simple. Anyone can enter. Who is allowed back out is a different matter," said the small man behind the desk in well rehearsed and performed, precise clipped tones.

"By meeting with me here in this hut you have chosen to enter the Old City. This you must now commit to. If you do take the exit door and then do not proceed immediately to the gatehouse, you are likely to be lynched by the adoring fans who await you outside." The 'Executor of Entrants' gave a peculiarly bureaucratic little wheeze which passed for a laugh. His really fresh mug of tea steamed away beside him as he reached into a cavernous open drawer of his desk and pulled out some paperwork.

"If you wish to exit the Old City, make your way back to the gatehouse. It is the only way in or out of the Old City. Most people usually run towards it," again the little gurgling wheeze, at least he enjoyed his job it seemed. He probably made the same jokes about ten times a day. Tumbletick and his friends were just staring at him blankly, waiting to answer his questions.

"You will be known as Party 'Twenty Six, slash, Two, slash, Aardvark Feathers' from now on. That will also be your password should you wish to exit. I will repeat it once more. Twenty Six, slash, Two, slash, Aardvark Feathers. Do not repeat it to anyone else inside the city. Now if you will all tell me your names after I ask you, I will write them down on your entry form and write a brief description about you. I have a discerning eye and the guards at the gatehouse appreciate my poetic nuances when it comes to describing returning adventurers. Despite the fact that they may have some new scars or fewer eyes then before." Gurgle. Wheeze.

One by one the 'Executor of Entrants' took down their names and wrote a description of each of the group. He did not show any sign of being impressed at any of the full titles of the groups. He probably did not actually know that he had in front of him some of the finest warriors the world had ever seen. He did know however that he had seen impressive groups and individuals before who had never been seen again, lost to the hell that actually existed within the walls of the Old City. However his descriptions were actually quite brilliant. Some rhymed, some scanned perfectly, some were masterpieces of classical rhetoric woven into sonnet or haiku form. Very few of the guards ever did appreciate it but he did. He took great pride in his role and knew that 'Executors' following him would look through the archives on quieter days and secretly be jealous of his prestigious talent.

When he came to write the description of Tumbletick he desperately wanted to write something ludicrously beautiful to contrast to the creature that was in front of him. A sense of vision into the nature of the strange being seemed to come to him. This is what he did write, simple and only two lines.

"Mellifluous name if mirrored to visage.

A small creature with a too true heart."

The man felt pleased with himself with that entry. This creature was a very strange one indeed and of all the entrants who had ever passed through his hut he could not seem to remember one that belonged to a similar looking race.

"Well, time for you to make your way to the gate," the executor stated. He nodded towards the only other door and the way out.

Mr. Battfin pushed it open and they exited in single file and into the light of the square. As they left the old man finished his mug of tea which was now a pleasant drinking temperature, just slightly too hot to gulp down but not too much as to scald. He put down the empty mug as the door shut behind the incredibly large hare and he sighed in satisfaction of a great mug of tea and another set of adventurers recorded in his files for the ages.

Chapter Fifteen

"Right straight to the gatehouse," ordered Egremont. He set off purposefully, conscious of the theatricality of heading toward what for many was certain doom. The bars and restaurants around the square were reasonably attended and the party looked grim faced as they strode towards the great gates that led into the gatehouse yard and the second set of gates which opened into the Old City itself. Tumbletick scampered faster than a trot to catch up to Egremont and pointed out that he actually carried no weapons and they were heading into a very dangerous environment.

"Would it make you feel better if you did have a weapon?" enquired the wolfhound. "You are right it is likely to be exceptionally dangerous but Is-Is and I will be your bodyguards. You would only have to fight in an extreme situation."

"I would feel better if I did have some sort of personal protection afforded to me," replied Tumbletick. Is-Is heard the conversation and as they continued walking towards the gatehouse bounded beside the little man and pulled out from a sheath on his thigh a long hunting knife. Straight and broad, made of steel with a blood letting gash worked into the centre of the blade. Nasty looking saw teeth were on one side of the blade, the other was a clean lined razor sharp edge. Is-Is tossed it in front of him, one flip like a skilled juggler and caught the blade flat in his paw. He stopped walking and handed it, hilt first to Tumbletick. The leather bound hilt was hard for Tumbletick to fit in his very much smaller hands and he had to hold it with two. It was like a sword to the small deformed man. Is-Is, unbuckled the sheath from the top of his leg and fitted it around Tumbletick's waist. Tumbletick looked at the blade, a little in disgusted awe about the damage this would do to another individual if used in combat and sheathed it.

"Feel better Tumbletick?" asked Egremont. He knew the answer was a resounding 'No'. "At least you will be able to defend yourself if we do get into a tight spot in there. Let us make sure that it does not come to that hey?"

Is-Is rubbed Tumbletick on the top of the head and gave his huge, one toothed grin. This was indication that he at least, would not let it come to anything in the Old City that threatened Tumbletick.

Now the gatehouse loomed above them. It was formidable, solid, squat looking in its massiveness, yet tall. A vast set of double gates, thick wood with black metal banding, would soon open into the central courtyard beyond. Full of murder holes above and to the left and right, this was the staging area where final preparations were made before entering. Also it could be the zone where returning adventurers could be assessed of their passwords or easily dispatched by guards with crossbows and boiling lead. The first gate would then be closed, pulled shut by ropes from within the gatehouse attached to great winding wheels. Then huge links of iron, in long chains, would rattle through controlling hoops of stone, deafening all as a portcullis fell behind the now shut gates. Next, hidden mechanisms within the depths of the gatehouse would be turned so as to raise the weights which lifted the next portcullis, slowly in front of the final gate which led to the Old City. If there was any sign of a potential attack from within the Old City the weight would be released and the portcullis would snap back down. The final set of gates were always locked and bolted from within. The final barrier to the horrors beyond it was best to keep this firmly closed. Entry to the Old City was not theatrically rewarding or allowed. The vast gates would not swing open to allow the grand entry of aspiring adventurers. It was fine to see groups enter the gatehouse by such manner and allow the audience around the plaza a last moment of respect. Here, however, security was paramount so access was via a small door which opened within the gate itself. It was thick and studded with iron and it allowed one person through at a time.

The whole gatehouse had the feeling of a lock on a canal. You waited and acclimatised between the two different levels.

There was a reasonable amount of people about to watch the gates swing open on the outside of the gatehouse. The party of Egremont the Lord Seau du Duvet, Is-Is, Lord Jackson of En'Tuk, Vixen, Campbell the Weasel, Mr. Battfin and Tumbletick disappeared into the shadows within. There were no large cheers, only a couple of shouts of encouragement. Most voyeurs had seen parties enter before.

As soon as they were beyond the line of the gates they started to close and the first portcullis slammed down behind them. Suddenly darkness was around them. They waited and a little light afforded itself as their eyes grew accustomed to the dank surroundings. They checked that their weapons were all securely fitted, their armour was all in place and that their backpacks were on tight. None smiled or talked. Then the sound came of the next portcullis rising, straining and creaking. It ascended only enough to be able to walk under it and push open the small personnel door.

Is-Is took the lead. He drew his broadsword, pushed open the little door, stooped and stepped through. A shaft of light split the darkness, dust from the floor rose as Is-Is disturbed it and it sparkled. Tumbletick heard other weapons rasp from their sheaths, drawn by his companions. He saw them disappear in turn, swiftly through to the Old City. Egremont followed Is-Is, rapier in hand. Then Vixen skipped, swift and graceful. Lord Jackson of En'Tuk, with a dagger in each hand, smiling sallied forth. Campbell flitted through then Mr. Battfin darted with his cutlass, into the light and Tumbletick was alone. His stomach turned and he exhaled a snort of fear through his nose, his mouth grimly set. Fear and anticipation combined as he held onto the hilt of his new knife, then he ran after his friends and heard the portcullis immediately crash behind him.

Here ends book one of the Tumbletick Trilogy.
Book Two, 'Tumbletick Too', continues with;
The entry into the Old City
And the continuing quest to Kenai.

BOOK TWO

TUMBLETICK TOO

Chapter One

Is-Is burst through the open door and into the Old City. His broadsword drawn and in a raised position behind his leading left paw, so he was ready for combat should the need arise. He was on a wide boulevard heading straight east. In the ancient past this was a glorious highway, neat flagstones perfectly fitted and smooth. Carefully carved channels allowed rainwater to be swiftly carried away and ruts at a standard wagons width would control industrial traffic as it moved through this part of the city. Trees, once lush and manicured were spaced evenly along the road, to offer shade and enjoyment to the eye. Now however, weeds cracked the flagstones, litter clogged the channels and the trees were dead with dead things nailed to them in varying states of decay and recognition.

Is-Is quickly surveyed the scene and thought it safe as the others emerged from the gatehouse. Next came Egremont with his sword flashing, then Vixen, Jackson, Campbell and Mr. Battfin. Finally Tumbletick came running through the small door, not needing to stoop at all. He was holding the hilt of his new knife with one hand allowing the other to shut the door neatly behind him as they all heard the portcullis crash down.

Buildings in various states of repair were set behind the trees and it was obvious that this city crammed many buildings within its walls. Rooftops and towers stretched away in all directions but east, where the boulevard ran straight off into the distance.

Running toward them now darted two figures. They had just sprung out from a darkened alleyway about two hundred yards away and were sprinting, arms and legs pumping down the road and towards the gatehouse and the group. What was this, an immediate threat? Only two, no obvious weaponry and dressed in leather armour they didn't seem to pose much risk. Soon the real threat was very obvious indeed. A very large, feline looking creature came racing after the figures. However, feline made it sound delicate; there was nothing subtle about this beast. Sandy coloured with tan speckling, huge hairy paws with claws scraping and chipping the stone road, its fur on its body looked short but around its vast head the fur was in a shaggy mane. Its head was broad, with large yellow forward facing eyes with vertical slits of black for pupils. Its lower jaw was bearded and wet with saliva from the gaping maw. It probably had loads of teeth too but at this very moment only the two prominent incisors were visible. Visible because three foot spikes of enamel like that always draw the eye. These two teeth curving down, puncturing pick axes of pain, and they were approaching very swiftly towards the two individuals, panting and pounding towards the gatehouse and potential escape.

"Interesting!" said Egremont as he took a firmer stance.

A roar came from the fifteen foot feline and from the crowd on the battlements near the gatehouse. Tumbletick remembered that some people paid an entrance fee to climb the battlements in a hope of getting to see a scene like this.

The two runners were now about a hundred and fifty yards away and it was obvious that the snarling sabre-toothed creature was easily going to catch one of them. It bounded along, took a huge leap and with its large clawed front paws landed with precision directly in the centre of the back of the poor unfortunate prey. He smashed to the ground, probably dead already from the crushing weight of the cat and the hardness of the flagstones. What happened next would have killed most living things. The creature rearranged the man with its paws so that it lay more accommodatingly and rammed its fangs into the neck and lower spine. Then it retracted its teeth and started to pull away at the leather armour with its claws doing further damage in the process. Finally with the flesh revealed the creature hunkered down and brazenly began to feast in the middle of the street.

The other man continued running, no thought for his erstwhile companion. He was soon close enough to Tumbletick that he could see the panic still clear in his eyes. The man paid very little attention to this group of seven adventurers or the cheering from the crowd on the battlements who had got what they had paid for. He skirted round Is-Is and Egremont, who still had their weapons drawn, with no eye for anything but the door to the gatehouse that Tumbletick had just shut. He ripped open the door and finding the portcullis down started screaming, "Let me in, let me in!" The sound of groaning guards was nearly audible as they had to go to work again on the gatehouse mechanisms in order to raise the portcullis. They did not have to raise it very far though because as soon as a little space afforded itself, the man had dropped to his belly and he was scrabbling to get under. Tumbletick thought about joining him but instead, as soon as the man's desperate feet were clear, he shut the door again to which Mr. Battfin gave an approving nod.

"I think that caution maybe the better part of valour in this instance," observed Egremont. "Why don't we leave the creature to its dinner and find some cover to the north?"

The group agreed and they turned left and skirting the battlement walls trotted into the alleyways and paths formed between the buildings. The structures they passed were nearly all vandalised, burned out, fallen down or damaged in some way in this part of the city. Roofing tiles lay smashed in their path where they had fallen in earlier storms or maybe been thrown by inhabitants. Wooden boards were nailed across windows instead of neat shutters; most doors were laying where they had been pulled from hinges. A smell grew stronger as they walked, of filth, decay and death. They passed a pile of bones, heavily gnawed, that had been stacked into a neat pyramid by some intelligence.

"Pleasant place," said Jackson dryly.

"Let's hope we are not here for too long," replied Vixen. "Just get to the castle, get down to the Sea Cave and get out."

They were now heading East again after working their way into a dense area of old houses. Every now and then a completely destroyed building would allow a view of the sky to open a little wider and a glimpse of the castle could be caught. Moving at quite a pace and with a sense of dedication they did not move around the city like most adventurers would, who were more methodical in their search for treasure.

Is-Is, who was leading the way suddenly stopped and raised his left paw. The group halted and bunched up, Tumbletick finding himself corralled to the centre of the seven. A little way ahead a figure darted across from one building to another. They heard a sharp whistle, then silence.

"This is not good," said Campbell, deliberately quiet.

"I think that we should find some cover and quickly," Jackson advised, nervously looking left and right, pointing his daggers as he did so.

Tumbletick, stuck in the middle could not see very well in any direction so he looked up. Coming towards them along the rooftops were figures dressed in black, two on each side of the narrow gap between the three story buildings at this point. Between them, at each of four corners, these shadowing scampering forms held a large net, looking light weight but very entangling.

"Jackson's right. This is an ambush," Tumbletick yelled with all his little voice.

Mr. Battfin was the second to see the threat and the first to respond. He burst away from the group and kicked down a boarded up door with a deliberate placed violence.

"In 'ere," he beckoned and they ran into the lower level of an old house and into a large open room with a doorway leading to another space just as the net fell down into the street, almost catching Egremont who was last in.

Is-Is bounded through to the other room and Tumbletick could hear him pounding up some stairs that must lead to the other levels.

"Do not worry about Is-Is," said Campbell. "Secure this room and defend the doorways. Egremont, Battfin and I will take the front door. Tumbletick, Vixen and Jackson you take that back room."

Is-Is had obviously found something, or something in his way, up towards the top of the building because there suddenly came the loud noise of smashing splintering wood and debris hitting the floor in a vacant echoing room.

Then two solid dull thumps came from the street.

"Is-Is found his way to the roof and to two of our potential ambushers," stated Egremont, looking out through the door and seeing two of the black garbed figures. One no longer had a head and the other was still pumping blood from a large rent to the stomach.

"And a third," noted Campbell peering over Egremont's shoulder. Another body from the other side of the street plummeted to the ground with a throwing dagger embedded in an eye.

They heard thumping upstairs as Is-Is jumped back through the hole he had created in the roof and he came back down stairs. He entered into the room and shook his head, indication that no other assailants were available at roof level.

"One got away then?" said Vixen.

"I'm not so sure," interjected Tumbletick as he watched Is-Is leave the building and retrieve his dagger from the face of the third. The whole face could not be seen due to the ninja style headgear. As Is-Is had his right foot on the chest of the deceased to gain extra leverage while pulling out the dagger, Tumbletick ran next to the hare and despite the potential for gore, pulled off the headgear of the corpse.

He revealed the face of a Wolf.

"I've said it before and I'll say it again. Interesting, " stated Egremont with a little venom.

Tumbletick stepped back from the body and then, as a second thought, decided to ravel up the net which still lay in the narrow street.

"I think you will find that there are three more Wolf assassins about," he said as he was gathering up the net. Is-Is lent him some aid in bunching up the well made entrapping device and guided him back into the building, always keeping an eye on the roofline. They piled the net away into a corner.

"You had better explain how you know that," said Jackson.

Egremont and Is-Is kept a sharp lookout at the front door, Vixen went through to the backroom in case any extra wolves decided to come down through the gap Is-Is had made in the roof.

"Well, in case you didn't notice, when we were queuing to enter the Old City there was a group of six dressed in very similar gear who went in a little before us."

"He's right," said Campbell.

"I wonder if it was chance or design then that led them to wait and attack us?" enquired Jackson.

"I think we know the answer to that," snorted Egremont. "You don't get a pack of wolves attacking a group like us, looking to hunt down their leader, at random."

"Well, if Tumbletick is right then we need to hunt down the remaining three very quickly," stated Campbell.

"What about Captain Fenton?" observed Tumbletick. "If six wolves could get into the Old City before us, well it would not be such a large leap of imagination to think some could be going after him too!"

"Cap'n Fenton can look after hi'self," said Mr. Battfin grimly.

"Well we are not going to achieve anything debating the issue in this hovel," added Egremont. "We all knew it was going to be dangerous within the city walls. Admittedly a few wolves added to the equation makes it a different scenario."

"A few maybe an understatement," pointed out Lord Jackson. "We can be pretty certain another three are loose nearby but who knows if other packs did not go in earlier or are on their way in as we speak?"

"Rampart authorities are definitely slipping if they do allow wolves to walk the streets. Strictly though it is a neutral City State and as such they have no quarrel with the people of Kenai," said Vixen sauntering back into the room and the conversation.

"Right. Let's get going and ensure we end up with at least three more Wolf heads rolling in the street," ordered Egremont. "Stay sharp, keep alert and show no mercy to any threat."

They started moving out of the bare, dusty room and back into the street and headed East. As they left and passed the dead bodies, Lord Jackson found himself beside Tumbletick. He patted the hunched back of his companion and said,

"Welcome to the Old City of Rampart, hey Tumbletick?"

Chorus One

Fenton finished his flagon of foaming ale at 'The Black Bull' and watched as his seven friends entered the gatehouse and the huge wooden doors shut behind them.

Their final conversation at breakfast at 'The Swan' had concluded that he would head back to Tetterton and buy a small boat that he could easily navigate to the entrance of the secret sea cave. The secret that almost every smuggler and thief knew about. He was to give them a full five days to negotiate their way through whatever dangers lie ahead and then find their way down through the catacombs.

It would take him a full day and night to get back to Tetterton, half a day to find the right boat and then about two days to sail to the right place for the rendezvous. That gave by his reckoning a full day and a half rest and relaxation for Fenton. Time he intended to use well now he was alone.

A large roar of approval came from the crowd atop the battlements near to the gatehouse and Percy wondered what they were so impressed by.

A pleasant looking serving girl with dark hair tied into a pony tail with a purple ribbon came over to his table and asked if he wanted anything else.

Fenton looked her up and down, noticed the promising curves and attractive freckling across the bridge of her pretty nose and thought that perhaps another flagon of ale might be nice.

He flashed her his most practised smile, asked for the beer and whether or not there were any rooms free for a weary traveller. Perhaps a full day might be worth spending here, just to make sure he was fully relaxed before heading off to Tetterton.

Chapter Two

Egremont was leading the way at quite a pace and Tumbletick and Jackson were finding it difficult to keep up. The Lord Seau du Duvet was notorious in certain circles for his hatred of wolves. Internally he was feeling almost desperate to find and despatch a grey furred adversary. Although he loved Is-Is as deeply as you could a giant hare, he was also feeling slightly jealous that it had not been him that had eliminated the three wolves as quickly as Is-Is had. Then he checked these negative thoughts as he remembered that no-one had known the assailants were wolves as the ambush had been launched. Egremont knew Is-Is well and therefore knew the next time a group of ninja wolves were within range the hare would step back and allow the wolfhound to leap into battle.

The light started to darken, clouds were crossing the sun. Egremont slowed the pace through the tight winding lanes. He realised his internal thoughts were distracting him from being fully alert to potential dangers so he stopped the group and looked to the sky and the potential for rain.

Warehouses and rough tenement buildings closed in on them from all sides. The area was less vandalised than the first section of the city they had passed through. Thoughts flickered through more than one mind that this may have been because fewer adventurers went through this area where nearly all must have passed through the first part of town before dissipating around in search of treasure.

A wind picked up and the silence of the street was broken by a creaking sign. At first it was just a slight whine but the wind grew and the sign began to sway back and forth on the metal arm that held it with increasing vigour. The group looked up as one at the distracting wooden board and saw a picture of a severed deer's head with the inscription, "Hind's Head Brewery, founded 18/2/6." The first spits of rain came plummeting down upon them.

"Well we maybe hunting wolves but there's no point in getting wet is there?" enquired Lord Jackson, pulling his cloak around him a little tighter.

"We seem to find ourselves in the environ of a brewery gentlemen. And Vixen," Egremont added in haste. "Although I suspect they may have been out of business for some time."

The brewery building was large and very tall. Gravity is the brewer's friend, not just as a way of improving taste when in its specific form but also as a helping hand in getting materials through the brewing process. The first two levels were of stone, then two levels of brick, then two of wood. Large doors were still intact at ground level, their locks still in place from when the city had been closed and walled up. However, somewhere in the recent history of the brewery someone, or something, had broken in at some loading doors which were at the fourth floor. Initially grain and hops would have been pulleyed up to here; now an intruder had felt the doors at such a height provided an easier access point to break in through rather than the forbidding grand gates at street level.

"Some enterprising thief must have been very agile to get in up at that level," said Campbell. "However, I am much more enterprising and able." He pulled out a neatly rolled up set of lock picks from an inside pocket, unloosed the little leather tie and as the tools unfurled within the canvas holding, he whipped out a precise looking metal pick. Campbell then got to work on the lock of the large doors. After a couple of curses and begrudging comments of admiration for the lock maker a loud click was heard and the thief pushed hard on one of the double doors.

"Let's hope they didn't bolt it from the inside," Campbell said as he strained. Mr. Battfin stepped over to help with his considerable bulk and the door began to give way a little, pushing into years of dust and detritus on the floor behind. It opened slowly and resentfully but soon enough of a gap was revealed so that the group could enter and out of the increasingly heavy rain and ensured they closed the door behind them, which Campbell promptly locked, feeling his way as the limited light from the street extinguished with the sealing of the door.

It was very dark inside the 'Hind's Head Brewery'. The increasingly thickening clouds and the lack of windows at ground level meant that backpacks had to be taken off and lanterns searched for and lit. All carried a lit lantern except for Egremont and Is-Is who could see exceptionally well at the best of times and very well in this gloom with the aid of five lanterns casting their glow. The lowest room of the brewery was cavernous, vaulted and here and there iron beams added extra strength for the roof. Most of the area was empty but along one wall hundreds of stacked wooden barrels were still in place. The size of the room was such that even with several hundred barrels stacked to the ceiling along the one wall the room still felt empty.

"I suppose it would be too much to expect that those barrels maybe full," said Jackson walking over to them. He rapped one firmly with the hilt of a dagger and was rewarded with a hollow boom in return.

"Lord Jackson," protested Egremont. "You have just announced to any inhabitants our arrival better than sending in a butler with a calling card!"

Now very alert they scouted out the rest of the large room. They found some sectioned off offices in one corner, the doors unlocked, led to a series of three small rooms. Vixen flicked through some dusty ledgers still on a desk which spoke of barrelage production and delivery schedules. At the far end of the hall, furthest away from the doors they had entered through, a wide set of industrial cast iron staircases led up. Two staircases to the next floor that looked imposing and well made. Historically one was probably used for ascending and one descending, to aid easy movement around the busy brewery.

"Unless there are some monsters hiding in those barrels, this room is secure," said Campbell the Weasel. "Looks like we had better search the next level, seeing as we are here."

"I suspect the wolves will not be in this building. They are probably holed up somewhere else," said Egremont with a hint of disappointment in his voice.

"Still adventure might avail itself on some of the upper floors, Lord Egremont," offered Jackson, positively enthused by the amount of thrilling encounters he had had within such a short time.

Egremont took the first step of the left stairway, Is-Is led to the right. They ascended slowly, if anyone or anything was waiting on the next floor it was bound to know they were there. Cautious step after cautious step on the iron stairs came and went and the two warriors crouched and positioned themselves to be able to look up onto the next floor and found that nothing was waiting for them. As Egremont and Is-Is made it to the top of the steps they gestured for the others to follow. Another huge room revealed itself to the group as each of them arrived next to the wolfhound and hare. Again it was vaulted and similar iron beams supported the roof, this room however was dominated by four vast copper kettles. In a smart brazen line they formed wonderfully rotund images of industry. The lantern light bounced off their curves and resentfully made it far enough to the wall and completely grimed up windows above the street. The windows were leaded and also had bars as thick as Is-Is' wrists protecting from intruders.

"Well here lies a real treasure, make no mistake!" gasped Campbell. "If you could melt that copper down, get it into ingots and get it out of the city you would be well set!"

"I estimate the value to be ten thousand, five hundred and thirty gold coins," informed Lord Jackson. "But as always I would be open to negotiation Mr. Campbell. Should you wish to open up a smelting works you know I have offices in Tetterton who would be happy to purchase your ingots."

The group continued their caution and made their way along the room, skirting the kettles and ensuring that nothing was in the brewing hall as well. Campbell prised open one of the coppers and had a look inside for any lurking creature but nothing was resident not even an old aroma of a final brew.

"Don't you go banging your daggers on those!" laughed Vixen to Jackson.

"That would send a whole army of butlers ahead to announce our arrival," he joked back with the sumptuous spy.

They made it to the other side of the vacant space and found a steep set of steps, again iron, with a single handrail leading up. Each step was honeycombed with holes in a hexagonal pattern and there were no risers to allow a foot to rest against as you climbed.

"Do you know why so many breweries around the world have motifs of bees or use the old hexagonal patterns of the hive?" asked Jackson to no-one in particular. "It is because they were such hives of industry and the brewers wanted to reflect the busyness of bees often in their businesses, buildings and beers."

"Interesting fact Jackson but seeing as you encouraged us on this exploration I suggest that the third floor awaits," stated Egremont. "Is-Is goes first."

Is-Is, confident in his body's muscled balance and agility climbed what really amounted to a ladder rather than steps and slotted through a square open hatch in the roof to the next floor. Egremont was following as they heard Is-Is start to run above, away from the hatch. Egremont picked up his speed to help Is-Is in whatever he was doing and was just in time to get his coiffeured mane through the access hatch and into the darkness above as everyone heard a high pitched squeal. The rest of the group, not knowing what was happening, all piled up the ladder in rapid single file following the wolfhound. When they were all up they were greeted by Egremont, tapping a foot, arms crossed with a scowl on his face, he was starring at Is-Is. Is-Is was walking back with a grin on his face and a rat skewered on a throwing dagger in a triumphant trophy like pose. He stopped and held the rat aloft, it's little legs splayed in shock.

"Target practice?" enquired Egremont. A ripple of laughter flitted through the friends in relief that nothing more serious had occurred.

This room had a much lower roof than the previous two. It had wooden floorboards and around it were scattered hessian sacks that had once held hops. Pipes and funnels led from here to the floor below. Opposite where they stood was a solitary door, in the direct centre of a peeling plastered wall. Campbell walked up to it and had a brief look.

"Not locked," he revealed and turned the handle and pushed. The door led to a corridor about eighty feet long. Doors were staggered on either side. A few old paintings of the brewery and old men in imperious stances still hung on the walls. Dust lined the corridor floor and rat tracks criss-crossed each other in a chaotic dance. Another steep stair was at the far end leading to a closed hatch. Large bolts on three sides firmly held it shut from this side.

"We need to check each of these rooms," said Egremont and he walked to the first door which was on his right hand side. It was a solid door of wooden planks. Still legible on it were the words "Under Assistant Brewer", scorched into the wood. Egremont tried the handle but it was locked. Campbell took a couple of steps forward and went to work with his tools and within a couple of heartbeats the door was swinging open. A single desk was in the small room, an empty bookcase and a musty smell, nothing else of interest.

Mr. Battfin went to check the other doors, "Assistant Brewer" and "Head Brewer" on the right hand side, were also both locked. To the left Is-Is tried "Buyer", "Mr. Savage" and "Meeting Room", all were locked.

"Couldn't you just break them down?" sighed Campbell, then he methodically unlocked each door in turn, allowing them to be searched.

Each room was similar to the under assistant brewer's, devoid of any interest or value. Each had a dusty wooden desk and various pieces of furniture that once would have held files and records. The meeting room was larger than the others and it also boasted a vast open fireplace. Jackson took particular interest in the impressive dominating table in the centre of the room. He leered over it, brushing away dust with his sleeve pulled over the whole of his hand. The master merchant kept passing comments of superlatives between sighs before he finally turned to his companions and said.

"Campbell, you really should go into furniture removal as well as smelting. Here lies a true treasure. I suspect at the time of evacuation this was a modern piece but now it has matured to an antique. Well, the value! I'd give anyone who could get this back to Tetterton double what I would have finally paid for all that copper downstairs!" He avariciously continued removing dust and a wonderfully patterned table was revealed. Thick carved legs held aloft the perfect rectangular top. Suddenly Lord Jackson of En'Tuk cried aloud, clapping his hands in exuberance.

"Ah ha, I knew it, it is a Christopher Stanton-Smith. Wonderful. Look Tumbletick, come over here I have found his charming motif."

Tumbletick sauntered over to Lord Jackson. His previous life living in a hut had hardly schooled him well in the world of fine antiques. Jackson, still beaming hugely under the light of the lanterns, picked his own light up from the dusty floor where he had placed it. With one arm round Tumbletick's shoulder and the other holding forward the lantern he spoke.

"Look under the edge of the table here. Do you see it? A carved Coeur, an embossed heart? The sign of the master cabinet maker. He did this piece himself. See on the heart the initials C.S.S. above the shaft of a sunken arrow and the letters C.W. underneath? Oh it dates it perfectly to when the master was still engaged to be married. A tacky icon of affection, make no mistake, but well meant."

"Is this a good table then Jackson?" said Tumbletick looking back at his friend inquisitively after finding the wooden heart.

"Good Tumbletick? Why it is the very best. The product of a great artisan and a wonderful romance," Jackson was still smiling.

"I wish Egremont and Is-Is had had this Christopher with them when they built my hut!" Tumbletick observed. Jackson laughed and led Tumbletick back to the rest of the group standing around the door just inside the room as well as just inside the corridor.

"Master Campbell, please lock this room back up. When we have finished on this part of our quest I will be sending word back to some stout fellows to come and retrieve it," Jackson looked genuinely pleased and amazed at his find.

As Campbell locked the room back shut all thoughts turned to the steep stair at the end of the corridor and the bolted hatchway at the end of it. It must have been raining extremely heavily outside with a stiff wind galing as within the enclosed space they could now hear the building creak and splatters of water lash the outside. The lanterns competing light in the narrowness of the space meant the floor was very well lit but the ceiling was swathed in shadow. They moved slowly along to the foot of the iron steps. It was identical to the one on the floor below. Mr. Battfin lifted his lantern aloft to cast its light on the hatchway. It was painted white and made of solid short planks of wood. Cobwebs clung around the corners of the ceiling and crept across the face of the hatch. On the side of the hatch closest to the end wall of the corridor, four large industrial hinges were screwed in. The hatch lifted up into the room above. On each of the other sides there was a similarly robust bolt, drawn across into the locking position. Campbell took a couple of steps up and brushed away at the cobwebs and checked the bolts a bit closer.

"This hatch has not been opened in decades," he proffered professionally. "The bolts have started to rust but look very, very firm. Do we want to keep searching this place or wait out the rain in one of the offices. I could get a good fire going with some of that furniture!"

Jackson spluttered a protest but was soon stopped by Egremont who stated, "We should go on, unless there are any major objections."

Campbell tried to draw one of the bolts but he could not move it. He attempted another and the third with the same results. He stepped down and Mr. Battfin had a go with his greater strength and rougher hands. He failed to move them too. Pride hurt he stepped down and made way for Is-Is, who also had no joy despite his massive muscular ability.

"Right," said Campbell enthusiastically. "Time for a different method." He clambered up the stair and got his shoulder under the hatch and rather than heaving at it he revealed his tool kit again, selected a piece and started to unscrew the bolts from the wood. The others waited in silence as the thief worked. As a screw came free he threw it down to Mr. Battfin who caught it and placed it neatly on the floor under the bottom step of the stair. Campbell's skill with his tools was awesome but it still took time to do. Rusting screws would lose their heads as he worked and cause frustration but eventually he threw down the final screw and the final released bolt.

Campbell climbed back down to the floor and said, "Right my bit done. I'm not going to be the first one through that trap door to the fourth floor. I kept thinking something huge and brutal was going to rip open the hatch and drag me through."

The group stood and stared at the white hatch. Vixen's lantern went out suddenly, spluttering as the last of the oil burned out. It grew a little darker. All knew they were now leaving the first three floors which had been sealed shut by the very secure trapdoor. The front gates to the brewery had been designed to keep people out and they had succeeded for decades before they were confronted with Campbell's lock-picking abilities. The access door on the fourth floor had been broken and this hatch led to the fourth floor. They stared at its white square face as the creaking of the building grew as the storm outside increased.

Jackson's lantern went out too, the flame coughing and dying as the last of the oil burned. The shadows moved violently with its death.

"We better add some more oil, "observed Mr. Battfin. "Those lanterns were all lit at the same time and were all new."

"What sort of shoddy merchandise did your people get for us Jackson?" complained Campbell. "They only lasted about an hour!"

"Perhaps we shouldn't have lit them all at once then," retorted Lord Jackson. "Just add more oil and be done with it!"

"Did we order extra oil? I haven't got any," worried Tumbletick, looking at his own lantern which was beginning to flicker, the flame skipping around trying to find fuel.

"Time to make a move then," said Egremont, also watching the three remaining lights and the diminishing golden glow.

Tumbletick's light died too, quickly followed by Mr. Battfin's. It was now extremely dark in the enclosed corridor. Only the lantern of Campbell remained alight and it did not look confident.

"Quick light one of the remaining two!" shouted Vixen. "Both Is-Is and Egremont have lanterns in their packs too."

"That might be a good idea but without any extra oil and the fact that we have got to go underground at the castle, perhaps we should keep them for an emergency," replied Campbell, focusing on his flame.

"I'd say this is a bit of an emergency," Vixen spat back. "We'll be able to find something to light the way by the time we get there."

"But we can not be certain of that," replied Egremont. "We should keep those two lanterns for when absolutely necessary."

"I think it maybe necessary very soon," said Campbell, the flame in his lantern was getting very small.

Is-Is made a sharp move and began to climb the stair determined to smash his way through and deal with anything on the other side.

"Wait," whispered Egremont with urgency. "We maybe able to see my bright eyed friend, but these others can not."

The group all turned and stared at the solitary flame then looked aloft to the hatch as the flame went out.

Chorus Two

Fenton finished his fourth flagon of ale still sitting outside 'The Black Bull'. His booted feet were now well ensconced upon the seat beside him and he had just lit his pipe. He had a pleasing ounce of tobacco that he had been keeping for a time of relaxation. The ale meant that he kept smiling very easily at passers by and the 'Viking Mango' tobacco added an air of nonchalance to the pirate.

The pretty serving girl had finished her shift and pulled over another chair and delicately placed herself beside Percy. She undid the purple ribbon that held her hair in a ponytail and let it cascade over her bare shoulders. She breathed deeply to take in the aroma of pipe smoke.

"You are booked into room seven, Mr Fenton," she said sweetly.

"Hmm. Excellent," he replied. "Would you like a drink?"

"Yes I would, a glass of red if you please."

Fenton looked around and raised his hand, still with pipe burning gently, to summon over the new waitress. She was a dumpy and surly looking girl with black hair tied tightly into a bun. Fenton scowled momentarily, commenting internally on the hiring policy of the premises that could be so right and yet so wrong when it came to selecting staff. As the new girl got close enough to hear him he broke into a smile and ordered a bottle of claret with two glasses.

"Looks like rain," stated his pretty companion, looking up at some very black clouds scurrying across the face of the sun.

"Why yes it does," he replied. He suddenly swung his feet off the chair and sat up facing the attractive off duty serving girl.

"Do you know," he continued with a new intensity. "That one of my favourite things is listening to rain lash the window pane as I lay in bed?"

"Really," she mused. "I have a very similar view on that."

"What say you on taking your drink with me on the inside and discussing the matter further?"

"I'd be delighted."

They walked into 'The Black Bull' just as the first spits of rain came plummeting down upon them. The surly looking waitress saw them going and tapped her feet as they selected a secluded table in a quiet corner of the pub.

Chapter Three

The group stood in the dark listening to each others breathing. Tumbletick noticed how each of them could be identified by their own ways of inhaling and exhaling. Mr. Battfin, usually tight lipped anyway only breathed deeply through his nose. Vixen was giving quick little pants, perhaps in tune with her heartbeat, was she nervous? Egremont panted too, as was the way with wolfhounds, Tumbletick was not surprised by that, he could imagine him in the dark with his long tongue drooping out to the left. Jackson was wheezing slightly, indication of a life mostly led indoors across a negotiation table. Campbell, impatient and edgy was taking in huge gulps of air then rapidly blowing out, and then he would wait a while before breathing again. As a trained thief, being able to keep still in times of tension and pressure was obviously a part of his life. Is-Is however was quiet. Tumbletick could not hear the hare here but he was aware of his bulk in the corridor. Is-Is was breathing normally, unconcerned, completely calm, unstressed and waiting for someone to make a decision.

Tumbletick offered a solution. "There were some old sacks back beyond this corridor. Perhaps lighting some of them wrapped around a broken bit of furniture would serve as a torch?"

"Or myself and Is-Is could go up through the hatch, deal with any troublesome circumstances and then call for you guys. We can both see fine," replied Egremont.

"It should be a bit lighter on the next floor up. At least some light should get in through the broken access door," said Campbell. "Why don't you guys rush up through the hatch and we'll follow whatever. Naked flames are dangerous and make me nervous, so I don't like the idea of climbing up a ladder while someone below is handling a conflagration on a stick."

"Okay," responded Egremont pensively. "Is-Is, are you ready?"

The giant hare nodded, though only Egremont could see it. Potential violence oozed out of his very being as he set a foot on the bottom rung and raised a huge paw to the hatch. A seconds pause to ready himself and then he pushed mightily, slamming the hatch wide open and over to fall back down to the floor with a very loud crash. Is-Is, bathed in a little grey light, flew up the steps followed swiftly by a clambering Egremont.

Is-Is emerged at an explosive pace onto a floor devoid of anything. This was a completely empty space, except for dust. It was a room designed for storing brewing materials but there wasn't even a sack left here. Broad floorboards, dusted grey by years of industrious feet and dragged goods, stretched off to blank brick walls painted white. The loading doors, now broken, creaked and flapped wildly in the gale which continued to rage. They banged on the inside of the room and one broke off and slammed to the floor, just as Egremont climbed into the room to join Is-Is. Rain splattered in in sheets, forced by the buffeting storm and the dust turned into a cratered, slate grey paste.

"Somehow I feel disappointed," remarked Egremont, sheathing his rapier. Is-Is clicked his tongue to his teeth in mute agreement.

Mr. Battfin then Campbell came climbing out of the dark corridor more tentatively after hearing the crashing from the falling door but confidence soon returned as they saw Egremont and Is-Is standing idly and the room did indeed have some light in it, despite the clouded sky outside.

Campbell and Mr. Battfin stood either side of the trapdoor and helped Vixen, then Jackson and finally Tumbletick to climb through the hatch and into the storage room.

"We'll just scout out the whole room but it looks empty," informed Egremont and he and Is-Is did a quick sweep, vanishing into shadow further off than the meagre light allowed. However, they quickly returned and Egremont said, shaking his head, "Absolutely empty, just another ladder leading up through an open hatch and there are some pipes leading down through the floor and also up through the ceiling."

"Well we know from looking outside that there are two more stories left, smaller levels built of wood. That must be where the ladder and the pipes go," said Campbell.

"I expect you will find a large pump and a water tank up there," proffered Jackson. "And little else."

"Okay, Is-Is and I will check that out, you remain here but stay sharp, just in case anything is lurking around on the upper levels," advised Egremont.

The wolfhound and the hare again vanished into the shadows. They could be heard climbing a ladder then moving around on the floor above. Tiny flecks of dust fell through the gloom to come to rest on the party and the floorboards. Some bits nearer to the open loading doors were blown around in a tumult of activity.

The five remaining adventurers stood around despondently. After the early activity in the city this felt very tame indeed. Tumbletick found that the thought 'Be Careful What You Wish For' suddenly swarmed around his mind and he turned to look at his friends all silent with their own inner monologues ranting at them.

Eventually stomping sounds again came from above and then footsteps on the ladder. Two figures emerged from the gloom, Egremont and Is-Is.

"The floor above has an office. The door has been broken down but the name on it said "Engineer"," reported Egremont. "The pipes and pumps are there as predicted. Then the ladder continues straight up to a room about half the size of the floor plan of the others. That one contains a gigantic black metal tank. Empty like everything else. However there are windows on that floor that command sterling views over the city. The storm is obscuring even Is-Is' eyesight currently. I would like to be able to stay here until the light returns and we are able to make a decent reconnoitre of our immediate environment,"

"Didn't the meeting room have a rather fine fireplace?" asked Vixen. "Perhaps we could go down there, break up some of the less valuable furniture, Jackson, add some sacks, get a really good blaze going and curl up and be comfortable."

"We could dine on the fabulous table with our meagre rations," joked Campbell. "Ride out the storm with a little style don't you know!"

They agreed and went back down a level. Egremont and Is-Is had to do all the work due to the dark, including reattaching the bolts back to the trapdoor for added security.

The fire was soon going and spirits lifted, faces looked friendly in the reds and golds of the flickering flames. The smell of burning wood bringing comfortable memories to Tumbletick of other nights he had spent with his friends by a fire. They settled down, ate their meal, talked a little and smoked then one by one fell to sleep as Is-Is kept a peaceful watch over all of them.

'The Hind's Head Brewery' had at times provided moments of high tension but fundamentally it was vacant of all life except for a single, solitary rat.

Chorus Three

Fenton awoke with a start to a slamming door and a still warm, empty bed. He lay rigid for a couple of moments with his eyes staring wide then as the memories of the night before returned he relaxed, smiled then writhed into a luxurious stretch. A slit of light sliced through a gap in the curtains like a blazing blade.

'Perhaps the reason one always finds the light in one's eyes is because the light has woken one up', Fenton thought. 'But then maybe it was the slamming door.'

The storm had blown itself out and the morning's weather looked promising for a days tramping along the plateau of Rampart. He lay under the comforting covers of the bed and planned his trip back to Tetterton. He would visit some shops and purchase a blanket and some food for the trip. Then he would have a leisurely walk through the countryside, find some farmer's barn to bed down in for the night and then make it to the cliff face above Tetterton early the next morning.

Percy Fenton spared a couple of moments thoughts for his friends in the Old City and wondered how their night had compared to his. He gave a hearty chuckle had a final joint cracking stretch, then he leapt out of the bed. He hunted down his clothes which were scattered around the room, dressed swiftly, picked up his backpack and weapons and decided a quick exit from the pub was perhaps best. He didn't want any accusatory or condemning stares whilst sitting over a long breakfast. As he jauntily danced down the stairs to reception he reached into a pocket, plucked out a gold coin and balancing it on his forefinger, flicked the rim of the coin with his primed thumb sending it in the direction of the clerk with his head in a book.

"That's for Room Seven, my fine fellow. Keep the change. Wonderful service!" he commended and then he was out through the front door, whistling and setting a good pace towards the city gates.

For a few copper coins he bought a breakfast of seed cake and hot treacle with a mug of small beer from a street vendor. Then he browsed around a merchant district to find the blanket which he rolled up and placed under his backpack straps so that it sat comfortably near his shoulders. Next he purchased some fruit and bread for his luncheon.

Crowds were beginning to build up as he got to the gates. Several people were also leaving the city at the same time as him but most wanted to get into the city. A few adventurers, farmers, black robed treasure seekers had to be dodged within the gatehouse as Fenton started his day long trudge over the rolling plateau amongst the grazing pastures and olive groves.

Chapter four

The night spent in the meeting room of 'The Hind's Head Brewery' had certainly been made more pleasant by the fire providing warmth and light. They had kept guard through the night as a matter of due diligence but had felt reasonably safe with locked doors and the hatch firmly bolted again. For some reason the rooms on this floor had no windows, light in the history of this brewery would have been provided by many candles it seemed. This probably led to intense myopia of the management.

Is-Is gave a huge sigh after a look from Egremont. The hare made his way back into the corridor to start undoing the bolts that held the trapdoor firmly shut, muttering very quietly to himself.

"Let us depart from here and take in the sight of the Old City at dawn," barked Egremont, sounding a little more his old self. He stood with his palms of his paws pressed into the small of his back as he stretched and arched slightly backwards. Bolts could be heard being thrown to the floor and as the group collected their equipment and went to the corridor they found the hatchway already thrown wide open and a vanished Is-Is.

The floor above which had been so dismal the day before was now blinding. The sun was positioned so that its entire glare burst into the old store room. Is-Is must have already made it to the top level of the building so they proceeded in single file to the ladder and began the ascent, straight past the engineers floor and to the water storage facility.

Is-Is was standing surveying the cityscape through one of the many windows of the top tier. All were broken, the remains of vandalism from whoever had clambered in through the fourth floor once upon a time. These windows virtually filled every bit of space from about three foot from the floor to the roof. Only thin strips of wood held them in place, it was obvious that light had been important for inspection of the water tank. The pleasing breeze, through the broken panes, did not carry any of the fetid odours at this height which were so pervasive at street level. They all stationed themselves at different windows in different

119

directions and gained a great view of the Old City. Tumbletick pulled out the compass he had ordered to gain further bearings; Vixen slinked up besides him and purred softly,

"Do you know Tumbletick that I keep a diary?"

"No Vixen," he replied in equally soft and conspiratorial tones.

"Well perhaps we could work together to draw up a map. I have a reasonable artistic ability and with your compass we could pick out some key features and reference them to this location."

"But aren't we just going to head for the castle and the catacombs?" Tumbletick asked. "We know where that is. In the centre."

"Oh I'm sure that is exactly where we will go but you should never underestimate the importance of intelligence and knowledge. I do not think that we have a recent map of the Old City back at the Service in Umiat. Or you and I could set up a little sideline business in the future and sell copies to adventurers looking to gain a little advantage." Vixen stood closely to Tumbletick, so close he could feel the top of her thigh and hip pushing into his own excuse for a waist. She swung off her backpack, bent over, her leather clothes creaking and stretching in restrained complaint. Vixen deftly removed her diary and pen and turned to the back blank page.

"Let's be quick," she whispered into his ear while she was still provocatively positioned.

Raven Hill's many skills had meant a rapid rise through the echelons of the Secret Service. Tumbletick held the compass in his hairy little palm so she could easily read it. He was very impressed by the speed of her eye and hand picking out landmarks and recording them.

On the other side of the water-tank, Campbell, Mr. Battfin and Jackson were hidden from Vixen and Tumbletick. They were in a muted conversation observing the castle. Egremont and Is-Is were also gazing at buildings to the south which appeared to be monumental structures.

"Do you know," observed Jackson. "That, that castle, where we are intending to travel, looks extremely unassailable and closed."

"Guess it was kind of naïve to imagine that whoever is Lord and Master at the current time would just leave the gates wide open for any passing visitors," quipped Campbell flippantly.

"Then it is our job to go a knockin'," stated Mr. Battfin. The trio returned to silence looking at the ancient castle. Fundamentally it was just a single block of a stone tower about the same height as the brewery. It had a curtain wall running around the enclosed courtyard area. Eight stone towers were built into that wall, quite large enough to house a staircase for troop movements and a vantage point at the top. The eighth tower to the south though was much larger and contained the gatehouse. A wide boulevard, like the one that had staged the tiger attack, ran directly south, bisecting the east west broad road.

Egremont and Is-Is were focussing on four large structures to which the southern road led. It was obviously an important civic centre of entertainment in the history of the Old City. What roles they played now could only be guessed at. The largest of the buildings was the first of three Romanesque entertainment venues. It was an ovoid building constructed in a grand style. A hippodrome or a circus depending on your point of view. Once great horse races, with coloured teams would have powered round to the roars of appreciative audiences. Next to that vast venue was a circular amphitheatre. Three tiers high it was still a gargantuan structure but small in relation to the circus. Gladiators would fight here, executions would be staged, animals slaughtered and even marine battles recreated with the arena flooded. The third building was a theatre, open air now but perhaps once covered with tarpaulins to help keep the sun off of spectators. These would have been operated by sailors, used to moving large canvas sheets. Built out of the obligatory stone blocks of the age, the multi-stepped wedge shape building was constructed so performers on the rectangular stage could speak with clarity and resonance backed by the good acoustics and an impressive three story piece of permanent stone set design.

"Well Is-Is," conspired Egremont into the hare's ear. "Which of those fine buildings do you suppose I would prefer to perform in?"

Is-Is gave a little chuckle in recognition of his friends artistic temperaments but was himself focussing on the fourth large structure which by far the most vast of the constructions. Clustered around an ancient abbey, imposing with two large towers, were many buildings of monastic origins. The abbey alone was larger than any of the arenas of entertainment. Around the compound about the abbey ran a wall and on the wall were the obligatory reminders of a militaristic past, five large squat towers. Forts in their own right, Is-Is could see they all had numerous arrow slits, battlements and each was set with a thick pair of gates. Is-Is guessed that as the gates were on the outer wall of the towers, one would enter into another killing zone before passing through more gates and into the compound. These gatehouses were similar to the main set that they had passed through in order to enter the Old City. Within the protective enclave of that wall and in the shadow of the abbey in the early morning sun, Is-Is could see that there were large areas of grass covered with grazing goats and fallow areas, this being Frimaire, that were obviously more intensively farmed. He then spotted some more deliberate movement than the grazing goats and he picked out some other forms of life. A group of about twenty humans all dressed in very colourful patchwork robes, thick leather belts around each waist, walking at leisure along a stone path towards the abbey. They followed a solitary figure, hood of his robe down, he had flame red hair, back brushed into shocking spikes and clumps. Energetically he cavorted as he walked, animatedly regaling some tale of immense mirth as he seemed to be laughing with great enthusiasm. The other patchwork monks seemed to be laughing heartily too by the movement of their shoulders and the hands reaching under their hood in an action that looked like they were wiping away tears of mirth. Is-Is' eyesight was superb to be able to pick out such details from such a distance but he kept the observations to himself.

Egremont walked over to the trio of Campbell, Mr. Battfin and Jackson, skirting around the hard iron edges of the black water tank.

"You might want to check out those buildings to the north too," offered Campbell to the noble wolfhound. "Interesting looking shanty town seems to have sprung up."

"Hmm, yes," pondered Egremont. "There are some extremely interesting entertainment venues over in the southern section of the city."

"We have been evaluating our chances of a full scale affront on the castle and it does not look promising," said Lord Jackson. "That fortress is sealed up like one of my vaults."

"Oh there is always a way into a vault. Just like a woman. Find out what weaknesses it has or what makes it tick and those gates will open right up," joked Campbell, reasonably proud of his allusion.

"Let's just go an' knock," said Mr Battfin.

"A man of such supposed resourcefulness, offering such a simplistic solution is hardly fitting," chided Jackson in condescending tones.

"Jus' the way I deal with vaults and women," he replied in a matter of fact way. "You never know what yur gonna get, if you jus' knock!"

Campbell started laughing, huge bursts of panting peels, interspersed with wheezing whines as he tried to get his breath back. Mr. Battfin shrugged and gave a little twitch of a half smile from one corner of his mouth.

"Well I don't think it was that funny Campbell," said Jackson in a business like manner. "We have got to find a way into that castle and meet with Fenton in four days."

Egremont returned to the discussion as he had wandered off to cast his eyes over the sprawling slums which filled the northern section of the Old City. He twisted his moustache with a paw and looked like he was missing a monocle.

"Time to formulate a plan though gentlemen. Time to formulate a plan," he said with a touch of whimsy. "Is-Is, are you still looking at that monastic collection?"

Is-Is turned, nodded and returned to looking through the broken window, transfixed by something within the abbey's grounds. Tumbletick and Vixen moved in beside him, working on their map together. Egremont noticed the cartographic creation and noted mentally that it may well come in useful.

"Actually," said Egremont. "I quite like Mr. Battfin's suggestion. A brazen, yet calm perambulation up to the gates might be just the ticket to gain entry. If we get a hostile reception we can always beat a tactical retreat."

"Fine," responded Jackson, shaking his head a little. "If we do get turned away, what are we going to do then? There is no storming a castle with just seven of us. I'm no warrior but promises of money might work."

"What would they want with money?" called over Vixen, listening to the conversation though her eyes were firmly on the map. "They are in a prison."

"People always want money, it brings them hope and power," he replied.

"To my mind Lord Jackson, albeit a militarily cultured one, I think that there would be some intelligence in that castle," observed Egremont." And money is always an incentive as you say. They are also obviously maintaining it and that suggests that there may be workers as well as a Lord. To the south too, there are buildings which look in a fine state of repair."

"I'd probably want to keep my gates firmly shut and well maintained if there were monsters like that sabre toothed beastie roaming the streets," said Campbell fully recovered from his comedic seizures.

"Yes," agreed Lord Jackson. "We know that the Rampart authorities often import terrible monsters into the city as well as prisoners to combine with volunteers like us. So if you were a prisoner let loose within an open prison like this, where would you want to go?"

"To a place where I could meet with fellows of a similar disposition and world view and where I could feel safe under lock and key again," concluded Egremont. The four of them all turned and looked long and hard at the castle and it's firmly shut gate.

Vixen and Tumbletick sidled up to Egremont and continued recording their map. A nice routine had developed between them; Tumbletick describing landmarks and the direction in which they lay by referencing from his compass, Vixen would look up briefly, capture the image and quickly sketch it in her diary. To the east beyond the castle they could make out some large wooden warehouses, then the two moved on and had the detail to fill in of the north of the Old City and the massive maze of tiny shacks and dilapidated housing. Soon, however, Vixen had completed her sketch and she patted Tumbletick on the head and purred a praising comment to him as she put her diary away. Tumbletick blushed outrageously as he carefully packed the compass away into his own backpack.

Egremont called the group together and explained the plan. He had chosen the simple one, a calm approach and a demand for entry. Any sign of trouble and they would beat a swift retreat to shelter before promises of vast sums of money via a message sent by one of Is-Is' arrows over the wall.

They clambered down to the engineer's level and then the storage hall. Descending to the corridor and the offices was fine as light filtered down with them. They did not bother to lock the hatchway again by re-screwing in the bolts much to the annoyance of Lord Jackson who claimed he had visions of thieves scampering in as soon as they left the brewery in removal man brown overalls carrying off his table.

Then it was a single file procession, shuffling in the dark, being led by Is-Is and followed by Lord Egremont, chuckling at the weakness of humans in the gloom. The last two flights of iron staircases at least had hand rails and when they finally made their way back to the robustly locked front gates of 'The Hind's Head Brewery', Campbell the Weasel proved his skill as a thief by picking the lock in the dark. He boasted that he did it with his eyes shut too just to enhance the dexterity of his long slim fingers. Even though there was just enough light sneaking in under the crack of the gate to give a source for vision and had he been peeking through his claimed sealed eyelids he would have been able to make out a great deal. The lock clicked, the doors swung inwardly, easier this time as the dust and detritus had already been pushed into a neatly heaped line by the gates on the preceding day. The group stepped into the street, responsibly pulled the doors shut again and with Lord Jackson pleading for security, Campbell locked them with a courteous comment.

Chorus four

Percy Fenton had been cutting quite a pace on the plateau, the bright morning sun washing the back of his head with warmth. His backpack and new blanket sat comfortably at first but eventually the blanket began to bunch up and niggled away in discomfort at Fenton's thoughts. 'Surely a rolled up blanket should be more comfortable than this,' he considered. So he stopped on the well trodden path to take off his pack and see if he could place the blanket elsewhere, either in the backpack or fastened by a strap on one of the outside pouches. As he knelt at the side of the track he noticed that another traveller on the road behind him, maybe three hundred yards distant, had also decided to take a break. They were sitting cross legged on a little stone wall, marking the boundary of a particularly sparse olive grove and they appeared to be eating or maybe biting their nails.

Fenton frowned as he could not make space in his bag for the blanket. The straps that acted like a belt in holding shut one of the four pouches, two on the back and one on each side, were not long enough to loop over the rolled up blanket before being buckled again. 'Unless I carry it, there is no other option,' he thought. So he rolled it up, placed it across his shoulders and swung the backpack onto the blanket and his broad back. It felt a little more comfortable but it still nagged away with its uneven lumpiness.

He got to a standing position and headed off towards Tetterton. A brief look over his shoulders showed two individuals, darkly dressed talking to the traveller who appeared to still be taking his luncheon.

Step after step he strode onward, trying to entertain himself with memories and future plans. He tried whistling but lost interest. He kicked some stones on the road, seeing how far he could kick one so it bounded and skipped along but always stayed on the track and did not bustle and spin off into the soft mud in the gutter from last night's storm. He looked for wildlife to amuse him but none seemed present. Percy Fenton grew very bored but still he trudged on and then it struck him that this was the first time in a very long time that he had been alone. Yes there was the loneliness of command and the captain's cabin but there had always been people around him, nearby, someone always close, making noise, asking questions, demanding attention.

He quickened his pace, lifted his head and attempted to crack into a smile and a song but found that he could not. Looking back again, he saw that the two had joined with the solitary man and they were all heading west together, following Fenton.

Chapter five

The group found themselves skirting along the edges of the hemmed in streets of a grotty quarter of the Old City. The street was broader at ground level than the gap at roof level as terraces, brothels and townhouses all became wider as they rose. The structures all seemed to be leaning towards each other, leering and hulking. Egremont and Is-Is led the way, unerring, straight along the road they believed led to the castle. Mr. Battfin and Campbell were in the second row, weapons drawn, they were both watchful and edgy. Then came Lord Jackson of En'Tuk beside Tumbletick, his daggers were drawn as he stayed close to the little form of his deformed friend, ready to defend him if the need arose. Bringing up the rear was Vixen, she held no weapons openly but Tumbletick suspected she was dangerous without them.

Eventually the closed in quality of the structures ended with another path crossing theirs at right angles forming a crossroad and natural boundary to this part of the city. A quick look to the left and the right and Is-Is led them across. The houses in the next quarter were larger and designed to imitate architecture of renown. The buildings were not linked, they were large detached villas, properties of ancient merchants, mercenaries done good and men of inherited wealth and snivelling prestige. All were fortified and were solid looking at ground level except for the ubiquitous hard wooden doors, studded with black square ended nails of iron. The walls at the lowest level had been painted bold colours in the past but now they were faded and decayed to pastels of their former glory. Pinks, pale yellows and greens were all common, all mottled by splotches of cream coloured plaster, the guts underneath, where the paint had fallen away making the buildings look diseased and rotten. The second levels were usually of large blocks of stone and the windows were all secured with vertical iron bars. Most had third floors and some a fourth. Various materials were used here, brick, plaster, even rough hewn beams placed like a log cabin. Roofs were either flat to enable gardens in the sky or steeply shaped and covered in intricate tiles. Many still looked secure but several that they passed by had obviously been ransacked. All had large amounts of graffiti daubed on them. Tumbletick noticed a few recurring designs among the scrawls and obscenities and he wondered what they meant. There was more light available here as each of the compounds made up its own city block. Privilege and wealth bought space this close to the castle. Egremont held up his paw as they approached the corner of one of the peeling palatial residences. The group came to a swift halt as he addressed them in a slightly calmer tone to what they were used to from the big gregarious wolfhound.

"Esteemed adventurers. We are now close enough to the battlements that anyone on watch will soon be able to see our approach. Within about five minutes we will be in the open spaces in front of the fortifications. Let us put away our weapons and set off looking leisurely and unworried."

They nodded in agreement and put away the accoutrements of war. Tumbletick was struck by the sound of sheathing metal blades in scabbards. Just as Egremont took the first step to lead off toward their goal there came a distant sound of hollow rhythmic banging, echoing around them. Several glances indicated nervousness from all, before sounds of guttural laughter and jeers came to them on the breeze.

"It sounds like a large group some way off," informed Campbell seriously. "I'm pretty sure of the direction, stay here, I'll investigate. The role of guide, pathfinder and scout often falls to the thief."

With that the weasel looking man sprinted off so silently that the redrawing of weapons covered any noise he did make. The remaining group tucked in a little closer to the wall of the once grand building beside them. Tumbletick started to think of places to hide in case of trouble, he knew that one of the villas they had just passed was one that had a front door that had been broken open. They remained, quietly listening to the warped sounds of thumping and roars coming to them. Within sixty of Tumbletick's rapid heartbeats Campbell suddenly came rushing back, leaning low as he cornered round the edge of a mansion, legs covering great strides even though he was in a stooping posture to remain as small as possible.

"There's only a frigging small army of blokes all dressed up like harlequin monks or something, about to attack the castle!" he panted in haste to report back. "About two hundred, before you ask Egremont, all armed with enough weaponry to knock down the gate. Big hammers, clubs, maces, ladders and battering rams. Most of them are in fits of giggles too!"

"Multi coloured monks you say?" replied Egremont. "Me thinks we have stumbled into some form of turf war. Those monks of mirth probably come from the abbey we saw to the south." Is-Is was nodding firmly.

"Then I say we hole up somewhere until the battle blows over," said Jackson.

"Well I'm not going all the way back to that brewery again," retorted Campbell, still gaining his breath.

"How about one of these merchant houses?" suggested Tumbletick quickly. "The last ones door was open. Maybe we could secure ourselves in there?"

"Sounds like a plan. Better than staying in the street," added Vixen quickly.

"Stay alert though people," ordered Egremont. "We have no idea what might be lurking in one of these mansions." He started to lead the way back the way they had come.

"Don't know why I don't just pick a lock and get us in one of the secure houses," Campbell offered a little grumpily.

"No time Mr. Campbell," comforted Mr. Battfin as they picked up the pace. "Even for a thief of your skills."

They arrived at one of the imposing structures with an open door. It was a three storey variant covering a full city block. It was pale pink at ground level, with the peeled plaster and graffiti giving it a sorry look. The second floor was neater, in granite blocks that had once been painted white. Now the colour had been given a greyish hue by years of rain and green black moulds had taken root in the well cut grooves. Imposing windows, the height of the floor, were still in place, each protected by closely set iron bars. The third floor was exposed brickwork, with smaller square windows regularly set on all sides. The roof was made of black tiles, set at a shallow angle and it sat squarely and neatly atop the structure with only a few missing tiles, testimony to the original roofers skill at his trade.

The entrance was two solid looking wooden doors that opened inwards to reveal a wide corridor, solid walls on either side. They proceeded with caution, Is-Is leading the way. The wide corridor was about twenty yards long and it opened into a courtyard which was open to the elements, a large atrium with no roof to the sky. An elegant marble pool was placed in the centre of this space, once ideal for entertaining, filled with statues, pot-plants and ornate garden furniture. Now the pool was slurping with scummy water, weeds grew rife through the untended lawn and gravel paths. The buildings three floors looked in on the central courtyard, doors at ground level were all in place and shut, the windows on the middle floor were not barred. In its heyday this would have been a wonderful place, an austere and forbidding exterior hiding and protecting a glorious palace on the inside. Tumbletick looked up to the sky, revealed through the large square opening with a crinkled edge made by the shape of the tiles design. He noticed that there was actually a fourth floor, under the roof, made by the slight rise from the outside of the building to the central walls. Small windows in these eaves spoke of tiny rooms that once would have housed the staff and storage rooms. Tumbletick realised that only four others of the party were now standing looking at the atrium courtyard and inside walls of the house. He turned around and saw Mr. Battfin holding the doors at the end of the entrance shut while Campbell was working on the lock with his toolkit. Tumbletick turned back to give his attention to the vista in front of him, he started looking for more details. The ground floor had columns painted on the wall to give a pleasing effect of a cloister. There were wooden shutters too on the ground floor, all closed over the windows behind and they had a rustic and utilitarian feel compared to the large leaded windows of the middle floor. One of those tall windows was smashed, glass lay shattered on the ground at least ten feet below the sill. Heaps of little white bones made mini mounds amongst the shards of glass. Tumbletick looked around and saw more of these little bones, they were everywhere. With the bones he often found many small furry, mouldy tubes, all hidden amongst the weeds and undergrowth. He shrugged it off to large owls making their home here now and not being discerning as to where they left their pellets and remains of rat. The others were looking around too, Tumbletick wondered if they had spotted his ornithological observations as well.

Campbell and Mr. Battfin returned to the group.

"The doors are shut and I managed to put some of the bits of lock back in place," Campbell conferred. "It is completely cosmetic. The doors look shut and locked but I fear anyone who comes a knocking would gain entry at the first polite rap!"

"Well let us explore this fine old house, who knows what treasures await?" invited Egremont. He turned in a smart military manner and proceeded to the nearest door leading into the house. He turned the large iron ring that acted as a handle and to his obvious surprise he did not need to call upon the talents of Campbell as the door swung with an ebullient eerie creek.

The room was a kitchen. Large workstations, fireplaces, sinks and cupboards all indicated this could produce food on an industrial scale. Egremont pushed open the three shuttered windows to the room as soon as he was inside, to allow easier viewing for his less optically able companions. Spiders and beetles scurried away from webs and darkened corners, more little white bones were revealed covering the floor by the shafts of light.

"Well I don't think much of the menu here!" scoffed Egremont kicking at some of the rat bones. "But someone, or something, clearly does approve!"

"Shouldn't we check these cupboards for olive oil or for candles?" suggested Tumbletick. "We've only got the two lanterns left and I'm sure olive oil would burn well."

Jackson nodded sagely in agreement and he was the first to start looking for additional supplies. They ransacked the kitchen but nothing was left of any use. There were two exits from the kitchen above and beyond the door into the garden. A swing door was in the centre of one wall and a flight of stairs on the other side of an archway led both up and down in a wide spiral.

"Which way?" said Campbell. He went to the swing door which had a small window in it so servants in the past could see if anyone was coming through. Useful when the kitchen must have been busy. Campbell peered through and reported back that it led to a corridor.

"I think that perhaps up might be a fortuitous direction," remarked Egremont. "'Down' looks decidedly dingy and cellar like, what with our current lighting situation."

"Up it is then," stated Mr. Battfin and with a swish of authority he drew his cutlass and started up the stone stairs and was out of sight, around the central column before the others could join him.

The spiral stair continued to climb but at the second floor another archway was present. A curtain that could be pulled to cover it had been drawn and Mr. Battfin was found staring into a grand dining room. The large leaded windows meant the room was bathed in light, revealing an ornate quality that again spoke of a grand past. A long table with chairs all pushed under in regimental fashion, dominated the room. A plush carpet, now faded, nearly covered the entire floor plan. Mr. Battfin entered the room and was first to gaze around at portraits still in place, an imposing fireplace with mantle and well proportioned bureaus standing empty of any items that had once been on display.

"They didn't leave the silver service then?" questioned Campbell in hope, sneaking into the room with a sneer and an inquisitive look.

"Well we don't know if they did or not," remarked Vixen looking at the portraits. "They might have done and some treasure seeker has already lifted it."

Jackson joined her in appreciation of the art. "Ugly bunch, wonder if they were the family who resided here?"

"Those with money often lose their looks through avarice and inbreeding," she replied coyly. "I have often found that the face of a pure bred peasant child is infinitely more appealing than what the upper classes would classify as good looking."

"You must have been looking at the wrong kind of peasant then," sniffed Jackson. "Those in my employ are genuine beasts." He flounced off on a swiftly turned heel and a flick of his cloak into a billowing retreat.

Egremont was talking with Is-Is by one of the windows, Vixen remained with a smile looking at the portraits, Mr. Battfin and Campbell had pulled out a couple of chairs and a hipflask for a sit down and Tumbletick was examining the table for engraved signatures. Jackson joined Tumbletick muttering something when abrupt sounds of loud scratching came from the floor above.

Mr. Battfin and Campbell jumped up from their seats, Campbell instantly had a blade drawn in one hand and the hipflask in the other. Mr. Battfin's chair tried to balance for a while on its rear two legs, tottered for a moment and then crashed to the floor. The noise was long, drawn out, deliberate, a sound of bone like talons gouging into wood. Looking at the ceiling they could all sense an imaginary line of the deep scratch being drawn and stretched along the floorboards above. Then there were muffled shouts, voices, definitely voices, defiant. More scratching, thumping of running legs, something heavy. A deafening screech, squawks, more shouts and continued thumping stomps moving across the ceiling.

"Whatever's going on is going on right up that staircase and I doubt there's a door to stop it getting down here," said Campbell calmly.

"Let us engage and capture the element of surprise," enthused Egremont, already running towards the stairway, rapier revealed.

Is-Is was quick to follow his companion, then Mr. Battfin and Campbell were striding up the spiral stairs. Vixen turned to look at Tumbletick and Jackson to see if they intended to join the investigation.

"If there is danger to be had, I think we should stick together," she purred. "You two go first, I'll bring up the rear."

She slipped out two long knives from sheathes strapped to her thighs, twirled them twice and with a single shake of her head indicated that they should move.

Chorus five

Fenton had been trudging along, alone with his thoughts for hours now. The odd traveller who approached in the opposite direction had always been wary and hesitant to talk to any other stranger on the road, exchanging nothing more than furtive looks and grunts of acknowledgement. Perhaps news of the attack at the Court of Rhyell had well and truly spread now and people had grown suspicious and fearful. 'Terror getting what it wanted,' thought Fenton.

He often looked over his shoulder to see if the figures that had been following him were still there. No, following was not right, he needed to get that out of his head, there was only this main track from Rampart to Tetterton. Anyone travelling back west would have had to travel that way. Often though he saw the trio behind him, sometimes further away, sometimes closer, depending on who was moving faster at that particular moment he thought. Occasionally, if he picked up his pace to a brisk walk with the odd few steps at a canter he could get far enough in front that his shadows would be left behind the bridge of a rolling hill and he would be unable to see them when he turned around to check.

Fenton decided not to stop and linger over luncheon. He just took enough time to get his pack off, opened and fished out the fruit and the small loaf of bread he had bought to snack upon at about midday. Quickly the backpack was back on, the blanket loosely just draped over his left shoulder, he did not have time to roll it and stow it correctly under the straps. Then it was eating on the move but he decided to run for a distance first, to make up for the time lost in stopping to get out his food. It was not elegant running with the blanket placed precariously on his shoulder and two hands clutching his food. Yet he made up the distance and he began to chomp into the bread, his left arm managing to bunch the slipping blanket against his chest as he held onto the fruit. A piece of the fruit rolled free and dropped to the ground, bounced limply and picked up some mud on its skin. 'No point stopping for that,' thought Percy. 'It will be a nice treat for a rat or a crow.'

He looked to the horizon ahead and saw another trio of figures walking towards him. A quick look behind and he found that the threesome which had been dogging him for most of the day was gone. 'What's this? A trap? Have they got round in front of me somehow or have gone out to flanking positions?'

Percy checked himself, he was thinking too much. Maybe he missed his companions more than he would have credited himself. He wondered where they were right now. He slowed his walk to a wander and gazed more carefully at the approaching group. A man with two teenage boys, quite clearly. They carried a large sack each, perhaps olive farmers. As they drew within about five yards he hailed them with a hearty 'hello' and they mumbled something in reply.

Chapter Six

Egremont burst into the room above though another vacant archway, it was large and bare with stripped wooden floors, and no trappings gave any clue as to its old use. The sources of all the noise were engaged in a battle at the end of the room to his right, fighting in another open doorway. Two large birdlike creatures were violently attacking a human shaped figure. The monsters were dark brown feathered things, standing about seven foot tall on thick scaly legs, feet with three clawed toes at the front and a wicked looking talon at the equivalent of a heel. Their bodies were large and round with small nearly useless wings tucked firmly against them. Thick necks made up a lot of their height and were too covered in the stubby brown feathers of their breed. Their bald heads were of a knobbly, oily, leathery, dark brown skin, hideous to look at and contained black straining eyes, bulging out of the skull. Their beaks were very long, curved and only opened slightly to emit their squawks of rage and a long lacerating tongue which was their main form of attack. 'Stirges', thought Egremont. These were nearly flightless creatures, although whether they were on the way up the evolutionary scale towards flight or were becoming totally land based animals no one knew. They could easily still, however, leap large distances and heights and aid the bound with a little flapping. Their clawed feet could be used as weapons too and could disembowel a man, yet they preferred the precision of their serrated proboscis it seemed, with which they could accurately skewer a rat with one wicked impaling stab. They were both currently screeching and stabbing at the figure who was defending the doorway, duelling with a dangerous looking dagger and a long sword, unwilling to give quarter or retreat. Other figures could be seen in the room behind the fighter, two were close by shouting, trying to find space to launch their own attacks against the vicious bird like creatures.

Is-Is joined Egremont and surveyed the scene in an instant. The fighter in the doorway was a very fair faced individual, proud though and set with determination. Is-Is frowned trying to discern a gender in its androgynous qualities, then realised it must be an elf from the

Western Lands across the oceans. It was definitely a male elf from its height. The warrior was hacking at the beaks with his blades but the stirges were made of tough stuff and the beaks only seemed to be knocked away rather than damaged by any attacking action. A stirge gave a darting thrust and its tongue dug deep into the chest of the elf who screamed through gritted teeth. A man behind the graceful adventurer shouted 'retreat' but was met with a response of 'never' in injured tones as blood fell to the floor. The sight and smell of blood seemed to excite and encourage the stirges, another head butting motion thrust a spiked tongue into the elf's left shoulder. The other stirge who had first drawn blood, lifted a talonned claw and stomped it deep into the middle of the fighter's leg. The elf sank down onto his wounded knee, screaming in rage and fear, he lifted his sword and dagger into a defensive cross above his head to try and fend off the attacks. The two companions behind now had some space to try and thrust though attacks with their own swords but it was difficult to get any really effective gouges through to the stirges. The elf would not move by his own volition and the warriors who stood behind him looked as if they were about to push their way past him to enter the fight.

"You must retreat!" a man in full plate armour shouted and then tried to pull the elf clear of the doorway by his uninjured shoulder, sword still in hand and holding a shield with his other the knight could not get the grip he needed to pull the elf away.

"Never," came the stubborn reply again, violently shrugging off the hand.

Is-Is and Egremont were now rushing towards the large monsters, deciding that aid would be useful and appreciated. They had taken about ten seconds to assess the situation. Usually it would take about five but launching in against two stirges from behind was a dangerous encounter. Mr. Battfin came charging in and took no time at all to be racing in behind them.

The elf looked up, after shrugging off the armoured mans help, towards the new sound of charging hare, wolfhound and muscle bound pirate. He looked right up into another talon attack as one of the stirges large reptilian feet was stamped into the delicate and androgynous face. Claws cut into his eyes and cheeks, the force from the bottom of the claw smashing his graceful nose to an instant pulp. He buckled forward and the other stirge punctured straight through the lower back and into a kidney with its blade like tongue.

"No!" shouted a barbarian looking warrior, dressed in skins and leather boots but naked from the waist up, his solid, hulking, physical strength defied his speed as he leapt over the elf's body in a berserker rage, hacking at the birds with a double headed, double handed battle axe, just as Egremont, Is-Is and Mr. Battfin joined the fray from the rear. What the elf had shown in bravery or stubbornness the four warriors now engaging the stirges showed in vicious savagery. Hacking, stabbing violence was countered with attempted kicks and spitting tongues. The barbarian caught one stirge on the neck with his axe, cutting deeply into tendon and muscle until it reached bone, just as Mr. Battfin stuck his cutlass solidly under a wing and into the chest cavity, clipping the monster's heart with a good inch of blade. The creature stumbled and fell, pulling Mr. Battfin's sword out of his hand as it landed on the wooden floor. The barbarian looked the pirate in the eye, no sign of thanks but in a continued rage, pulled his axe free, heaved it above his head and executioner style slammed it down into the main body of the remaining beast as it was fencing with Egremont and Is-Is. The immense blow crippled the bird, its legs buckled and it went down in an ungainly lurch forward. Is-Is was in next with an attack with his two handed broadsword, he thrust in from a long way back, all his weight behind the stab into the flank and the creature twitched violently as its long neck snaked and slumped down with it's death.

The barbarian fell to his knees and dropped his axe, lifted his arms aloft and howled. Mr. Battfin retrieved his cutlass and looked on as the armoured warrior silently gazed at the body of the dead elf through the gap in his visor. Is-Is was wiping his blade clean on the feathers of the carcass and Egremont was standing with a paw on his hip, rapier on the floor like a walking stick. This was the scene which greeted Tumbletick, Jackson and Vixen as they finally made it up the stairs and into the room. Tumbletick remained in the shadows by the top of the stair with Vixen and Lord Jackson, his jaw hanging open and his eyes wide at the vicious vignette.

The armoured warrior removed his helmet to reveal a handsome middle aged face, short, dark cropped hair, slight flecked with grey. His blue eyes were sad at the violent death of his companion.

"Dear friend, it would have been wiser to retreat a few steps to allow us all to have engaged these fiends. No shame would have been afforded to you or your race," he said solemnly, dropping to one knee beside the body of the fallen elf as he finished speaking.

Two other men now emerged from the further room to stand beside the kneeling paladin, both were older and they looked first at the body of the elf, then the stirges and then the six adventurers in the room containing the carnage, Tumbletick still obscured by shadows was unseen.

The armoured knight looked up at one of the men, who had a long white beard and inky blue robes.

"These warriors helped dispatch the foul fowl," he said in a rich and well educated voice.

"For that we are grateful," replied the ancient bearded man looking at Is-Is, Egremont and Mr. Battfin. "But now we wish to be left to our grief thank you."

The other older man was dressed in chain mail covered with a tabard with a religious device emblazoned upon it. He was a well built man still and was obviously a cleric who had not taken vows to renounce violence as he had a warlike countenance and an iron mace hanging at his belt. He had a hand on the shoulder of the barbarian, in sympathy perhaps but it roused the muscled warrior from his solace and he raised and stood beside the cleric. The barbarian puffed out his chest, set his feet to a defensive stance and hefted up his battle axe into a ready position, both hands holding the shaft, the weapon forming a barrier in front of him.

Is-Is' eyes narrowed as he looked at the solid looking warrior monk, the barbarian and now the armour plated paladin rising from beside the dead elf to form a wall of three men standing in front of the bearded man.

Mr. Battfin too sensed the change in the encounter, his recently released cutlass was instantly gripped tighter and moved to his side, ready to slash back at any threat which may occur.

Egremont remained calm, paw still on hip, rapier in the position of a prop of a gentleman out for a stroll.

"Dear sir," he almost purred. "We pose no threat to your grief but we do not intend to currently leave this place."

The paladin was replacing his helmet, the sturdy cleric released his iron mace into his right hand and the barbarian started to ever so slightly growl.

The bearded blue robed fellow replied in tones of civility.

"Yet we do not wish your companionship. Just leave so that we are free to bury our dead."

"As already stated, we do not intend to leave the environs of this building," Egremont returned with only a hint of curtness. Campbell the Weasel stepped forward so now the odds were very much even in terms of numbers in the face off. The barbarian shifted the weight of his axe a little, Is-Is immediately picked up on the subtle movement knowing the barbarian was closer to a battle readiness and posed more of a threat.

"Hmm," Egremont mused out loud. "I wonder why you really want us to depart."

"I have told you why. I wonder why you won't."

"Perhaps it is a stubborn streak or a hint of suspicion about what is in the room you were defending from the stirges," Egremont revealed.

The paladin raised his broadsword to an en-guard position and from behind the visor of his helmet replied, "I took you for a gentleman originally with your chivalrous act of coming to the aid of our fellow but now I see you are nothing but a cad!"

Mr. Battfin's sabre rose simultaneously to counter the broadsword with a nearly touching blade.

"I would not question my courteous credentials, sir!" Egremont said calmly and he raised his own rapier to point towards the opposing group.

"Wait!" shouted Tumbletick as he came bounding over from the shadows. Jackson tried to make a grab at him to stop his headlong rush into an impending battle and he stumbled forward as he missed the little man. Vixen dashed to his side to steady him with a look of exasperation on her face.

"Wait!" Tumbletick shouted again. "Do we need to have more bloodshed after the death of your friend Vigor?"

The barbarian, armoured knight, bearded ancient and clerical warrior all turned away from the potential conflict to look with shock at the hairy creature who had mentioned their fallen comrade by name.

"We are not here to threaten your adventures, we should be friends. I know you are good people," Tumbletick continued as he worked his way between the two aggressive groups, feeling uncomfortably close to the corpses of elf and monsters.

"You were behind us in the queue to get into this god forsaken place," said the cleric in sudden recognition. "Yes, you are a very memorable little fellow."

"Thank you Nazar Grant," replied Tumbletick, the man looked less shocked than when the misshapen dwarf had mentioned the name of Vigor but a degree of amazement crossed his face.

"Well you are not only memorable you are obviously of good memory too!" said Nazar Grant.

Egremont sensing a change lowered his rapier, Mr. Battfin followed suit and the armoured knight returned the etiquette and sheathed his broadsword.

"Thank you Beran," Tumbletick said towards the knight who nodded his helmet in return. "Now if Seton Rax will put down his battle axe I am sure we will be able to leave you in peace to bury Vigor."

"Well said little man," said the barbarian Seton Rax and he lowered his axe and his gaze which had been fixed towards Is-Is.

The old man then stepped forward and offered his hand to Tumbletick.

"You seem to have us at a disadvantage as we do not know your given name."

"Well neither do I really. You venerable sir are Garraday and I go by the name of Tumbletick," Tumbletick took Garraday's hand and shook it.

The sound of sighs from both sides was audible as held breath was released and tensed muscles loosened. Hands were held out on both sides, taken and shook. The groups moved away from the remains of the elf and stirges and into the centre of the room where the battle and potential battle had taken place. Tumbletick took the lead and did the introductions.

"I have the pleasure of introducing the Lord Egremont Seau du Duvet, Mr. Battfin, Campbell the Weasel and Is-Is," as he indicated the first three of his friends. "Now these two fine people are Lord Jackson of En'Tuk and Raven Hill, otherwise known as Vixen."

"We seem to be in the presence of nobility," said Beran. He removed his visored helmet again and dropped to one knee, as he was now close enough to Vixen, took her hand and kissed it.

Groups started to form and chat with each other. Beran seemed rapt in the charms of Vixen and Lord Jackson. Mr. Battfin and Campbell were examining Seton Rax's battleaxe who seemed pleased to show it to them and the size of the arms you needed to be able to wield it. Egremont was already questioning Nazar Grant as to his ecclesiastical credentials and the use of a mace as a weapon designed not to draw blood. Is-Is was standing quite still, looking through the door and into the other room with a quizzical look on his face. Tumbletick found himself talking to the elderly Garraday.

"I am sorry for the loss of your friend," he said softly.

"Oh I have lost many friends over my time. We knew the risks upon entering the city. We shall remove his body to the garden and bury him so that he does not fall to ruin as carrion for other creatures." His voice was solid and controlled, thoughtful, yet swift.

"Where is Lambert?" blurted Tumbletick.

Garraday bent down to Tumbletick, his long white beard swung forward and touched Tumbleticks own hirsute, unshorn face.

"He is back in the room we were defending, opening a treasure chest," the old man almost whispered. "If you can convince your friends that any loot we find is ours then it will make the possibility of another fight very greatly reduced."

He smiled and his eyes widened and twinkled.

Chorus Six

The sun burned brightly as it dropped towards the horizon causing Fenton to look distinctly at his feet in order to avoid the glare. His thoughts were focused too, on finding somewhere sheltered to spend the night. Somewhere with a roof and walls would be good, somewhere where he could closet himself away from the elements and any other potential threats. He was sure that a barn would avail itself, he may have to share with some cows but at least they would provide extra warmth.

The sun was visibly moving now as it hit the horizon and slumped beneath it, very bright but very pale light giving way to darkness racing in from behind Fenton. He turned and looked to the sky in the east, already a deep murky blue. 'Got to find somewhere quick, can't afford to be stumbling around in the dark,' he thought.

He moved from an urgent walk to a jog as the sun completely vanished and only a semblance of sun bathed the sky with any light. Fenton knew that the plateau's horizon was higher than the natural horizon of the sea so he had very little time left before complete darkness. Then his luck paid out as it usually did as he saw a barn off to his right, the roof just visible in the darker shadow in front of a shallow hill.

He immediately left the road, decision made, footsteps running on spongy farmland, sodden with water from the previous day's storm. The grass was cropped short, eaten by browsing beasts, maybe goats, maybe cows he briefly thought. The barn small, more of a long shed with rickety doors at one end, just barely visible now in the scantest of twilight. Fenton was flying at full pelt, feeling that the barn would offer some solace from the thoughts of being watched, being followed, imagined touches on his shoulders of clawed hands reaching out from behind him. The doors yielded with a boom to his outstretched arms as he careened into them, bursting inwards to an inky void of rural storage. No animals here, just piles of hay, even though he could not see, he knew the smell and it was comforting. Memories of his orphaned youth violated his mind and took the comfort away. He entered the barn and pushed the doors back shut, slumping against them as they closed, exhausted from his run. He then walked tentatively in the dark to a pile of hay, reaching with his finger tips for the dry grass heap and then he threw himself down upon it. He was still breathing deeply when he blindly removed his backpack and felt around for his blanket. He covered himself with it and then pushed his way further into the hay. Although he was hungry no thoughts of a fire or cooking entered his mind, just the sounds of a rising wind, creaking of the wooden barn and his own breathing. His eyes were open in the dark and he found no sleep, just fear.

Chapter Seven

Tumbletick broke away from the twinkling gaze of Garraday and scampered over to Egremont who was in an eager conversation with the clerical warrior Nazar Grant. Tumbletick bobbed a bit at Egremont's side then started tugging on his tabard.

"Yes Tumbletick, what can I do for you?" enquired the lordly wolfhound.

"I'm sorry to interrupt but I do need a quiet word in private," Tumbletick apologised. Egremont put an arm around Tumbletick's shoulder.

"Never apologise to me old chap. Would you excuse us for a moment Nazar Grant?" he said, sounding like the host of a party being dragged away from an important guest.

The two sauntered over to the corner of the room and became enveloped in the increasing shadows which were growing as the afternoon took hold. Egremont's countenance now changed to one of more urgent interest than that of a phlegmatic courtier.

"What is it Tumbletick, something important?" his voice was hushed as he bent a little to bring his face closer to his friends.

"The group we have just met are nervous that we are treasure seekers too! They have another member, if you remember, from the queue. He is called Lambert; I think he is a thief. Well he's in the other room right now trying to open a chest they have found and well, Garraday, who I think is their leader, thinks there might be trouble if we were to know there might be a horde of coins or jewellery in that chest," Tumbletick paused for breath and looked into Egremont's deeply thoughtful eyes.

"Well done Tumbletick. You seem to be able to get people to trust you very quickly," Egremont said then stood tall again, put a smile on his face and walked briskly and with purpose over to Garraday with his arms open wide in a posture of universal openness.

Garraday had been standing alone watching the conversation in the shadows with interest, he knew immediately that Tumbletick had conveyed the correct message. He too opened his arms to mirror the posture of the gregarious wolfhound.

"My dear Garraday," boomed Egremont. "Please let me explain our reason for being here to you in utmost clarity!"

"It would be much welcomed my Lord Egremont," replied the sagely old man. He placed his hands together with Egremont's paws in a double handshake.

"We are not interested in any treasure that might be found. Our goal is a noble quest, yet we seek no item here. We must, without fail, gain entrance to the castle of the Old City," Egremont offered openly in a voice loud enough to carry to all in the room.

"Then why do we find you in a merchant's house, likely to be laced with loot from ancient times or placed by the authorities of Rampart as one of the many lures offered to those who seek treasure?" Garraday enquired.

"That is simple. The castle is currently under attack from a sizeable mob and we were merely seeking solitude and respite from any danger when we heard the sounds of another battle above our heads."

Garraday moved his head closer to Egremont's and in quiet tones, looking him straight in the eye said.

"Do I have your word as a knight and as leader of your group, that any treasure that we might have just found will be uncontested?"

"Indeed you do. Any that you have just found and any that you currently have upon your person at this instant, will be yours," Egremont replied immediately.

"This is a moment fraught with tension, Lord Egremont. You may have seen Vigor be easily defeated by two stirges but he was an inexperienced warrior eager to prove his worth. Beran and Seton Rax are very dangerous men indeed, very experienced. Nazar is a solid defender of the faith and I have some peculiar talents," Garraday was holding Egremont's paws with a grip that surprised the wolfhound. The grip of his eyes was surprising too and Egremont found that he could not turn away.

"I absolutely must have your strongest oath on this matter my Lord Egremont," Garraday instructed.

"I, Egremont, the Lord Seau du Duvet, swear unto you Garraday, in front of these witnesses, that any treasure you or your party find whilst in our company will be yours. Indeed to avoid any room for equivocation or misinterpretation, any treasure that my party find whilst in your company will be yours too. I hereby state that we have no interest in treasure, we just wish to get into the castle," Egremont was very precise and stern.

"Well that seems clear then," said Garraday with a chirpy tone as he released his grip and looked away with a smile towards the rest of his companions. "Gentlemen, we have reached a binding agreement of the finding of any treasure. It will be ours and ours alone."

Beran and Seton Rax visibly eased. It seemed that although they had been engaged in conversation it may have been a contrivance to position themselves with more space for any potential battle. Nazar Grant looked to the ceiling and mouthed something just as a huge scream came from the adjoining room and shattered the moment of goodwill. Feet stomped on the floor as everyone drew swords and weapons and ran through the door, leaping over the dead bodies of Vigor and the stirges. The room into which they emerged was another long cavernous space. It was bare of any furniture, the windows to the left were letting in a fading light and in the gloom a small ferrety man was writhing around in agony in front of a large dark brown chest with metal straps and a large keyhole and lock.

Nazar Grant, despite his heavy solidness was the first to get to the little thief whose body was now contorting into forms that looked like his legs and arms were broken and his spine had been snapped. His mouth was issuing forth foamy spittle and his eyes were bulging in terror and pain. Nazar attempted to hold him down but found even his strength and burly bulk was not enough to keep the smaller, lighter man still.

The rest of the group were looking on now with faces ranging from fear to concern to disgust at the agonies and contortions of Lambert. Only Campbell showed no interest in the man, he had run instead instantly to the chest and was now kneeling before it, scrutinising the lock.

"Can he be helped?" barked Garraday to the struggling Nazar Grant.

"I doubt it," he shouted back with a hint of aggression. "If someone could hold his legs still rather than just watching we may be able to figure out what is wrong."

Mr. Battfin was the first to respond and fell quickly to the aid of Nazar Grant, placing his knees on the fitting man's ankles and holding his legs around the lower thigh with his swarthy and calloused hands, his strength hardened by years at sea and fighting.

"Has he had fits before?" Vixen interjected loudly above the thumping of his body on the floorboards and the screams. Nazar Grant and Mr. Battfin were still unable to keep him still.

"Not that I know of," replied Nazar through gritted teeth. "More help please, I am meant to be the healer not the ward orderly!"

Embarrassed a little Seton Rax stepped forward and brought his own mighty strength to bear upon the chest of the man. With Mr. Battfin just about controlling the legs and Seton Rax upon the torso, Nazar Grant moved away and started rummaging in a pack he had on a belt around his waist.

"Somebody put a stick in his mouth to stop him biting his tongue off," said Nazar still concentrating on the contents of his bag. "Please," he ordered looking up.

"Err, Nazar. Where are we going to get a stick?" said Beran slightly sheepishly.

Campbell the Weasel was sniffing the lock of the treasure chest when he suddenly turned around.

"Very little point in looking for the stick I'm afraid," he said. "He has been struck by a poison needle within the lock. It has retracted back in but I can see it there. From the complete absence of smell and his very violent symptoms, I would suspect that it has been laced with Ceracktic venom."

"He hasn't got a chance then," sighed Nazar Grant.

"You can let him die in agony or dispatch him to the afterlife," said Campbell calmly. "Depending on his strength he may survive like this for a couple of days but death is inevitable. If it was me, I'd want a quick and well placed blade."

Seton Rax looked at Mr. Battfin over the body of the poisoned man as they attempted to hold him still. Beran turned to Garraday and drew his sword a couple of inches from the scabbard an indication of willingness. Jackson looked at Vixen with a quizzical tilt of the head that made her think he thought she wanted to do the deed. Tumbletick turned away and placed his face into the body of Is-Is who put a comforting arm around his friend. Egremont stood stone still and solemn.

"I think perhaps this is something better done without an audience," said Garraday.

"Perhaps we could carry him down to the garden and do it there," proffered Vixen.

"I think it would be a bit of a struggle to get him down two floors and through the kitchen," said Egremont to grunts of approval from Mr. Battfin and Seton Rax as they maintained their laboured grip upon the thrashing thief.

"Take him to the body of Vigor. He can die by the side of his erstwhile friend," Garraday ordered grimly. "Beran, are you willing to provide the mercy blow?"

The armoured knight nodded several times, never removing his eyes from the vision of agony before him. Mr. Battfin and Seton Rax then really struggled to move the man, half carrying, half dragging and regularly dropping the wildly jerking, convulsing, screaming and frothing thief. They got him through the door and placed him with as much tenderness and respect as they could on the floor near to Vigor's corpse. Then they returned to the rest of the group as Beran marched passed them with purpose and determination jutting from his squarely set jaw. As the sun was beginning to set outside the larger group left in an empty and cavernous room, stood facing towards a treasure chest which taunted them with its trap and unseen contents. With their backs toward the door they remained quiet as they listened to the last horrors of Lambert come to an end. The voice of Beran could just be made out offering a prayer for forgiveness and the thief's soul, then a sword was drawn, the screaming ended and two thumps were heard hitting the floor shortly spaced with silence.

"So we've agreed that you guys get any treasure we find?" Campbell questioned breaking the atmosphere with professional zeal. "Cause, I reckon I could pick this lock you know."

"You want to pick that after what you have just seen?" said Egremont.

"Absolutely. I am a pretty high ranking member of the Thieves Guild you know and if I just left this chest sitting here when I know of at least one of the traps and there was a large treasure inside it would be, embarrassing, if it ever got back to anyone. The needle on the spring that retracts after firing is an easy one to circumnavigate. This chest is intriguing, up here in the middle of a bare room."

The conversation stopped with Beran coming back into the room looking dejected.

"I cut off his head. I thought it would be the quickest death."

"You have done a brave and noble thing," calmed Garraday walking over to him and putting an arm around a metal encased shoulder. He walked the paladin back towards the group but rather than looking at the knight who had just helped his friend to a quick death, Garraday kept his eyes firmly fixed upon Campbell fixating over the large chest. Campbell had his tools out again, laid beside him while he took a moment to scratch the inside of a nostril, deep in thought. He reached down and selected a pick, twirled it with his agile fingers and ran it across the front of the chest where the lid met the body. The pick's sharp point was thin enough to drag through the front of the joint and Campbell's tongue protruded slightly as he concentrated, feeling for something that only his thieves training knew.

Seton Rax and Nazar Grant walked over to Beran and Garraday and formed a small huddle of condolence and momentary melancholy before they swiftly turned and fixed their attention upon Campbell and the chest. Tumbletick was bemused by how such people could so easily be interested in the contents of a curious chest rather than pouring out emotions of grief after so recently losing two companions. He thought his own emotions were stunted after his childhood in Egremont's castle tower and living in his hut pretty much alone apart from the odd visit by his wolfhound and hare friends. Perhaps, however, his own feelings were intensely condensed by his lack of experience. Perhaps these adventurers had casually tossed away companions before from their group, an occupational hazard where only the best survived. Perhaps the remaining four were actually the core of a long standing group and were best of friends. Tumbletick turned his own attention to Campbell, it seemed riveting stuff watching the thief work on the one item in the bare room.

Campbell frowned slightly and closed his eyes, moving his ear to the faint join he paused with the pick at the corner of the chest and then dug the pick in deeper into the seam.

"Yep, think I've found a second trap here. Whoever put this in place certainly wanted to make the contents worth dying for," he stopped speaking in an awkward silence realising what he had just said was particularly uncouth but a quick and furtive look at Garraday and company highlighted they were more interested in his lock picking skills or the potential contents of the chest rather than his insensitive words.

"What form does this trap take do you think Master Campbell?" enquired Beran.

"Well it is sprung when the lid is lifted. Whether it is a poison gas cloud or a blade or a spray of acid, I don't know but I would suggest we do not stand in front of the chest when I open it!"

"Will you be able to open it then?" enthused Garraday.

"Oh yeah, without doubt. The lock is quite standard, once you have identified and bypassed the threat of the needle laced with Ceracktic venom it is actually quite an easy process. So when I have unlocked it, it is just a case of opening the lid from behind, no one in front and watch out. If gas is released a quick exit from the room for a couple of minutes should be enough for any poison to defuse. A blade or acid thrown out and we will, within seconds, be able to see the contents of the chest."

Campbell now turned his kleptomaniac skills towards the lock with a new tool selected from his roll of thieves equipment. Deftly he worked at it and when a slight click was heard and a needle shot out he had been ready and his fingers were far enough away to avoid the same fate which had befallen Lambert. He went back to working on the lock until a larger and more significant click was heard as it opened. Campbell, with only the slightest amount of sweat showing on his temples from the strain of concentration, broke into a significant smile.

"Step one complete," he informed. "Now if you could all stand back to a safe distance I will reach over from the back to lift open the now, unlocked chest and we shall see what we shall see."

Garraday was smiling broadly at the news Campbell imparted. Seton Rax was already rubbing his hands in anticipation of the contents. Beran still had a haunted look from his earlier actions but an interest in his eyes firmly fastened on the wooden trunk. Nazar Grant broke the anticipation with a sensible comment.

"Shouldn't we light our lanterns? It is going to be dark soon."

"I think we have got a little time to see what is in the chest first," replied Garraday.

Egremont raised an eyebrow and Mr. Battfin turned his head in interest.

"You've got lanterns then?" piped up Lord Jackson.

"Well obviously. You can't go adventuring without the right equipment," responded Garraday.

"I wonder if you managed to bring some extra oil with you too," stated Egremont calmly. "We would be very interested in purchasing some off of you. Seeing as we seem to have none with in our own supplies." He continued with a suave modesty at their own negligence.

"Yes, yes, yes. No problem at all, you can have some oil. Let's get the chest open," snapped Garraday. Campbell was looking frustrated too that the conversation had taken such a turn and the focus away from his work and the sense of high drama. Garraday was almost twitching and bobbing in eagerness as Campbell the Weasel leaned over from behind the chest with his arms outstretched to take hold of the lid. His thin face and scraggly beard lifted towards the ten figures in front of him, waiting for just that little longer and his moment of glory to reveal the innards. He toyed with them for a while, winked and tensed his muscles.

"Shall we proceed?" Campbell asked. "Just be ready for the trap."

The thief gave a last smile, took a deep breath and heaved open the lid of the large trunk. As it opened the earlier identified trigger was released and the sound of gas under immense pressure was heard escaping. Campbell was quickly scuttling away close to the floor like a frantic lobster towards the edge of the room, his cheeks puffed out, holding his breath. The rest of the group instinctively put hands and paws in front of their faces and backed away and out of the room. There was no way of knowing just how dangerous the gas was or for how far it would extend but it was obviously designed to inflict the most damage on someone in front of the chest who was breathing normally.

Campbell had swiftly crawled to a corner and was sitting hunched now looking back towards the treasure chest and the rest of the group.

"What's in it?" he shouted to the others from the shadows.

Is-Is made a start to walk and investigate the contents but Garraday promptly strode in front of him, one hand covering his nose and mouth and his other arm flapping wildly with the large drooping sleeve of his cloak. It made an effective fan against any remaining miasma. The others were quick to follow not wanting to miss out on the first view of whatever lay in the cavernous coffer.

Within the light that was left a golden glow arose from the chest. Eyes widened in the gloom to take in extra light in the twilight and with hope. As confidence grew against the remnants of the gas a view of the treasure was taken in by all as they approached in a semi circular line of greed. Seton Rax broke rank and he sprinted the last few yards and fell to his knees in a long skid on the wooden floor. His hands dove into a depth of golden coins as glee exploded onto his face. Garraday was there next, speed in his ancient legs a surprise to some. He was audibly moaning in pleasure at the sight of Seton Rax cascading coinage through his fingers. Beran and Nazar Grant had their arms around each other and their grins would have enveloped each other too if they could. Campbell did not need to shout his question again as he could make out the sound of falling coins from Seton Rax's hands. Egremont, Is-Is, Mr. Battfin, Tumbletick, Jackson and Vixen were all further back, each with their own thoughts of the avarice for treasure that was on display. Jackson thought how people could be so weak in their pursuit of wealth that they needed to turn to adventuring and death of friends in its search. Mr. Battfin thought of many similar chests that he had buried on islands all around the Circle Sea during his pirate career. Vixen was musing on how fallible people had been in her spying career for a handful of metallic discs. Tumbletick was only wondering about any remaining gas which may be harmful. Is-Is was ruminating on the glory gained in battle rather than in treasure. It was Egremont who broke the treasure seeking celebrations of their new companions.

"I trust that you are happy with the find?"

"Oh yes, extremely happy," replied Garraday, looking back over his shoulder briefly.

"How much do you think is in there?" Egremont continued with his questioning.

"At least ten thousand gold pieces," said Seton Rax not even bothering to turn away for a couple of seconds.

"This is the very essence of our adventure," added Garraday. "And we found it so quickly too!"

"Do you think this is a placement of the Rampart authorities or a remnant of the merchant who once lived here?" asked Egremont, keen to understand what the other group felt.

"Oh with out doubt this is a placement," stated Garraday. "We know they place treasures as lures to keep the adventures traipsing through their city. Well we have found one and defeated the monsters and the traps that were left to guard it."

"Undoubtedly. But at what cost?" retorted Egremont.

"None that we were not willing to pay Master Wolfhound," Beran added to the conversation, turning to face Egremont with a face contorted with desire for the gold.

"How do you propose to carry such a large amount of gold out of the city? Ten thousand in coin is a hefty weight for any treasure seeker," Egremont asked.

"Indeed," Jackson entered the conversation. "The reason we use promissory notes in trade and business is because coin is so cumbersome. Tumbletick here would have been unable to walk into Geiger's with the amount he would have needed to buy the fine watches we all carry." He winked at his hairy little friend.

"Well we will leave a guard here and three of us will head back to Rampart. Then we will find a hotel with a reliable safe then come back in to take the next five hundred or so pieces," Garraday said with a logic that seemed very reasonable to himself in a flush of treasured happiness.

"And I suppose you will then have to leave a guard back at the hotel. So two of you will return through the dangerous streets of the Old City and back to this Merchant's House. Casually carrying sacks of five hundred coins at a time, back and forth. You'll probably be able to do it in about ten or so such trips. No chance of you drawing any attention from the other vagabonds and cutthroats that roam these loathsome lanes," Egremont was cool in his analysis of the situation and the smiles on the four faces of their new companions evaporated as they realised the logistical difficulties of their find.

"It seems there was one final trap then," said Campbell walking out of the shadows. "That of the weight of the treasure. Are you rich now or is this just a worthless hook that will keep you here with the ghosts of your companions who died in revealing its wealth?"

Seton Rax's muscled bulk looked crestfallen as he realised what was being said.

"Yet we are where we are and we have only the solution of transporting the coin to the city of Rampart where there we could realise the wealth by converting it to promissory notes at a bank. Should we choose to do that," said Garraday with a hint of resentment at Jackson's earlier comment.

"Is this money so extremely important to you?" asked Lord Jackson.

"Obviously it is," said Nazar Grant. "This is two decades worth of work for a priest such as I."

"Then I have a proposal for you all," continued Jackson, looking at Egremont to trust him to carry on with his freshly formulated plan although he had not discussed it first with the wolfhound. Egremont pulled a slightly grudging grimace but thought he knew where Jackson may be going with his proposal so nodded that he should proceed.

"My proposal is that we need some oil for our lanterns and some more physical support, potentially, to get into the castle, which it appears is currently locked up against attacks."

"Please go on," implored Garraday. "For we do have extra supplies of oil that we are willing to sell, especially as I had already promised you some for free and any adventurer can easily turn their hand to mercenary or bodyguard, should the fee be right."

"Then the proposal is this. Your chest of gold we believe contains an estimated ten thousand gold pieces. I will pay you in much easier to carry promissory notes the same amount to fuel our lanterns and come with us until we release you from our service. That releasing of service will be when we are in a position to make rendezvous with a ship we are planning to meet at a secret location. Although we must gain entry to the catacombs under the castle in order to get there. Plus you are of course then free to come back here and claim whatever gold you see fit, by what ever method of transportation."

"Okay. Well you obviously plan to make it to the cave on the south side of the island which is so often used by smugglers and pirates," said Garraday. "But do you really carry such sums of money with you? For we would want payment up front."

"Indeed yes," said Lord Jackson and swinging off his backpack he untied a pouch and pulled out a leather wallet which he opened. Quickly flicking through a wad of notes he selected eight. Four two thousands and four five hundreds, he then handed one of each individually to Seton Rax, Nazar Grant, Beran and finally Garraday. They stood looking down at the value of the cash in their hands and gawped slightly.

"This is five years work," said Nazar a little stunned.

"Well, yes, that would be the right calculation based on your earlier comment," said Jackson, putting away the wallet.

"Does this new agreement override our earlier pact that if we come with you that any treasure that any of us find will be counted as ours?" Garraday said, seeking clarification.

"That conclusion has been made and will be honoured by us," responded Egremont, joining the negotiation. "We have no desire whatsoever for treasure. We just need to gain access to the castle."

"And the definition of treasure is?" probed Beran.

"Anything that you deem it to be. You have first choice on anything we find," Egremont stated with a slow deliberate certainty in his voice and with a solid stare. "Your pay will take you to a point where, as Lord Jackson said, we are in a position to make rendezvous with our other companion. Then we can choose our own paths."

"What is your true path Lord Egremont?" Beran asked.

"One of the noblest quests that you can imagine that as yet we can not reveal," Egremont replied.

"Yet we trust it is a quest for Good?" Garraday was keen to ask.

"Do we strike you as followers of Evil?" Egremont replied.

"No, you do not," Nazar Grant entered into the discussion with a religious authority.

"Then do we have a deal?" asked Lord Jackson, conscious that he had already handed out a fair amount of cash.

There was a slight pause as the three warriors looked to their leader, an old man with a long white beard, inky blue robes and the chance to double their money for a little bit of work.

"You sir have just bought yourself some very expensive lantern oil and some very cheap personal guards," stated Garraday. He turned back to the chest and doled out fifty coins to each of his crew. Then he shut the lid and started to recite some arcane language whilst making gestures over it with his hands and fingers contorted into mystic shapes just as the sun dropped beneath the rooftop.

"That should protect it from anybody else until we get back," he said. "Right, Seton Rax, give our new masters some oil and let us discuss the next steps in our mission."

Chorus Seven

The barn creaked in the wind, the sound of straining beams and planks gave no solace to Fenton. It was not the same sound as his beloved ship and there was no comforting roll of the sea or snorts of sleeping crewmen on the deck below. The dark however was the same as a cloudy night above a deep and churning sea, absolutely no light at all. Pitch black. Devoid. Fenton had lain awake despite his lethargy from the day long walk. His eyes wide and his hearing desperately alert to every sound he could pick up. He had never felt so uncomfortable, so alert and so unable to move to try and bring on the pleasures of sleep.

Then in the dark it struck him that this was the first night he had spent alone in years. Yes, aboard ship he often slept in a solitary fashion in his cabin but the crew were nearby and the ship herself felt like a comforting companion. That lack of emotional comfort started his heart pounding as only fear in the dark can, wide awake with no solace of sleep he could feel his whole body pulsing in the trepidation of his impending stretch of solitude in the dark. Fenton began to tremor more as his mind raced with all sorts of fears creeping in at the edges. He imagined noises louder than they were, scratching in the rafters above, howls of the wind or of beasts outside in the void of the night. He started to imagine himself a condemned man, in the death row cell the night before the dawn destiny with the gallows. 'How must that feel? Could you be brave the night before?' he asked himself. As he imagined the frights and terrors that must abound his mind decided to give him the added intimidation of a torturer entering unannounced to soften him up with some agonies before the blessed release of the noose was craved.

Fenton shook his head and tried to clear his mind of these nonsensical fantasies. He turned over in the hay and bunched up his blanket and clutched it to his face in a childish act of comfort. He focussed his thoughts toward pleasure, trying to remember last night and an altogether different experience. Then he found himself thinking about the others in the Old City and wondered what their adventures had brought them. Seven friends in difficult circumstances, relying on him to make it to Tetterton and bringing a ship and longboat around to their escape via the Sea Cave. His wits then turned to imagining, no seeing, seven dark forms encroaching on him out of the dark. These figures were blacker than pitch and their gaping mouths were darker than that, hollow screams with a rasping spectral haunt, their claws reaching out to taint him with death in a unison of orgiastic frenzy to kill. They were floating towards him now and then hovered above and around him before one dived down at his throat as Fenton attempted to bat the phantoms away with swinging, swiping arms at nothingness.

"Damn it Fenton, sort yourself out," he said aloud and sat up.

Then he knew that the disturbed silence and constant black of the barn was not going to cease until the sun brought the comfort of light. He only had to get through this night and he would be at Tetterton by midday. Then he could check on 'The Ardent Panda' before purchasing the new vessel he needed for his mission. He thought about dispelling some of his fear of the dark by lighting the lantern in his backpack. Yes, that would provide some solace. As he fumbled around in the pack he found the lantern and his pouch of kindling and fire lighting equipment but he could not untie the knot that held the pouch shut. The thin dark leather straps were tightly bound in a double sailor's knot. Fenton pawed at it and attempted to pull the right strand or pick the right piece loose but try as he might he could not undo the pouch and he whimpered and swore and prayed until he threw it away in disgust, hearing it thump softly into the dirt of the barn floor. He was a captain and should be able to untie knots in the dark. This was pathetic; he threw himself back down in the hay and searched for his blanket again.

"Sort yourself out Fenners!" he shouted, punching at the dry straw stack.

He focussed firmly on the pains in his thighs, calves and feet from the day long trudge across the plateau. Dull, weighty aches and cutting pangs of pain combined throughout the length of his legs. His eyes hurt too with tiredness, feeling dry and heavy even when closed. His thoughts turned to other ways of inducing sleep and he landed upon alcohol as potentially the best option. His hipflask that he had shared with Tumbletick was in a side pocket of his pack. He reached out and easily found the backpack, a couple of quick gropes in the dark and he found the pouch containing the flask. It was half empty and he unscrewed it, holding on securely to the cap as he slugged down the remaining half pint of whiskey from Noatak. Knowing that it was not the way to treat such a fine product he felt a pang of guilt and made a solemn promise that he would savour a bottle in the future and raise a toast to the distillers for what his was to bring him now. The heat of the liquor warmed his throat and brought a cutting heat to his gut. He got himself into a position where he could feel safer when alcoholic unconsciousness came to claim him. The faithful friend drew a haze around him and soon the intense tiredness and stupor swirled into a pit of exhaustion and forgetfulness.

He slept but it was unrewarding and filled with vibrant and disturbing dreams. Climbing steep stairs towards a too small door with a crazed ape, slathering and screeching behind him. Small pebbles alive and playing childish games together, fine and friendly. Then medium sized boulders mothered them away whilst sniping at each other with catty comments. Then vast rocks crushing each other, shouting, angry with warlike claustrophobia. Switch to unborn children, kidnapped from the womb and dismembered. 'Horror, horror, horror' cried the loyal subject at finding his liege and master murdered in his bed. The unexpected step on the stair as you awake in a previously empty house at midnight. The dreams went on, disjointed, his own nightmares, things that made him fear.

Fenton was still a warrior and when the barn doors opened just before dawn he had jumped up, fully alert but unaware. Sword drawn to fight the demons of his mind, the figure standing with a pitchfork in the murk made an easy target. Fenton was crazed and staring, bleary eyed, screaming he shoved the blade into the guts of the fearful farmer as the pitchfork moved far too slowly in an attempt to defend against the manic vagrant in his barn. The bucolic yeoman gasped his last and slipped backwards off the blade in a tense arc to the ground. As the man's back and head hit the dust at the same time, Fenton was stabbing at his chest with a separately drawn dagger, hacking away at the threat which had presented itself. The unwanted knock at the door.

All of a sudden the heavily side-burned face of the farmer became clear and a moment of clarity struck Fenton. He looked up and around at the vacant landscape, sheathed his weapons and quickly dragged the bloodied body into the barn. Less than a minute of frantic haymaking with the pitchfork had covered the remains in a shallow heap. Grabbing his backpack, blanket and fire lighting pouch, now found, Fenton sprinted out of the barn and back towards the track leading to Tetterton.

Chapter Eight

Campbell returned from his second scouting mission to the castle. He had departed after a meagre breakfast but that was to be expected. Running back, weapons drawn in case of any dangers presenting themselves, he made his way back to the garden and ground floor kitchen where the companions awaited him.

"It's all locked up and devoid of any signs of life after the battle," he reported.

"Right," said Egremont. "Our turn to find out if we can get in. Let us adopt the strategy of just walking calmly up and knocking."

Packs were shouldered and preparations made for the short stroll to the environs of the castle. Egremont and Is-Is led the way through the broad streets of the wealthy quarter of the city. The large merchant houses loomed and drifted by as the party of eleven made their way towards the ancient fastness. The day was bright and clear and the carrion birds wafted in wide circles above the centre of the Old City. Obviously some of their previous days feasting was still available after the conflict. Their distant, high cawing sent a shudder to Tumbletick. Behind the wolfhound and hare came Lord Jackson walking beside Vixen, a strange pairing thought Tumbletick who would have preferred to walk with his friend. Then came Mr. Battfin and Campbell who were becoming inseparable. Tumbletick walked alone and Garraday and Nazar Grant strolled behind him. Beran and Seton Rax brought up the rear as a formidable guard.

The last houses before the open plaza surrounding the castle were truly magnificent affairs, five stories high, ornate and turreted, all the obligatory city block and all completely covered in graffiti. The view that took in the entire castle across the open flagstone area was inspiring. As each member of the party passed the last house they each faltered momentarily in their strides as they took in the sight of the grey edifice. Before only snippets of sights had been caught of the keep, rising above the heights of the curtain wall. Only one large gate sat in the defensive outer perimeter and it faced south, traditionally it was made of the same thick dark wood with black iron bands and deep wide studs. Tumbletick

161

found himself thinking if this was some kind of historical fashion or if there had only been one man designing doors and gates in Rampart and he was loath to bring any creativity or design to his portal construction. The defences of the wall were topped with regularly spaced battlements and the face of the granite blocks were regularly gashed with arrow slits. The keep itself was set slightly back from dead centre to the north of the complex. It rose about eighty feet into the air, grey and uniformly square. Again it was topped with battlements and there were also several poles upon which were shapes which looked like, and were, skewered bodies in various states of decomposition. As the group got closer to the heart of the Old City it became clear that the building like many others here was not in perfect repair. Battlements were actually chipped and not fully squared off; moss grew in large, diseased looking patches over the face of the fortifications. The gates had been repaired with planks and wooden shields, bolted or nailed on. The keep had tattered flags hanging down the face of the fastness and Tumbletick felt that the designs crudely painted upon them were reminiscent of the devices he had seen painted amongst the graffiti of the Old City. A simple to draw diamond shape with loops at each of the points. The rest of the castle's facades were also deeply scarred, pock marked and shattered in many places, dents, cracks and craters in the stone after centuries of attack and decades of neglect.

All eyes were casually scanning the warlike structure looking for signs of life, the odd helm of a sentry moving between the gaps in the battlements, an archer on top of the keep scanning the horizon. Nothing appeared and there was also no noise, except for the distant caws of the scrounging vultures.

They slowed a little in their approach, to adopt a more sedentary manner, with Egremont and Is-Is leading it was easy for them to control the pace. Egremont's eyes narrowed as he tried to focus in on any sign of life, any clue as to whether just going and knocking on the gate was the best plan. Clouds scudded across the early morning sun and darker shadows painted contrasts that shifted over the greys of the castle walls. It was colder too without the direct sun light; they all noticed it was colder. The clouds left, the light returned and a small glint twinkled in an arrow slit next to the castle's gate. Is-Is' ears suddenly twitched and jerked, a slight fizzing followed in the air and the giant hare threw himself to the ground, flat on his belly, his paws beside him as if he was about to start a push-up.

The angle of the crossbow bolt's flight meant that it missed the supine Is-Is and slammed solidly into the solar plexus of Lord Jackson. Vixen turned quickly to her left and made a grab to stop him as he stumbled backwards and into Mr. Battfin. Jackson slumped against the pirate and collapsed clumsily to the ground, his hands clutching the shaft and his eyes wide with horror and shock.

Is-Is was back on to his feet, a dynamic push had launched him directly upright and he was already in the process of shielding Egremont with his own body as the wolfhound was shouting the order to retreat.

Everyone but Tumbletick started racing back to the cover of distance and the merchant houses. Tumbletick, a lone deformed body, stood a couple of yards from the body of Lord Jackson, unable to find the purpose of mind to leave his friend and head for cover as well. He looked at Jackson, there was no thrashing, no frothing at the mouth, just the dead body of a man he considered a friend. Alone, Tumbletick ignored other crossbow bolts and arrows that started to skip off the flagstones around him. He walked slowly to the body of Jackson and crouched down beside it with a quizzical look on his hairy face as he enquired into the dead eyes of the master merchant.

"Lord Jackson..?"

With no response, Tumbletick pulled at the dead arms, releasing them from the wooden shaft of the bolt. He desperately tried to pull on the dead weight of his friend in an effort to drag him to safety too. The body would not move and Tumbletick strained and heaved to get even the slightest budge. Tears started to form in his eyes as he realised no-one was going to come and help, he looked over his shoulder and saw them scarpering away. He turned back to Jackson and put a hand to his dead friend's cheek as the tears fell freely and blotted the flagstones. He was aware of other projectiles nearby but did not find that he cared. His face fell into the chest of his companion and he deeply sobbed. It might have felt like forever but it was barely seconds before a hand was placed on his shoulder and he was turned round to find that he was looking up into the face of Vixen.

At first he couldn't hear her screams as he was too consumed and focused on his grief. He was oblivious to the sounds he knew must be emanating from her rapidly moving mouth. Slowly his concentration slotted on to her slight freckling and red hair bounding with the breeze and the urgent movements of her head. She was indicating that he should move away from Jackson's body by moving her head, Tumbletick found that curious. She ducked in a rough movement and Tumbletick saw a crossbow bolt fly close to her. Suddenly the sound of her voice cut through the grief and dullness that he felt.

"...get away from him now!" she was blaring at him and tugging as well but Tumbletick was still grabbing onto Lord Jackson's corpse.

"No, we must get him to safety," he replied in a steady and convinced tone.

"Moron, he's frigging dead. Get away now!" the Master Spy yelled with a vehemence that startled Tumbletick. She pulled extremely hard on the deformed man and he snapped away from the body. Tumbletick broke into a deep frown of confusion and resentment.

"He was my friend and I will not leave him," he stated firmly.

"He was an immoral, foul and fatal man, leave now," she punched Tumbletick in the arm to make her point and rouse him.

"You what?" was all he could splutter back.

"Not now, just come with me," as if to punctuate her point she ducked again as another bolt lacerated through the air near her shoulder.

Tumbletick attempted to blurt some sort of retort of resentment and rejection of her command but he found himself stumbling behind Vixen as she forcibly pulled him by the wrist. He turned his head to gain a last look at the laid out fallen form of his friend, gave a quick cry of remembrance, then turned back and focused on running with Vixen, away from the projectiles and towards safety.

Within seconds Vixen and Tumbletick had rounded the corner of a vast merchant manor and the red headed purveyor of intrigues dragged Tumbletick into a skidding halt against a decaying wall with a slam. She held him there with the palm of her hand shoved firmly against his chest.

"Listen very closely you scrote," she grimaced through gritted teeth. "You were not meant to die wasting your life in mourning for a scab like Jackson of En'Tuk."

"What are you talking about," Tumbletick snapped back and he swiped hard at Vixen's wrist with the base of his hand, knocking it away.

"You don't get to be the richest man in the world without doing several terrible things," she smiled. She did not look at Tumbletick directly in the eye; she just let the inference hang as she briefly rubbed her recently walloped wrist. She walked away, back towards the alleyways. "We need to get to the others. They are back at the place we explored before. Most probably."

"Don't leave it like that Vixen! Tell me what you know," he shouted after her.

She turned sharply back and caught his eye with a nasty slant.

"Oh that would take far too long little man. His dossier is one of the thickest back at the Academy of Central Intelligence."

"Then I will consider it all slander and libel if it was compiled by you."

"Oh really. Well let me tell you a few facts about him. Consider them libellous if you want. Hmm, where shall I start? When he gave the order to starve a village to death by burning their crops then besieging them with mercenaries so that he could easily gain their land which he believed may be valuable in a future negotiation over access rights to a hardwood forest. Believed maybe valuable in a future negotiation. Do you get it Tumbletick? He'd trade lives of innocents to make a speculation on a gambled profit. Or would you prefer a more involved approach to a crime? Like when he directed his retained 'enforcer of contracts' to interrogate a competitor with pliers and a wicked wit as to the location of a stolen cache of silk. Or how he'd increase peasant taxes on his estates above and beyond the rate of inflation? Yes he was well known for donations to the poor but never out of charity. Always for a personal gain. Or how about his delight in breaking the confidence of those in his employ? I mean what more do you want than that? You don't get to be the richest man in the world without doing several terrible things."

"Yeah you've said that before."

"Do not mourn for him. Do not mourn for him. Do not mourn for him," she stood hands on hips lecturing him.

"You know what Vixen? He didn't treat me like that. He was always pleasant, attentive, interested and caring. He taught me things that I will never forget and I will mourn for him. Now unless you want to tell me some more of your dossier facts, or maybe what we would find if we read the dossier on you, let's get back to the others and figure out what we are going to do next."

Vixen made a little sneer then spun round and strode off with vehemence and purpose towards the merchant's house they had only recently left.

Chorus Eight

Fenton considered himself a fit and capable athlete but sprinting as fast as he could down the track to Tetterton he could only manage four minutes pushing hard in the twilight of dawn before he had to stop and pant and fall to his knees in remorse and desperation for air and for forgiveness.

Fenton had killed before, he had definitely killed. Easy executions like Whispering Bob, brutal butchery in close combat boarding a boat, duels at dawn with husbands of disgraced wives but it had always been with a reason, for a reason and within reason. What he had just done was a reaction against an innocent to the fears of the night before. Like a scream, roaring out in instinct at a sudden face appearing at a window in the dark.

While his need for air was quickly being fulfilled Fenton felt sure the forgiveness factor might never come but he would keep the sin internal, no-one would find out, no-one could find out. Within hours he would be aboard a newly purchased boat in Tetterton. If 'The Ardent Panda' was still docked he could have a night of drinks and camaraderie with his pirates before he had to set off for the planned rendezvous with his companions. No, he'd be alright, less than half a day to Tetterton, no-one would miss the farmer by then and he could slip into the mass of merchants and stevedores and the life of the port.

He stood up from his knees, now fully recovered and started to stride off down the track. He had left nothing behind that could be tracked to him so he adopted a casual air and whistled as he walked. For a while it worked but the face of the farmer returned, the look of shock, the gasp, the pain, the death, the resentment, the innocence. 'But I don't know if he was truly innocent,' Fenton tried to convince himself. 'Maybe he was an evil man and I was sent there to deliver him to Hell with vengeance for all his wrongs.' Fenton shook his head in his idiocy of the internal monologue. He picked up the pace, tucked his chin into his chest with the now noticed chill of the early dawn and struck out along the path. With no noise around him his boots sounded loud crunching on the rough path, his whistle returned and he decided that time and a lot of whiskey in his future would remove the guilt of the murder from his mind. After a couple of hours trudging Fenton could see the fortifications appear on the horizon that marked the cliff that loomed above the port. Soon he would be busy and purposeful again.

Chapter Nine

Tumbletick followed Vixen back to the familiar kitchen of the merchant's house where they had first met Garraday and company. A deep melancholy pervaded the room; death had now come to both groups. Individuals slumped in corners or leaned on dusty worktops, dejected by the foolishness of walking openly up to a castle that had been the scene of a full frontal attack the day before.

"Are we going to retrieve Jackson's body then?" asked Tumbletick immediately with an iron strength in his voice that surprised a few.

"You know, I think we should," agreed Campbell. "There is the very tangible fact and benefit that he is still carrying a hell of a lot of money."

Campbell gave a look which spoke of pragmatism but volumes as to perhaps his true concerns. Tumbletick and Mr. Battfin, both of whom had honour as a very strong personal value looked the most disgusted at what Campbell had said. Garraday nodded sagely in agreement the others just looked dejected.

"We will retrieve the Lord Jackson's remains because it the right thing to do," said Egremont with a calm and steady voice. "Campbell, should you wish to ransack and rifle those remains then so be it. I too am very sad to lose one of our companions and friends to such a random method but we must do the right thing and lay him to rest in this garden and not leave him for the carrion crows."

"I will go to claim his body," offered Seton Rax, his muscles flexing communicating his ability for such a mission. "It is not honourable to leave him to the vermin that would pick his bones or the inquisitive hands of those in the castle who killed him. But we must move swiftly. Is-Is will you aid me in this quest?"

Is-Is looked up from where he had been staring at the floor and nodded decisively. Then he moved off with a couple of bounds and was out of the door and off to the garden and the streets. Seton Rax raised his eyebrows and sprinted off in pursuit. By the time the barbarian had made it to the street he could just see the hare about forty yards ahead absolutely flying along. Seton Rax put his head down and with

169

arms pumping and long legs straining he tried to match Is-Is for pace. When Seton Rax made it to the open area in front of the castle, Is-Is was already scooping up the body of Jackson from the floor, arrows and bolts were piecing the air again but more significantly the gates were creaking open.

"Is-Is, quick, get away," Seton Rax yelled as a group of five figures came recklessly running from the gate. They were dishevelled and mismatched in various pieces of armour and they did not run as a unit but as individuals at different speeds. Is-Is turned his head and took in the new threat and went to put Jackson's body down but Seton Rax, closer now, shouted again.

"No Is-Is these are mine, get him back to safety!"

Then his battle axe was pulled from the leather device that held it to his back and Seton Rax was running by the giant hare and towards the group sallying forth from the castle.

'Uneducated warriors,' thought Seton Rax to himself as they dispersed into a wide line, some closer some further away depending on their pace. Their weaponry was as diverse as their armour. One had a sword and small buckler shield, another a dagger and an axe. The third was wielding a mace hanging by a long chain and number four had a poleaxe and the last man swished the air with two scimitars. They were all human, slightly underfed, grotty looking with bad teeth showing through their smiles of contempt for the one man confronting them.

'Easy,' thought Seton Rax as he suddenly swerved to his left and went for the thug with the poleaxe first. The enemy presented the long weapon in a defensive pose, pointing the blade directly towards the sprinting Seton Rax. Seton Rax responded by diving into a forward roll on the flagstones, ducking under the blade of his adversary and coming to a rising stand leading with his own battleaxe right into the space between chin and throat. The ragged gash formed by the wide blade of the axe was enough to ensure death and the barbarian peeled away to the right leaving his foe standing with a lolling head and a stupefied look before he crumpled heavily into a clumsy, dead heap.

Next in the melee was the brigand with sword and small shield who was standing close to the wretch with the single headed axe and dagger. No time for any subtleties or play, kills would have to made quickly and brutally. The enemy with the sword lunged forward, left knee to the ground, leading with his right leg, Seton Rax swung his battleaxe into the sword arm, severing it below the elbow. Then with the butt of the axe's hilt in the right position Seton Rax jabbed it with great force into his opponent's eye as his amputated arm hit the floor still holding the sword. It was a fluid move well practiced but Seton Rax added to it by then spinning round to his left and embedded the battleaxe blade into the belly of the other warrior, ripping deeply into his guts across the entire breadth of his stomach.

The two remaining challengers stood dumbfounded. Here was a semi naked barbarian who had just dispatched three of their companions in nearly as many seconds. They stood still, looked at each other and turned and fled straight back to the castle. Seton Rax thought for a moment about following up for the final kill but the correct decision was to follow Is-Is and return to their makeshift headquarters.

Even though Seton Rax had not taken long in his work he still did not have time to catch up with Is-Is despite his burden. By the time the barbarian had made it to the merchant's house the body of Lord Jackson of En'Tuk was laid in the garden next to the recently dug graves of Vigor and Lambert. The atmosphere in the kitchen was much the same as when Vixen and Tumbletick had returned earlier. Campbell the Weasel looked up when Seton Rax entered and with an apologetic look on his face began to speak.

"If no-one is going to help me then I suggest that you leave me to it and do not interfere. Jackson does have money secreted about his person and we do not know when we may need such a resource in order to complete our quest. Do not worry though. I'll leave him as I find him."

With that Campbell ambled into the garden with a resignation, perhaps more for the others sensibilities than his own concerns of desecration. Campbell was notorious and well versed in all elements of robbery and thieving, he had plundered tombs and pilfered corpses before in order to turn a profit.

"Well while Campbell busies himself we must make a decision about what we are to do next," said Egremont. "We know we must make the rendezvous with Fenton by the cave. Therefore we must gain entry to the castle and the catacombs beneath. But how do we get into the castle?"

"No point trying a casual full frontal again," responded Vixen.

"It was an agreed plan and considered sound," snapped Tumbletick.

"Thank you my friend," said Egremont solemnly knowing the pain he felt.

"So what are we going to do then?" asked Mr. Battfin.

"Why do you need to go through the catacombs to the cave anyway? Why didn't you just get on the boat like any normal people in a harbour?" asked Seton Rax.

"There are certain prying eyes about and we want the owners of those eyes to believe that we have disappeared, thought dead. That is why we came into the Old City and that is why the passages beneath the castle are pretty perfect for moving around unseen," said Egremont. "So let us try and understand the situation again."

"Umm, large battle earlier leaves inhabitants of castle feeling twitchy!" said Vixen with a flouncing wit.

"Cuttingly obtuse but well observed my dear," retorted the suave wolfhound.

"We do not have the men or the equipment to assault or siege the castle," said Beran.

"Exactly why we thought just walking up and knocking would work," said Tumbletick looking at Vixen as he did so.

"So what do we know at the moment?" asked Egremont.

"That a battle took place between a large group of people dressed like multicoloured monks and the inhabitants of the castle," said Mr. Battfin.

"True. And we thought that this was likely to be a battle over territory and power and that the Harlequins came from the collections of buildings to the south," continued Egremont.

"Then perhaps," offered Garraday. "An old adage may well be employed, that 'my enemy's enemy is my friend'."

"Why would we expect a better welcome from them?" asked Mr. Battfin.

"For exactly the same reason, we are the enemies of the crew in the castle," Garraday replied.

"We could carry a flag that shows their design and then burn it in front of the abbey, or monastery or what ever it is," said Tumbletick.

"Design?" asked Egremont immediately, his bushy eyebrows rising sharply.

"They have a design that they use to mark their territory. A gang symbol or something. It is a diamond with loops at each point. I've seen it on their castle flags and drawn in the graffiti around the city," said Tumbletick and with that he marked out the pattern in some dust on a worktop.

"I saw the same design on the armour of the wretches I just beat in battle!" exclaimed Seton Rax excitedly looking at the tracings of Tumbletick's finger.

"It could well work as a sign of a non negative intention," mused Egremont. "Burning a flag is proof positive of a pretty poignant position."

"So we are in agreement. We should march from one local stronghold after a battle to go to another one?" asked Garraday. "I'm not so sure that our payment is sufficient enough to ensure such a trip. I believe the agreement was based on gaining entry to the castle and the catacombs. This does seem a tortuous route to reach that point."

"Ah, Garraday, but our honour is at stake. We have received payment and we still have had very little chance to quest for treasure," pointed out Beran.

"I'm up for heading off with our new friends, agreement or no agreement. Some good hunting seems to be drawn to them," enthused Seton Rax, still flushed with post battle adrenalin.

"Why wouldn't we expect a similar reception from the monks?" enquired Vixen.

"Because when we get within range of arrows and crossbow bolts we will raise a flag with the design upon it and burn it," said Egremont.

"We'd better find something to use as a flag," said Tumbletick.

"There's the curtain in the archway on the floor above," responded Mr. Battfin.

"Well recalled Mr. Battfin," praised Egremont. "Could you get it for us please?"

Mr. Battfin sprinted up the stairs from the kitchen and soon returned with the curtain. He spread it out on a work surface, drew his sword and cut the cloth to a more manageable size. The curtain now in more flag like proportions was a faded purple, almost lilac and while a white or a cream would have made a better base colour it was light enough that a thickly painted design would be visible at a distance.

"A bit of burnt wood should provide enough ashes. Let us light a fire, have some lunch and then mix the ashes with a bit of lantern oil to make a paint," said Egremont just as Campbell came back into the kitchen looking unrepentant.

Wood was soon found, either from dead bits in the garden or from other rooms of the house where furniture was broken and donated. The large kitchen hearth was soon blazing and spirits rose as always happened when there is a good size fire on the go.

Once they had eaten some of their supplies Mr. Battfin scooped away some ashes and taking some of the oil that Nazar Grant offered to him he mixed it all together on a work surface. It swirled together into a patch of sticky mess which soon turned to a jet black paste as the carbon from the burnt wood was held in suspension in the oil.

"Tumbletick, can you draw that design for me again please?" asked Mr. Battfin. Tumbletick ambled over, still wracked with grief, he dipped a finger into the paste and in one graceful move marked out the diamond shape with a loop at each point without his finger leaving the design once. He turned and walked away, wiping his wet finger on part of the discarded scrap of curtain. Standing in front of the fire looking into the flames he hung his head and threw the cloth into the blaze.

Mr. Battfin then took a broken stick which he had used to mix up the paint and cut the end so it was a regular shape. He then remade the design on the curtain using the stick like a large pen. Again and again he went over the shape making it thicker and thicker, more and more visible on the lilac background.

"Well before we leave we need to bury Lord Jackson of En'Tuk. A shallow grave and some deep words from friends will have to suffice for now. Eventually his family may want to retrieve his corpse should any of us live through this to tell them where he is," said Egremont.

"What did you use to scrape the earth away for Vigor and Lambert?" Campbell asked Seton Rax casually. Before they had left for the castle that morning Seton Rax, Beran, Nazar Grant and Garraday had quickly said their own goodbyes to their friends.

"Oh I found a spade in a corner of the garden. Thought for a minute that I was going to have to use my axe. The earth was quite soft but I was only going down about a foot. Lay the body in and the spare earth can be piled on top," Seton Rax replied.

"Okay," said Campbell. "Did you put the spade back?"

"Yeah. It's in the far corner on the wall with the broken window where the lovely ivy has been growing wildly."

"Right, well I'll go and get that done then," volunteered Campbell and he went back into the garden looking for the patch of 'lovely ivy' and thinking it curious that a barbarian should have such a horticultural viewpoint. He turned back, poked his head around the door and said. "I'll give you all a shout when it's done."

"Do you want to go and help?" asked Egremont to Tumbletick.

"No. I said my goodbyes when everyone else was running away."

"It was a dangerous situation Tumbletick and there was no point in others dying the same way. Thankfully Vixen noticed you had not come with us and she returned, risking herself, to get you."

"Yes and I shall never forget what she said to me Eggers," Tumbletick replied. "Listen, I wonder if we might be able to have a private word together? Upstairs where the others can not hear us. Just while Campbell is digging the grave."

"Of course Tumbletick. Is it about what Vixen said to you?"

"No, something else."

Tumbletick and Egremont climbed the spiral staircase and set themselves at the large table in the room above. They sat down and could look out of the large windows seeing Campbell going to work with the spade that was exactly where Seton Rax had left it.

"What's on your mind my friend?" asked Egremont.

"Well, we have seen a lot of death just recently and it got me to thinking that one day I may not be around, or worse you and Is-Is might find a trip with the grim reaper sooner than any of us want."

"Yes, the chances of meeting that fine fellow are always with us but I agree a meeting would be more likely in the current situation."

"The thing is Egremont, I want to know who and what I am. Sorry to put it on you now but I have gone too long never ever badgering you for knowledge and well, I think that I should know."

Egremont gave a deep sigh and with his paws firmly placed on his knees he looked down between his feet and was silent for a while.

"Ah. Are you sure you want to know? You are who you are and no amount of history or explanation is going to change the fact that you are good and honest and decent and true. You are my friend and my companion and Is-Is and I will always love and protect you."

"I do not want to be in a shallow grave and not know Egremont."

"It might upset you more than ignorance."

"It might. But I promise it will not change the way I feel about you and Is-Is. Nothing could change that. But we are in extreme circumstances and I wish to know why I am being swept along."

"I will ask you one more time. For this is a day I have been expecting and I will reveal all to you, full and true and fearsome if you truly do desire it. Do you really want to know about your heritage Tumbletick?"

"I truly do desire it Egremont."

"Then I shall tell you."

Egremont stood up and walked to the window. He looked down on Campbell as he continued the grave digging chore. He could see that the thief was swearing and sweating, perhaps his slight frame found the earth a little harder than the barbarian had found. Egremont placed his paws behind his back and began.

"Tumbletick, what I told you about you being Bartle Rourke was essentially true. Sir Bartle Rourke was indeed the greatest warrior of his age. He was a nobleman of immense worth and prestige and he was my closest friend. We were both officers in the army of Umiat together and fought in the Ahrioch Wars with distinction. That is how we met Is-Is as well. He was once just a common foot soldier but his ability saw him rise through the ranks to the highest of any non commissioned officer. He became the standard bearer for our regiment and he never ever lost it."

"I think I remember you telling me before how you and Is-Is met, Egremont. One night beside a fire by my hut. I want to know where I came from."

"Trust me Tumbletick I will get there," the wolfhound paused. This was difficult for him. "Sir Bartle Rourke as I said was a great man, Tumbletick. You must remember that. He was loyal, funny, a wit, well educated, a perfect knight on the battlefield and it was he who taught me in arcane laws and wisdom. It was he who made me Master Elect of the Nine in the knowledge that one day I would lead a quest that would contain nine pure and true souls. He had sight of the future and knew of things that none of us will ever know. He was my leader and my friend but he had flaws too. We all have flaws Tumbletick. Well here we go then. Before the second Ahrioch War, Sir Bartle was staying at my castle. We had some of the regiment staying and I threw a vast feast.

We caroused for about three days and Bartle got very, very drunk and it brought out more of his dark side."

Egremont stopped again, he unclasped his paws from behind his back and wiped a forming tear from his eye. Then he turned and came back to Tumbletick and sat in front of him again and he took the little, deformed man by the hand.

"Bartle Rourke took a fancy to one of my staff. A serving girl from a local village. He had been flirting with her for a while and she had always been polite but as he grew drunker his ability to flatter left him and he became cruder. I laughed with him at first, thought the profanities funny, droll, arousing perhaps. I did not know what he was planning to do. On the third night while most of us had passed out, he went on a drunken walk about the castle looking for the girl. He found her room in the serving quarters and he took her, beat her savagely and raped her. Other servants went to her aid when they heard her screams apparently. But would not interfere when they saw who it was who was attacking her. I did not hear about it Tumbletick, the servants did not come and rouse me from my stupor. It was the girl herself who told me what had happened months later. She was with child and said she wanted to be able to stay in my employ. She told me who the father was. At first I did not believe her and accused her of being a liar and a whore but my housekeeper, a trusted employee, told me what the truth was. The girl would not visit with a woman who could give her certain roots to end the pregnancy and thank Fate that she did not. I wished her to visit with that woman and I have felt guilt and anger at myself every day since I suggested it. All to protect Bartle. The girl however wanted nothing from him. His sin was great at attacking her. She just wanted to be able to stay safe at the castle, have the child and bring it up in an environment where it could be nurtured and loved, educated and protected. I swore to her that I would do that Tumbletick. I swore."

Egremont had lost all of his usual flamboyance, tears fell to the floor as he struggled to maintain a steady voice.

"Where is the girl now?" Tumbletick asked.

"She is buried in the chapel at my castle. She died during the birth my little friend. It did not go well for her, it was a very difficult labour and the complications affected the child too but I kept my promise. I kept my promise. Despite the fact that the baby was not the prettiest thing in the world," Egremont laughed through his tears and placed his paw on the side of Tumbletick's misshapen face, his words were thick with emotion now. "Is-Is helped me keep the promise too. You do remember playing with him in the tower don't you? And learning to read. Oh, Is-Is would read to you for hours reciting plays and romantic quests in far off lands. And I protected you. Kept you secret and safe. Only Is-Is, I and the housekeeper knew of who you really were. All the staff were told that both mother and baby died. They were replaced and the three of us brought you up until it was time for you to become the guardian of your father's bones and the Umiat Stone."

"Thank you Egremont. I can see it was hard for you to tell me. But I feel stronger for knowing. I love you more now for knowing what you did."

"I don't know how to take it myself though, Tumbletick. I have obviously always known what Bartle did but he was a good man. He was a great man. He just did a terrible, terrible thing. But look what we got from it. We got you. Oh my, everything sounds so trite now when it is was all so momentous then," Egremont broke down in to huge sobs, he shook with regrets and realisation and love for his friends, both Sir Bartle Rourke and Tumbletick.

Then Is-Is was there, huge, steadfast and silent. He patted the wolfhound on the back and Egremont jumped up, turned and hugged the hare, crying into his chest. Tumbletick, just sat and thought for a while whilst Egremont sobbed. He waited for the tears to subside.

"What was my mother's name?"

"Faith."

"Well, time to get yourself back together Egremont. I suspect that you will be expected to say a few words at the funeral. Let's not have tears before an occasion such as that," said Tumbletick. "Seriously though, thanks. It doesn't change anything between us."

The trio walked downstairs and found the rest of the group standing talking with a heavily perspiring Campbell. A few looks were exchanged but no-one enquired as to what had been said upstairs, so they all walked into the garden and gathered around the trench in which lay the body of Jackson. Tumbletick looked solemnly on as Campbell picked up his spade once more and began shovelling. He thought to himself how before he would not have been able to watch but something had happened which somehow made him feel stronger and more complete. The sight of Jackson being buried was completed in silence as gravel and mud fell upon his body and face. When he was completely covered all ears and eyes turned to Egremont who cleared his throat.

"Lord Jackson of En'Tuk was a friend and companion who was a giant in the commercial world of Umiat. As a giant his reach spanned the known world with influence and power. He touched many lives and businesses with his dealings. As a result his wealth was second to none and he became one of the First Men of Umiat. Valued at court and beloved by the mob, who he often fed with donations of bread and entertained by paying for shows around the country all out of his own personal pocket," Vixen coughed loudly and Egremont's eulogy paused for a while.

"Recently," he continued. "He has become even more of a friend, not just someone whose finance has aided our expedition. We have found that his wit has lifted our spirits. Also his guiding of Tumbletick has helped bring that fine furry gentleman out of his shell and..."

"Oh please," spat Vixen. "Can we cease with the sickliness? Let me tell you about Lord Jackson of En'Tuk." She seemed irate and intensely bitter.

"Don't you dare Vixen!" Tumbletick ordered. "Sully his name and I will not consider you part of this quest."

"Sully his name little man? Won't consider me part of the quest? What kind of a sanction do you think that is to me? Your original companions all know the sort of things he has done, perhaps Garraday, Nazar Grant, Beran and Seton Rax should know them too."

"As I said Vixen, do not dare," Tumbletick retorted and walked off towards the exit and the streets of the Old City. Mr. Battfin was first to respond and strode off beside Tumbletick.

"Okay Vixen, end of the funeral speech," said Egremont and he followed the pirate first mate and his deformed ward. Is-Is was soon off and Campbell joined him leaving Vixen standing with the quartet who stood in anxious anticipation in hearing of Jackson's past. They all looked towards her for a little while with enquiring faces, seeing if she was going to let them know.

"Oh...he was just a very, very bad man at times," she gasped dismissively and headed off too, shouldering her pack roughly.

"Was that worth interrupting what I thought was a very pleasant graveside speech?" asked Beran to the remaining men. "I don't think it was really."

The foursome looked briefly again at the other two graves and also shouldered their equipment and left the merchant's house for the last time. They caught up with Vixen who was walking alone. Ahead of them five figures were sauntering south, potentially towards more death and disappointment at the monastery where the harlequin attired monks were believed to be based.

Chorus Nine

enton decided to pay the toll to take the basket down the escarpment into the port of Tetterton. Clambering into the wide wicker basket cradle he felt quite ecstatic as the plateau disappeared and the rock face moved slowly above him as he descended. As the occupants in the rising basket drew near, Fenton found himself deliberately turning his face away from them and then looking down as they drew level so if they had of glanced his way all they would have ever seen of the lone occupant was the back of his head. 'Guilt still very much present,' he thought to himself.

As the ground approached the basket slowed and came to a stop with only the slightest of bumps. Fenton hopped out, hands on the side, legs swung over together in a graceful move, then he quickly made it through the gate of the ground station and into the teaming mass of people that harangued the streets.

He thought about taking a trip to 'The Grobbling Smith' and checking on his favourite receptionist and was kind of pleased with himself that some of his more innate habits had not left him. The thought though was dismissed and his mission took priority, he headed straight to the docks.

Fenton knew his way around docks and he easily fitted in with the tough and rugged characters that plied their trades there. The notes that Jackson had given him could easily have been traded in at one of his offices for coins by anyone but as they were in several denominations he would be able to negotiate a trade for a boat easily enough.

He made his way to a wharf that had plenty of boats in and started striking up conversations with the local types as to people who might be looking to sell a decent sized schooner with a launch. The schooner he could handle by himself and the launch would need to be the right size to row into the Sea Cave at low tide.

After a few hours of chatting and questioning large bearded fellows, a couple of ladies with a lot of make-up and inquisitive minds, fishermen repairing nets and stevedores with evil looking hooks pulling crates off of docked boats, he found what he was looking for. Ironically it was a merchant down on his luck, who was prepared to sell his small coastal vessel, with all its contents at a very reasonable price. The cash the merchant raised would be used to buy some weapons and armour, have a good time and then try to hook up with some other fortune hunters and enter into the Old City. A price was agreed and Fenton handed him the notes along with his best wishes for the Old City.

Fenton spent the rest of the day buying supplies of food and materials for the trip and what he imagined would be of use for the journey into Kenai. He thought that the rest of the group might appreciate some good food and new clothes after five days of adventuring. He also ensured his own particular needs were well met and he purchased a couple of bottles of whiskey.

He then made a brief visit to 'The Ardent Panda' and told the crew to wait around for a couple of days further rest and relaxation before returning to patrol the Sea of Kaltag.

With the supplies purchased and stowed he found himself aboard his new boat sailing it away from the dock on the lightest breeze within the confines of the harbour. The boat was named 'The Brazen Manticore' and soon she would be on the open sea. Then Fenton would swing her to the south and when he had cleared the headlands to the western end of the island he would hit the trade winds and race east. He felt confident that he could reach the rendezvous with time to spare, drop anchor and have a decent length smoke and a couple of beers from the seven crates he had purchased.

Chapter Ten

Y'Bor Kaz lounged in a large wooden chair that had once belonged to the abbot. He was surrounded by a group of laughing men in multicoloured robes and habits. Y'Bor was smiling and often he would let out a raucous laugh at a joke or an antic of one of his men but at the current time he was not talking or joining in whole heartedly with the frivolity. Despite the outward appearance, internally he was seething. The attack on the brigands at the castle had not gone well and his 'Monks of Delight' had been thrown back by volleys of missiles. They had managed to hack at the gates but had not broken in this time. He had lost twelve men before he ordered the retreat. A quick hit and run was probably never going to work. He would have to build some larger engines of war. At least a battering ram, hung under a canopy next time, something where his men could shelter from the arrows and bolts.

'The Monks of Delight' were the war band that controlled the whole of the southern sector of the Old City. Y'Bor Kaz was their charismatic leader. He had red hair which he waxed with animal fat and moulded into three large points, one on either side of his head and one on the top. He was slightly freckled but hugely muscled and he had won his way to leadership with humour and prowess in battle. Y'Bor Kaz was kind and fair when he needed to be but he was also wonderfully addicted unto wrath. He fought with two large warhammers. Lesser men would have to heave these mallets about with both hands, Y'Bor could swirl the two solid lumps of metal on the end of four foot shafts smashing and crushing his way through his enemies with skilful violence. His enormous strength and energy meant a frantic flailing of fear for his foes. The Monks of Delight were his crew and their philosophy was simple; to laugh at fear, smile at pettiness, chortle at bigotry and generally have a good time as prisoners of the Old City. Yet domination, revenge and turf battles was a serious business, the Monks of Delight had just decided to dress as harlequins, base themselves in an abbey and have a jolly good time doing it. The sowing and growing of a mild narcotic in the grounds of the walled monastery was also a major part of their time, a major industry and a major reason for their constant laughter. Protecting the crop was a constant concern but Y'Bor Kaz had successfully done so for three years. Now he was very much thinking about expanding his influence to the centre of the Old City and maybe one day he could then hold sway over the northern slums as well. Total control would bring about more wealth but Y'Bor had wealth a plenty, more would have no value. Power and influence was key. Those were the main things worth fighting for now. Those and his other hobby of hosting gladiatorial combats. For that hobby, which really caused him to laugh naturally, he had to have good stocks of captured men and monsters. The Coliseum nearby was always well defended by his mirthful men and the prisoners he caught were managed like the monsters they managed to trap, in cells with the promise of release or recruitment after ten victories. Y'Bor Kaz dreamt of a day where he would be overlord of the entire city and then he would be able to manage his resources more effectively and actually allow audiences in for the gladiatorial games rather than just the private performances for his own men. His life was full of fun and frolics and so he would persist in both aims.

Y'Bor's thoughts turned back to how he had first entered the Old City, five years ago as a fortune hunter. His trusty warhammers at his side as well as his four comrades. He was more drably attired then, in leather armour and with his hair cropped short. He remembered how the first few days had gone well with them, the odd fight, a bit of treasure and then they had decided to head south towards a group of extremely large buildings.

He had stared in awe at the amphitheatre which rose high above the surrounding rooftops. He and his companions had got to within a few feet of its columned walls and high alcoves, complete with decapitated statues, when they had been attacked by an ambush of laughing fiends. Y'Bor Kaz fought with prowess and skill, shouting for his companions to flee as he held off the horde for a while. Death was certain to take him as he had crushed the skulls and spines of several of the enemy in the bravado of a last stand. He smiled to himself as he knew his friends had managed to break away and off into the nearby tangled streets. Y'Bor Kaz though had been surrounded by grinning multi coloured wretches with various weapons trying to keep him cornered and at bay. Y'Bor Kaz strangely found that he thought back to his youth as he believed he was about to die. The young affable lad called Kaz from the river town of Bor. His father had been mayor of the fishing community and that had brought wealth and privilege but little adventure. So Kaz had decided to apprentice as a blacksmith, 'in order to build up muscle and trade', he remembered confronting his father with the indisputable logic. Politics was not for him. As he grew in strength and skill he had joined the militia to teach him the ways of war and now he was standing in the Old City of Rampart, several dead around his feet as his enemies brought in a large net and slung it in a wide, canopied arc and captured him.

The year he had spent as a gladiator in the amphitheatre had become a very enjoyable time for Y'Bor Kaz and he looked back upon it with an intense fondness. At first the fear of a solitary cell and no knowledge of what was to happen to him had brought on fears that led to thoughts of suicide. He knew not if he had been dumped into the darkness to be forgotten and left to starve or if he was to be taken out at dawn and executed for his killing of several of his captor's companions. However after a while a guard had brought food and drink and conversation. Fat with a hairy, naked torso, a leather apron and a lantern, the bald man placed some food on the dirt floor with a flagon of weak beer.

"Seems like you impressed with your soldiering boy!" The guard had said. "You's going to be on the bill at the next games. Pretty red head like you could win the crowd over if you perform well." The laughter of the guard as he had left had been strange, not flirtatious or mocking, just genuine.

The next person to come and visit in the dark had come into the cell and unlocked the chain which had held him by the ankle to the wall. He was a small, wiry man, with a pointed nose and a grin that shone out from within the limited light from the flames of his spluttering torch.

"Now you can attack me immediately if you like," the little man said as the key went into the lock of Y'Bor Kaz's chain. "But that won't get you very far. What will get you a long way is to follow me to the armoury. We've kept your warhammers should you wish to use them, or you can choose from the classic gladiator kits that have been laid down in antiquity. However, you have been billed as a barbarian 'from the grim western hills' and as such can fight with whatever you like." The little man gestured to Y'Bor Kaz to follow him as he skipped and giggled along the subterranean corridors of the amphitheatre to a room full of weapons and pieces of armour.

"My name is Krell, by the way. I'm really the Animal and Monster Maintainer. But barbarians also come under my remit. So it is in my interest to take care of you should you prove to be any good out there in the arena."

Y'Bor Kaz said nothing as he picked up his warhammers. He choose no armour, other than his leather which he liked for its flexibility and he wore no helmet so he could maintain full vision.

Krell moved very lightly and sprightly, still with his skipping gait and took Y'Bor away from the armoury and along a corridor that was ten feet wide and ten feet tall. The square tunnel was lined with neatly cut blocks of granite and flaming torches. Y'Bor Kaz could feel that the tunnel was ascending slightly. Krell's giggling seemed to be intensifying as they came to a lowered portcullis across the space of the corridor. The little man took his flaming torch and placed it in an empty bracket.

"Well young man, here we go. A little way up the corridor from here you will enter into the arena. Now it's night at the moment so when you get out there it is going to be lit by torches set into the top of the arena walls. There will be a crowd of about a hundred, probably whacked out and revelling in the night's entertainment. Now you are going to be fighting another prisoner tonight. No idea what he is going to choose to be equipped with, all I know is he is a seasoned veteran, been in the ring a fair few times and is a nasty piece of work. But you'll figure that out by the look of him. Just get out there and fight to the death. Easy really. As soon as this portcullis goes up his portcullis is going to be rising as well, so it might be a good idea to run up to the arena and be certain to get your bearings," he gave a little wink and a big smile. A sudden clanking came and the portcullis lurched upwards in the rapidly flitting shadows of the torchlight. Y'Bor Kaz ducked under the metal gate as soon as he could and sprinted up the passage and out into the cool open air.

The arena was circular, covered in sand and lit, as promised by Krell, by torches set into the top of the enclosing wall. Y'Bor saw a decent amount of people sitting about in little groups, some paying attention to the imminent combat, others laughing and joking between themselves. Mostly, the huge amphitheatre was empty and the tiered stone seating looked haunting in the dark.

Y'Bor Kaz turned and focused on the figure running towards him, out of the black tunnel that was opposite the one he had entered into the arena from. He was wearing a silver metal helmet with wicked looking spikes over the smooth dome and a grid like mesh to look through. His naked torso was oiled up and glistened under the sparse flame light that reached him. Y'Bor thought to himself that the oil was probably there to stop any grappling rather than just to make the warrior look good. Otherwise his opponent was only dressed in black leather shorts, he was even barefoot. For weapons he had a toothed sword, evil looking and serrated, it would cut and rip as it slashed flesh. The warrior also had a small metal shield with a spike set in the centre which itself could be used as an offensive bayonet.

"Decided for speed then," said Y'Bor Kaz to himself. "This could be interesting."

That first battle in the amphitheatre of the Old City was one that went down in legend. The pace and ferocity of the two combatants attracted the eye eventually of every single member of the crowd. The audience began to leave their seats and swarm to the limits of the auditorium, at the very edge of the arena wall, to gain a closer view.

Sparks rained in the half-light as sword strokes hit the cleverly parried blows of warhammer heads. The enemy's shield became more and more cratered and dented as it blocked Y'Bor Kaz's mashing blows. Both the warriors could see the whites of their opponent's eyes, smell their sweat, and hear their increasingly strained breathing but it was Y'Bor Kaz who caught the sight of fear behind the metal mesh of the silver helmet. His strength and speed with two warhammers was amazing and had never been seen before. Few warriors could have experienced what it was like to have that much mass of metal flying around in lethal combat. Y'Bor Kaz's enemy found that out when he got cracked on the side of the head and he instantly fell unconscious to the sand of the arena floor.

It was the first time that the death blow was not called for by the crowd because the entire crowd believed the opponent was dead as he was dragged off by the attendants and Y'Bor Kaz stood in the centre of the ring. His warhammers aloft he took the applause and cheers of the crowd and found that he adored it. It turned out that the unconscious warrior was fighting his tenth fight and as a technicality, as he did survive, he was entitled to release within the brotherhood of the Monks of Delight.

The next nine combatants who faced Y'Bor Kaz were all despatched with slightly less ceremony. Some were timid wretches who fell quickly in pulpy heaps to loud boos from the crowd and disdain and contempt from Y'Bor. Others were more skilful warriors with tridents and nets who found their weapon's wooden shafts smashed and the red head too quick to ensnare. An ogre in pieces of mismatched battered plate armour and scraps of chain mail soon found its ankles crushed and on its knees howling with incomprehension as a warhammer silenced it for ever with a blow to the back of the head as Y'Bor Kaz flamboyantly played to his ever increasing fans. It was another light and agile fighter with two long knives that provided the most danger, actually getting a couple of deep cuts against Y'Bor, one viciously across the back of the neck, which looked life threatening at the time and another in the thigh. The fight again had the audience swarming to the perimeter wall and raising a large cheer as Y'Bor Kaz got a dramatic uppercut in which ended the fight as the metal block head of the warhammer shattered the chin and snapped the spine.

The ten fights were spaced out over about three months but Y'Bor chose to take a role working with Krell rather than join the Monks of Delight immediately. He enjoyed the smells, ways, people and atmosphere of the theatrical amphitheatre. Krell had indeed looked after Y'Bor Kaz with food and training and medical care so he wanted to return something as an assistant and gain something as he learned about monster management. Monsters were mostly used for executions but occasionally they featured in staged hunts or one on one combat in the arena. Sometimes the word hunt was not a technically correct one because the billing often called for fair fights and the monsters were often capable of hunting the men pitched against them. The creatures used for this type of activity were caught by special parties sent into the Old City to retrieve stocks from the regular monsters sent in by the outside authorities. They ranged from vicious baboons enhanced with steel tipped claws and a diet of unsuccessful gladiators right up to large scale creatures with unique attributes, one off horrors caught and imported from foreign lands.

Y'Bor Kaz spent nine good months working with Krell until he was convinced by the then leader of the Monks of Delight to come and live in the monastery. There Y'Bor found that the monk's admiration of him as a warrior led him to a position of influence, his skill as a blacksmith meant he was invaluable to the community and his affable nature ensured he won many more friends. It came as no surprise to his fellows that he was elected leader when the old abbot, a man by the name of Elias, died whilst in the north of the Old City looking to recruit new gladiators for the games.

Y'Bor Kaz had not protested at being elected leader. He found he enjoyed the life and he was keen to keep the amphitheatre well stocked and the monks constantly entertained yet Y'Bor found himself again drifting back to his well known harboured desires to take the level of influence of the monks further and wider than just the southern section of the Old City and that he would do so with a laugh and a smile.

Y'Bor continued to lounge in his large wooden throne, mostly unaware of what was going on around him as he reminisced. The atmosphere in the room rose when a party of monks came bounding in and Y'Bor was suddenly roused from his happy memories by a stocky monk whose boisterous loud voice was brimming with jocularity.

"We've caught a party of ten adventurous types. They just walked up, burned a flag and then waited to parley as we went out to them!"

"Good potential?" Y'Bor asked immediately, his thoughts turning to the arena.

"Oh yes," laughed the monk. "Lots of potential, couple of real gems. It's just that they came so calmly and this well groomed wolfhound simply asked that he could speak with the leader of the operation."

"Where are they now?" enquired the intrigued Y'Bor Kaz, now sitting more upright in the abbot's chair.

"We've got them in one of the larger holding cells at the amphitheatre."

"Okay, take some of the boys down there and split them into separate pens," ordered Y'Bor.

"And the wolfhound? He was quite polite about wanting to speak with you."

"Well then bring him to me. Sounds interesting."

The stocky monk headed off with a leap followed by a large bunch of coloured priests. Y'Bor Kaz started pacing up and down the hall, extremely curious about the 'well groomed wolfhound'. He reached into a leather pouch on his wide belt and pulled out some dried, dark olive coloured leaves and started to chew them. The first taste was always bitter and there was a slight stinging around the edges of the tongue and the roof of the mouth. Then the sweetness swirled and the elations began. Y'Bor closed his eyes in pleasure and decided to pluck from the pouch again and ensure he was in a most excellent mood for the audience with this wolfhound that would simply give himself up and nine of his companions.

When Egremont entered the chamber, flanked by a couple of monks, Y'Bor Kaz was languidly draped in the abbot's throne, laying on his back he had his legs over one of the arms and the back of his head on another. He managed to sit up a little to face Egremont and the grin he conjured up was huge and welcoming as the wolfhound walked to the floor in front of him.

"My, you are a fine looking fellow aren't you?" chirruped Y'Bor.

"Thank you. And you sir are obviously a man of impeccable taste and observational skills."

"True, I am that indeed," then leaning forward Y'Bor added. "But I am also extremely dangerous, mordant and intensely interested in gladiatorial combat. I think that you and your crew are going to provide some much needed entertainment for my men who are a bit low at the moment. There was some unpleasantness the other day that needs rectifying."

"Ah you talk of your defeat at the castle?" Egremont deliberately needled.

"Defeat!" Y'Bor Kaz scoffed with a guffaw. "Merely a set back that will be corrected when my boys are happier after a decent set of games."

"Were you not told of my requests?"

"Requests? Yes. That you wanted to speak with me. A request that I have met."

"Ah, you were not told everything then," said Egremont phlegmatically.

"Come on then Wolfy, what is it?" Y'Bor joked, some of his men laughing loudly.

"Never call me that!" Egremont spat with disgust. He stood tall and proud, not looking like a captive at all. "I am Egremont, the Lord Seau du Duvet and I have a proposition for you."

"I don't care who you are Wolfy. But I am interested in a proposition from a prisoner. Is it that you will do whatever I want you to do? Yes, that is probably it. Like fight a battle with a Nine Win champion who is hungry for release and a bit of dog flesh?" the harlequin monks in the room fell about with massive amounts of barking mad laughter and back slapping.

"No it is not. And I will forgive your slip of an insult for the second time," the crowd gave a few loud 'ooos' at Egremont's impertinence.

"Then what is it because that seems the most likely outcome to me, don't ya know!"

"It is that you let us join you in an assault on the castle."

The crowd of monks again fell about the room in a cacophony of derision. Only Egremont and a suddenly sober Y'Bor Kaz were quiet and they were staring at each other.

"What could you possibly bring us Master Wolfhound?" Y'Bor said in a serious steady tone.

"Seeing as you ask so politely and we are so keen I will tell you. I would bring you warriors of great renown, remorseless barbarians, knights of immense strength, thieves of deviousness and masterful minds."

"Some big claims there Egremont, the Lord Seau du Duvet. Why do you want to attack the castle?"

"We need access to some of its secrets. Why do you?"

"Power and influence over the whole of the Old City and the castle is key to controlling the centre. Well I am actually interested in your offer. But I am also very interested in entertaining my troops. It is important to keep their spirits up by other methods than just the leaf. Tell you what, there may be a way we can both be satisfied. I will stage two fights tonight. You get to choose two of your party to stand their ground and prove your claims in the arena. If you can impress my men and me then we can look to fast track your application to join the Monks of Delight. Usually it takes ten fights and ten victories if you were captured like you were.

"Fine," said Egremont immediately holding out his paw to clinch the deal. "I accept your terms for enrolment."

"Whoa, not so fast there my friend. You do realise these are fights to the death, don't you?" Y'Bor smiled and raised a finger of warning.

"I would accept and expect nothing less to join such an auspicious group of people. But two fights to the death are so much more efficient than the hundred the ten of us would have had to have completed."

"Do not worry," Y'Bor said with a smile and a far off look in his eye. "I'll ensure that they are fifty times harder to redress the balance and to test your claims of prowess. After all, I want my men to have a real spectacle and your men a real test."

The Monks of Delight all gave whoops of joy in a stylised and well practised salute and they left the monastery in a gang. Egremont walked with them calmly and engaged Y'Bor Kaz in conversation. Egremont had already ascertained that he would have to choose the two of his companions who would have to fight. He asked Y'Bor if he could talk to them all first. Y'Bor conceded with the condition that once he had decided whom he would have fight, Egremont would then join with Y'Bor to view the spectacle from the stands. Therefore he could not volunteer himself to face death in the arena in lieu of a companion. He would have to go through the pain of potentially picking a friend to die.

Chorus Ten

' The Brazen Manticore' was almost falling off the crest of the waves as it leapt along under the masterful control of its new captain. Fenton felt huge joy with the wet whipping wind, the lilting yacht and the familiar sounds of straining, taut rigging and the cracking of canvass sails.

Fenton let out a huge roar of relief, so loud it rose above the noise of the sea. He felt energetic and sparkling again after the time alone on the plateau. 'The Brazen Manticore' was large enough to have a wheel to stand behind and Fenton relished in adjusting the course to keep a steady path to the east with the coastal cliffs of Rampart imposing and parallel to his portside.

He still had plenty of time to make the rendezvous point and would probably have to have a couple of nights at sea. Safe from interrupting farmers he thought to himself. Dusk was approaching as the sun set behind him so Percy felt he would lower the sails and throw the anchor overboard a little early. With the canvass ravelled away and the anchor keeping the ship in position, Fenton raided the stores he had bought and selected a few bottles of rich dark ale and some new tobacco for his pipe. Facing the plunging sun Fenton drank and smoked and watched flocks of flying fish skipping along the surface of the sea. The moon was out too as the sun set and lights of gold and silver played on the fins of the flapping fish and broke and merged and broke again on the surface of the sea.

Then the night set in and Fenton focused on the reflection of the moon on the heaving water, watching the myriad of maritime mirrors. Although the night was chill on the open water, Fenton was well wrapped up for the journey and he had his blanket around his shoulders too. The beers brought warmth to his belly and the pipe smoke was a strong comfort too. He enjoyed blowing long streams of thin grey smoke through pursed lips, head tilted back, directly into the evening air.

A few hours later and six bottles of beer, the gentle rocking of the ship had Fenton fully content and relaxed. His thoughts again turned to his friends. By now they should have gained access to the castle and probably should be making their way through the dungeons and death filled catacombs.

He thought of their increasing claustrophobia in the caves that would follow and he allowed himself a selfish grin as he breathed deeply of the night sea air. Fenton decided than an early night would be of benefit so he made his way to the cabin and wrapped himself up on one of the perfectly pleasant beds in the well appointed schooner. As he fell asleep he was thinking how it might be a little crowded when the rest of the group was on board. There were only four beds in the cabin and another couple of covered areas that would serve as protection from the elements. Otherwise there was always the hold which he felt sure would not be a popular place for a rest. He smiled a guilty smile and drifted into a deep sleep.

Chapter Eleven

Tumbletick and his eight potential gladiatorial companions were all kept in little cells with wooden doors, thick and bolted with tiny windows in them with four stumpy iron bars. Slimy clumps of substance held onto the wet, grey black blocks of stone that made up the walls. The darker areas of glistening wetness recalled shapes like shadows of stalactites.

A little earlier Egremont had talked to them all individually through the bars about what the plan was. He apologised that they would not be able to see the two battles unless it was them who stood alone on the sand before their adversary. He had had long talks with some and shorter chats with others who felt that gladiatorial games may well not be their particular strength. Then he had left, escorted by a thin and wiry, giggling man with a spring in his step. The group had mainly been silent as they waited and listened to the sounds of combat and earlier entertainments that filtered down to them.

"Do you think they are going to feed us before we fight? I'm starving!" said Campbell suddenly to no-one in particular but out loud so most of his companions could hear in their row of cells as it was really quite quiet down in the dungeons.

"What do you think they'll provide?" asked Tumbletick, his head to the grilled gap.

"Oh I'd expect that they would have a selection of pies," Campbell replied with jest in his voice.

"What, like Shepherd or Cottage?" Tumbletick continued.

"No, I was thinking more like a nice pork pie or peppered beef," Campbell mused, his stomach gurgling in anticipation.

"Well isn't that interesting?" Tumbletick blurted full of excitement.

"What is?"

"Well my perception of a pie is that it is topped with mashed potatoes and maybe a bit of grilled cheese and yours is a collection of meat completely surrounded by pastry!"

"Hmm, that is interesting. It probably stems from the fact that as I come from good working class stock, my ancestors would have preferred the type of pie which was a totally encased variant which was designed to be portable. So the farmers in my ancestral past could carry their food to the fields very easily. Like a pasty as well," said Campbell sagely and with a degree of historical insight into food technology that impressed Tumbletick.

"What about apple pie?" added Mr. Battfin.

"Oh now that is interesting. Is that a completely encased pie, pastry on all sides, top and bottom as well?" asked Tumbletick completely enthralled.

"Aye young Tumbletick, mother always made apple pies with pastry on all side. Shaped them into rectangular pockets of pure pleasure."

"Mine didn't," said Campbell. "She just whacked a load of apples into a dish and added pastry to the top as a form of lid."

"Like the potatoes on a shepherd's pie," said Tumbletick emphatically.

"What about fish pie?" Seton Rax jumped in excitedly. "That has a mash topping!"

"Good point," said Mr. Battfin. "You've also got the interesting variants of Admiral's Pie, Mariner's Pie, Ocean Pie..."

"But it becomes a fish cake if it has bread crumbs on all sides," observed Beran. "Does anyone make a fish pie with pastry or potatoes on all sides?"

"What about Banoffey Pie, that hasn't got any crust or potatoes," said Tumbletick.

"Ah ha! Lemon Meringue Pie has a meringue topping," added Mr. Battfin.

"Which leads me to ask the very obvious question. What is the definition of a pie?" asked Tumbletick.

"Well I reckon it has got to be encased on all sides," said Mr. Battfin.

"Hmm, I think it can probably be both, with a lid on or encased," said Campbell.

"Don't forget a meat or fish based filling where the dish itself keeps everything together and a load of mashed tatties are spread on top with maybe a little cheese and parsley," said Beran.

"Will you lot just shut up!" screamed Vixen. "Here we are, some of us about to face single combat and you are talking a load of nonsense. You're doing my head in!"

"Oh go and stick it in a mud pie then!" returned Tumbletick. The others all roared into fits of laughter, Tumbletick was aware that his insult was perhaps not the most cutting but he was certainly glad to have continued the mass pie debate.

Egremont was having another kind of debate. He had to select two to enter the arena and face whatever challenge Y'Bor Kaz had chosen for them. His first choice was easy, no doubt at all. The second was harder and he was basing it all on the conversations he had had with his companions in their cells. He found himself disturbed by thinking of some of the new members of the group, as he did not have a true understanding of their capabilities, but one in particular had urged him that he would be able to cope easily with anything that the arena could throw at them. He cogitated a little longer then made up his mind under the stern gaze but broad smile of the watching Y'Bor. It was decided then, first choice easy and second choice based on the confidence of the individual concerned and it meant that the risk of death was therefore less for his original companions. They had just better be as good as they said they were. Egremont looked down into the arena at the current victor of the last bout. The crowd numbered about four hundred, which he had been informed by Y'Bor Kaz and the wiry man called Krell, was an incredibly good turnout. The audience applauded and cheered as the heavily armoured man who had just won raised his arms aloft to receive their adulation. The body of his vanquished foe was being dragged away by attendants who had slung hooks, attached to long ropes, into the dead meat of the corpse. Bloody tracks were trenched into the sand as the dead weight was pulled towards an exit opening within the wall by a rising portcullis.

"Well, fight number one for you tonight is a particularly interesting match I think," said Y'Bor Kaz leaning into Egremont and speaking with enthusiasm, his eyes never leaving the scene in the arena. "I've got five guys who are on eight or nine wins each and they've been told that they just need to work together to beat one of your chaps in order to win their final victory. Now, who are you going to pick to win that little confidence booster?"

Egremont replied calmly, not turning his head in any way towards the leaning Y'Bor.

"Is-Is."

Krell went sprinting off with a hearty giggle and a spring in his heel to release Is-Is and take him to the armoury where all their weapons had been stored. Meanwhile Y'Bor Kaz gave a heavily weighted nod to another attendant who also departed with pace to release the five who would face Is-Is.

The rumour of an engagement of major significance had pervaded the collective imagination of the crowd and the atmosphere was enhanced by the low murmur of engaging conversations about what would be revealed.

Y'Bor Kaz went to stand at the front of his private viewing platform where leaders of old had always held the attention of the crowd. A group of attendants blew loudly on long horns to indicate an announcement.

"Gentlemen," Y'Bor roared. "Tonight I have for your delectation two major combats against some major claims. I have been told that we have some warriors of renown to entertain us. Let us hope for their sake that they do for I have decided to give you two very special matches tonight!"

Y'Bor Kaz listened with great joy to the guttural cheering that rose around him as he took his seat again next to Egremont. The long horns were blown again and the opposing portcullises were raised to reveal the protagonists.

The five came running out first, frantic to see what opposed them. A quick kill and all were free from the constraints of gladiatorial life. All had chosen armour and weapons for speed believing that as a group against just one this would be the best strategy. A couple had helmets and shields but the remaining three were all bare headed and in leather jerkins. For weapons those with shields had long swords and of the remaining trio, one had a long two handed spear to fend off an enemy if needed and the other two both carried dual scimitars.

From the other end walked in the huge hare in his full chain mail suit and a smile revealing his one buck tooth. His golden earrings picked out glints of firelight from the illuminating torches and all he carried was a couple of crooked kukris. All the way to the five in front of him Is-Is just walked, slow and steady, measured and controlled. Strength oozed from his limbs and a self knowledge of brilliance in battle was displayed in his every move.

The five fanned out into a pre planned formation of two swordsmen either side of the warrior with the spear. The audience was whooping either in derision or expectation, Egremont found it hard to discern but he too had the confidence which Is-Is displayed. He knew that this was an unfair fight. Is-Is came to a complete stop and then dropped to one knee and bowed towards Egremont and therefore, by default, Y'Bor Kaz as well. His paws touched the sand and he dropped the kukris for less than a second before grabbing them again in a repositioned grip and then he sprang into the air and towards his first fight.

Is-Is landed at the feet of a shocked warrior who raised his shield to fend off an attack and quickly found his guts ripped out by razor sharp blades, criss crossing through the leather armour and stomach to his own startled screams. Entrails quickly unravelled through the rented gap left behind and began piling up around the feet and ankles of the dying man. He stood for a while and then slumped to his doom. The hare immediately departed, one foe discarded and ran at full pelt towards the spear wielding warrior. Is-Is jumped long and high towards the spearman. The enemy tried to lift the spear in the hope of impaling the hare as he fell from his vaulting arc but Is-Is was moving faster than the man could move the eight foot shaft and as he came down he kicked out hard into the face of his enemy. The head was smacked back and the neck snapped. On landing, Is-Is took a couple of steps to reposition himself and before the dead man also hit the ground the hare had dropped a kukri, blade first into the sand so that the handle stood proud and plucked the spear from the dead man's grasp. The three remaining gladiators were looking at each other and trying to understand what had just happened. They decided to rush Is-Is en mass in a screaming, roaring group. Is-Is tilted his head in disgust and disappointment at their decision. He simply tossed the spear about three foot horizontally into the air, grabbed it again in an over arm position and flung it like a javelin through the torso of the middle assailant. The crowd roared in appreciation as a full on running gladiator suddenly changed direction and flew a few yards backwards, dead as well before he slammed to the ground. Now Is-Is was only faced by a double scimitar warrior and a fighter with a sword and shield. He threw his other kukri to the ground where it quivered for a while next to the other.

"Not bad, not bad. Good boy you've got there," said Y'Bor into the ear of Egremont, his words mumbled a bit as he was chewing on some leaf. "Not bad at all. Fancy a bit before he finishes them off?" He offered Egremont his open pouch.

"No thank you. I would rather enjoy the evening with a clear head."

"Suit yourself. Looks like your boy is about to make a move!"

Is-Is was deciding what to do next. This was too easy. Should he play to the crowd and finish them with his fists? Or do a back flip, pick up the kukris and sling them into the throats of each in a wonderful display of ambidextrous knife skills and accuracy. There was a stand off for a while which the two swordsmen mistakenly took as an opportunity for them. One suddenly ran off to the body of the fallen comrade with the spear sticking out of his chest. He started to tug the shaft free thinking his best option was to select a different weapon. The other with the sword and shield thought he could take on Is-Is and he advanced with the shield tucked in close and the sword in a position to be able to put in a short, strong stab.

Is-Is was annoyed at their petulance and decided to show off to the crowd. He opened his arms and twitched his paws indicating that the enemy should come and have a go if he thought he was tough enough. The universal sign of contempt enraged the swordsman and he lashed out towards the awaiting hare. Is-Is moved with immense speed and simply clapped his paws around the blade, capturing it between flat palms. The gladiator was so startled and confused by this approach that he immediately tried to pull the sword back but Is-Is was so much stronger even holding the sword in this unorthodox manner. Is-Is pulled on it bringing the enemy to the right side of his body. Then he let go of the sword and smacked his palm into the front of the helmet, whilst placing his leg behind the ankles of the warrior. The foe fell awkwardly on his back. Is-Is jumped directly up, span three hundred and sixty degrees and landed on two heels directly on to the prone man's chest, crushing his rib cage and heart.

The last remaining gladiator now had the spear free and he advanced towards Is-Is very slowly, blade pointed at the hare with very little conviction. Is-Is stepped down from the crushed form beneath him and walked towards the kukris. He simply bent down, plucked one up, turned and with a swift underarm action tumbled the blade through the air and into the forehead of the final enemy. Already walking towards Egremont's position in the crowd before the man had hit the ground, dead like the other four, Is-Is paused slightly to take the adulation of the raving audience. Y'Bor Kaz had been one of the first to his feet applauding maniacally; beside him Egremont merely caught the eye of his friend and smiled a warm and knowing acknowledgement.

"Wonderful, wonderful, wonderful!" enthused Y'Bor. "So good. Well that lives up to your claims Master Egremont." The red headed monk was clapping constantly, shouting to get his message across above the roar of the crowd. Eventually Is-Is was shown the portcullis he should leave by, by one of the corpse removal attendants and the crowd returned to the bubbling hubbub of the excitable conversation of fanatics.

"Well done, really very good indeed," said Y'Bor Kaz. "Now for fight number two. I have decided to use one of my favourite monsters for this one. I feel sure that you could not possibly have anyone who could deal with him. Even your marvellous hare, Is-Is, would struggle I'm sure."

"What type of monster is it?" asked Egremont, looking for information which may be able to influence his selection.

"Ah ha, no no no. No clues this time. Suffice to say he's big," came the cagey reply.

"Well then, I have received certain guarantees that one of our party can deal with anyone or anything in a one on one encounter. He has the utmost confidence. So I select Garraday."

Y'Bor Kaz sent one of his men off down to the cells to get Garraday. He then stood up and held his arms aloft to the cheers of his men.

"My Monks of Delight," he roared, turning left and right to take in the full spectacle and to ensure he could be seen by all. "My glorious Jesters of Death. What a display we have just seen from the fierce warrior by the name of Is-Is. Glory in his name and skill." He waited to allow the cheers to build and come crashing down in waves. Then he rose his arms aloft and an eventual hush came to the crowd.

"Now my men, I have a special treat. Tonight we shall open the large portcullis!" A huge howl of ecstasy went through the crowd and Egremont's eyes were attracted to the portcullis opposite the royal box which was about three times the height of the one through which Is-Is had entered.

"And we all know what lies behind the large portcullis, don't we?" bellowed Y'Bor.

The crowd started up a great chant in a rhythmic and tribal unison.

"Eblis, Eblis, Eblis, Eblis."

"Who or what is Eblis?" Egremont asked in slow concern.

"Well it was the name of one of the old abbots. Now it is the name of my favourite pet," came the proud reply. "I think you will find him quite...stimulating."

Garraday came walking into the arena, his dark robes swaying to the rhythms of the chanting crowd. He came to the centre of the sand covered floor and stood there, unarmed and unencumbered by armour but looking supremely confident.

Then the beast came. It was preceded by an awful smell of death and decay. It was sweet and sickly, cloying to the senses. The smell was disgusting but so was the creature. It pulled its way out of the opening by two large crablike claws. They were a pale red with intermittent white spots and they grated against the stone wall as it heaved a corpulent body through the gap.

Its body had rolls of fat which looked disturbingly humanlike in its nakedness. Its legs were squat and sat on the sides of the podgy body so that it dragged its rump as it moved in a strange combination of scuttling and heaving. Its head was pointed and conical and merged into the body through a short neck, flabby with folds of skin. Its face had a toad like appearance, with a wide mouth, darting tongue, dead reptilian yellow eyes with black pupils and mangy, stringy black hair clinging to the very top of the crown of the head.

The crowd hushed again. Egremont was amazed by the faces of all he could see in the crowd. Their voyeuristic desire about to be appeased, mouths open, eyes wide as they leaned forward to gaze upon Y'Bor's pet.

Egremont felt concerned, how could Garraday cope with a creature such as this Eblis that must have come from one of the very lower levels of Hell? Garraday however looked calm as he stood, looking small and infant like before the creature which now was standing to its full bulky height of about twenty foot tall. It had barely been able to squeeze its way out of the passage and portcullis from its pen. The creature knew what its role was in the ring. To savage and destroy anything that was put before it. To succeed meant that it would be fed with the scraps of the evening's entertainment. Remains of sweet gladiator and beast meat, usually with the bones removed to make the devouring so much simpler. Eblis had not always been so large but the feeding here was good and it had grown fleshy and outsized from its victories and the butchery of other battles.

Garraday started to mutter some words quickly under his breath and held his arms in front of him with his palms facing each other. Then he started to move his hands in small circular motions in the opposite direction to each other. A difficult enough trick with arms at full stretch in most situations but with a monster like Eblis coming towards him the concentration needed was quite phenomenal. A spark of light appeared between the circling palms and it began to grow in size and in brightness. Garraday moved his hands further apart and made the movements larger still, like he was massaging and caressing the light hovering within. The light grew into a ball about the size of a human head, bright red, flames flitting off in little tongues of vapour. Now it looked like a sun in its intensity and the crowd were drawn to it and away from the magnetism of Eblis' horror.

"Ah ha," said Y'Bor Kaz, his eyes attached to the scene in front of him but talking to Egremont. "You have a Magic User in your ranks. A rare commodity indeed!"

"Indeed," retorted Egremont also watching with interest as the fireball grew and Garraday suddenly drew back his right arm and threw the ball of fire towards the monstrosity confronting him.

The throw was perhaps for theatricality or perhaps for aim but the fireball sped away straight and true with a trail of roaring, burning flames leaving the night air shimmering with its immense heat.

Eblis saw the fireball coming but it felt no fear. It took one of its huge claws and simply batted the attack away. The shell and structure of Eblis' claws was strong and thick and fundamentally impervious to most things. The fireball was struck and changed direction and massively crashed into the sand floor by the arena wall. The resulting explosion lit the entire area and picked out in perfect detail the expression of shock upon the face of the aged man in the centre of the ring who stood aghast in his failure to hurt his enemy.

Eblis then moved with a rapidity which belied its bulk. Its stocky legs pumping quickly the body rose off the ground from where it had been squatting seconds before. It leaned forward and reached out with one of its long arms. The claw opened and snapped back shut around the body of Garraday. The pincers were so large that the breadth of them covered the wizard from his chest to his knees. The vice was so tight in the snapping that bloody froth immediately burst forth from the old man's mouth. Eblis lifted the body high into the air and gave an alien, mutant roar for its imminent victory. The crowd started to chant again in adulation of the beast.

Y'Bor Kaz was cackling and hooting with spasmodic delight. Once again his pet had proven itself unbeatable. Then the beast squeezed the claw a little more and the body of Garraday was severed. Head, shoulders and arms fell in one piece to the floor with the two stumps of his legs. Eblis opened his killing claw revealing a sticky, pulpy mass of magician's midriff. It brought the claw close to its wide mouth and began to devour the mashed meal with its long, slurping tongue while it was still warm.

"Well, there's no coming back from that," exploded Y'Bor Kaz in joy. Energy and enthusiasm in his voice, encouraging Egremont to join in the celebration. Y'Bor was so wrapped up in the rapture of the event that he was totally oblivious to the fact that Egremont had just had one of his party wiped out.

The crowd was on its feet too, cheering and applauding the victory, despite the short timescale of the fight it had been entertainment and spectacle at its height. Magic and a gory death combined with a feeding frenzy from Eblis.

The beast handlers that cared for Eblis came running into the arena with buckets of fresh meat which they scattered about for its reward. The crowd went wild as they could watch further feeding time and the eating habits of Eblis were an entire diversion in themselves. The demon went into a minor frenzy and the beast handlers did their best to avoid his sweeping claws and massive heaving bulk.

Y'Bor Kaz put his arm around Egremont.

"Come Master Wolfhound, I think it is time to discuss our agreement."

He led Egremont out from the stands and to a large private chamber where more pleasant food was laid out on tables with flagons of ale. The red head started picking at pieces to eat and then poured two large wooden tankards of a rich brown beer and handed one to the steely wolfhound who found that his appetite was intense despite the recent scenes.

"I believe," said Egremont between chewing bits of meat. "That the agreement to join the Monks of Delight was based upon impressing you and your men."

"That was part of the wording, I did not actually say anything at all about two fights and two outright victories it is true but that was very clearly implied my dear Egremont."

"Ah but not very clearly stated."

Y'Bor Kaz took a long drink and mused for a while. He turned and walked to a chair where he sat down to continue thinking. Egremont remained silent, standing and still but did occasionally drink some of the beer, which although a home brew was of a very fine quality, with a hint of stinging nettle bitterness that he found very conducive. The monks had clearly adopted some of the skills that the brethren who had originally inhabited the abbey would have had in abundance.

As Y'Bor Kaz sat thinking he too drank and found that the addition of leaf to the beer was, as always, a perfect compliment. He had decided what he wanted to do and that was to invite Egremont and his party to join with them. The hare, Is-Is, had been exceptional and although the Magic User had been a loss, it was truly an impressive spectacle. Perhaps he could find a way of getting Eblis to be trained to attack castle gates and he could join in the next battle against the brigands who resided in the fortress.

Y'Bor finished his beer in one long draught, stood up and set the empty tankard aside. He reached to his pouch and took out some leaf to chew. The sympathetic stinging was a much missed friend.

"Well Egremont. I think that I am extending an invitation to join the Monks of Delight."

"Excellent, we shall be delighted to do so," Egremont replied with grace. "I take it that it shall be for the duration needed to gain you victory over the castle."

"Exactly my dear wolfhound. That is the deal. Only one other thing needed to be a Monk of Delight and that is to laugh a little. I think that your beer should help with that in a little while."

"I did indeed find it an amusing number," Egremont smiled broadly. Satisfied with the result and not feeling anything negative about the loss of Garraday at the current time. The wizard had very strongly urged Egremont to select him. He took the risk upon himself with such pleadings and had paid for his confidence with a gory death.

"Then let us send for your friends and crack open a fresh cask," Y'Bor boomed with a friendly tone. He went to the door and called for one of his men whom he sent off to the holding cells. It was not long before they all returned and were joined by many monks.

That night much beer was drunk. Beran, Seton Rax and Nazar Grant at first were much aggrieved by the loss of their leader and they asked many times for Y'Bor Kaz to relate the tale of his final fight. As the beers went down they found themselves more inclined to laugh and feel that actually it had been a good and glorious way to die. Garraday had entertained and ended his long life in a blaze of gory glory and a magical firery light and the roar of an appreciative crowd was the last thing he had ever heard. Also with the leadership of Garraday gone the three men found themselves closer to Egremont, Is-Is, Tumbletick, Campbell, Vixen and Mr. Battfin.

The Monks of Delight celebrated with them, many much in awe of Is-Is. They also thought that all these new companions looked very handy, full of potential and danger. The monks however were slightly confused by the small, ugly, hairy little creature that was with them. They liked the way he enjoyed drinking a lot of beer and how much he giggled and guffawed. Perhaps it was another Magic User from an exotic part of the outside world. The monks felt certain that these nine could be the key to securing the victory their leader so wanted.

With their weapons returned to them 'The Nine', as the monks had decided to call them, were shown the way from the amphitheatre and to the monastery. There they were given an old monk's cell each to sleep off the beer and gain some rest. On a peg, on the back of each of the cell doors there hung a multicoloured hooded robe, just the right size for each of the occupants, should they select to wear them.

As Egremont was about to enter his room and gain some much needed sleep Y'Bor Kaz caught his paw in a strong handshake of respect and burgeoning friendship.

"Egremont, now that we are to be on the same team, perhaps you can tell me what is it you wish to find in the castle?"

"Sure. We want to gain access to the dungeons, then the catacombs beneath them and then to the subterranean passages that lead down to the smugglers cave. We need to make a rendezvous with another companion who should be meeting us there soon," Egremont was slurring a little with the effects of the leaf laced beer and was surprised at himself for being so forth coming.

"Really?" said Y'Bor Kaz. "I wish you'd told me sooner and not made an agreement to help attack the castle. You see we have got access to those underground passages too. In fact we used to try and attack the castle from underground as they all link up. The brigands though grew wise to the potential attacks from that route and they caused a deliberate cave in about three months ago. No one can get down to the cave now and a lot of the old benefits have since dried up because of it."

Egremont suddenly seemed sober.

"You are absolutely sure that the passages are blocked?"

"Oh definitely, we can't get down and there is no way they can. See you in the morning my friend. I'll send for you at dawn when we take breakfast. We can have a Council of War and discuss our tactics for taking the castle!"

Y'Bor Kaz left with a big smile and headed off for his own quarters. Egremont walked into the cell and shut the door behind him.

Here ends Book Two of the Tumbletick Trilogy.
Book Three, 'Free Tumbletick',
Focuses on how they make their way to Kenai
And what occurs there.

BOOK THREE

FREE
TUMBLETICK

Chapter One

awn broke upon the Old City. Egremont was already awake having had very little sleep in his cell. Y'Bor Kaz's comments on the blocked passages beneath the castle was devastating news. No way down to the rendezvous point and an oath made to help attack the castle. Egremont knew that to risk an assault without the benefit of the route to meet with Percy was an extremely rash one. He would have to convince Y'Bor to release them from the agreement.

Egremont heard footsteps and rapping on wooden doors to rouse the companions from their slumbers for breakfast. The wolfhound opened the door himself just as a grinning monk was about to knock, his clenched fist paused in the air in front of the muzzle of Egremont.

"Nearly caught you one on the snout there my Lord Egremont," the monk chattered.

"Yes. Tell me how to get to breakfast. I need to speak with Y'Bor Kaz."

"Sure. Down the end of the corridor. Doesn't matter which way you go really. You'll find yourself in the cloisters. Take a little amble around the columned courtyard and you'll see some double doors to the refectory," the monk paused as other doors opened and yawning occupants emerged. Egremont, however, had already began moving towards the end of the corridor where he found an open door and the flagstone floor of the cloister surrounding a surprisingly well kept square lawn.

"Must be goats keeping that well cropped," he thought to himself and then grew agitated that he had let his mind slip to such mundane matters when there was serious business to be taken care of.

Egremont arrived at the double doors and with one paw on each he gave an expansive push, flinging them open on well oiled hinges. The refectory was large, filled with many long wooden tables and equally long wooden benches for seating on both sides. A few monks were already present, dipping wooden spoons into a gruel and smiling in between mouthfuls. The distinctive form of Y'Bor Kaz was sitting next to Krell. They were talking quietly as the doors had burst open and fell to silence as Egremont made his way directly towards them.

"My dear Egremont," Y'Bor proclaimed. "Come and join us in our Council of War!"

"Not a very large council," replied Egremont swinging himself onto the bench next to the red headed warrior. "However, I wish to address this gathering on a matter of utmost importance."

"Address away my friend," Y'Bor replied.

"I know I made an agreement to help in the assault upon the castle," Y'Bor's face changed quickly to a frowning visage of thunderous black.

"That sounds very much like you are about to renege on an oath Master Wolfhound!"

"Not really much on the table for me though was there? We promised to give you two fights to the death so we could entertain your men and thereby join the Monks of Delight. Upon joining we could then fight with you to take the castle and were then free to go our own way."

"That was the deal Lord Egremont," Y'Bor said sternly.

"Well the deal was in place in order to gain access to the catacombs. Now, you told me last night that the passages we need to gain access to are completely blocked."

"You should have ensured you were in receipt of all the facts before you bargained your way into an agreement."

"But we have given the life of a companion and I wish you to release us from the full terms and conditions of the oath."

"Well I wish you to remain true to your honour and aid us in the attack. Upon victory you shall be released from the Monks of Delight. Until I have that victory, you are and will remain part of my merry troop."

Y'Bor pulled his fixed gaze away slowly from the wolfhound, looked into his bowl and began to eat some of the gruel in front of him. Krell continued to look seriously at Egremont.

"Listen Y'Bor. We are on a quest. As I have already told you. We needed to gain access to the tunnels underneath the castle. You now tell me they are blocked."

"Yes blocked," Y'Bor interrupted in an angry burst, gruel spitting out in between the words. "And I have already told you that you should have gathered all your facts before making a deal."

Y'Bor returned his gaze again to the bowl and slowly began to eat again. Egremont paused for a while, conscious that Krell was still staring at him with his head fixed in position like a hawk.

"The quest we are upon is one of the utmost importance to the continent of Umiat," Egremont spoke slowly and calmly. "I urge you to release us from our bond so that we can leave the Old City immediately and find another way to meet our companion."

"Quest," Y'Bor spat out his gruel again directly into the bowl. "I have met hundreds of men believing they were on a sacred quest of 'utmost importance'. Most of them are dead. Their intentions and honour ghosts in the graveyard with them."

"I have met many more men whose intentions were power and influence," Egremont replied. "The two sirens you seek Y'Bor with the dominion of your micro empire. If you achieve them and have the knowledge in your heart that you have the power and influence over the whole of this mighty Old City, what would it truly bring Y'Bor?"

"Fame. Legend. Self satisfaction. Glory," Y'Bor threw the wooden spoon into the remaining slurry in front of him. "Maybe some better food. Do not doubt my motives Master Wolfhound. They are noble because they are untainted by any lies. I seek power and influence for what they are. Pure and simple."

"Fine. Good. I hope you find them. But we will not be risking our lives in helping you to attack the castle. You must release us from the agreement for we seek the Umiat Stone. Stolen from Umiat and smuggled to Kenai by Ahriman."

Y'Bor Kaz's jaw dropped at the same time as Krell gave a mighty blink of surprise. The two men then sat staring at Egremont with vacant expressions. Krell spoke first, quietly, the increasing noise of others taking breakfast and talking raucously almost covering his comment.

"Quest my Lord Egremont? Quest hardly seems the right word. Sounds more like you are taking a trip in a dream. Ahriman is long dead. Killed by Sir Bartle Rourke in one to one combat. Everyone knows the old poetic tale that did the rounds of the globe. That epic story even reached us old lags in the Old City!"

"'Twas no tale Krell," said Y'Bor Kaz in a hushed manner. "Some of the battles of the Ahrioch Wars took place near my home town. My mother spoke of horrors walking the streets of Bor. Demons that had found their way out of the battle and looked for easy prey in the wilderness. Terribly wounded men struggling back from the carnage."

"Many of those men would have fought with me Y'Bor. For I was fighting alongside Sir Bartle Rourke as he killed the demon loving Ahriman," said Egremont calmly. "True they were your mother's words. All real, bloody guts and terror. However a few days ago when the Umiat Stone was being presented to Princess Annabella Blaise at the Court of Rhyell, a man who looked very much like Ahriman led an attack with wolves and skeletons summoned from Hell. Hundreds were killed. The stone was taken and the murderous thieves left in a strange black boat from the harbour. Heading, we surmise, for Kenai. We are the people selected to go and retrieve the stone and exact some retribution."

"Kenai is a big place," said Y'Bor.

"Yes it is. However we have a good idea of where to start looking," Egremont replied.

"Sounds like a foolish and un-thought out piece of heroism to me," said Y'Bor with a smile.

"Perhaps. But we have to do something. The most important thing is the morale of the people of Umiat. You can control a population in only two ways fundamentally. Fear or contentment. The type of fear they will be feeling at the moment though is that of impending disaster and demons taking them in their sleep. It is not the right type of fear. We prefer it when the population feels fear for the next harvest, fear of foreign invasions by men not monsters. Combine that with contentment of a full belly, fine ales in the local late opening pub and a tax system which leaves them with enough money for a few little luxuries and everything is just fine. We all get on with our lives and develop and grow. The stone plays a big part in keeping the fear element at the right level and the contentment level balanced with it. We have to return the Umiat Stone so that they feel safe and content. The stone has no real power to protect the population from attack but the People believe that it does. Anyway, it is a debate that has been had many times. If you want to believe in the stone then believe. The real quest is actually to find out who this villain is that has decided to adopt the look of the evil demonologist Ahriman. Find him and destroy him with extreme prejudice."

"How about we change the deal slightly?" Y'Bor offered.

"You are going to release us from our pledge?" asked Egremont.

"Not in the slightest. I am a man of my word and I expect you to be too despite the change in the parameters. My offer in the form of a slight change to the original deal is this. We still attack the castle and we must win. But I will use Eblis to aid the attack. He is a very favourite pet of mine but I am prepared to risk him. I'm sure he will sway the battle if we utilise him effectively. Upon winning I will pass the title of leader onto Krell."

Krell looked at Y'Bor and his eyes filled with the waters of emotion and respect. Loss and gratefulness combined.

"You have been a great tutor and a loyal friend Krell," Y'Bor said. "But if we can be successful it is time for me to leave. You deserve the chance to lead the Monks of Delight, Krell. You will be a worthy leader. However, I still remember my password. I entered as a free man and I can leave as one too and embark upon another great adventure with my new friends. That is if you will take me Egremont?"

Egremont paused only slightly, he was taken aback by the offer of loyalty and companionship from Y'Bor. The wolfhound looked at the red headed warrior with a solemn countenance.

"Yes of course we would. And, I must add, I feel that with your offer of Eblis in the vanguard then victory should almost be assured. He is a great beast and I am sure he would be able to breach the gates of the castle."

Egremont held out his paw and Y'Bor spat into his own hand.

"This will be binding Master Wolfhound. No opportunity to find ways around this solemn pledge," the red headed warrior said holding out his hand close to the extended paw of Egremont.

The wolfhound pulled his arm back and with as much nobility as he could he spat onto the leathery black pads of his own paw.

"I know," he said and looking Y'Bor Kaz in the eye shook his hand vigorously. "But you do realise that our number is already nine with our off shore friend counted as part of the party. You know that I am their leader. The Tenth. I am the Master Elect of the Nine. You will be the eleventh but an equal member in our quest."

"As I shook you hand, I knew Master Wolfhound," came the reply from Y'Bor Kaz as he bowed his fiery red head before the noble Egremont.

Chorus One

Percy Fenton awoke on board 'The Brazen Manticore' and stretched in the comfort of his bed. Dawn had long since departed and the strong early morning sun was bright upon the calm seas. The pirate languidly sorted himself some breakfast and took it out on deck to eat. He wasn't fully dressed and the morning air felt cool on his naked, well defined torso. Percy slowly chewed on the breakfast and regarded the calm seas with a deep pleasure. He had made good time and had a full day to himself before the planned rendezvous. He decided that he would take the schooner to the meeting point early on, making further good time but not pushing the boat to its limits. Then he would drop anchor and spend the rest of the day fishing. 'The Brazen Manticore' had some basic equipment on board for piscatorial pursuits, some rods, line, hooks and lures. Sailors would often supplement their preserved foods with fresh fish, if they could catch them. Fenton felt that such a delicacy would be nice for his supper and his companions might enjoy the addition of some day old variety to their diet when they hooked up. Then he planned to have another relaxed night of contemplation, beer and pipe smoking. A final piece of relaxation before he and his friends would head south for the cold, hard and rugged land of Kenai. The challenges, threats and terrors that would await there was definitely something that contemplation was bringing to the forefront of his mind. The land was filled with monsters beyond that of the followers of Ahriman. The earth itself would rise into shapes of fear that could kill with falling rocks or cut with razor sharp obsidian edges. The passes and ravines would form natural mazes in the mountains that could confuse travellers and lead to starvation and weakness. As you awaited death through exposure your hopes would rise that a monster would pick you off quickly thinking you a piece of carrion or easy prey. Fenton gave a shudder in the breeze and began swallowing his food.

Chapter Two

Y'Bor Kaz had summoned his senior monks and joined with Egremont and Is-Is in the main nave of the abbey. Conversations had been focussing on how to ensure a successful assault upon the castle and its main gate, they needed an excellent plan to succeed.

Seton Rax, Beran and Nazar Grant had been informed of the new plan and the news of the collapsed passages. Egremont had released them from the agreement to come further with them but suggested that Y'Bor Kaz fully expected them to be part of the attack on the castle. The three had wandered off for some solitude and discussions about what part they would play in the plans.

Mr. Battfin and Campbell were lounging on some pews listening to Egremont and Y'Bor discussing their strategy. Vixen had returned to her cell to write in her diary and Tumbletick had been taken by a young monk to the top of the abbey's bell tower after expressing an interest in taking a view from that vantage point of the city.

Y'Bor was pacing back and forth, deep in thought but massively enthusiastic for the planned assault. His monks were wide eyed and smiling in anticipation of the glorious plan that would guarantee victory and plenty of fresh prisoners from the brigands holed up in the castle. This time they felt sure the attack would work with the help of the newcomers, Eblis and their leader's mind; many new gladiators would be performing in the arena soon.

"Eblis will be the key," said Y'Bor. "But how do we get him to take out the gate?"

"What is 'its', I struggle to say 'his', general level of intelligence?" asked Egremont, picking at one of his claws.

"Oh, extremely low," Y'Bor replied. "Let's ask Krell but I would suspect it is something akin to that of a snail."

"Indeed Eblis is a pretty primitive monster," Krell proffered. "He fundamentally responds to the instinct of killing and eating only."

"But he does respond?" asked Egremont.

"Yes. We reward him with buckets of left over gladiator when he has killed in the arena. We seem to be in a virtuous circle now of expected reward after a good performance. Do you know, I swear I sometimes detect a smile as he sees the buckets coming with the titbit contents," Krell said.

"How do you think it would respond if it had made a kill and then did not get the promised bucket contents?" Egremont said.

"Extremely badly. Tantrums on a colossal scale," came Krell's reply.

"Then I think I may have a suggestion," said Egremont. "Let us stage a short gladiatorial combat. Get all your troops into the arena to watch it as a rousing pre-cursor to the day's main battle at the castle. Eblis is brought onto the main stage and finds a small bunch of wretches in the ring. You know the type, snivelling wretches, third rate weaklings that he'll make short shrift of. No real opposition, can't risk any potential bravery, but equipped with swords and armour so Eblis 'thinks' he's got a fight on and a spectacle to create. Well Eblis comes in, does the business, hears the roar of the crowd has a bit of a starter from his victory but then is expecting his reward buckets. We then get some willing volunteer with a bucket to lure Eblis out onto the streets and run up to the castle and smear the contents onto the gates. Eblis, who will have been chasing them, will then rip the gates to bits in an effort to gain his reward."

Y'Bor and Krell looked at Egremont dumbfounded.

"What a terrible idea," said Y'Bor. "But there maybe a kernel of a plan there."

Egremont looked dejected but quickly changed his outlook so not to appear too precious about his thoughts being dismissed. Y'Bor pondered for a while and then spoke.

"I think the trick would be not to smear the contents on the gate but to throw the bucket over the castle wall so Eblis would naturally want to break the gate down. Your idea risks Eblis just slurping the wood with his tongue like an overgrown toad," laughed Y'Bor. "Yes. Yes. I like that idea a lot. We could get him into a real frenzy by having lots of monks running with lots and lots of buckets and throwing them all over the walls of the castle in an arcing rain of charnel pots."

"Are you sure you could guarantee that all the buckets would get over the walls?" asked Egremont. "They were at least forty feet high. If a few missed Eblis might just start scrabbling around for buckets which bounced off the walls. Leaving himself open to a counter attack from missiles from the battlements."

"Hmm. I think then if we got ten good lads with a big dose of leaf inside of them they would find the courage and the energy to run towards the castle with only one bucket of gladiator slop. Yes, we need to ensure they have the speed to outrun an angry Eblis and a forearm to lob the bucket that high. Eblis can be quite quick you know."

Mr. Battfin and Campbell exchanged a glance over the backs of the pews as they lolled on the wooden benches. The look spoke of exasperation and madness in the minds of the men discussing tactics.

"Then," continued Y'Bor. "After Eblis has smashed down the gate we let him go to work on the inhabitants of the castle. Eventually they will probably kill him but we will have already rushed in through the breach and be causing merry hell and havoc. Should be a very successful sortie!"

"Fine, let's do that then," agreed Egremont. "Got to move quick in matters like this. The 'How' is decided. When do we do it?"

"Tonight. No, this evening. Time it so the buckets are lobbed at dusk. That way we get the benefit of a hungry Eblis and twilight to help mask our attack."

"Okay," said Egremont. "And upon victory at the castle, you hand over to Krell and then join with us and we have to find some other way to Fenton and his newly acquired boat."

"That sums it up," replied Y'Bor.

"And if we fail in the attack at the castle?" questioned Egremont.

"Then you are bound to the Monks of Delight until we finally do prevail or upon your death. Whichever comes first."

"Well then let us ensure that it is a successful night's work."

Y'Bor, Krell and several of the monks headed over to the arena to select come prisoners for either a round of combat with Eblis or for the buckets that would be needed as bait.

Egremont and Is-Is went to sit with Campbell and Mr. Battfin.

"I've got a bad feeling about this," said Campbell. "I reckon we should all make a bolt for it as soon as we can. I don't think we need to take a serious risk in a full scale battle just to keep our word and gain the support of Y'Bor Kaz in our quest."

"Certainly cowardice would be an option that could be explored," Egremont replied. "But I do fear that sometimes I have an over exaggerated sense of honour and I did give my word."

"I reckon old Eblis will sway the battle in our favour," said Mr. Battfin, chewing on a splinter of wood he had pulled from the pew. "That is if it all works out and he smashes those gates. Besides, I could do with a good fight. I've missed out on everything so far, except for a thrust into one of those stirges."

"I think you'll probably get a gut full of thrusting in the castle," said Campbell. "Well, I'll tag along but I'll try and stay near the back. Any sign that it is going badly and I'm off I tell you."

"Hmm," mused Egremont. "I think that you would be safer with us."

"Don't count on it," replied Campbell. "Look here comes Seton Rax and company."

Seton Rax, Beran and Nazar Grant ambled along the aisle of the abbey until they came to the group. They sat round on the pews and it was Seton Rax who was first to speak.

"Me and the boys have had a chat and we would like to stay with you. Help out on the assault of the castle and then, if we are victorious, come with you to Kenai. I'm sure we would be of use."

"You will be more than welcome," enthused Egremont. "I'd be delighted for you to come with us. I kind of thought that you would make that decision. When our party became the number we became I kind of suspected that you would stay with us for a very long time."

Egremont stood up and went to hug the barbarian, metal plated paladin and cleric each in turn. Then they shook hands with Is-Is and Mr. Battfin. Campbell the Weasel leant back on the pew with his hands behind his head.

"Well," muttered the thief. "I guess the chances of victory have just improved. But only by a little."

Chorus Two

Fenton felt reinvigorated. The coastal breeze had been behind 'The Brazen Manticore' and a single sail had been more than adequate to buffet the boat ahead of the waves. Percy knew these waters well and he knew exactly where he was going to drop anchor. He was looking to the port side for well known crags and fissures in the cliff face that would tell him he was near the cave that could only be entered during low tide.

Fenton made tiny adjustments to the wheel, port and starboard, to keep the schooner efficiently in front of the wind. He loved the feel of the deck pushing up onto the soles of his boots and then dropping away again after the swell. Tomorrow, if everything went well, he would be seeing his friends again and the quest would become even more serious than it had been. There would be no opportunities for beers in the wilderness of Kenai. No inns with pretty receptionists or buxom wenches to please his eye. No beds to sleep in at night. It would be rocks and cold, black obsidian edges sharper than broken glass. Fenton realised he was visualising his fears again just as he had done when he was recently woken by the farmer. He shook his head free of the image of a dark shape hiding in the corner of the prow or of his mind he was not sure which. He looked again at the front of the boat and all was clear of any shadowy forms lurking there. He was nearly where he needed to be. It was time to furl in the sail and sling the anchor over the stern.

He could see the dark entrance to the smugglers cave now. It was small, almost semi circular, appearing and disappearing as the waves covered and then revealed what was there to be seen. Fenton selected a rod and a lure and made a cast over the starboard side. His back was to the Isle of Rampart and he faced the open sea ahead. If the fish were not biting then it would be another evening of ale and pipe tobacco.

Chapter Two

Eblis snapped at a fleeing sacrificial prisoner with his huge claw, just catching the victim with a snip of the pincer point which was enough to gouge into the naked back and sever the spinal cord. The man continued to run as he died and the stumbling fall that followed the demon's attack became an amusing crash into the dust for the audience.

The crowd of armed monks cheered with jubilation and lifted their weapons aloft in pumping appreciation. The bloodlust was building and Eblis had now finished the last of the individuals chosen to die. The monster scooped up the twitching form and began to feed. This was the sign. Doors to the arena swung open and ten monks came sprinting into the arena, each with a large silver bucket filled with the kind of easy eating pieces of flesh Eblis so desired. The beasts eyes twinkled and he dropped the body and started to move towards the ten monks. They were yelling and swinging the buckets in a taunting manner. Completely filled with as much leaf as they could stomach the monks were raucous and pumped up with adrenalin as well as the mildly narcotic leaf. As soon as Eblis broke into a run, lifting his bulk from the sand of the arena the monks turned and sprinted out of the amphitheatre and out to the boulevard heading north to the centre of the Old City. Eblis gave a piercing roar, seeing freedom and his reward racing out into the dusky evening air. He followed the monks growling in indignation and hope.

The monks remaining in the crowd whooped. The plan seemed to be working thus far. Hordes of warriors ran down to the walls of the arena and started leaping over the edge and swarming after Eblis.

Y'Bor Kaz looked at Egremont who was part of the group upon the ceremonial platform where they had been watching how things transpired.

"The plan seems to be working Master Wolfhound," he said with a smile. "We had better not get left behind."

Mr. Battfin led the way and sprang down from the dignitaries' area, a cutlass in each hand and started pushing his way through the throng of enthused monks.

"Let's get this over with then. Someone needs to keep an eye on that pirate. He can get carried away," said Campbell with a degree of resignation and caring. He was next down and off to the potential assault. Y'Bor followed closely, snatching up his two warhammers as he ran and jumped down to the arena floor.

Seton Rax, Beran and Nazar Grant were next, then Is-Is made his way, calmly at first then taking a gigantic bound down to the ground which had him a fair way ahead of the trio who had preceded him.

Egremont turned to Vixen and Tumbletick who remained on the platform.

"I want you to stay with Vixen, Tumbletick. She will protect you in case things go badly. Stay at the back of the assault and I do not want you entering the castle if we gain entry."

"I'm not overly eager to enter into a fight Egremont but I'm not exactly excited by your choice of bodyguard," Tumbletick replied.

"It might give you some time to overcome your differences with Vixen. She is part of the group and was selected for a reason," Egremont said.

"Guys, I'm right here you know," said Vixen. "Look I'm sorry for what I said about Lord Jackson of En'Tuk. If that makes any difference Tumbletick? I'd also remind you that it was me that came back to get you away from the danger of the multitude of missiles we faced when our first plan to get into the castle went so badly wrong."

Vixen walked up to Tumbletick and put her arm around him. He could feel the curves of her body uncomfortably close. It was a completely different feeling to the one he had had when she had stood so close to him at the top of 'The Hind's Head Brewery' and they had made the map together. He found that he was holding onto his resentment of her very deeply and perhaps did not want to let it go as a way of protecting himself from the deeper grief of the loss of his friend.

"I will do anything I can to keep you alive Tumbletick. You were the defender of the Realm of Umiat for a decade, although you knew it not. As such I will defend you from all that could be a threat. Be it with skill at arms or knowledge or intrigue. My honour demands it and I swear that I shall do so on my God given soul."

"Well said Vixen," Egremont commented. "With that sorted out, if you would excuse me there may be very little opportunity left for me to find some revenge for the loss of Lord Jackson."

The wolfhound turned and with an uncharacteristic bark of excitement he leapt down to the amphitheatre floor and careered after the last of the monks who were flowing onto the boulevard.

"Come on Tumbletick, let's go and see how the battle goes. Eblis should be quite a sight assaulting the castle," said Vixen.

She jumped lightly to the arena. Tumbletick found that the height of the wall was a little intimidating for a man of his stature, so he lowered himself down the wall and held onto the ledge for a while before dropping.

Eblis was in a rage. His small mind was finding it difficult to understand why he was not being rewarded with his favoured treasures. He had done well in the arena by destroying all that was put in front of him. The ten monks ahead were running fast but when Eblis slowed down they did too. Looking over their shoulders at first, some might even fully turn around, walking backwards and then sway the buckets in wide arcs holding them with two hands. The aroma of the contents was driving Eblis on, he looked up. In front of him at the end of the wide straight road they had been following there was a large building. It was nearly night. Perhaps this was going to be his new home. A resting place as a final reward for so many battles to the death? The monks in front of him started shouting, drawing his attention back to them. He looked down and slipped out his tongue in a brief movement, tasting the air. Tantalised by the promises of raw meat and encouraged by the yelling men, the demon put on a turn of pace, determined to get some of the contents of the buckets.

The monks seeing Eblis come charging towards them, turned and ran full tilt towards the castle. They could hear cries of alarm ringing out from the battlements, more fearsome than the shouts that had been raised during the previous battle at the gates. It was now very much murky in the twilight and the long shadows of the massive merchants houses to the west reached out and covered many of the monks and Eblis' bulk. The odd arrow began to fly from the walls and arrow slits of the fortress. All ten of the monks ran as fast as they could now. It was imperative that none of them fall and spill the contents of their bucket as a distraction for Eblis. Should one of them get hit by a missile a companion would have to stop and take their bucket as well. Unencumbered by anything except their putrid pails the monks were fast and confusing targets. Fifty yards to go and the missiles were thickening. Crossbow bolts joined the flurry of arrows. A monk sunk to his knees when a bolt landed solidly in his guts. Despite the pain he still took care to place the pail carefully on the flagstones of the piazza in front of the castle. Another harlequinned hero ran to his side and snatched away the container as the wounded man slumped to his side, clutching the sunken shaft and moaned in pain and regret that he had failed in his mission and so he faced death. He though it would be from the fatal wound in his stomach but it was Eblis who scooped him up from the floor and quickly ended his life by gnawing off his head to suck the pumping blood from the torso.

The nine remaining monks called and hollered at Eblis to end his snack. The demon dropped the body after only a couple of gulps and he sped off again after the men.

They were close now, only a few more yards and the lobbing could begin. Only one of their number had been taken out and that had to be considered a success. Now they had to rely on the strength that the overdose of leaf had given them. In a line, the nine faced the wall and the gate of the castle and swung with all their might. Arrows and bolts were close and grazed a couple. Eblis was drawing near and roared as he saw his rewards arcing high into the night sky and over the battlements and into the courtyard behind the walls. Eight monks whooped with joy and began scattering in all directions, the lucky ninth took his second projectile and lobbed it just as high as his first towards the castle walls.

"Eblis, fetch!", he roared. With a giggle he too was running away from the fortress before the bucket had reached the zenith of its flight.

Guards on the battlements looked up and backwards following the arc of the objects. They were expecting them to be crude incendiary devices but found themselves surprised when they landed with only a slight thumping noise and began oozing on the floor. A final object came over the wall and one upturned face got splattered with some congealed liquid. The man smeared it away with the back of his hand uncertain as to what the substance was. He was not too concerned though as now all attention and alarm was focussed on the abomination that was clawing and roaring and hacking away at the gates with massive crablike claws and with a bloodlust in its reptilian eyes.

Chorus Three

Fenton's fishing had gone well. Obviously the lures aboard 'The Brazen Manticore' were well chosen ones for the coastal waters of Rampart. He had five large fish of about ten pounds each. He did not know what they were called but he felt certain that Mr. Battfin would and that his first mate would know how to skin, gut and cook them. Despite not knowing their name he knew they were heavy, healthy looking and probably delicious so he sealed them up in an air tight pottery container he had found in the galley. It had a lead seal on it that would help keep the meat as fresh as possible and he felt happy that it would represent a change in diet for his companions as he put the fish safely away.

"Time for another pleasant night," thought Fenton.

He selected a couple of bottles of ale from the supplies and went to sit and watch the sunset. The ale was dark brown, with hints of caramel and a strong, hoppy finish. Fenton smacked his lips in delight after the first taste, it was a perfect ale for him. He already loved whiskey from the Noatak region and he suspected strongly that the hops for this beer probably came from the higher altitudes of the foothills from the northwest of Umiat. He took out his pipe and removed a small pocket knife from the inside of his jacket. Releasing the small silver steel blade from its casing he scraped away a thin layer of burnt wood from the inside of the pipe bowl. Maintenance was essential in a good pipe. If the wood on the inside was too thickly charred then small holes in the carbonated areas could allow in too much air during smoking and the tobacco would burn too hot. There was even risk of the pipe bowl splitting if it got too hot during a particularly lengthy burn. Fenton finished the scraping and tapped the upturned bowl right into the palm of his hand so the scrapings could be tossed overboard and into the breeze. He then rubbed the outside of the deep coloured cherry red wood on the sides of his nose. The oils from his skin polished the bowl and added to its deep and reflective shine.

Satisfied with the ritual Fenton added some 'Viking Mango' tobacco to the bowl and lightly compacted it with his thumb. Too tight and the drawing of air through the lit tobacco would be a chore, laboured and the tobacco was likely to go out too easily. Too lightly packed in and the leaf was likely to burn too fast, especially in the open air conditions of a boat at sea where the winds would fan the flames easily. He took out his special pipe matches, long and made from cedar wood. These were extremely expensive and he took care to strike the match precisely and shield it from the wind. The match was well made for the money and the cedar wood would not give off any tainting aromas to mask the flavour of the 'Viking Mango'. He lit the top layer of the tobacco and let it burn for only a short while, giving only a couple of brief tugs with his lungs. The tobacco on top was burnt now and would form a lid of charred leaf to protect the burning below from the sea breeze. He lit a second match and drew the flame deeply down into the body of the leaf with some really deep inhalations. Fenton enjoyed a long smoke, along with several more ales than he had originally expected to drink. There was something so very pleasant about a good quality blended and aromatic tobacco combined with the natural flavours of the beer. He stayed up late contemplating the stars in the ink black sky and imagined himself the most content man in the world.

Chapter four

Eblis did not just focus his massive rage and bulk upon the gates. When guards started shooting bolts and arrows into his fleshy form from the castle walls the demon would swipe with the back of his claw at the irritating foes. Chunks of granite snapped off the battlements, the merlons in particular came crashing down like knocked out teeth, some falling inside the castle perimeter causing havoc for the defenders inside as they dodged the huge chunks that earlier had been there to defend them. The gates did not put up much resistance either, despite their bulk and reinforcement from behind, the weight, strength and continued frenzy of Eblis meant they bowed and splintered and soon looked extremely vulnerable. Cries of panic could be heard rising from within the depths of the fortress. The horde of gathered monks kept at a safe distance but grew hopeful of a break through and started chewing more leaf to bolster their bravado. Eblis was in a frantic rage now and his unearthly screams only added to the terror of those defenders who could not see the beast. The demon was no longer concerned with the pleasures of gladiators with the bones removed; now he only wanted to get at the men that were attacking him with missiles. Eblis kicked at the gates with his strong stubby legs and started pulling deliberately at the walls around the entrance. Huge slabs started peeling away, buckling as the sheets of stone were removed like a demolished tower. The walls although hugely heavy were not a match for a demon. Eblis might have looked soft and flabby everywhere but his shell like claws but he was immensely strong and the bits of stone that did land on him merely fell away not harming at all.

The gates suddenly gave way to a back handed swipe of one of the huge claws. With the wall weakened from the sustained onslaught and the gates now destroyed the battlement that had been above them collapsed too in a deafening roar of rubble and screaming defenders. The sound was so loud combined with the rage of Eblis that defenders were seen covering their ears as the demon clambered over the debris and into the castle to attack a row of helmeted guards with pikes. A vast swipe with a claw caught the weapons, knocking several out of the grasp of the brigands. Suddenly Eblis was not the only concern of the terrified inhabitants, swarms of the Monks of Delight came running and leaping through the breach, went around Eblis and headed off into the courtyards and passages of the castle.

Other defenders appeared from towers, doorways of buildings and from around corners to counter the attack and many melees ensued. Egremont found himself behind a charging Mr. Battfin and soon saw the pirate claim his first kill. The first mate of 'The Ardent Panda' slashed his cutlass across the stomach of an attacking wretch with a devastating back handed swipe as he ran passed, despatching the assailant as their own weapon was still raised in the air in a slow and clumsy move.

Egremont nodded in approval and went to find his own adversary for one to one combat. Mr. Battfin ran on with his two cutlasses and engaged against two warriors armed with swords and shields. Showering blows with rapid sweeps the two men held off the raining attacks with their shields barely having the opportunity to find time or room to offer counter blows. Mr. Battfin with a deft flick of a powerful wrist lifted his cutlass so fast that the weaker of the two enemies lost his grip on his sword and saw it fly several yards away. Grasping his shield with two hands he cowered behind the defensive armour then found his knees hacked at deeply by the pirate's blade in a move that then countered a thrust from the other opponent with a parry. The wounded man stumbled back and fell, writhing in pain, to then be stabbed through the throat by Campbell the Weasel who suddenly appeared. The scraggly bearded thief looked for some thanks from the pirate but found none.

"That's one to me," said Campbell.

"There's no way I'm getting into a competition with you, you assassin," replied Mr. Battfin, never once removing his eyes from the warrior in front of him. "My kills are face to face. Now leave me be, I'll be fine."

Mr. Battfin gave the slightest of smiles which the observant Campbell picked up. The thief disappeared as quickly as he had arrived into the shadows to rid the world of other brigands though none would ever see him arrive or depart. Mr. Battfin's remaining prey was more proficient and was returning several clashing blows as the fight went on. The pirate realised that something less orthodox might be needed so when the attacking move was right he fell to one knee and crossed his cutlasses above his head and caught the blow in the intersection of the two blades.

Then moving one of his swords to the horizontal to hold the opponent's weapon aloft he hacked his remaining cutlass into the exposed right flank of his enemy, digging deep enough to cause a fatal blow.

All around the sounds of battle and dying rose into the night, it coughed and screamed and clashed and panicked in a cacophony of death. The Monks of Delight with Eblis as a major distraction were able to make good headway in the fight.

Seton Rax, Beran and Nazar Grant were fighting as a unit. They made a strange trio of barbarian, paladin in full plate armour and a warrior priest. Many would have expected them to be individual warriors on the field looking for honourable one on one combat but they fought together, protecting each other and dealing out death, Seton and Beran with blades, cutting and stabbing, Nazar Grant smashing and crushing with his iron mace. The barbarian was swift and unencumbered, moving with great fluidity to deflect a blow or make a kill. Beran was slower in full plate but was ruthless and determined. He would take blows on his armour from attacker's weapons without much concern, concentrating on quick retaliation when a combatant left an opening. Nazar Grant stayed slightly behind the imposing Beran acting as a guardian, due to the knight's visor causing certain blind spots. Nazar would take on assaults from the flanks with a grudging strength and religious prayers of forgiveness on his lips as he killed.

Is-Is had clambered up a broken wall caused by the rage of Eblis and then leapt onto the battlements. Men there were armed with bows and long knives. Is-Is pulled out two kukris and started to move along the wall with stealth. Archers were picking off monks within the compound or firing upon Eblis who was still causing devastation. Is-Is' appearance on the battlements had meant an instant and unseen death for the man who was first in line. When his body fell the focus of the longbow-men turned on the huge hare with the crooked knives. An archer turned to aim along the wall, in the darkness the grey hare in chain mail flittered like the most shadowy of ghosts but was still a large and relatively easy target. An arrow was already notched and the man pulled on the bowstring and curved the longbow into bent tension. Is-Is' eyes narrowed and focused purely on the man's fingers, the hare stood still. A twitch in the knuckles and Is-Is stepped swiftly back and to his left and pressed against the ramparts. The arrow shot by a foot wide of the hare's broad chest. The man swore, unbelieving as to the assailants speed. Quickly he reached over his shoulder for another arrow in the quiver on his back but he never found it. Is-Is was already at his side and a kukri was stabbed deep into the armpit that was revealed by the reach for the arrow. Metal found the heart of the archer and the body slumped to the edge of the parapet and then rolled into the air for the short drop to the enclosure below. Four other archers, surprised to see their comrade fall all turned and aimed at the warrior responsible for his death. The hare's ears flicked back and then he jumped high into the air and towards them as two fired. Those arrows missed but the third archer managed to get a shot at a better angle and anticipated a moving target. The feathered shaft flew straight and true towards Is-Is' head. The hare tightly shut his eyes in anticipation of the pain and turned his head slightly away from the flight. He felt the arrow pass right through his right ear. Another gold ring needed. Landing between the archers, Is-Is stabbed backwards with a kukri in each hand mortally wounding two men. He then pulled his right paw forward with pace and punched the fourth archer, who still had his arrow notched, full in the face with his fist wrapped around the hilt of the dripping kukri. The archer flew back a couple of yards and found there was no battlement to break his fall, just air above the ensuing battle below. He fell, landing badly among some Monks of Delight, who laughing set about hacking at his broken body.

The remaining archer was the one who had scored the lucky hit on Is-Is, bringing the number of holes to thirteen in his large right ear. Is-Is brought his face right up to the man's own terrified visage. The hare blinked away the water in his eyes that swelled due to the stinging pain. He stared the man directly in the eyes and saw a deep fear in the face of what was undoubtedly a prisoner who once thought he was tough. Is-Is snorted out a spit of air from his nose and the man turned and ran along the parapet, knocking another archer off further along. Is-Is sheathed his kukris and selected a throwing knife. A flip of the wrist followed and the knife spun only once in the air with a juggler's precision. Is-Is caught it in the grip he needed and then threw it over arm after the fleeing man. The knife tumbled as its broad and heavy blade sought its target. The weapon sunk through the man's thin leather armour and into his liver. He fell flat and twitched a bit before dying. Is-Is approached the fallen form and tugged out the knife.

Eight other archers remained on the battlements. Another warrior appeared atop the rampart on the other side of the eight enemies. He had flame red hair and a warhammer in each hand.

"I'll meet you in the middle!" Y'Bor Kaz yelled to Is-Is.

With that yell, Is-Is and Y'Bor went to work on the lightly armed and armoured men. A couple tried to let loose an arrow or counter with a long knife but the blades and fists of Is-Is and the thumping metal hammers of Y'Bor had the archers dead in a few violent seconds. With the last archer nullified Is-Is and Y'Bor clasped each other in victory then turned to survey the scenes of carnage beneath them in the fortresses enclosed courtyard.

With the threat of sniping removed from this section of the wall the horde of harlequinned monks moved even more freely around the grounds of the castle.

Eblis was still raging in the centre of the main courtyard, keeping a large group of brave defenders occupied in a forlorn hope of victory. Y'Bor Kaz gazed with loving admiration towards his favoured demon pet as the beast scooped up another unfortunate and crunched off a screaming head, blood spilling from the creature's maw, dark in the now night filled sky lit only by a dull yellow moon.

Suddenly Eblis dropped the remains of his victim and simply turned around away from the defenders. The creature pulled its bulk along lethargically with his two huge claws and pushed half-heartedly with his short legs so that he was leaning forward, taking a lot of his weight on his gut. Tired and now well fed, the beast headed off for the only home it knew, its pit beneath the arena, in the bowels of the amphitheatre.

Y'Bor and Is-Is turned to look over the battlements and view the shambling beast drag his way along the boulevard and to the south. They could just make out the forms of Vixen and Tumbletick moving away to skirt the side of some large merchant house. Eblis paid them no heed and continued heaving himself along.

Egremont appeared upon the wall panting heavily.

"See you two have found a safe place to survey the battle."

"We have been mightily engaged as well Master Wolfhound," replied Y'Bor.

"Well there seems to be a few fellows who fell foul of you here. Is-Is you seem to need a new ear-ring," laughed Egremont, flushed with the excitement of victory.

Below the castle was well in the hands of the monks. A few remnants of troops who been defending against Eblis were now surrounded and had thrown down their weapons to the monks in the hope of capture and a chance in the arena. Torches were being lit now and held aloft rather than weapons and searches carried out of the fortress.

"Looks as if it is just the great tower to take now," commented Y'Bor.

"A Keep keeping some secrets," mused Egremont.

"Well, keeping the leader of this rabble safe for a while. He'll be in there with a hand picked bunch of his favourites, some body guards and keeping final dominion of the city away from Krell," replied Y'Bor.

"And unfortunately, no longer a way for us to disappear down through the catacombs and passages. Still, we are where we are. One fortified tower to take and then free to explore other options with your added strength Y'Bor."

"Well now we are in I figure we either smoke them out or just besiege them into surrender. There's no real reason to risk anything else. The castle is taken Master Wolfhound and you are released from your bond," pronounced Y'Bor. "Well better go and find Krell and shake his hand. I'm not one for big goodbyes. Leave them while they want you to stay my father always told me."

Y'Bor walked off along the battlement and down some wooden stairs built on the inside of the wall and looked for Krell.

Egremont and Is-Is followed but made their way to the large throng of men securing the prisoners they had captured. Faces of joy and dejection reversed from the battle that had taken place a few days earlier.

They found Mr. Battfin and Campbell. The pirate was sharpening a blade on a whetstone in long deliberate strokes. Campbell was hunched down, leaning against a wall of a small stone building. The thief had a bad cut along his left cheek.

"What happened?" asked Egremont with a nod towards the wound.

"Miscreant caught me with the tip of his sword. Looks like my looks are ruined," Campbell replied morosely.

"I'm sure it will heal just fine," said Mr. Battfin not looking up from his cutlass maintenance.

"Have you seen Seton Rax and company?" asked Egremont.

"They are over by the keep with a bunch of monks," Campbell replied. "Trying to find a way in. The main door is on the second floor with a single set of steep stone steps up to it. They drop large rocks on you if you try and climb them to knock to say 'Hello'."

"Well Y'Bor is looking for Krell now to hand over responsibility of leadership for the Monks of Delight. Our part of the bargain is concluded and Y'Bor has released us from our oath. Unfortunately the way that we had intended to take is blocked to us. Y'Bor has chosen that he wishes to come with us as a free man who can leave the Old City at any time," said Egremont. "However we now need to formulate a plan to be able to contact Fenton. By this time tomorrow he is going to be relatively concerned as we will not be in the cave to meet him."

"We could sail a boat from Tetterton and meet him, I know where the cave is," suggested Mr. Battfin.

"But that will take, what? Four days," said Campbell. "I wouldn't want to wait alone worried for that long. No guarantee he'll still be there after that length of time either."

"Fine," replied the swarthy pirate. "You any good with that bow you carry around on your back Is-Is? I've never seen you fire the thing."

Is-Is bit his lip and tilted his head in reply, looking directly at the pirate with a serious scowl.

"Well then," said Mr. Battfin, drawing the whetstone very slowly along the now razor sharp blade, all notches removed. "Seems to me that we have to travel south from the city of Rampart, cross country, climb the battlement that surrounds the isle and fire a message to Fenton utilising the extremely brilliant archery skills of Is-Is. Fenton will be anchored quite close to the cave no doubt."

"Excellent," replied Egremont. "Seems a better plan than anything I could have come up with at short notice. We'll leave as soon as we've got everyone together. Head south, travel through the night, hope to see Fenton's vessel and put in the message that we fire to him that he should sail back to Tetterton and pick us up there. Seems like this whole thing has been a bit of a debacle really. If you see it only as trying to disappear from anyone who may have been watching us. We needed to get Campbell and that was a real imperative. But and we must remember this, I think we came here for reasons that perhaps I could not foresee. We've managed to pick up a few other members of the party who may prove to be extremely useful. Now the other option that would have been available to us, that I was thinking of, was heading south, finding Fenton's vessel, throwing all our kit into the sea and diving in after it. But seeing as the sea cliffs are particularly tall around these parts, I think shooting a message down to Fenton to come and pick us up in Tetterton is a much better idea, thank you Mr. Battfin and I'm glad I didn't voice my idea out loud."

Chorus four

awn again, all alone aboard 'The Brazen Manticore'. A long stretch, the rhythms of the sea. Fenton continued to find himself feeling happy. Solitude out here felt fine. The reassuring sounds, mellifluous to his mind. The lapping of the light waves on the hull, the call of a circling sea bird, the yielding creak of wooden boards.

Fenton knew that low tide was a little time off but he was keen to see his shipmates again. So he breakfasted and dressed quickly and went to check on the small launch. It was a neat vessel with a single mast that could be raised or lowered, ideal for entering a cave. With no wind present it had two oars for rowing and enough bench space to sit ten comfortably. 'Plenty of space,' thought Fenton, rubbing his chin on his handsome face. He looked over board at the movement of the sea and judged that low tide would be in about an hour.

He spent some time tidying 'The Brazen Manticore' and preparing for his expected guests. Then he packed together some food and drink to place in the launch. 'Supplies for my companions after their ordeals in the passageways,' he thought. Carefully he then lowered the launch over the side and down onto the surface of the sea. He leapt over the bulwarks of the ship and landed lightly in the punt. 'No point putting up the sail. I'll only have to lower it again,' perused Percy. He undid the knots holding the smaller vessel in place with the deft fingers of a mariner. Then he lifted the oars and slotted them into the rowlocks and leant back into a long, strong rowing technique.

Fenton turned around to look at the massive cliffs above him. The sea might be relatively calm at the moment but a mistake upon entry to the cave could see the small boat smashed against the sheer granite walls of Rampart or crushed against the roof of the tunnel to the cave.

With just Fenton in the boat, piloting his way into that tunnel would be tricky but he felt sure he had the rowing skill. He would have to enter with a reverse technique with the oars so he could be moving facing forward. Less power that way but certainly more vision was required to navigate this course. He turned round on the bench to face the prow.

The tunnel to the cavern was not wide, maybe five yards and when the tide was at its lowest you would get a maximum of a yard and a half of head room. Through this orifice, smugglers had for years brought in goods and services to the residents of the Old City. With no taxation on Rampart the authorities were fundamentally free from traditional smuggling crime but if an occupant of the largest prison in the realms of Umiat and Kenai wanted a particular luxury and could pay for it, then another market place existed on a small and slimy beach, bathed in a sparkling blue light from the rays of the sun refracted through the top layers of the sea and into a cave.

Fenton squinted and got ready to time his run. He wanted as much time as possible in the cave in case his fellow adventurers had not made it there for the appointed time. He judged that in a couple of minutes he would be able to make his move. He waited, bobbing on the surface, looking up at the cliffs. They must have been two hundred and fifty yards tall here. Fenton felt the weight of all that rock pushing down into the sea and deep beneath the waves upon which he floated. 'Slightly unnatural for a sailor to willingly enclose himself up in so much rock,' he thought. Then the time was right, he rowed on, with the technically backwards stroke so he could see all before him. The pitching of the prow became exaggerated the closer he got to the cliff as the waves became extremely choppy. He pushed on, picking up some speed and got ready to make the final adjustments for entry. Bouncing along now and feeling the current move he aimed to the left of the tunnel ahead of him then pushed hard and rapidly on the oars. The little launch sped on, Percy was proficient and he judged he would make the entrance. He heaved on the oars, pulling them into the launch and then slammed them onto the floor of the skiff. Then as the prow dipped into the tunnel he flung himself backwards so as to not crash his head on the roof. The boat was halfway in but the lateral current would pull it back out unless Percy used an old trick. He swiftly swivelled around on his back so his head now faced the prow and his feet towards the stern then he thrust up his arms and his legs. Lying on a small bench, his feet and hands connected with the granite roof of the half submerged passage, Percy Fenton proceeded to crawl along the rook and pulled the boat with him along the tunnel towards the sea cave and hopefully a rendezvous with his companions.

Chapter Five

It was nearly midnight when nine hardened looking adventurers and a small, grotty looking, hairy man stood outside the only gatehouse in the wall around the Old City and knocked loudly.

"The small door is open," came a loud shout in reply. "Enter one at a time and have your password ready to recite when you are asked. Failure to do so will be considered an escape attempt and you will be shot. There are several crossbows aimed at you at this very instant and will be continued to be aimed at you until credentials are confirmed. Also be prepared to be questioned further on any distinguishing features or marks if we can't see them."

The sound of the first portcullis raising came and Egremont pulled open the door. Is-Is, Mr. Battfin, Seton Rax and Beran were keeping a close eye out for any potential attack while they were at this vulnerable moment of thinking they were safe from the potential threats of the Old City. While the brigands of the castle had been thwarted many were particularly conscious of the monsters that roamed and vagrant prisoners who were not affiliated to any gang.

Egremont entered into the dark gatehouse which smelled damp and musty. The portcullis dropped behind him then he heard a noise of metal twisting on metal and a beam of light swung down from the heights of the gatehouse hall and found him in a spotlight. 'Obviously clever use of mirrors,' thought Egremont.

"What is your password?" came a gruff voice.

"Party Twenty Six slash Two slash Aardvark Feathers," he replied.

Egremont's acute hearing picked up some grumbling and turning of a page in the records that would have been transferred to the gatehouse.

"What is your name?" slightly less gruff.

"Egremont, the Lord Seau du Duvet."

"Fine. You are free to go through the next door then."

The second portcullis guarding the thick wooden gate to the city of Rampart started to rise. Another beam of light swung down from high above and focused on the handle to another small personnel door within the main sturdy entrance.

Egremont walked to it and through and found himself in the nearly deserted central square. A few of the pubs around the outside were still serving clients and a couple of scampering forms hustled across the flagstones of the piazza but ultimately there were few people about to mark the emergence of the noble wolfhound. The portcullis crashed back down behind him and Egremont thought about how long a process this might be as each member of the party was interrogated.

Y'Bor Kaz entered next after the first portcullis was high enough to allow entry.

"Password?" It was a resigned question from a man who had suddenly found that he had some unexpected work to do at the hour of midnight.

"Party Three, slash Fourteen, slash Bellomancer," Y'Bor was controlled and steady in his response. There was a long pause as the investigating guard had to turn back through pages and pages and finally go and find another book with records from years back. Y'Bor ground his foot into the dirt beneath his feet as he waited.

"Name?" the disembodied voice rang out finally.

"Y'Bor Kaz"

A moment of silence again as the guard conducting the check read the records deep in the new book.

"Lift up your top and turn so we can look at the tattoo on your back," came a command eventually.

"It's been added to a bit," shouted Y'Bor revealing an intricate pattern of thick black lines and curves.

"You're fine, off you go then," came the guard's voice and the portcullis to the outside world began its grudging ascent again.

Y'Bor did as he was told and made his way to the little door that Egremont had thoughtfully shut behind him. Y'Bor took a deep breath as he opened it, stepped through and left the Old City forever and found himself standing by an imperious looking wolfhound who was looking lonely.

"Well Master Wolfhound, I enter another chapter of my life."

"And an important one. A fool's quest to retrieve an object of no powers whatsoever except those of symbolism and faith."

"That, Master Wolfhound, would appear to be the case. But, as we both know, such symbolism and faith is absolutely the most important aspects of anything that has true power."

"Indeed we do Y'Bor Kaz. Indeed we do," Egremont paused then quickly shut the door that Y'Bor had left open. He then turned to face the warrior beside him with an intent look in his eye and a rapid pace to his voice. "Listen carefully and quickly before the next person arrives. Tumbletick is fundamentally the keeper of the Umiat Stone for these past ten years. He knew not that he was guarding it from terrible foes but guard it he did. He must be kept safe at all times not only as a reward for what he has done but for who he is and what reward he deserves. He is the son of Sir Bartle Rourke. The followers of Ahriman would give anything to kill him as revenge for their master's death. Sir Bartle bested him in single combat during the Ahrioch Wars. I was beside him when with a wonderful upper cut he chopped the Demonologist in half and then decapitated him. The Ahrioch Horde would dearly love to settle that with a piece of retribution. They failed when they stole the Umiat Stone as Is-Is and I could defend him. We must retrieve the stone and present it again to Princes Annabella Blaise and have Tumbletick claim her hand in marriage as reward."

Y'Bor looked a little aghast.

"Egremont, I swear I will do all I can to make this happen. Tumbletick is my sworn friend and I will be another protector of him."

The door opened behind them and Vixen stepped through. The trio waited in silence as next Tumbletick, then Campbell the Weasel, then Nazar Grant came through. There was a longer wait than normal for Seton Rax and Beran. Apparently a debate had taken place between the four remaining members about who should go next as it meant eventually someone would be left behind alone and could be vulnerable to attack from any watching cutthroats or monsters. Is-Is had been particularly vociferous in arguing his case the barbarian and the paladin informed just as Mr. Battfin stormed through as the penultimate adventurer.

Is-Is stepped into the gatehouse and faced the beam of light and the questioning gatekeeper.

"Password?" he asked from the darkness. Is-Is was about to speak when the voice continued. "Oh forget it. We remember you. Very distinctive. On your way Master Hare."

The party of ten adventurers hurried through the night filled streets of Rampart. The plan was to get to the south of the island as soon as they could and have a look to see if any boats were anchored near to the Smuggler's Cave. Confirmation that it was Percy by Egremont or

Is-Is with their superior eyesight would result in a message being shot into the deck of the boat by Is-Is. They would then make their way to Tetterton and meet Percy there. Supplies could then be restocked and any other necessities purchased.

A bevy of drunks staggering the streets were startled by the swift moving group, thinking it a patrol they decided to push right through the middle of the group in an act of universal bravado. As the group ignored them and continued on their march the drunks brazenly slung insults after them as they passed. When the seven drunken men realised it was not a patrol the taunts became more callous and threat filled. Luck was with them, the group was a lot more dangerous than any patrol. Had they been in a position where they had wanted to interact and engage with some bacchanalian thugs the drunks would have come off a lot worse than their alcoholic fuelled thoughts of prowess would have suggested.

The ten walked hard and fast straight to the main gatehouse on the west side of the city. When they got there they found that six guards were standing on duty in the entrance. More were housed in the guardrooms to the left and right of the gate. It would appear that news of the Ahrioch Horde being abroad and the attack in Umiat must be well known now.

"Good evening sir," said the Sergeant at Arms. "And what can we do for you at this time of night?" The guard was civil but alert and fully armed.

"We wish to leave Rampart and head for Tetterton," Egremont replied.

"I'm sorry sir but the city is now closed during the hours of darkness. There are notices all over the city. Have been for some time sir."

"Ah, I'm afraid that we have not read them. We have been … otherwise engaged in a place where perhaps notices are not posted."

"I understand sir," said the guard perfectly politely. "Then let me enlighten you."

Four more guards came out of each guard house to ensure that the numbers were in their favour.

"There have been a few incidents recently which have meant security has had to be tightened," the sergeant said. "Firstly it appears that the Ahrioch Horde is openly operating again and has instigated a commando raid on Umiat. Secondly there have been reports of more wolves in the land of Rampart than would usually be about. Our sources reveal that at least two dozen entered via Tetterton about a week ago. Now while Rampart is strictly neutral in all these matters we do understand that when there are wolves about tensions can become an issue with other guests of the island and the afore said mentioned wolves. Thirdly an innocent farmer has been found murdered just off the main track to the west. As such the city is closed during the hours of darkness as I have already said. The notices give a little more detail and dawn is about seven hours away sir, so if you don't mind moving along."

"I wonder if perhaps there could be any way to persuade you to allow an innocent party to leave who are anxious to get to Tetterton?" Egremont said with a slightly nervous grin.

"Those are just the kind of people that we don't want to leave sir. It's always the innocent and the anxious. The gates are closed. There are a few boarding houses and hostels nearby where you may be able to find lodging. Or you are welcome to hunker up against the walls of the city with some constant attention from my men to keep you company through the darkest hours."

"I think that perhaps we will seek out some accommodation Sergeant. Thank you for your time and the information," Egremont said.

Campbell the Weasel led the way to a tavern close to the city walls where he felt sure they would find the landlady still awake and willing to provide some hot food and some beds. The building was a three story affair deep in the tight and winding back streets of Rampart. Lights were still burning brightly at many of its windows and two extremely large men flanked the entrance to the establishment. A small and incredibly well painted sign hung above the door proclaiming it to be called 'The Last Dove'.

"Let me give you some 'Last Dove' advice," said Campbell standing still in front of the group. "This is not the kind of place where it is likely to be quiet at night but we will still be guaranteed a bed."

He laughed then strode quickly through the two doormen who both merely nodded and then said 'Evening Mr. Campbell'.

Vixen tutted and followed first, leading the rest who found Campbell paying a young lady who sat behind a small counter. She passed out five keys to him and a coquettish glare.

"You pay by the hour at this institution," said Campbell as he handed out the keys. "Two to a room. We've got them until an hour after dawn. I'll come and make sure you are all awake before we have to leave. You'll find that all the rooms are identical and extremely comfortable. If you want to there is a bar through that red curtain to your left."

No one took up the offer of a drink although both Seton Rax and Y'Bor did try to have a glance through a gap in the curtains. They selected room mates and made their way to the accommodation on the upper levels which was exactly as Campbell had described. Each room had a very large double bed and surprising, right next to it a very deep and wide bath. Vixen suddenly insisted on sleeping alone despite the quick invite from Campbell that she bunk up with him. Therefore Tumbletick found himself sharing with Egremont and Is-Is, which suited him fine. Seton and Beran took the room next door. Nazar Grant and Y'Bor Kaz were across the corridor. Mr. Battfin found that Campbell was thrust in with him upstairs and Vixen took the room which was furthest away from everyone else.

The building felt safe with so many people coming and going and the companions all relatively close by. Tumbletick realised that he had not slept on anything as soft as this bed in his entire life and he fell into a deep and heavy sleep disturbed by no dreams or fears. Egremont curled up beside him but the bed was large enough that his bulk did not shift his little friend. Is-Is remained vigilant for most of the night, sitting in a large armchair, he even felt secure in 'The Last Dove' and caught about three hours of much needed sleep.

Tumbletick awoke to the strong paw of Is-Is rocking him awake and he heard Egremont and Campbell the Weasel talking in the open doorway. The sun was just risen and it was nearly time to depart.

They breakfasted at stalls around the main gatehouse that had sprung up with the sun, eating little honey seed cakes. Although the gatehouse was well manned with guards no questions were asked of the group as they left. They were now just seen as part of the throng that made their way in and out during the early hours.

It was decided that they would take the road west until they were out of sight of the city, hidden by one of the low rolling hills. Then they would turn left and head south. After all there was very little point about being overly overt in their movements. Despite the fact that a group of ten warriors, thieves and an ugly little man of no discernable value would draw attention from anyone who did see then tramping through the pastures and olive groves of the Rampart Plateau, they had decided to act as secretly as they could.

When Egremont felt that the time was right he turned to the south with no conversation. The road ahead was vacant and the city far behind. Chatting with Campbell he knew they had a good ten mile walk until they would come to the southern boundary wall atop the impregnable cliffs. For most travellers this would be considered a good distance to walk in a day. Egremont however encouraged them that they should do it by midday. The terrain was not challenging, light farmland mostly and olive groves were not that thick with gnarled trees. The only diversions that would have to me made would be if they were obviously going to walk through a cattle yard of a dairy farmer. Their packs were relatively light, Is-Is carrying the main burden of the tent that could be quickly erected and sleep six. Yes, Egremont felt confident that they could make the wall in four hours. Even Tumbletick could make that pace on the lush pastures.

They tramped on throughout the morning. Conversation was light and easy. Y'Bor Kaz seemed young and invigorated. Seton Rax, Beran and Nazar Grant spent the time bonding with the party, chatting about their past lives, asking questions and telling of how they had all been brought together by their mutual friend Garraday. They had been adventuring for different reasons and the magic user had known how to appeal to each of them. Seton Rax it turned out was a barbarian from the grass deserts to the very northwest of Umiat. Beyond the vast mountains of Schwatka, his homeland was mainly used by the indigenous tribes to follow and manage vast herds of Elk. His father had been a strongman in the local tribe. Seton Rax was the second son and was encouraged to travel and to test himself in the wider world. A barbarian of impeccable breeding and manners he thought of himself as a protector of the weak and a thrill seeker.

Nazar Grant was a holy man from the Isle of Aklavik to the east of Umiat. The isle was to the north of the Porcupine Gulf and was a place of refuge and training for his order. The Rose Cross were fighting men who also focused on the arts of healing. They were wonderful warriors and great healers who were sort out by all sorts of people to also provide spiritual care. Their God was secret unto them but the fundamentals of their religion were based around, respect, wisdom, chastity and protection and healing of the weak. Poverty was not a vow though and the order had grown immensely rich over the years. Nazar was late middle age now, an experienced veteran of many battles. Garraday had quested with him for twenty years, from when Nazar had taken his first holy vows and travelled in the search of opportunities to slay demons and to heal the sick. He openly admitted as they walked to being more cynical now he had been on his quest of understanding for so long. He was harsh on himself for being too quick to hit out during verbal battles and on being faster to find himself questioning the nature of life and its ultimate purpose.

Beran was a paladin from Ve'Tath. He was a member of a rich dynastic family that had paid for his training in the military wing of the Church of Umiat. It transpired that Garraday had saved his soul when he had had un-virtuous thoughts about a lady in waiting at the Court of Rhyell. That had been many years ago too and for him the quests and adventures he found himself involved in had to be about forgetting that sin. If they could help him in that then their ultimate goal could be ignored. Questing for money with others was fine if the dangers involved helped him forget. If the quest he currently was embarked in had a pure and true calling and it could improve his possibility of noble standing at Court, then all the better. However, he had not been back to Court for over a decade and now Nazar Grant and Seton Rax were his main concerns as he considered them filial friends.

All three of them openly confessed though, that nowadays, if the truth was really told it had become about the money. Questing and a glamorous life was expensive, despite where your roots lay.

Chorus Five

Fenton found himself in the natural beauty of the Smuggler's Cave. The water here was clear due to a solid granite floor to the pool which formed at the end of the tunnel. The tunnel had run for about twenty yards. The pirate had found it relatively easy to push himself along its course. The roof was wet but not slimy as the sea never really touched it for any real length of time apart from at the very highest of high tides. Within the cavern itself light could make its way along the space of air that was left at low tide or refract and bounce its way in. Mixing with the strains of quartz in the rock and the blue light from the sea the atmosphere of the cavern tingled in an azure and golden haze. There were no stalactites or stalagmites present in the roughly hewn cave. An area sloped into the water where generations of traders had placed their craft. Here in the gap between high and low tides, algaes and slimes had made a grasp at colonisation and they slopped on the rock and made it treacherous to step there. Previous smugglers had hammered in iron rings to the floor to aid mooring and Fenton stepped into one of these rings for extra stability. His toe of his boot within the ring, his heel wedged against its thick circumference. He tied the little boat to another metal hoop so he could then move with confidence to the dryer parts of the cavern.

Fenton was slightly disappointed that the rest of the party was not already here waiting for him as he had half expected they would have been. Today was the appointed day but the appointed time of the rendezvous had not been landed upon as morning or afternoon. Fenton thought that the gentle lapping of the waves and the extremely pleasing light made this a magically pleasant and peaceful place. He could see the passageway that led to the upper caverns and catacombs. Here it was as tall as a man and afforded easy access to the sea cave. He suspected that further up its course there would be moments of intense claustrophobia where you would have to crawl and squeeze yourself between roof, floor and walls of granite. You would feel the solidness of the island and the weight of that rock pressing down.

Then there would be the catacombs and the dead all around you in their horizontal alcoves. Skeletons and rotten corpses combined with the recently passed wrapped in their shrouds. Finally on your progress up you would travel through the dungeons of the castle. 'What would you find there?' Fenton thought to himself. 'Pits of forgotten prisoners? Chained wretches craving food, light and water? In what order? A torture chamber with is screams and instruments designed to retract information or just to provide pleasure for the torturer?'

Percy pulled out his pipe and tobacco and quickly lit a decent sized plug of 'Viking Mango'. He delighted in blowing thin streams of blue grey smoke into the shafts and shimmerings of light around him.

Fenton felt relaxed, he would sit out in the cavern and wait. He knew that between the tides he would be dry here and the boat was well fastened. He had placed some supplies in the launch so he could have some luncheon if the others did not arrive until later in the day. If they did not arrive today then he would make his way back to 'The Brazen Manticore' to spend the night. So he sat and smoked and waited, listening to the little waves and thinking of past adventures and the impending trip to Kenai where things would get much, much tougher he was sure.

Fenton soon found that boredom was creeping in at the edges of his mind. Natural beauty was one thing to look at for a while and smoking bowl after bowl of tobacco soon left his tongue burning and the ridges on the roof of his mouth swollen and raw.

"No more smoking," he said out loud and put away the still hot briar.

He made his way to the boat and picked a hunk of cheese out from the supplies and then made his way back to the permanently dry area of the cave. Pulling out a dagger from inside his jerkin he cut away the thick waxy skin that kept the bright yellow cheese fresh. He rolled the wax scrapings into a ball and threw it into the pool and watched it sink to the bottom in rhythmic rocking swoops. He stuck the cheese onto the dagger and nibbled at it in an effort to prolong the taste and to take up some time. 'Tide's rising,' he thought as his front teeth quickly sliced and mashed a morsel. 'Looks like I'm here for a little while longer.'

Fenton quickly turned his head to the right and towards the passageway. He swore he had heard something other than the background noise of the water and his own chewing. He stared and focussed on the entrance. The light was a little less bright now with the surface of the waves getting higher.

All of his senses disappeared apart from hearing and sight. He frowned and strained to hear. What was that noise? A low rumble? Some talking in the passageway? Footsteps? No nothing, his imagination wanting to hear his companions on their descent. He turned again to the cheese and took some larger bites on the diminishing chunk. The final mouthful was left stabbed on the blade so he placed his mouth over it in one go and dragged his teeth along the cold, sharp steel to pull it off. As he chewed he heard noises again but put it down to the air in the twenty yard tunnel booming slightly as it was replaced by the rising waters.

He finished the cheese, stood up and walked over to the passageway and peered into the absolute darkness. The booming was not coming from the tunnel to the open sea, there was a definite noise coming down the fissure from above. It was a low noise, of voices, men speaking in anger and concern. It was his friends making their way down as arranged. Fenton smiled and listened closely again. Yes definitely voices but unrecognisable, corrupted by the confined space into echoes and mutations of memorable sounds.

Fenton could now pick out the very faint glow of lantern light filtering down the tunnel and the voices were louder as the group moved more swiftly down the passage now that it was opening up in height and width.

"Hello," Fenton shouted up towards them. "It's okay, I'm here."

The sounds stopped and Fenton's smile turned to a frown at the strange response. He had half expected to see Tumbletick come bounding down to greet him but what did appear as he peered up was a heavy and hobnailed boot attached to a thick leg coated in chain mail.

Fenton backed away from the opening in concern. He did not recognise that boot. His friends would have replied in the instant of hearing his salutation. He still had the dagger in his hand and decided to draw out another from a secret sheath attached to the small of his back underneath the jerkin and his long coat.

As he backed further away into the cave he could now see the bottom half of a very large individual with a sword drawn nearly emerging from the passage. If he was quick he could make the boat, cut the mooring ropes and push off into the body of water in the cavern. To get out along the tunnel though he would have to wait for the tide to turn and that was several hours away from happening.

Chapter Six

E gremont led the way across the rolling plateau. The going was easy and the wolfhound was pushing at a strong yomping pace. Tumbletick tried to keep away from Vixen and talk to the other members of the group but he was always aware of her presence nearby, shadowing him closely. He tried to rebuke himself for holding a grudge and remember her solemn oath to protect him on her God given soul but he was finding it difficult to forgive what she had said about Lord Jackson.

They were passing through a large olive grove with gnarled and twisted ancient trees all around them. The ground was much harder under foot than the springy meadow lands that were becoming vibrant as the winter season was fading away. The bark on the trees was rough and scabbed with years of growth, the canopy of branches not far above their heads. Is-Is and Beran often having to walk a little stooped as the tallest members of the party.

Campbell the Weasel went from the pace of a forced march to a sprint and caught up with Egremont.

"We are being tracked by a group of individuals in black robes," he said.

"Really?" came the reply. "How many?"

"At least eight to my reckoning."

"Recommendations?"

"If there are more and we face a serious threat than a stance in this grove of trees might be a good idea. Might not."

Egremont stopped walking and drew his rapier, the others responded to the sign and became agitated, militarily aware and alert with their own weapons drawn. Tumbletick was bundled into the centre of the group with Vixen standing behind him with her sword drawn. Quick whispers were passed to all the group from Egremont and Campbell and the group fell silent watching all around.

Tumbletick saw Egremont using some sign language and Campbell shot off in the direction they had been heading while Is-Is immediately bounded back the way they had come.

Although the olive trees were widely spaced the grove was large and soon Tumbletick could not see the forms of Campbell or Is-Is. It became darker as the sun moved into hiding behind a cloud. Tumbletick thought back to the safety of his hut in the middle of the copse that had kept him hidden and safe for years and he suddenly wished he was back there.

They waited and listened and looked in all directions. Those dressed in black robes had been dealt with in a swift and ruthless manner before as they had attempted an ambush. 'Perhaps if wolves were tracking them now the outcome would be a similar one for them, perhaps not,' thought Tumbletick. Shadows took on extra significance as the sun came back out from behind the obscuring clouds and the group strained to pick out potential enemies hiding behind every tree.

Tumbletick started to count his heartbeats as a way to take his focus away from the fear he felt. They still waited, six of them in a circle around Vixen and Tumbletick. Beran lifted his sword arm and pointed with the blade off to the northwest. They looked and saw nothing, whatever the paladin believed had been there had flittered away.

Then something, sounds from the south and Campbell came running back in the peculiar gait he used for scouting, his head and body low to the ground but moving faster than most could run. The thin faced thief was serious in his report.

"Nothing ahead but they were very definitely behind."

"Okay," replied Egremont. "Two volunteers to run back towards where Is-Is is."

"Me," said Mr. Battfin immediately and started running north. He was followed in short order by Seton Rax, the barbarian nearly as fleet of foot as the pirate. They were soon out of sight and Tumbletick felt more vulnerable with the two experienced and capable warriors off in support of Is-Is.

"If an attack is to come it is likely to be now," whispered Vixen into Tumbletick's ear. "They will be watching for the moment we divide our forces. Easier to cope with seven than with ten, hey? Don't worry though; I'll take care of you."

"I'm sure that any Wolf attack that came now, would be startled by the response from Egremont alone," Tumbletick said through gritted teeth.

Still they waited, the small circle looking off in all directions, especially south as Egremont and Campbell now suspected it would come from the direction they least expected. No sound, no birdsong, it was quiet, still. The trees were still too, solid in their age, no breeze could move them. Y'Bor Kaz had his two warhammers at his side, ready to raise them into a battle ready stance. Campbell the Weasel was twitching, quickly looking left and right, focusing for a period forward then turning his whole body to face in another direction. Beran in his full plate armour looked like a statue, still within the encasing he waited with the patience of a knight used to night long vigils of prayer.

Egremont was sniffing the air, his senses more attuned than any in the group. If the wolves came from the direction of the wind he would detect them but he suspected they would not make that mistake, so perhaps the attack would come from the north or the west.

The solidly build Nazar Grant had a grimly set face. He was swinging his black metal mace slightly. Tumbletick thought of how the weapon was designed not to draw blood but had slight ridges in it, like low and long pyramids that had teeth cut into its iron design. Surely if it came into contact with a skull blood would flow immediately and in massive quantities. He nearly asked Nazar about the principles behind the cleric's code of combat when he felt Vixen move in closer behind him and put a hand on his shoulder.

"Here they come," she whispered to him.

Tumbletick jumped and looked anxiously around. In the distance to the north, through the twisted olive trees three familiar figures approached.

Is-Is was shaking his head but Mr. Battfin was first to speak.

"Definite signs behind but gone now."

"Then I suggest we move on with caution," said Egremont. "If they know we know they are there they may try another method."

"What? Another method other than an ambush," Vixen replied. "I doubt it. They are wolves."

Egremont took time to consider a response but decided that a taciturn moment might be best after the tension in the grove. He led the group on, back to the old pace of a strong yomp. After about five minutes they were fully clear of the large olive grove and back onto the rolling grass plains. All were particularly attentive for followers or places ahead where an attack might be launched against them. They skirted any other groves and avoided the scattered communities of farmers. The final miles fell in this manner until just before midday the walls atop the cliffs of Rampart could be seen, solid and grey, a military testimony to the isolationism of the City State. They approached at a slightly slackened speed looking for guards patrolling the walkways but none were in view.

To climb to the battlements one would usually have to gain access via a regularly spaced tower with guards inside. The current plan would probably not be quite so well understood or appreciated by any men paid to defend the island's walls so some stealth was required.

Tumbletick removed the rope from his pack that he had suggested bringing when they had been in Umiat and passed it to Mr. Battfin. The pirate first mate quickly fashioned a lasso at one end then coiled it in the manner of a proficient sailor, between his hand and elbow in quick rhythmic loops. He then threw the rope aiming to lasso one of the merlons that should have been designed to protect a standing man rather than as an anchor point for a pirate trying to gain a vantage point. He pulled the rope and found that he had failed in his first attempt. The rope fell to the floor and Mr. Battfin recoiled it again in his well rehearsed manner. The second attempt missed again and he cursed. Essentially he was throwing blind up and over the wall. Seton Rax took a few steps backwards away from the battlement and started giving advice on direction and height. Mr. Battfin took the time to make the lasso loop larger in case the merlons were particularly thick. On the fifth attempt the rope loop landed neatly over a chunky piece of stonework and the pirate pulled it tight. Mr. Battfin then took the opportunity as he had done the rope work to clamber up the wall and heaved himself over the precipice of blocked stone. Is-Is followed next and both gazed over the crenulated edge and down the vast drop to the Sea of Kaltag below.

From their vantage point they could make out that a ship was anchored about a mile further to the east. No other vessels were in sight. Mr. Battfin undid the lasso and handed the end to Is-Is. With the hare bearing his weight with the rope wrapped around his waist, Mr. Battfin abseiled back down the wall again with a couple of springy bounds and approached Egremont relaying the news. Is-Is threw down the rope and Tumbletick started to pack it away. The giant hare then leapt down to join the group, such a drop being easily manageable for the magnificent mammal. They walked away from the wall a little then proceeded east for what Egremont judged to be a mile and then Mr. Battfin repeated the rope throwing exercise. Seton Rax acting as a guide earlier this time, Mr. Battfin with the larger lasso loop made it on the second throw.

Mr. Battfin pulled himself up first, the benefit of being the one who made the cast and still held on to the end of the rope. Is-Is followed him again. Beneath them almost directly the ship was anchored about fifty yards from the base of the precipice. The two warriors only had to move along the rampart about ten yards to be directly in line with the boat. Is-Is un-slung his bow and checked the tautness of the string.

Mr. Battfin went to the inside edge of the battlement and nodded to the group.

"I think we may need to borrow a page from that diary of yours," said Egremont to Vixen.

The spy reached into her pack and tore out a blank page from the back of her journal then passed it with a pencil to Egremont. He wrote the simple message of 'Head back to Tetterton. Meet at Grobbling Smith. Arrive there tomorrow. Egremont.' He handed it to Campbell the Weasel, who rolled it up, placed it in an inside pocket and climbed up the wall. Handing the parchment to Is-Is, the hare gave him a quizzical look. Campbell reached into another hidden pocket and with aplomb pulled out a small ball of string. Cutting off several strands he then asked Is-Is for the arrow he wanted to use, wrapped the parchment around the arrow and tied it extremely securely.

"There's no-one aboard the ship," Mr. Battfin shouted down. "The Cap'n must be inside the cavern. The arrow's ready for shootin' though."

Is-Is stood tall and notched the arrow onto the string. He narrowed his eyes, judged the wind direction and pulled the bowstring extremely slowly and hard so the blended pieces of wood strained into a tight curve. Holding the bow in a dramatic pause he took the fundamentally easy shot. Directly down the arrow sped, no curve of flight, just straight and true and forceful. The knots that Campbell had tied held the parchment in place and the deck of the ship was a large target. The arrow struck the intended area and dug deep into the wood. Is-Is turned to Mr. Battfin and raised an eyebrow. The pirate shrugged in return and mumbled something that sounded like 'Fair enough' but no-one was ever really certain. Campbell climbed down the rope first and let everyone know that the job was done. The rope was thrown down again by Is-Is after Mr. Battfin had repelled to the ground and Tumbletick gathered it up and stored it away in his pack.

"We'll partake of luncheon now, then head northwest to the escarpment above Tetterton," Egremont suggested. "We've got a good vantage point from here against any assault by the wolves so eating here is a good idea."

Supplies were still reasonably plentiful after the Monks of Delight had refreshed them mainly with vast slabs of dried goat meat. Rather larger portions were consumed than would normally be the case in the knowledge that they would have a chance to buy more in Tetterton again.

Egremont sat down with Campbell and did some basic maths on the expected distance to Tetterton if they proceeded in a direct manner. Fifteen miles from the port to the capital, they were ten miles south of there which meant that it was roughly eighteen miles across the plateau again to get to Tetterton. They would have to camp out over night and make it to the trading centre of the island early the following day. Caution and vigilance would be necessary with a pack of wolves tracking them and looking for an opportunity. If the attack was to come it would likely be before they made it to the sheer drop above Tetterton, in a lonely place, when they were asleep with only a couple of guards.

Lunch completed they headed off. Weapons were not drawn but hands were close to hilts and handles should the need to get them arise. The landscape was predictable grassland and more olive groves and they made reasonable time, meandering slightly to stay in shallow valleys and away from the trees where an ambush maybe slightly easier. It was an uneventful journey with only the odd cow to avoid and major obstacles being small stone walls to hop over. As dusk approached Egremont was keen to find a good defendable position to camp in. A location where any campfire could be hidden well and sentries could have the best chance of seeing any attack early on. Unfortunately the clouds that had been intermittent early on in the day now covered a good seven eighths of the sky so a dark night looked very likely. Their pace dropped to a slow walk as Campbell scouted off around them in an effort to widen the search for the good campsite they wanted and desired. He returned regularly to update them on his mission until he reported on an opportunity which Egremont concurred was satisfactory.

The chosen place was in a corner of one of a multitude of fields where the stone walls marked a boundary between two pastures. The ground lowered in this particular corner so a fire could be well hidden by the wall and their tent which could be erected on the other side of the flames. The wall was about four foot tall and the land rose gently in all directions for about half a mile, so visibility, if any at night, would be as best as they could hope for. They trotted off to the area and soon Is-Is, Seton Rax and Beran were putting up the tent. Mr. Battfin and Y'Bor Kaz prepared a fire from scrag ends of gnarled bushes that grew up against the wall in places. The others remained vigilant as the night took hold of the end of the day. It did indeed appear that the clouds would make it particularly dark. Tumbletick was shivering and asked if he could be one of the first to sleep and was slightly upset when he was told by Egremont that tonight he could rest fully as the others would take guard duty.

They took watches in groups of three, Tumbletick and the remaining six sleeping in the tent as best they could. The night was cold and the fire was small, weak and provided only enough light for the immediate area of the wall and the side of the tent. There was to be three watches until dawn and then the march would begin again. Conversation was low and muted between Egremont, Is-Is and Y'Bor Kaz on the first shift. Egremont seemed sure that the attack should come at the beginning of the night when most of their number was weary after the day of yomping. Over the course of their three hour watch no attack came though. Is-Is roused Seton Rax, Beran and Nazar Grant who were next on the rota. They rubbed their eyes and listened to a report of solitude and only the occasional lowing of a cow out in the enclosed pasture nearby. Seton restocked the bunches of wood by the fire, Beran said a prayer for a safe watch and Nazar boiled some water to infuse with some herbs he carried with him that would make an invigorating hot drink to promote awareness. The hour of midnight departed and still no alarm was needed. Seton Rax was twitchy and concerned as he did not like the fact that control had been taken by an enemy that could attack on their terms alone. A breeze grew into a bit of a buffet which flickered and stoked the fire into a brightened glow but still no attack came.

Vixen, Campbell and Mr. Battfin were woken for the toughest shift. It was the final watch and meant that it would be the coldest and was not ended with the hope of sleep but a morning of tramping the countryside. Nazar Grant made them the same herbal tea he had had to aid with their stint before retiring himself. Campbell walked a wide perimeter in a scouting hunt and Mr. Battfin fell to quietly attending to the cutting edge of his cutlasses with his whetstone. Vixen was very watchful and attentive. All passed peacefully and the occupants of the tent slept soundly until at the very moment of dawn breaking they were woken by the screaming voice of Vixen. They quickly emerged to find her leaning on the wall and blaring out across the empty countryside.

"Where are you, you cowards?" Why don't you attack?"

Mr. Battfin seemed unconcerned and was packing away his equipment. Campbell the Weasel was burying the remains of the fire with slabs of freshly cut turf.

"Vixen, please. A little decorum," said Egremont. "We are not safely to Tetterton yet my dear. Your request may still come to pass."

She turned to face the wolfhound and apologised. Then she aided the others in striking the small campsite and preparing for the remaining journey. No breakfast was taken as it was decided a brunch would be easily found in the port town. They headed slightly more northerly in an effort to find the east west road and a guarantee of a direct route to the cliff face. All the time on these last few miles of marching they were attentive to the attack of wolves. Campbell kept up his constant scouting of the area, disappearing over ridges, appearing from groves, hopping over walls and slipping out from behind solitary farm buildings. Keeping Egremont up to date on the landscape ahead and the chance of any ambush.

"I can find no trace what so ever of the wolf pack," he said after appearing following another sortie. "The road is ahead just over the next rise. It looks like we are alone out here."

"Let's strike out for Tetterton then with a brisk jog," Egremont encouraged and he broke into a light run over the shallow hill and on to the dirt track taking a westward direction.

They crunched over the stones and dusty earth and within a mile of their starting the jogging they could see the towers which marked the cliff face above the port town. The group decided to take the steep and twisting path down as it meant they could stay together and not be broken up by basket descents. The way down brought new pain to new muscles compared to when they had climbed it only a few days earlier but they made it to the bottom and were inside 'The Grobbling Smith' just as the sun was a quarter of its way along it daily track to the west.

Chorus Six

The man who stepped into the cave stood well over six foot tall. His chain mail armour and the large fur cloak which was draped over his shoulders were both filthy with mud and grime from the caves above. He had a short cropped beard, extremely square jaw and straight brown hair which was crudely cut.

"And just tell me why it is okay that you are here?" the man said in a deep voice of authority and confidence, his sword rising slightly. Three more well built and well armed men came out from the tunnel and lined up behind the initial warrior. They too had drawn swords and a grim disposition. Fenton had to think fast and get this conversation absolutely correct.

"Gentlemen, I am a trader offering the finest wares to the inhabitants of the Old City."

"Really?" replied the first man. "The way you shouted it sounded more like you were expecting someone."

"Exactly. Expecting customers with discerning taste."

"There have been very few customers in recent times. Why would you expect them now?" The man was serious but the three behind him were almost laughing.

"I am always looking for an opportunity to make a trade," Fenton replied.

The large lead warrior, pointed to the launch with his sword and one of his minions walked off to check it out for him.

"Doesn't look like you have a lot to 'trade'," the bearded man said.

"Just a bit of food guv," said the searching man stepping into the boat. He reached down and took a hunk of bread and ripped a large mouthful out of it. He then threw other pieces of bread, fruit and cheese to his companions who greedily scoffed it down.

"Why would a merchant be carrying a dagger in each hand if he was expecting customers?" the man asked and then took a bite out of the apple that had been thrown to him, the crunch seemed ominous.

Fenton looked briefly down at the daggers he had instinctively drawn and was pointing towards the group.

"Dangerous times. Buyer beware," he replied with a shrug.

"I think you were expecting someone else," the man spat out little bits of apple as he talked. He paused to swallow the chewed fruit that remained in his mouth. "And I think that perhaps you have been waiting for some time for those other people to meet you here but they never turned up. Also I think that there is a bigger boat anchored a little way outside the tunnel."

"Might be," Fenton replied a little frown of concern over the accuracy of the statements. "Might be a pirate ship rammed full with blood thirsty cutthroats, swarthy fellows just itching for a fight."

"He's by 'iself guv!" one of the men shouted raucously.

"What makes you think that Tan?" the governor responded turning slightly to the man who had just spoke.

"Well if you 'ad some mates on a ship you'd bring at least one wiv yer to pass the time of day. Wouldn't ya?"

"All right let's end this charade," said Fenton, his voice turning to a more commanding tone. "Who the hell are you?"

"I think that perhaps we are in the position to ask the questions."

"But I have you cornered," the pirate replied with bravado.

The four men laughed. The warrior who was rooting around in the launch clambered out of the boat and returned to the other three. Fenton was standing on a shelf of rock. If these enemies decided to attack they would have to approach him one at a time. He had the wall of the cavern to his right and the pool made by the sea below and to his left. Two daggers in his hands against chain mailed thugs with swords but no shields. 'Maybe,' thought the pirate. He knew he was proficient in close quarter combat; you had to be to be a successful pirate captain. A slash to the throat with his right hand, left forearm blocking a downward cut of a sword by hitting under his opponents bicep with his own wrist. Then left dagger into the exposed armpit and most men would be down. Fine against one man but another would then step up and they were all armed with broadswords and would have a long reach. Plus although the ridge was really only wide enough for one man at a time another could be close behind and thrusting with those long swords. Fenton was not wearing any armour, just a three quarter length coat, jerkin, leather trousers and boots.

"I think perhaps it is we who have you cornered," the man replied slowly.

"Technically, correct. But I am Percy Fenton and I have bested worse odds than these before. Now that I have told you who I am, who are you?"

"Refugees from the Old City of Rampart. Only one way out for us and looking for luck to find safe passage off this cursed piece of rock. Now that the good times are over," the men laughed. "Looks like our luck has come extremely good with you here. You should have heard the arguments we had about running away down some passageways to a dead end. But one of our number felt pretty certain there would be a way out. He's usually right. He'll be here in a second."

Percy shrugged off his jacket in a dramatic move, arms thrown behind him and both daggers slipping easily through the sleeves of the coat. He positioned himself into a fighting stance, twirling both blades a couple of times. He started to breath deeply and tensed himself ready for any confrontation to come. Behind the four men another figure emerged from the passageway dressed completely in a black robe, the four warriors turned and looked reverentially at the new entrant to the cavern.

"Hey guys," said Fenton. "Five to one is still okay odds with me."

The hooded black figure pulled back the robe to reveal a heavily furred wolf face with one milky white eye, a head length scar running right through the middle of it.

"Kill him," the wolf growled.

The men turned immediately and approached with sneers and eagerness to be first along the rock to fight. Fenton dropped the daggers and took a couple of quick steps to his left and dived athletically into the pool and started swimming underwater in the direction of the tunnel. As he made his way through the crystal clear sea he swore he could hear the muffled yells of men who had thought they were just about to make a lucky escape, have it taken away from them.

Chapter Seven

Campbell the Weasel negotiated on a price for their suite of rooms with the pretty receptionist at 'The Grobbling Smith'. They dumped their bags in the main living area and all went down to the large tap room, except for Vixen who said she wanted to take the opportunity to have bath.

"Seems you have quite a disposition for bathing," Egremont said.

"Well I don't know when I might next get the chance seeing as we are heading for Kenai," she replied and disappeared off to the bath room with a serving girl who would help with the preparation of the fire and the pouring of warmed water from large porcelain flagons.

As it was a little before luncheon the men ordered a round of ale. 'Three Wyches' was still on and was in excellent condition. Y'Bor Kaz seemed especially pleased to be having professionally produced and crafted beer again after his self imposed incarceration in the Old City. The beer the Monks of Delight had brewed had just had their mildly narcotic leaf and stinging nettles to help with preservation, bitterness and a kick. Y'Bor relished in the hoppiness of the beer in front of him and was soon off to the bar enthusiastically ordering an entire second round for his 'esteemed companions'.

Tumbletick felt relaxed for the first time in a long time. People were acting normally around him. Dock workers coming in for a drink at the end of or beginning of a shift. Traders taking a negotiation to the neutral and more pleasant ground of the hostelry. Staff were bustling around the tables, clearing glasses, plates and tankards and beginning to take orders for lunch. Tumbletick had been looking at the menu on a large blackboard above the roaring main fire of the public house and had noticed that 'steak and kidney pie with seasonal vegetables' was available. When a waitress arrived he was first to blurt out that that was what he wanted.

Mr. Battfin and Campbell laughed and also went for the pie choice. Egremont ordered a rare steak with lobster and a vegetarian option of a large 'Grobbling Smith salad' for Is-Is. Seton Rax wanted soup and a sandwich, Beran went for the salad as well and Nazar Grant selected rustic sausages on a mash potato base with mustard and onion sauce.

Y'Bor Kaz was returning with a third pint and a discerning eye for the waitress. He looked briefly at the board when she asked him for his order but he put his heavy set arm around Tumbletick's shoulder and said that he would have what 'he' was having and placed a big kiss on top of Tumbletick's hairy head.

Conversation turned to the quest after a while.

"Well it's not exactly going to plan is it?" said Campbell.

"Your plan of avoiding watchful eyes by disappearing in the Old City was fundamentally a bold one though," replied Egremont. "When we came to that decision it was right for that moment. Now we have to continue with a new idea."

"Seems foolhardy and risky now though," the thief retorted. "If we had just headed straight here when you found me in 'The Lillith Arms' we would be days ahead and Jackson would still be alive."

"Fundamentally, I'll say it again, it was sound and clever," Egremont said. "Plus, while we did indeed lose Jackson, we gained additional support with four new adventurers of strength and talent. Something tells me that was meant to be you know Campbell."

Tumbletick felt some sadness for the death of his friend again but looked up warmly at Y'Bor Kaz who was still leaning, rather heavily, on Tumbletick's shoulder. Y'Bor had given the little man a bearish squeeze at the mention of Lord Jackson but was now concentrating on the conversation and swaying only imperceptibly.

"So now we must await the arrival of Percy and continue in our quest," said Egremont. "We still arrive in Kenai by boat. How long would you think he will take Mr. Battfin?"

"This evening or tomorrow morning if tides and winds are with him," the pirate replied.

"Fine. So we rest and wait then," said Egremont.

"In full view of all those people who pass us by with wolves abroad who were hunting us," commented Campbell. "Do we think that anyone would actually guess our quest?"

"I'm sure many will believe something must be going on, even if it is just revenge for the atrocity committed at court," Egremont replied.

The conversation grew more hushed and conspiratorial under the noise of others in the room enjoying their lunch.

"What exactly is the plan now then?" asked Seton Rax.

"Exactly what it has always been," said Egremont. "A small and elite team move into the Kenai wilderness and seek out the Ahriman impersonator. Exact revenge and if possible retrieve the Umiat Stone."

"Do we know where we are going to find Ahriman then?" Beran asked.

"Vixen and the Secret Service say that the old centre of Ahriman and the Ahrioch Horde, with their disgusting demon worshipping, was based around the mountain of Kantishna."

"What is it about these evil types and mountains?" Nazar Grant questioned. "They always seem to base themselves near or on some vast and lofty peak. A mighty wizard and a volcano here, a feudal warlord and rather pointy hill there, mass murdering homicidal psychotic on every raised geological elevation you care to look at."

The cleric realised everyone was looking at him and he quickly lifted his tankard to his mouth and took a big drink.

"Is Kantishna a large mountain then?" Seton asked. The barbarian being from the plains beneath the mighty Noatak was not used to venturing into particularly demanding scenery, just looking at it.

"It is one of the main eight peaks of Kenai, which is all pretty much rough ground but those eight really stick out," said Egremont. "We have a map of Kenai but you can see Kantishna from the moment you get any where near the northern shore of the Kenai Peninsular. Apparently, I've never been there myself. Mr. Battfin?"

"Aye. Sailing out of the Tanana Straight, westward, you'd see it to port as soon as you pass Cape Hayze."

"So let's get this straight again," Campbell said. "We are a commando raid that potentially the enemy could be expecting. Heading for a place based on some pretty old intelligence, which just happens to be quite easy to find because it is so freaking big. Yeah, that's where I would set up my base, somewhere where everybody can find it."

"Campbell please?" hushed Egremont. "Our sceptical friend is right, we are a commando unit. So let us look at the six stages that make a successful operation. In case any of you have forgotten I was once quite a senior military officer."

"How could I forget," said Campbell. "While Is-Is rose through the ranks and found the military very much to his liking, I got busted out and found more appreciation for my talents in the underworld."

"Hmm yes Campbell. Talents that were also appreciated by the military on occasion," Egremont alluded.

"Well I don't like to talk about some of the unofficial engagements that you used to find for me while you were that senior military officer. Back to the six stages of your military genius Master Wolfhound!"

Campbell stood up and gave a mock salute, sloshing some beer over the side of his handcrafted pewter beer mug.

"You have had a few different careers haven't you Weasel?" said Mr. Battfin. Campbell sat back down and gave a nonchalant sneer, then placed his head in his hands in mock enthusiasm and interest in Egremont. The others laughed a little for they knew there was nothing malicious or truly mocking in Campbell's response.

"The six points of a successful commando raid are as follows. One, 'Clarity of Purpose'. Two, 'Appropriate Means'. Three, 'Intelligence'. Four, 'Insertion'. Five, 'Execution' and six, 'Exit Strategy'. I think you will all agree that points one and two are present and correct. One, we all know exactly what we have to do. Two and apologies to Tumbletick as Jackson still provides his support even though he is not with us, 'Appropriate Means' are well met with his money and our abilities in the field of operation. Three, 'Intelligence', is perhaps a little vague but we have two individuals with us who are expert at gathering it when we actually get closer to the theatre of operation. Currently knowing that they will either be at Kantishna or in the major city of Ende is enough. 'Insertion', we will land by boat in the secret cove that Mr. Battfin knows about and travel by foot to Kantishna."

"Correct," said Mr. Battfin. "Not many know about it but I do. A short walk through enemy territory from there to the mountain. About forty miles by my reckoning and they won't be expecting us if they are at Kantishna."

"If they are not at their old base then we try 'Plan B' and head for Ende. Either cross country or back by boat," said Egremont. "Point five, that of 'Execution' is simple. All of us have the skills we need to take out an enemy quickly and decisively. Plus we will have Percy with us and now we have the added backup of Seton Rax, Nazar Grant, Beran and Y'Bor Kaz."

The four men nodded with serious looks on each face, Y'Bor swigging another large gulp of ale.

"What about me Egremont? I'm not much use," said Tumbletick.

"Not much use!" exclaimed Egremont. "You brought us together, negotiated a peace with our party and Garraday's and you were the protector of the Umiat Stone. Who knows what you will do next plus you shall carry the stone back to Rhyell once we retrieve it!"

"What about point six? 'Exit Strategy'," asked Y'Bor looking at his now empty pint then into the faces of the other eight around the table.

"Ultimately we will have to deal with that when we have to deal with that. But let's be clear. The only objectives that have to occur are the death of the Ahriman impersonator and the return of the Umiat Stone to the roof of Rhyell Cathedral. I would like it if Tumbletick, at the very least, has the honour of returning the artefact into the hands of Princess Annabella Blaise."

They fell silent in resigned contemplation but then four waitresses appeared and started dressing the table with cutlery and then lavishing it with food. They started hacking away at and devouring their meals. It was extremely good after their time on iron rations and the best that the Monks of Delight could provide. 'Hunger is the best sauce,' thought Tumbletick, surprised by such a twee flitter of the mind after the gravity of Egremont's last statement.

"Why don't we come up with an inspirational code name for this mission," Campbell said in between some mouthfuls of pie. "Something like, 'Operation Eagle Claw'."

The comment lightened the mood again. They were all capable characters, seekers of adventure and veterans of tough situations. The plan was simple and they knew that if they confronted any threats they would be ruthless in the execution of dealing with it. It was time now to recover and prepare. To be at ease with each other in the knowledge that the future would test and maybe break their bonds of friendship and honour.

"What about 'Operation Bellomancer'?" asked Y'Bor Kaz now more than slightly affected by the ale.

Is-Is choked on some salad and Mr. Battfin laughed out loud with a guttural heave from the depth of his belly.

"Who or what is a Bellomancer?" enquired Campbell for the benefit of the group.

"Well, bellomancy is the art of foretelling the future by judging the flight of an arrow," Y'Bor replied. "Well not only has Is-Is used an arrow to convey a message but I figure we may need some precision arrows in the future. Plus if you are a good Bellomancer you would know exactly where the arrow was going to fly. And seeing as we want to be and will be an elite force that knows exactly where we are going to strike then 'Bellomancer' might be a good title. Unless you randomly want to just throw some dice to see what will happen. Telling the future by shaking some dice is known as cleromancy and I wouldn't want anything this important to be named after something as random and uncontrollable as rolling dice."

The others sat round the table not eating, they were sitting with their mouths hanging open. Campbell was the first to react and scraped the last piece of his pie together with some carrots onto the end of his fork with a deftly confident knife stroke.

"Well obviously I knew that! Who doesn't? And the plural of dice is die. Still think 'Operation Eagle Claw' is better," the thief stated calmly.

"What about 'Operation Blaise Blaze'? That has a certain cache," suggested Beran. Not many seemed to respond to that suggestion so he quickly swigged some beer to wash away the taint of badly selected words. "Sorry guys, that was rubbish," he concluded.

"Operation 'Get Stone Back' would have been better," said Mr. Battfin. Some laughter bubbled about from Seton Rax and Nazar Grant.

"We could go for a religious theme," said the cleric after composing himself. "I mean we are going up against the Ahrioch Horde. Demon worshippers. Something with the word 'Crusade' in the structure."

"But we aren't all religious Nazar," said Campbell. "No offence. I'm glad you are with us and all but for me this is a straight forward snatch and grab mission. You need something exciting and fast sounding like 'Operation Kestrel Strike', that would be good."

Tumbletick laughed the most at that suggestion. The others too were still laughing when they noticed that Y'Bor Kaz had left the table and was returning with a large tray with eight pints on it.

"'Three Wyches' is finished it seems. I selected some beer by the name of 'Corambis Best'. Apparently it is a 'powerful, full bodied, copper red, well balanced brew, with a moderate hoppy bitterness.' According to the landlord anyway. I thanked him for his recommendation and told him he could probably expect to sell some more to me. Hope you don't mind Campbell, I've been putting the drinks on the tab."

"No problem at all. Perhaps we could raise a toast to lost friends? Next round we'll put four whiskeys behind the bar in their memory hey?" Campbell said with a touch of class that touched Tumbletick and reminded him that the thief had made the effort for digging Jackson's resting place and that their new friends had lost three companions. "To lost friends."

"To lost friends," the chorus went in unison and great gulps of 'Corambis Best' were swallowed. Tumbletick again realised that many around the table may have been thinking of many more than just the four alluded to as he tasted the beer and found it pleasant on his palate. Some enjoyed its taste. Mr. Battfin wanted a dryer finish and Seton Rax felt that more malt was always needed but Y'Bor thought it was beautiful.

"Any other ideas for the christening of this mission or should we take a vote?" asked Egremont, leaning back into his chair and rubbing his stomach expansively.

"I'm all for 'Operation Bellomancer'," said Mr. Battfin. "It has a certain ring to it."

"Eagle Claw," shouted Campbell, then more quietly. "No, I'm not precious. Bellomancer is great. Clinical, slightly arcane and no-one will know what the hell we are talking about if they over hear us. I go for 'Operation Bellomancer' or 'Hawk's Beak'."

"Bellomancer is good with me too," agreed Seton Rax patting Y'Bor on the back in a congratulatory gesture or to help him belch, Tumbletick was not sure.

"I am in agreement after my attempt," said Beran.

"I think it is a well thought out name Master Kaz," complimented Nazar Grant.

Egremont looked at Tumbletick who nodded, as did Is-Is.

"Well I agree too, although the democratic process had already swung it," said Egremont. "Looks like we have a wordsmith in our midst, hey Y'Bor Kaz?"

Y'Bor finished his pint, flushing slightly, either at the happiness of acceptance of his title and crafting of words or from the effects of the beer.

"Thanks guys. Anyone want another beer to celebrate? I'll put those whiskeys on the tab too..." he stopped speaking in mid sentence and stared across the tap room. "Egremont, do not turn around but six black robed scum have just walked into the bar."

Tumbletick, next to Y'Bor looked up and saw them too. Definitely wolves, he could see the muzzles under the shadowed hood of the cloaks. Is-Is was quick to put a paw on a throwing knife, Seton and Mr. Battfin had their swords slightly out of their scabbards in case of trouble. Campbell quickly left the table, running up to the room to check on Vixen, Beran was swiftly after him in case support was needed.

"Everyone stay calm," said Egremont. The edge in his voice belying his own desire to hack some of the enemy to pieces. "Remember we are in Tetterton and the City State rules of neutrality are extremely strict here. What went before in the Old City was fair game. If they had attacked on the plateau no-one would have likely known of our vengeance upon them for days, here it is different. I can't believe they have the audacity to come into the bar in broad daylight though."

Egremont had his back to them and was in an agony of rage at the restricting rules. He knew the other warriors around the table had him covered if anything was to happen. The six cloaked wolves moved into the main area of the room and forced their way into a pack, standing at the bar, where the landlord quickly served them up some beers with a face that belied neither condemnation or appreciation of their custom.

The lupine group were raucous and bawdy. They appeared celebratory and slammed pints together in their own unknown toast. Egremont sat almost rigid, chewing on his bottom lip with his great fangs. Is-Is never once removed his gaze from them, his paws under the table, a throwing knife now in each. Beran and Campbell did not return, perhaps they were protecting Vixen, even she would need a guard if she was vulnerable in a bath, thought Tumbletick.

"Oh this is a crock," said Y'Bor dismissively after about five minutes of the stand off. "I need a beer and I'm not letting them get in the way of another Corambis."

The red headed warrior, secure in his own bravery, skill and confidence, aided by the courage of Corambis stood up suddenly letting his chair fall behind him with a crash. The wolves turned to look at him as if expecting and waiting for one or all of the group to approach. A couple pushed back their hoods to reveal their fierce lupine faces but

Y'Bor walked steadily up to them and purposefully pushed his way directly between them and to the bar.

"A pint of 'Best' again landlord and four shots of your finest whiskey to be placed behind the bar please. You see we're having a bit of a wake," said Y'Bor loudly between the pack.

None of the wolves said anything and none of them seemed impressive in stature next to the hugely broad warrior. Y'Bor turned and looked at each of them with a long stare, a challenging stare, a knowing stare. He took his pint when it was placed on the bar, sniffed it and took a gulp.

"Seems a bit tainted by something, smells a bit like mangy wet fur," he commented. "But it will do."

He then walked back slowly to the table, reset his chair with an easy lift of a powerful arm, keeping his pint stable, and sat back down.

"We'll see if they want to make anything happen now," Y'Bor said sounding more sober than he was.

The two groups continued to look at each other occasionally. Ignoring wolves was difficult for Egremont but he knew that this was not the time or place for a violent encounter. He was utterly convinced that he and Is-Is alone would be able to defeat six wolves but he did not know the other variables at play here. Were there more outside, had they captured Vixen upstairs and now had Beran and Campbell as hostages? Was their leader nearby, maybe in the bar right now ready to unleash the undead form of some beast against them or the innocents within 'The Grobbling Smith'. Plus there was the issue with the enforcement policies of Rampart. While it was widely believed they secretly favoured Umiat over Kenai, the island had prospered with strict neutrality and a zero tolerance of violent crime. To be caught meant either summary execution or addition to the criminal stockholding of the Old City with no password. If they did kill the wolves and then make a run for the boat in the harbour and try and sail away there were two main problems with that, firstly Percy was not necessarily even here yet and secondly there was no chance of making it under the Rampart Harbour Portal as wanted men. The huge balls of iron shot would cascade upon them meaning a certain destruction of the vessel and very likely death for the crew by crushing or drowning. 'No,' thought Egremont. 'Now is not the time.'

It was only after about five more minutes since Y'Bor had gone to the bar and boldly stood between the wolves that one of their number approached the table. He came and sat confidently down at the space left by Campbell as if joining a conversation with friends. No other inhabitant, except maybe the landlord, suspected the potential for violence that could erupt. As the gateway to Rampart, Tetterton was always filled with exotic types looking for adventure or trade. Wolves were rare but not unknown and as long as they abided by the rules, like everyone else, they were free to travel, to talk, to trade and to drink in the bars of the island.

Everyone stayed quiet and waited for the wolf to speak. For his race he was handsome with a well defined muzzle and clean sharp white teeth. His fur was mostly dark grey but with flecks of silver about the eyes, ears and snout, defining him as nearing middle age. His eyes were a pale blue, quite stunning in his creed. His neck was broad and strong, this was an alpha male no doubt, the pack's leader, not a whelp sent with a message.

"You have done well in besting us so far Lord Egremont Seau du Duvet," his voice was measured and educated. No trace of an accent as he spoke in the common tongue. It was also deep with only the slightest indication of a growl in the depths of his chest.

"You know my name?" Egremont replied, fixing those pale eyes with his own.

"Of course, what wolf does not? Yes you have bested us so far. A pack in the Old City with three left dead, your handy work I believe Is-Is," he turned to the hare who made no sign of any acknowledgement. "And you managed to avoid the other pack that was sent to harry you as you traipsed across country yesterday."

"We knew they were there," Tumbletick blurted out. "Ran away when we went looking for them." Egremont winced slightly due to Tumbletick being drawn into a conversation so easily.

"Ah my little keeper of the stone, you truly are as ugly as everyone says you are. Disgusting wretch. They did not run away, your friends failed to find them or even track them properly. If they had meant to attack you, you would have been attacked," the wolf smiled at Tumbletick and leaned a little closer towards him across the table, sniffing slightly. "Just as if had I wanted to attack right now, I would have done so too."

The wolf paused breathing more deeply, slight amounts of drool started to form on his canine lips as he looked at Tumbletick.

"Yes sometimes I wonder why we abide by the rules of Rampart. When we are dominant there will be a very different kind of rule everywhere. Then your type will find it a very, very unpleasant place."

"You speak as if you expect a change to occur," said Egremont.

"The change of rule has already begun. We took the Umiat Stone so very easily with Ahriman with us. So easily and at the time when you were conducting your pathetic little ceremony to hand it back to your whore princess," the wolf let out a growl of anger but quickly calmed himself to just dripping venom with his voice. "Yes right into the very heart of your land. We took your talisman at the time you wanted everyone in the realm to see that it was safe and that the bastard son of Bartle Rourke, curses on his name, was there to give it back. Pathetic."

"What do you want wolf because I grow wearisome of your rhetoric?" Egremont was stern. The others moved so as to show hands were readied near weapons and the rules of neutrality may not last much longer. "You have said much that angers me blue eyes. I repeat, what is it that you want?"

"I want you to know that the pack has risen. The Ahrioch Horde has risen. Ahriman is with us and you will fail in your attempts to retrieve the Umiat Stone. Go back to Umiat. Prepare for War. For when we come again it will not be as a raiding party but as a tide of death. The stone is ours and we will carry it at the head of our demon armies watching your people crumble and die before us in fear and forlorn of hope."

"Well I suggest that you race back to Kenai for we are coming too. You seem to know a lot about what our plans have been so you probably know what they are. We are coming and we are going to kill any of you that gets in our way. I will take particular pleasure in making the fatal blow that dispatches the Ahriman impersonator back to hell," Egremont was vicious in his speech and the blue eyed wolf listened to it all without flinching.

"Ahriman impersonator? My Lord Egremont, you could not be more wrong. This is Ahriman. The one your feted Bartle Rourke killed those years back was the impersonator. He was sent in place of our glorious leader. You have no chance. Run back home to your kennels and hovels for He will have no mercy for you when we arrive."

The wolf rose quickly and walked straight out of the bar. His followers left their drinks and tailed him immediately out and onto the streets of Tetterton.

Chorus Seven

Percy broke the surface of the water about half way along the tunnel. He rose slowly so as not to crack his head on the rock but he knew there would be a little layer of air here for him to breath. He was fit and a good swimmer. There was no huge intake of breath to revive screaming and painful lungs. The sway of the sea was exaggerated in the tight tunnel and he had to have one hand raised against the roof as he trod water with strong kicks. Fully clothed apart from his discarded coat he knew he would have to swim hard for the ship but he couldn't resist looking back. Vision was very much restricted by the choppy little waves and the rock but he could make out the legs of the men getting into the launch left in the cavern.

"They'll have to wait a while before the tide is low enough for a pursuit," he said out loud and then fell to thinking. 'So where are the others? Things must have gone wrong up top. Chasing these thugs down the passages now. How come that wolf seemed so confident that someone would be waiting with transport? No time to find out now, Situations like this call for only one solution, self preservation.'

He turned around and began a steady breast stroke down the tunnel towards the open sea. Upon reaching the Sea of Kaltag he was pleased to see 'The Brazen Manticore' where he had anchored her and he switched to a powerful crawl. He was surprised that his main thoughts as he struck out for the ship concerned his boots he was wearing. He had been fond of the coat but there was no way he was going to kick off his boots and lose them too. The ship was not that far away. The daggers could easily be replaced; he felt no sentimentality for them, just a couple of concealed weapons for emergencies. The coat was good but he knew many a fine tailor in the major cities of Umiat. The boots however were superb. Extremely comfortable, fantastic looking and had been with him for a long while. A good soaking in sea water might even improve their suppleness. He kicked out and crawled on, a deep breath to the right every third pull through the sea. He reached the anchor chain, taut in the water with the high tide and flung his arms around it. This would be the toughest and most important part of the whole escape. He knew he was strong but he also knew he had just swum, fully clothed, a good distance and his clothes would add to the weight he would feel trying to heave himself out of the water. There was no-one on board to help him up or to throw a ladder down. 'The Brazen Manticore' was not a large vessel but the rail that he had to reach was a good six foot above the waves. He manoeuvred underneath the chain, hands above his head and he started to move along by reaching in wide swings. The chain did not stay taut, his weight was enough to bring the ship slightly towards him and the chain got steeper until eventually he could only progress by moving one fist in front of the other. It was an effort as his shoulders and chest started to be pulled out of the sea, he felt bulky and cold as the air chilled his wet clothes. It wasn't going to work this way round with his chest facing the boat, so he dropped back into the sea. He tried wrapping his legs around the chain and pulling himself up and along again but that did not work as the chain soon got too steep and his weight and the wet chain was too much of a combination so he splashed back into the waves again. He then got himself into a position where the chain was under his chest as if he was laying on top of it and he began to heave himself forward using the chain to bear his weight. Now he found the true value of his boots and he thanked the gods that were precious to him for those wonderful pieces of foot wear. Due to his intense love of fashion Percy had boots with a strong point to the toe, useful not only to impress the discerning eye of a lady but also to administer a painful kick to an opponent. The toes of the boots were just right to fit into the eyes of the links and Percy found that he could aid his movement along the chain with them. Inching along he pulled with his fists and pushed with his boots until he was fully out of the water and almost in a standing position he was able to grab the hand rail and pull himself into the stern of the boat. He slopped onto the deck and breathed heavily for a few minutes.

"Why is there never anyone around to see it when I achieve something like that," he quipped to himself and then he saw the arrow stuck in the middle of the deck.

Chapter Eight

With the wolves leaving 'The Grobbling Smith', Egremont and company moved with haste to their suite of rooms and found Campbell and Beran with swords drawn as they opened the door into the living room area. Faces looked relieved that their friends were there.

"Is everything okay?" Egremont asked.

"Well yes," replied Campbell. "She is still, believe it or not, in the bath. We thought that perhaps the thumping lumps up the stairs was a pack of our lupine friends, hence the drawn swords."

"I don't think we will be getting any trouble from them while we are so public. So let's all rest up here for a while where we can defend easily if they have tried to lull us into idiocy. Then it's the public bar again tonight to see if Fenton turns up. That will nearly be a day and a half," Egremont said.

"What happened after we left?" asked Beran. He was out of his armour seeing as they had thought themselves safe in 'The Grobbling Smith' but he was reattaching his breast plate as he spoke, buckling it tightly around his ribs.

"Oh we had a bit of dogma and diatribe from one of their number. Handsome fellow. His head would look good fixed upon our battlements," Egremont said.

"I think he was trying to save face after Y'Bor Kaz fronted them all," Tumbletick added.

"Really? Did we miss a potential skirmish?" Campbell asked.

"Not really," said Y'Bor, slumping into a well furnished armchair with a high back and broad arms. "They seemed bothered by the quaint traditions of Rampart being a neutral zone. As if they couldn't risk themselves. If we had of had a fight all of us would have been in a spot of bother but if you are a zealot for the cause shouldn't they have sacrificed themselves to get rid of us permanently?"

"Y'Bor might have landed upon something there you know," Egremont said.

"Ah you know, sometimes I am perceptive. Anyway, I've got a bit of a headache coming on. I might have a little doze before dinner and a few more ales when I awake," Y'Bor replied. His eyes were closed by the last word and his head began to totter forward a little as he sprawled in the chair.

"And they didn't attack in the woods either," said Mr. Battfin. "Plus they only tried to capture us with a net in the Old City."

"Something to ponder on for certain. If there are a minimum of three packs on the island they could have attacked us with a decent numerical advantage," said Egremont. "Well, let's stay vigilant and get to Kenai as soon as we can and not let any of them follow us to the Peninsular although they now know we are definitely coming."

"I think Y'Bor's dropped off. Would anyone mind if I had a nap too?" asked Tumbletick. "I didn't knock them back as fast as he did but you know, smaller frame and all."

"Certainly my friend. If anyone else wants to fully rest up now it could be a good idea. I will be posting full watches again tonight so sleep might be worthwhile," replied Egremont.

Seton Rax and Nazar Grant took the option to sleep as well. The barbarian was used to fresh air and exercise to keep his excellent physique toned. A few pints at lunch were great at inducing lethargy. Nazar being the oldest member of the group had also found the effects of the beer superb in summoning sleep. Mr. Battfin was fine. He was used to heavily caning rum when ever he had the chance to. Egremont and Is-Is were also quite immune to the beer and they moved a little table between a couple of chairs and Egremont dug out a small but intricate travel chess set that no-one had seen before. He began to set up the pieces as Is-Is formulated defence strategies from the wolfhound's attacking style. The game that ensued was closely followed by Campbell the Weasel while Beran and Mr. Battfin had a long conversation about blade maintenance. Vixen it appeared had fallen asleep in the bath and had involuntarily therefore volunteered for the night shift watch with the other soporific souls. The afternoon passed by pleasantly for all but some had dreams of hardship in the Kenai Peninsular or thoughts that the near future was going to have moments of violence that would be greater and more heartbreaking than the encounters they had already had.

The afternoon dragged on and noisy snores were a disruption to quiet conversations or concentrations on chess. Vixen had emerged from the bath and was now reading her diary after moaning a little about gaining the nightshift. Thoughts turned to Fenton. It must surely have been his boat anchored off the sheer cliffs. He must be heading back now and would arrive in Tetterton soon. Surely he would not have just waited in the cave. He would have returned to the boat and found the arrow and message.

Beran asked if he could play a game of chess against the winner of the current encounter. When Egremont moved his bishop into position causing check mate Is-Is retired gracefully and went to maintain his knives with Mr. Battfin. Beran it turned out was a much tougher opponent for Egremont than the giant hare. Is-Is had enjoyed playing as a young warrior in the Umiat Army, passing hours of boredom like this in his barracks. His opponents had been other rank and file men for years. As Is-Is had risen through the ranks so had the quality of his challengers and when Egremont had become his commanding officer their games had begun. Usually the wolfhound was victorious but Is-Is had his moments. Beran however was a different class. As a child he had had private tutors who schooled him in history, warfare, politics and chess. A gentleman should be required to play a powerful game whether it be in the debating chamber, on the field of combat or across the board. Egremont's brow soon became furrowed after the first few opening moves while the paladin retained a calm and smiling disposition. Soon Egremont's paw moved with less certainty and would often hover over a piece, touch it briefly, maybe move it a little, then return it to its originating square and withdraw his arm.

"You seem to have other skills than that of the blade," said Egremont.

"Thank you Master Wolfhound. I have studied hard to gain them," Beran replied.

Vixen looked over at the two chess players and decided not to interrupt them so she walked over to Mr. Battfin and Is-Is and asked them about the encounter downstairs so she could update her journal. Mr. Battfin was happy to relay his interpretation of events. Vixen listened with interest then returned to her chair and began to write.

Campbell the Weasel was becoming impatient and began pacing the room. He investigated the tapestries of mythical beasts and the paintings of naval battles and famous seamen. This was his first stay at 'The Grobbling Smith' and he found the works an extremely interesting diversion. He thought the sea battles were a little formulaic in their approach to the genre, with representation of that form of warfare he wanted to see more action than just clouds of canon smoke. He did think though that they had reasonable depictions of choppy waters and chopped up mariners floating in them. He enjoyed studying the craggy, leathery faces of famous admirals in their finery but it was the tapestries that really contained his attention with the woven skills showing warriors of elder days fighting and trapping monsters. It looked like the land in which they fought must have been Kenai as there were plenty of black rock mountains, deep cut passes with raging rivers tumbling over massive boulders. Campbell found a scene of men with tridents fending off a behir. The snake like, reptilian monster with twelve legs and a crocodilian head clung to a cliff and was snapping at one man with its many toothed maw. The weaving was so fine that the thief could see upon staring very closely that the man was screaming with fear. He moved around the perimeter of the tapestry with his eyes and found another interesting vignette. A warrior was in full plate armour engaging a three headed chimera in solitary combat. He was wielding a double handed sword which had flames raging around the razor sharp edge. The creature with a body of a large lion had a tail which ended with four spikes. It had large feathered wings like an eagle and was muddy brown in appearance. The beast was flapping to gain some height advantage over the knight. Its three heads were all looking to attack, the lion, the goat and a great long necked pit cobra. A large front claw was sweeping down to bat away the flaming sword. Campbell could see movement and grace in the artisan's work and he hoped to see who would win the fight but they were locked for ever in that moment of the artist's mind. Campbell kept on with his scanning of the tapestry now utterly enthralled by the work and completely unaware of the others in the room. He leapt over a scene of men with nets snaring a large black bear destined for a pit to be baited by dogs. He then gazed with prolonged interest at an ice giant from the Elias Ice Flats, the glaciers to the far southeast of Kenai. The bearded brute must have stood five fathoms tall Campbell thought. He could see icicles hanging from its eyelids and its broken teeth from chewing on too many boulders. Campbell was really close to the work now, his long, twitching nose almost touching the woven twines. He looked with interest as a group of men, clad in furs and with only sharpened flints attached to roughly hewn poles were attempting to fight the giant who had a small uprooted tree in his hands to swipe at the irritants in front of him. While Beran and Egremont were wrapped in their own world of intellectual duelling, Mr. Battfin, Is-Is and Vixen had all been staring at the wiry thief for some time and his intricate inspection of the art work.

"Never had you down as a critic," Vixen said aloud to him.

He did not respond, unhearing her glib verbal swipe due to a complete obsession with being able to see the tension in the ice giants biceps as he was about to crush one of the assailants in bear fur with his trunk club.

He could see the veins in the giant's arms, the shadow on one side of the blue ridge represented by just a skilful twist of twine. So delicate, so precise, he felt he was being drawn into the tapestry, pulled into the material; he wanted to be a part of it. Campbell's gaze was completely focussed on that delicately placed piece of thread for the giant's vein, he saw how it was shaded different blues on either side, this was purely amazing quality.

Mr. Battfin grew concerned and suddenly strode up to the thief and pulled him roughly away from the wall hanging. Stupefied, Campbell's head shook and came still again with his eyes staring directly ahead, motionless and directly into the face of Mr. Battfin. Campbell's jaw dropped, hung for a while and then he spoke in a slow and deliberate manner.

"Well cut my guts out and wrap 'em around a post. That is the most amazing piece of art I have ever seen," he said and tried to turn again to look at the tapestry but Mr. Battfin stopped him with an iron hard grip to the shoulder.

"It looked like you were drifting off into the realms of obsession there," said the pirate.

"What was in the beer we were drinking? I seriously found myself contemplating the blood flow of an ice giant. I could feel the stuff pumping through his arteries. Seriously intense my friend. It's so precisely done. Come and have a look at it," the voice of Campbell picked up in pace and enthusiasm and he tried to guide Mr. Battfin towards the woven scenes. The large first mate resisted and pulled

Campbell completely away and placed him in a large armchair next to the snoring Y'Bor Kaz.

"I think that perhaps you had better have a bit of a rest," said Mr. Battfin.

Vixen came over, she was not smiling now. She knelt next to the thief and looked into his eyes. Concerned she gently pulled on his lower eyelid to get a better glance at his pupils.

"I don't think he's been drugged," she said. "Probably just been staring too hard in picking out those minute details he seems so fond of."

"Aye but half our number are passed out. Seton, Nazar, Y'Bor, Tumbletick and now Campbell is in a bit of trouble," said Mr. Battfin. "And wolves are abroad."

"Coincidence linked with the fact that they are probably not used to drinking," replied Vixen. "And you were all drinking at lunchtime weren't you? Wolves don't usually employ poison or drugs. So in answer to Campbell's earlier question about 'What was in the beer we were drinking?', I would have to say, alcohol. That and the fact that a little art appreciation can be a strain on a usually uncultured mind like Campbell's. But let's make sure we all stay alert when as you say half our number are now pretty much useless for a few hours."

Mr. Battfin and Is-Is nodded in agreement. Egremont had not noticed the exchanges at all. He was completely focussed on his few remaining chess pieces on the board in front of him. Beran was relaxed and confident in his ultra aggressive attack. When Egremont finally made a move, the paladin responded with an instant move of his own, screwing the piece with a final twist on its square for an added theatrical effect, indicating its solidity and robustness. Egremont winced each time Beran did it and Beran knew that each time he did it, Egremont winced.

Time dragged on. Campbell had fallen asleep and sunk into a rhythmic cacophony of snores with Y'Bor. Vixen had gone to check on the other men all sleeping in the separate bedrooms around the suite and was thoroughly convinced now that it was purely the benign effects of beer. She did though have a quiet word with both Mr. Battfin and Is-Is about their recklessness. She seemed sure that those two must have led all the others astray and was not satisfied by the pirate's protestations that it was Y'Bor who been the instigator of the midday session.

Beran beat Egremont with an elegant move, his knight leaping a remaining pawn and revealing a pin from his bishop. Egremont conceded with grace and goodwill and asked for another game just as Is-Is' ears twitched and rotated forward towards the closed door to the rooms and the corridor beyond. He heard, before anyone else, the heavy tread of boots in the corridor approaching with determined thuds.

Mr. Battfin sensed the hare's ears moving first and drew his cutlass quickly and moved to the side of the closed door. Is-Is stood directly in front of it but about ten feet away. He selected his favourite kukris for close quarter combat. Egremont left the setting up of chess pieces and decided to move to a defensive position, his back to the wall and rapier drawn. Beran following the lead of the wolfhound, left his white pawns slightly scattered and went to the side of Is-Is, broadsword snatched out of the scabbard which had been lying on the floor by the table used for chess. Vixen went to rouse Y'Bor and Campbell but then decided against it. She stood in front of the two snoring men with a long knife in each hand, picked from a side table where she had neatly laid out her arsenal before taking her bath. All this positioning took a few seconds as the thuds continued.

The footsteps were purposeful, direct, loud to the keen senses of Egremont and Is-Is, solid, muffled tramping on the carpet of the corridor to the other warriors. Only one set of footsteps surely? They approached the door and immediately the handle turned and the door swung open with pace, determination and aplomb.

"Well you'll never guess what happened to me!" Fenton beamed. He quickly took in the scene of warriors with weapons readied, a snoring red head in an ornate chair, a handsome middle aged knight next to Is-Is, both of whom he did not recognise. He saw Mr. Battfin step out of the cover of the blind spot to his left and re-sheath his cutlass and greet Fenton with a broad smile.

"Have I missed something? Who were you expecting?"

Chorus Eight

Fenton stood still for a couple of seconds dripping onto the deck of 'The Brazen Manticore'. He stared at the arrow with the parchment wrapped around its shaft. Quizzically he looked around for other ships that might have had an archer on board to fire it but then he slowly looked up at the magnificent cliffs and the battlements above.

He took the couple of strides necessary to reach the arrow, bent down and grasped it firmly by the shaft, below where the parchment was wrapped and just above the surface of the deck. A firm pull and the arrow yielded from the wood with a satisfying reluctance to depart from the embedding. He quickly undid the ties that Campbell had fashioned and dragged away the parchment that scrolled around the arrow. He read Egremont's message:

"Head back to Tetterton. Meet at Grobbling Smith. Arrive there tomorrow," Fenton thought for a moment then said aloud, "Well I wish they'd shot this arrow down before I entered the cave. I'd have kept my coat."

Fenton knew that when low tide came his erstwhile attackers in the cave would be emerging along the tunnel. He could wait and exact revenge upon them as they faced the open sea in the launch. It would be a simple matter to ram them with 'The Brazen Manticore' and leave them to drown in the Sea of Kaltag but that would mean lost time and would serve no real purpose. Another launch could easily be bought in Tetterton by Lord Jackson and his wealth. There would be no point in attempting to pick off the men and the wolf with a crossbow that was in the cabin and then salvaging the little boat. Egremont's note sounded urgent in its truncated writing and Fenton knew that something must have gone wrong for the unexpected men in the cave to appear and for an arrow to have been shot down from the south side of the island.

The pirate busied himself by raising the anchor, unfurling the sails and turned the ship around and sped off west towards Tetterton.

Chapter Nine

Fenton was slumped in an armchair in the suite at 'The Grobbling Smith'. He was being debriefed by Egremont about all the events of the Old City. His shock at the loss of Lord Jackson was deep set. He had liked the highly skilled merchant and wonderfully naïve, to other ways of the world, man. That grief however was offset by the fact that Jackson's support was still present after the corpse rifling skills of Campbell and the additional sword arms that were provided by Y'Bor Kaz, Seton Rax, Beran and Nazar Grant. For now the quest was to be one where violent men would be useful.

Egremont asked when the best time for tides was to leave. With wolves openly walking into bars in Tetterton and obviously having links with the brigands who had been in control of the castle in the Old City, Egremont felt that speed was now necessary.

"Tomorrow, just after dawn," said Fenton. "I'll take Mr. Battfin with me now to the docks and we'll buy another launch. We'll also get as much supplies as we will be able to carry plus crossbows and bolts for all except Is-Is."

"Crossbows?" asked Egremont.

"Yeah, I reckon we are going to need to increase our missile fire capability, plus it might be useful if we need to hunt any other prey over in Kenai."

"Fine," said Egremont. "Take care of black hooded groups with one volley hey? Do you think we should leave some guards on the ship now?"

"It's a fair question but it will be safe in Tetterton. The Harbour Master and his Port Keeper Guards will not let anything be taken out without the correct paperwork. I think it will be better with us all here together tonight."

"Excellent. Head off now then. The two of you will both also get the chance for a full nights rest as we have some volunteers for the night watch after their long afternoon reposes!" Egremont chortled a little, looking at those in the group who were rubbing groggy eyes and lightly

281

complaining of pains in the back of their heads caused by too many lunchtime beers.

Fenton left by the door that he had entered a couple of hours earlier with his first mate and capable bodyguard, Mr. Battfin, by his side. The two trotted quickly down the stairs and left 'The Grobbling Smith' by the reception door. They took the straight streets directly to the docks and to one of Jackson's offices as some coinage was needed to procure another boat to land in Kenai. It was now late in the afternoon but Jackson's empire was always open very late to take advantage of trade which rarely ceased. Fenton pulled out a wad of promissory notes that Campbell had handed to him and pushed open the door to the office, ringing a bell hung on to the frame by a shaped piece of flat metal, announcing their arrival.

The clerk behind the desk looked at his customers above the wire frame of his spectacles. His pen stooped writing in the large ledger in front of him as he took in the view of a couple of flamboyantly dressed and intimidatingly muscled pirates who were striding confidently towards him.

"Ah my good man," said Fenton. "We need to acquire some coin please for some transactions we intend to make this very evening."

Fenton handed ten of the notes across the desk towards the thin faced bureaucrat who took the pieces of paper and examined them.

"Just a moment sir," he replied and turned around to a bookshelf behind him where he selected an anonymous looking ledger and brought it back to the desk. "If I am not mistaken, and I rarely am, you are part of Lord Jackson's little expedition?"

He opened the book and started examining a list of numbers that corresponded to identifying numbers on the notes.

"Well yes, that is correct. Has he spoken of us?" Fenton replied.

"We have been advised that Lord Jackson is travelling with certain nautical and militaristic types. Is he well?" the clerk replied.

Fenton paused for the slightest amount of time before responding in an extremely conversational manner.

"I believe that Lord Jackson has found the trip most exhilarating and I honestly believe that he could not feel any better than he currently does."

Mr. Battfin looked at Fenton out of the corner of his eye but knew to stay quiet. Fenton said nothing else but waited as the clerk checked his book, running thin fingers along rows of numbers.

"Well everything seems to be in order," said the man. "Rather than making the trades yourself this office could easily secure your needs and have them delivered to wherever you wish."

"That seems like a much finer idea than us having to procure everything," said Fenton giving the man with the wire rimmed spectacles his most debonair tone and most thankful smile. "We need a small launch that can land on a beach and carry eleven. We need ten sets of crossbows that wind mechanically with a batch of sixty bolts for each, of the highest quality. We need rations for eleven hearty souls that will sustain them on a dangerous trip. Oh, and I also need a fine three quarter length, leather coat that will suit my build. Can you have them all taken to 'The Brazen Manticore' before dawn? You'll find her docked in the harbour."

"Absolutely sir. Consider it done. May I suggest black leather for the coat?"

"I think that is a very fine suggestion sir!"

"Then it will be in the cabin with the other equipment and rations by dawn. The launch will be attached to the stern," the man replied and put away the ledger back to its original place on the bookshelf.

"Come Mr. Battfin. It seems that Lord Jackson's reach extends further than any man and with more class than even I could have expected. One last evening of pleasure and comfort awaits us before we continue with our latest expedition."

With that Percy nodded to the clerk and left, ringing the bell for a second time with their exit and they headed straight back towards 'The Grobbling Smith' confident and certain that their order would be delivered. As they walked back to their base Mr. Battfin gave his captain a look akin to a frown of disapproval.

"Well I didn't tell any lies did I? And we get an easier evening than the bartering with trade types I had expected," Percy said with a stunned tone at his first mates accusatory stare.

"You are a great equivocator make no mistake," replied Mr. Battfin.

"But never a liar, Mr. Battfin. Never a liar. Let us return to the others and say no more about it."

Night was now not far off and the straight streets of the well planned Tetterton were becoming less crowded as the mass of peoples in the port headed off to homes or hostelries. The solid laid out blocked buildings struck Percy Fenton as cold and hard facades but he knew the mountains of Kenai to the south would be colder and harder with no promise of a welcome within.

"Well Mr. Battfin, are you ready to guide 'The Brazen Manticore' to Cape Hayze?" said Fenton as they walked on. "I've spent enough time sailing recently. I think it is time for my first mate to take command for a while."

"Aye Cap'n. No trouble at all. Direct south, then south southwest to the beach I know of and then I'll pilot the launch too. It will be a very rough ride in the peculiar waves on the approach to that coast."

"I assume we are going to try and get back to Umiat at Rhyell when we retrieve the Umiat Stone. How do you reckon we'll make it back?" asked Fenton.

"Well I should think that a standard piece of pirate procedure should apply. We'll anchor 'The Brazen Manticore', drop all sails and raise flags of disease and quarantine. The launch we hide in the rocks of Kenai."

"Good answer Mr. Battfin. I've got some fish on board that I caught in expectation that you would have wanted some fresh meat if you had made you way down the tunnels to the Smugglers Cavern. We can catch some more on the way down…"

"And then we leave them to rot in pots covered in mesh to protect them from gulls but allow the aroma to pervade the immediate environment," continued Mr. Battfin doing a fair impersonation of his captain. "The smell should keep any inquisitive types away when combined with the flags of universal warning."

"I'll also send a message to the lads on 'The Ardent Panda' who are not at sea just yet to drop by now and again, check the ship is still there and restock the pots. What think you Mr. Battfin?" Percy smiled a huge grin.

"Good answer Mr. Fenton. It's standard pirate procedure for a long jaunt on land. Are there a couple of extra anchors on board already or should we pick some up early tomorrow?"

"I think a couple early tomorrow should ensure a solid tethering Mr. Battfin. Consider it done. I will select a couple from nearby traders who should be up for that early morning opportunity of a sale."

Mr. Battfin gave a large grin and the two pirates trod on through the streets unaware that the remaining people on them moved out of their way as do waves against a cutting prow.

They entered 'The Grobbling Smith' by the reception door but rather than heading straight up the stairs to the rooms they decided to head to the tap room for a couple of pints so as to appear as if they had been working a little harder on securing supplies than they actually had. A small slice of pleasure afforded to them by the professional skills of Lord Jackson's business empire.

The room was filling up with individuals seeking recreation, company or just the pleasures of beer. Mr. Battfin led the way straight to the bar. The landlord gave him a friendly look which said 'back again?' and then raised his eyebrows, a question universally understood in this environment.

"Two pints of Corambis please. I found it very fine at lunchtime," said the vast pirate.

"Glad you enjoyed it sir. We are doing very well with it. Half a barrel today already," said the landlord pulling firmly on the pump and taking care that the spout did not touch the glass or the rising beer. He continued in a friendly yet conspiratorial manner, "Don't worry though. I've got a couple of extra barrels well settled and cared for down in the cellar if you and your party are coming down again this evening."

"I'm sure we will be back down again for a while," said Fenton chipping in.

"Glad to hear it sir," said the landlord passing over the first pint.

Mr. Battfin indicated that Fenton should take it which he did with gusto and quickly slurped half the pint down his throat. He smacked his lips and his eyes twinkled in enjoyment of the ale.

Mr. Battfin rubbed his jaw thoughtfully with his large left hand waiting for the next pint to be served up. As the landlord put the pint onto the bar Fenton asked if he could have another as he passed the now empty tankard back. The landlord smiled knowingly and instantly reached for a fresh mug into which to serve the beer. As Mr. Battfin enjoyed his ale a little slower, Fenton handed over some coins which he deftly stacked into a tower of copper and silver.

"Keep the change. Wonderful beer. Well kept real ale in a cellar by a man with your prestigious skills is so much nicer than the bottled variety I have been imbibing these past few days," said Fenton with the graceful tones of an appreciative gourmand.

"Thank you sir. There's quite a lot of change from that stack of coins sir," the landlord replied eyeing the coins up and down.

"I'm sure you'll look after us for it. You know if the bar gets busy tonight."

"I will keep a look out for you and your party and instruct the staff to do the same."

"That will be most appreciated as it is our last night in town and therefore the final chance to enjoy your fine hospitality and beer."

"Taking a trip sir?" the landlord enquired.

"Absolutely. One where we might not have the chance of an ale for a while."

"Now that is a crying shame sir. One should never have to be away from the chance of an ale for too long," the landlord took on a serious tone. "Let me pour out a couple of extra pints for you gentlemen now. These shall be my pleasure. On the house if you will. I'm sure it won't take you long to get through the ones you have now. Then I must attend to my other customers. The bar is filling up nicely tonight sir."

With that the thick set man with his grimy stains poured out two more drinks and set them alongside each other on the bar. Then he turned his attention to other clients with coin in their hands and a thirst in their throats.

Mr. Battfin and Percy Fenton remained at the bar with their beers and engaged in deep conversation about what had transpired since they had split and Fenton had taken his lonely journey to Tetterton while Mr. Battfin had entered the Old City. As they slowed down their drinking with the increase in conversation the bar continued to fill with workers finished with work and residents of the inn emerging from their rooms for an evening in the bar. Rough faced dock workers with heavily canyoned skin, delicate merchants swathed in purple silks, the typical mix of adventurers just arrived in town all sat and stood in their chosen groups and the noise of many voices and various accents filled the bar in competition to be heard. Fenton was listening intently to Mr. Battfin's description of how they had first met Seton Rax and company in their battle with the stirges, Campbell's opening of the treasure chest, the terrible plan to walk up to the castle gates, Jackson's death and burial and the meeting and gladiatorial negotiations with Y'Bor Kaz before the first mate then described the victorious attack on the castle. By the time Mr. Battfin had efficiently filled in more details than Egremont's briefing they had ordered another couple of pints and the evening was solidly in place.

"How about your journey then Percy?" asked Mr. Battfin.

"Oh, very quiet really. Had a nice night at 'The Black Bull' then it was a simple jaunt down to Tetterton. Bought the boat and made my way east. You heard about my little encounter in the cave and then I raced back here when I found the arrow," Percy shrugged and finished his pint with a great forced gulp. He wiped his mouth dry. "About time we head back upstairs, get the others and come back down here for a meal."

They left the tap room and took the stairs to their rooms, knocking on the door which they had expected to find locked. It was opened by Beran.

"Successful afternoon?" the knight asked, glancing briefly behind them and down the corridor.

"Oh yes, everything sorted out and we can all be on board by dawn," Percy replied.

Egremont looked up from the chessboard where he sat alone, obviously deep in thought at the situation confronting him. He gave a slight sniff and returned to looking at the pieces.

"Successful enough to stop off for a quick half, hey?" he said.

"Well it's been a while since I have had the opportunity to have a beverage with my first mate," Fenton said coming into the room with Mr. Battfin.

"There's still a little time left," said Egremont. "I resign Beran, you've beat me again and easily." The wolfhound knocked over his king with a clip of his claw.

"Thank you for the opportunity to play," said Beran closing the door behind Mr. Battfin who headed straight for a view of the end game position while Percy slumped himself down in the chair where he had earlier sat.

The group gathered itself together and headed down to the ground floor of 'The Grobbling Smith'. They decided on having a last more formal meal together in the dining room. Waitresses brought drinks to their table and they all selected to have a starter, main course and pudding when the chance came to order. Despite the knowledge that the following day would take them to Kenai the atmosphere was filled with joviality, fuelled by Corambis and a single bottle of wine which was enjoyed by Vixen. Hangovers in the morning were to be an issue for those with shaky sea legs, tonight was about the knowledge that it was the last safe night for a very long while and the trials of Kenai would be more demanding than the dangers that the Old City had thrown against them.

Chorus Nine

The night slipped by uneventfully, the guards untroubled by wolves or the noises of other guests in 'The Grobbling Smith'. Most slept peacefully, aided by a comfortably full stomach and a restful amount of ale.

Vixen however found that she was having vivid dreams of Ahriman and his pack of hand picked wolves. She saw him on board the deck of a black ship without a sail. She felt it was propelled by many oars below the water line but she could not be certain. She saw the ship enter the harbour of the capital city of Kenai, Ende. The city was old, rotten, peeled plasters and decayed reds. Large public buildings with thugs lolling around the entrance, busted up pubs with poor quality sour ale and patrons sloshing around. The docks were solid though, huge slabs of concrete, mixed up in ancient times by people who knew how to build for a thousand years. The black ship eased up against an edge and came to a stop. A group of swarthy, opal eyed men with jet black hair, greasy and unkempt stood at the dock. They were heavily armed and in well made leather armour and they waited silently and with discipline. Ahriman leapt off the ship and into the middle of the men. The group instantly marched off at a purposeful pace into the city of Ende. The warriors pushed any fool that got in their way, out of their way. Sometimes a punch or a thwack with a sword hilt to the face, sometimes a more violent thrust from a weapon that left the individual writhing in the street for other witnesses to ignore. Then she could see no more of that group as her thoughts moved to black cloaked figures following her though woods as she flittered slightly above the ground and floated towards a pile of clean picked bones of victims from some slaughter.

Fenton was dreaming too. The boulders were back, rolling around his mind with their play as little children, bickering as mothers and bellicose cries of violent intent as large crushing rocks of death left no space in his mind for him to escape.

Chapter Ten

Mr. Battfin piloted 'The Brazen Manticore' through the harbour of Tetterton and towards the portal and the open Sea of Kaltag. Only Y'Bor Kaz and Tumbletick were otherwise on deck, excited to see the man made arch and supreme defence of Rampart. The others were in the cabin, examining the crossbows and supplies that had been delivered, just as promised, with the additional launch. The sun was just beginning to rise far to the east and the chill of the air refreshed Y'Bor and Tumbletick as they gazed at the portal and its delicious array of weapons. The chill also reminded both of them that they were heading south towards the colder continent of Kenai. Y'Bor looked directly up with Tumbletick and their heads moved in fixed unison to take in the view as it drifted along in the half light.

"Well I wasn't sure I'd ever see that again when I saw it last. It surely is a mighty monument for memory as well as defence," said Y'Bor.

"I wasn't so sure I would see it again either a couple of times in the Old City," Tumbletick replied.

"Yeah, it got pretty hairy for you in there I guess," Y'Bor paused, aware of his faux pas. "You know what I mean. A little tense. Scary. Sorry, I did not mean to say anything that implied anything about you being such a hirsute fellow. Sorry Tumbletick old chap."

"That's okay Y'Bor," Tumbletick laughed. "The hairiest part was when we lost Jackson. I shouldn't joke when talking about that. I miss him very much you know? I haven't had that many friends."

"Ah but you've got lots now Tumbletick. And you've got some friends among the great and the good. We all think very highly of you and you know that we have all been sworn in by Egremont to protect you at all costs don't you?"

"Yeah, all of you. I guess I even have to accept that Vixen has taken the oath too and made it very clear that she's going to be about. I did not like what she said to me about Lord Jackson. When he died. It didn't seem to be the time and the place to go into things like that."

"I heard about that. Probably a bit obtuse but I'm sure she had her reasons. You know, like needing to get you away from danger and

290

then probably defending herself in front of everybody. From what I can make out she is a very capable woman with many talents that will come in useful. Plus she was the one who did indeed come to your aid before anybody else and under a volley of missile fire too," Y'Bor turned round with Tumbletick to look back on the Isle of Rampart as it was left behind and 'The Brazen Manticore' entered the choppier waters beyond the man made reef. They were aware that the sun was rising to the east but it was hidden behind the island of Rampart and the boat was gripped by an early morning gloom hunkering over the sea.

Mr. Battfin swung the wheel to port with a strong sweep of his right arm. The wheel spun freely until 'The Brazen Manticore' faced south, then the pirate grabbed the wheel into a sudden stop and the prow started splitting the steep waves ahead.

"How long until we get to Kenai then Mr. Battfin?" asked Tumbletick, kind of hoping for a response that would indicate a very long time.

"With the wind as it is and it being just under a hundred nautical miles to the bay I know, I would say we will be anchoring late tonight or in the very early hours. Then we will attempt a landing on the beach tomorrow. The tide is best a couple of hours after dawn."

"Why is it we always seem to do things about dawn?" Y'Bor moaned a little.

Tumbletick already knew that Kenai was drawing close but somehow the pirate's answer to his question meant that the nerves welled up in his stomach again but now the feelings of panic fluttered and heated his chest and head with great poundings of fear. He decided to try and stand a little taller and blow out the emotions in a purposeful sigh.

Y'Bor sensed the nerves and patted Tumbletick on the back with a broad hand. Tumbletick felt that Y'Bor was saying that it was going to be hard but that he would be there with him. His warhammers would be a lot more use that the knife Tumbletick had with him. If, as they all said, they were now moving into a phase of raiding and butchery, it was lucky that the group was incredibly well equipped. All Tumbletick had to do was stay away from any violence and then be used as a courier once the stone was retrieved. Simple really, as all great plans are. Success would depend on the individuals involved in the mission and Tumbletick reminded himself again that the group was, really, incredibly well equipped for what lay ahead. If that mission was a raid with the possibility of escape. He felt that the positive affirmation statements of the brilliance of his companions helped a little but he was still unsure of where they were heading and what truly lay ahead in Kenai.

"Let's go and join the others below deck shall we Tumbletick?" said Y'Bor. "Keep ourselves busy with packing the equipment correctly and passing the time with a little less sea breeze."

Tumbletick trotted after the tattooed and red headed warrior, across the wooden boards of the deck and down to the crowded cabin below. Is-Is looked up first at his approaching companions and gave a great gregarious wink as he repositioned the supplies in his pack.

Otherwise the tone was quiet as each sat with their own thoughts of the challenges ahead. The cold of the southern continent was a major concern. Although a warm northerly wind sped their passage south now, the gusts were likely to shift and bite and freeze in the chasms of Kenai. If an easterly should take them it would be coming straight off the vast Elias Ice Flats, which fed the Kenai Sea with great bergs and growlers from its multitude of glaciers. The mountain of Kantishna was several hundred miles west of the Elias Ice Flats and permanently frozen Lake Isana but the myriad of mountains between them but was an insignificant barrier to the winds of Kenai.

Tumbletick found himself sitting next to Percy. He rubbed his newly formed scar from the wound which bound them in friendship. Fenton noticed and gave the little man a big smile as he looked into his pack and pulled out a seed cake.

"Hungry Tumbletick?" the pirate said offering him the food.

Breakfast had been a scant and snatched affair as they had left before dawn. The heavy tipping of the landlord and the big spend on their final meal had meant that he had risen early and prepared it himself but his skills as a cook were nothing as compared to his craft as a cellar man. Breakfast had therefore been only bread, butter and slices of dry meats and chunks of cheese. To some like Seton Rax this was a typical breakfast of the nomadic tribes of the Noatak plains, to others used to city influenced hot breakfasts it seemed the first of several hardships ahead. So they had eaten and quickly left 'The Grobbling Smith' before first light, by a side door, fully armed and vigilant for wolves.

Tumbletick took the seed cake. It had a little glazing of honey that had gone hard in the cold of the open sea. He held it in his small hands and nibbled on the corners, turning occasionally to whittle it away with his teeth. Fenton smiled again. The image of a defenceless and naïve creature was not lost on him and he wondered how fate could have swept up Tumbletick in a pointless quest of the retrieval of an object of political, if no magical, importance. That was a ridiculous debate to have with oneself though. They were where they were and the stone had to be recovered and returned. If anything the mission was important as a piece of retaliation for the massacre at Court. If they could kill Ahriman as well and bring back the trophies of his head as well as the Umiat Stone then both would look good in the Nave of Rhyell Cathedral. Fenton thought for a moment. Until recently they had believed they were going after an impersonator of Ahriman. The wolf down in the common room had apparently told Egremont and company that the man killed a decade ago had been the impersonator sent in his place. Maybe the others had discussed this at length but everything seemed quite quiet about such a large piece of news. The pirate went to sit by Egremont, continuing to readjust belongings in his pack as he leant across to the wolfhound.

"Egremont, old chap," the pirate whispered. "I've been having a bit of a think about what the blue eyed wolf told you about Ahriman."

"What? That they sent an impersonator before?"

"Well yes. Quite a big bit of news really."

"If it's true, then yes I guess it would be huge."

"What you don't believe him then?"

"Not necessarily," Egremont replied looking down into his pack. "What are the facts in a situation like this? We have a man called Ahriman who leads the Ahrioch Horde against us in a time of war and is seen raising huge demons and knights of Hell from the very ground during the Ahrioch War. That man, my comrade in arms, decapitates in front of my very eyes. Then we have a raiding party, lead by another man who looks like Ahriman, who has a successful attack on a bunch of scrummed in defenceless dignitaries and all he can summon up are a few baboon skeletons. Then we have 'old blue eyes' tell us that what we are actually facing on our quest is the great and mighty Demonologist Ahriman. Well I would tend to think that the wolf may well be lying in an attempt to scare us off. Deconstruct it Mr. Fenton and it actually provides hope. But I congratulate you on thinking it through. No-one else has mentioned it. Either that or they did not care. The job still has to be done. Personally I don't care either way. In a little while we are going to be in a position of retribution and I look forward to being in an onslaught of fear and vengeance."

"I'm happy with my pack," announced Fenton, suitably satisfied and a little quashed by the response from Egremont which he felt sure others had heard as his voice had become a crescendo of violence towards the end of the speech. He stood up. "I'm going up on deck to support Mr. Battfin. I'll get the spinnaker unfurled and we'll make better time."

The pirate strode off and up the short steps out of the cabin. The door only had to be opened for a short time, as the handsome sea dog swaggered quickly through despite the vicious pitching of the vessel, but the cold air burst into the cabin during that moment and induced several shudders. Egremont and Is-Is were fine with their fur under their armour, Tumbletick was well covered with hair and large amounts of clothes however others in the room felt the cold a little easier.

"You know," said Campbell. "It might have been an idea if we had decided to get some of those black hooded cloaks that the wolves all wear, or taken the multi-coloured robes Y'Bor offered us."

"We'll collect some black ones when the slaughter commences then," said Y'Bor. "Might be an idea not to use blades on those we want to keep. I wouldn't want a great big rent in any cloak I was wearing."

"Your clubs and my mace then," said Nazar Grant. "I'm sure that between us we will be able to acquire eleven of varying sizes."

"Good idea," said Beran. "I know you guys got clothes for cold weather when you planned this expedition but I don't think we have really got enough for everyone now. My plate mail is not going to be particularly good at keeping the weather out."

"Well let's share what we have got to those who will need it most," said Egremont looking at Seton Rax with his bare torso but fur boots.

"Oh, I'll be alright," the barbarian replied. "Tough as nails me!"

"You might want to cover up a little," Egremont said. "Here's a rather nice top that will still allow you to fight with the freedom you like."

The wolfhound dragged out a garment from his pack and slung it across the cabin. Seton Rax caught it and put it on quickly despite his earlier protestations of immunity from the cold. His muscled chest and shoulders bulged out the tan coloured fabric that was cut for the slimmer wolfhound. Seton looked a bit sheepish as his belly button and midriff still showed.

"Let's definitely take some time to get at least one of those cloaks when we find them," the barbarian implored of the group. "If the guys back home could see me now."

"At least your feet will keep warm," said Campbell. "Those fur booties are just divine!"

Campbell's comment generated general mirth and the group fell into easy conversations now that all the packing was done. The day dragged on as 'The Brazen Manticore' ploughed a direct southerly route. There was not much that could really be done until Mr. Battfin could take reference points when land was sighted and then head close to where the cove was and the beach suitable for a landing.

Vixen spent most of the day in deliberate slumber, conserving energy for the trials ahead. Beran and Nazar Grant spent quite a bit of time on deck asking plenty of questions with a nautical bent in an effort to learn the names of ropes and sails. Percy was happy to answer them but Mr. Battfin was particularly focussed on holding the course. Tumbletick found himself gravitating towards the protective charms of Is-Is who was engrossed purely on blade maintenance. Y'Bor and Seton found themselves talking about the finer points of fighting with weapons that were often considered as out of fashion by most warriors. However they felt that the warhammer and the battleaxe both had their place as heavy weapons, especially in a commando unit with an over emphasis on swords, it added balance. Not all enemies ahead might be easily dispatched with the thrust of a blade; heavier damage might be needed, especially if wandering monsters might be encountered. They did however both feel that the crossbows could be a benefit on this expedition. Campbell the Weasel and Egremont were talking quietly so as not to disturb Vixen who lounged close to them. They were intent on ensuring that ruthlessness would be applied by all and that Tumbletick would always be protected by one of their number.

After a late luncheon of some of their fresh supplies more of the group started to fall asleep, rocked by the boat and seduced by the warmth of the cabin over the shivering of the sea. They dozed and fell into private thoughts as the day came to late afternoon and then drifted into night. The journey was taking a little longer than expected and most did not mind falling into deep sleeps in the cabin of the boat. Mr.

Battfin and Percy shared responsibility of a slow night sailing south, taking naps when they could they piloted their way through the night. The others slept soundly and deeply with no watches needed until a cry of 'Land Ho' from Percy at the bow woke everyone at a little after dawn. They all left the cabin to go out on deck and for many it was to be their first view of the Kenai coast.

The mountains were black and sharp. No trees to blend and blur round the edges, just hard, dark granite cliffs, impervious to the sea. The tors and crags were dominated by escarpments and mountains looming behind but all were dwarfed by two gigantic peaks to the left and right of the total horizon which was now filled by the growing wall of rock ahead.

It was noisy out on deck. The waves grew larger and more erratic as they approached the coast, crashing down on themselves and also being burst by the boat, the waters roared. The wind too was howling in the southern seas it lacerated the rigging and raged in their ears.

"The two huge mountains you see are Hayze and Kantishna," shouted Egremont, straining above the competing sound of the sea. "Two giants of the eight great Kenai peaks. Hayze is on your left. And our destination, Kantishna is on your right."

"We're lucky to see them," bellowed Vixen. "Usually both would be obscured by cloud. Hayze in the haze."

"I wish I could sail us closer to Kantishna," shouted Mr. Battfin. "But our journey must begin at the cove. Not long till we anchor but we must be ready to move quickly if we are to catch the tide."

Mr. Battfin turned to port slightly and Percy dashed about the deck unloosening knots to let sails go slack and then be grabbed again by the wind to burst and ripple into tautness and take the ship south southwest.

The cliffs, brute strength of rock, crept closer, fending off the sea by bashing back huge swelling waves that could never rise and break as on a beach. Spray could now be seen in the distance by the walls of rock rising and spewing above the surface of the water. The rock seemed impervious but eventually time would tell in the war of erosion.

Within an hour, Fenton and Mr. Battfin both started furling the sails and preparing to throw the anchors overboard to secure 'The Brazen Manticore'. They had explained the idea they wanted to employ, about hoisting the flags which would indicate plague on board. Campbell had been given responsibility to prepare the fish pots and with his tools he secured a piece of spare sailcloth over the top of each container with the lid removed. He then liberally perforated the cloth with many holes to allow the aroma of festering fish to grow while protecting the contents from ravenous sea birds. The pots were then placed around the decks in order to enable the smells to emanate over a wider area and send broad swathes of decay wherever the wind desired.

"Right, everyone into the launch then," shouted Percy and the group started to board while it was still hanging off the bow of the ship. The longboat rocked with clambering comrades and the swell of the ocean. Mr. Battfin remained on deck and untied the knots of the ropes holding the launch hanging high above the sea. The tough looking pirate had the ropes soon re-hitched via pulleys that would enable him to lower the little boat into the water. He lowered the launch with great skill and it made an easy decent until it splashed lightly onto a slapping wave. He then strode to the bow and leapt the six foot down into the back of the boat where he instantly grabbed the tiller.

"Release us from 'The Brazen Manticore', Mr. Fenton, please!" Mr. Battfin ordered. Fenton swiftly moved from bow to stern of the little boat, nimbly skirting and evading the bodies which packed it and undid the remaining ties to the ship that they all hoped to see again. With its anchors set, pots ripening and its flags fluttering, 'The Brazen Manticore' screamed its warning. The yellow flag with a bare white skull indicated plague and the other a deep blue square with a single red star meant quarantine.

"Y'Bor, Seton! You are rowing!" Mr. Battfin gave an order that was a relief to some. "You had better be fast if we are to catch the tide."

The two powerful warriors gave a slight moan to this most recent command and they lifted the long oars and placed them in the rowlocks. The oars were heavy and broad, usually meant for two men to handle each. The heavily muscled men though were easily capable and with Y'Bor sitting centrally in the first third of the boat and Seton in front of Mr. Battfin at the tiller, they started to pull hard and propel the launch forward.

Egremont sat right in the prow of the little boat, his paw on his brow and his tongue lolling slightly out in the strong wind, he gazed towards the cliffs ahead of them.

"Don't worry chaps," he said. "It's only about a mile."

Y'Bor and Seton flexed their muscles and buckled down to large sweeps, the launch picked up rhythm and pace and Mr. Battfin smiled a toothy grin as he directed them towards the cove of which he knew.

Tumbletick negotiated his way around bodies and the scything shaft of the oar pulled by Y'Bor Kaz until he found himself next to Egremont.

"Can you see the cove?" Tumbletick asked. "Doesn't look like there are any bays or beaches at all in that coastline."

"Well I think that is why it is a secret cove and cove might be a bit of an over description for a tiny little inlet," Egremont replied. "I think this one is a lot less known than the smuggler's cove on Rampart. That one is visible at low tide to anyone who might be sailing by. Not many come by this route. The straights to the east are lethal and Ende and therefore the trade routes are all further west and north. From what I know the cove is basically hidden because a spur of cliff juts out and over laps the entrance. You really have to be right upon it to see the way in. Then it is a sharp turn to starboard to head up the small stretch of water to the beach. Mr. Battfin says it is likely to be extremely rough on the approach."

"Oh," said Tumbletick. "Where do you think it will be safest to sit?"

"Somewhere in the middle I would think. I'm going to stay at the prow though and enjoy the ride," Egremont had a glint in his eye as he spoke.

The sea was growing much choppier as they got closer to the intimidating crags of Kenai. Tumbletick looked back towards the commanding Mr. Battfin. The man looked terrifying Tumbletick suddenly realised. He had been such a protective presence for so long that his real visage was missed. Bald and extremely dark skinned, grimacing as he scanned the precipices for landmarks. He was actually broader in the shoulder than either Y'Bor Kaz or Seton Rax, with natural bulk and strength rather than the kind of sculptured muscle the other two warriors possessed. The pirate's face was scarred in ritual patterns of lines and swirls which lent him an almost demonic look. His eyes were of the darkest brown framed with pure white and they moved quickly with the alertness of a dangerous man. His thick lips were slightly sneering and his jaw was squared and similar in scale to his massive frame. Tumbletick thought of all the men who had seen Mr.

Battfin as their last sight in life as the pirate attacked with his cutlasses or his fists. The little man gave a shudder in the sea breezes and turned back round to Egremont.

"I think I'll stay with you and enjoy the ride as well."

"Well said Tumbletick. Don't worry, were in safe hands with Mr. Battfin at the helm."

The rowing continued, they were now within a hundred yards of the massive cliffs, the swell was sickening as it volumed around them and then collapsed back down into temporary troughs and canyons in the sea. Several were suffering with the monstrous motions and held on to anything that seemed solid, be it boat or companion.

"Nearly there," yelled Mr. Battfin as they drew within about twenty yards of the rock face. "Y'Bor, Seton, when I say so I will need you to row with all your strength. You had better rest for a couple of minutes now. When the command comes you must be ready. I'll just ask you to row at a basic stroke at first but then you must be ready for an explosion of power."

The two warriors heeded the pirate's word and slumped upon their oars they breathed deeply to recover. Mr. Battfin was making small adjustments to the tiller to keep the launch facing the way he wanted. He could read the currents well and along with Fenton, was not unnerved by the rolling of the waters. Ahead of them now in the darkness of the rock there stood out a column of space. Behind this space a channel could be seen leading away tucked behind a vast spur of rock that concealed it from the sea until you were right next to the cliffs. The sea was being pushed and sucked into this watercourse at the same time in vast amounts and Tumbletick's eyes bulged more than usual as he realised that Mr. Battfin planned to pilot their little launch into a strip of water that was heaving like that with brutal granite crushing jaws on either side. Above the noise of the spray and wind and defeated waves Tumbletick could hear Campbell the Weasel sucking in a gasp of horror between his lower lip and top teeth. What caused most fear in Tumbletick was the fact that the water ahead of him was being forced into such a narrow space that it actually rose like a hill into the channel before forming higher waves again cascading along it. He turned around to look at his companions and noticed that they had a lot less colour in their faces than usual. Beran the Bold was the first to vomit over the side of the boat which set off Vixen and Nazar

Grant in short succession. Fenton laughed out loud, patting the cleric hard on the back to help him empty the contents of his churning guts into the hungry sea.

"Y'Bor, Seton! Are you ready?" shouted Mr. Battfin. "What we are about to travel down is fundamentally a funnel. The sea is forced down a narrowing channel. We have unforgiving rock on both sides but a pleasant pebble beach for us to land on at the end. However, if you don't get us the speed we need to get up that slightly strange slope of water ahead of us, then we either get spat back out or crushed into a cliff. One chance only everybody. I've done it once before. They say you've got a one in ten chance of getting it right, so?"

Campbell threw up as well, Egremont put his arm round Tumbletick.

"At least we shall have the finest view on the way in hey?" the wolfhound said.

"What speed do we need Mr. Battfin?" shouted Seton Rax.

"All you can muster," Mr. Battfin replied. "When I shout stop though, you stop as well. We are aiming to hit the peak of a wave and then we just get pushed all the way to the pebbles."

"And if we get to the beach in one piece, retrieve the Umiat Stone and get back here, we are then going to come back out this way?" asked Vixen wiping some final sticky strings of spit from her mouth.

"Coming back out is easy my dear Vixen. If you are facing the right way," said Fenton. "Just a matter of timing with a riptide."

Mr. Battfin nodded in agreement but was scanning the swell ahead. He suddenly shouted to Y'Bor Kaz and Seton Rax to row.

The red headed warrior and the barbarian started to row getting ready for the order to fly into their ultimate pace. Mr. Battfin was reading the waves, adjusting the tiller and leading the launch into a line heading towards the column of space between the rocks. Angling the boat now towards the dead centre of the entrance to the channel he suddenly shouted.

"Row! Row for our lives you dogs!"

Y'Bor and Seton burst with intent and power and pulled on their oars with a violence and a desire to move as fast as they could.

"Wish we had a couple of more oars," said Campbell nervously. "I thought we needed to be moving quickly."

The boat heaved and lurched with each stroke and did move faster but the sensation was more of being sucked up and towards the channel rather than real control of rowing from the warriors.

"Row! Row you slacking cracks!" Mr. Batting roared choosing to use the strongest swearword of Umiat to shock some action into them despite of the very obvious need for a response. "Pull till your backs break and your hearts burst!"

Their muscles strained and they dug in, oars deep in the water and the boat moved a little swifter. Mr. Battfin manoeuvred the launch to the direct centre of the channel judging the swell of the waves in front of them and then he suddenly shouted to stop.

The wave they were on lifted the boat and started to sweep it forward. Tumbletick and Egremont at the front of the launch could see the pebble beach about eighty yards ahead and the tall granite walls on either side closing in. The sensation as more water tried to get down less space was unnerving as the wave rose higher and sped up.

"Stow those oars gentlemen!" ordered Mr. Battfin. The warriors lifted them in and placed them on the floor of the boat. It felt now like the wave was going to topple forward on to the waters slipping back down the channel deeply beneath but it kept its form, just growing gradually more steep. The prow was now tipping forward and was noticeably lower than the stern. Tumbletick and Egremont leant back feeling conscious that if this continued then they might fall out. All in the boat started to get the same sensation and moved towards the bow trying to balance the launch. The cliff face on either side was rushing by as Mr. Battfin kept the vessel on a steady course but soon the rudder became useless as the boat was completely at the mercy of the tumultuous surge. The boat began to twist slightly and Mr. Battfin cursed again and then struggled forward to grab one of the stored oars. He pulled it out and swung it out over the wave. The others thought he was going to attempt to row without a rowlock but were amazed at his strength and skill as he jabbed at the granite wall in an attempt to straighten the boat. The boat stopped in its slow twist but was still in danger of eventually becoming side on and capsizing in the wave. Mr. Battfin pounded at the cliff again trying to get the launch straight. Seton Rax's barbarian brain gained the insight of the boat not facing purely forward as they hit the pebble beach so he too grabbed an oar and made a lunge at battering the speeding cliff face. Mr. Battfin struck for a third time with his oar and the boat definitely shifted back towards a true and straight course down the channel. The wave above them was beginning to crest and barrel into a potential tube as the beach ahead of them was now rapidly approaching. Seton Rax smashed the nearby cliff again with the oar and the boat grew straighter still as Mr. Battfin followed with a fourth strike. Seton again made an attack against the rock wall and to his surprise the oar got caught on a spur of granite and the wooden blade splintered dramatically, sending a shock wave up the shaft which caused the barbarian to lose his grip and the oar fell into the cascading wave and was quickly sucked under by the rip tide and back out to sea.

The beach was now little less than twenty yards away and the rushing surge of wave was now rising above flatter waters that were slipping back down the channel. The launch was now extremely steep on the wave and all within it were leaning back so as to almost be lying flat. The pace was exhilarating as the beach approached all could see that it was flat, made of pebbles and then rose steeply towards the granite walls that surrounded it on all sides. The constant breaking of waves forced the pebbles towards the dead end and they kept trying to slip back towards the water when they had the chance. Then a couple of yards before the beach the wave suddenly lost its height but none of its pace and the boat lowered, became flatter and neatly slipped up the stones and eventually came to a complete rest before tilting a little to the left as all momentum was lost.

The party looked at each other in relief before Mr. Battfin ordered everyone out and to start pulling the launch further up the beach carrying it away from the potential pull of further breaking waves.

"Come on," shouted the pirate. "There is a chasm to the south where we can make our way to the mountains of Kenai and store the boat above the level of the tide."

All started pulling and pushing the boat which moved well on the wet stones making a rasping, constant clicking of pebbles under dragging wood. They directed the boat towards the chasm and away from the high water line. As they heaved it the last few yards to the final resting place, Egremont turned to Tumbletick and Mr. Battfin and said;

"Well that was a little easier than I thought it was going to be for a minute."

"Well it's not really as hard as I made out," said Mr. Battfin. "Just wanted to add a little excitement for the non seafaring types. All you've really got to do is get the boat up the swell and keep it straight. Nature will get you to the beach every time."

Tumbletick gave a little chortle and reached over the side of the launch to pull out his belongings just as the others of the party started to shoulder backpacks and secure stored weapons at their rightful place on their bodies. Tumbletick gave a little check to his pocket watch to ensure it had survived the ride and found it in perfect condition.

The chasm was dark, shadowy and cold, protected from a weak southern sun. Bare rock closed in on both sides and rose to the south in great jagged chunks of granite. This was no natural staircase to the mainland of Kenai, it was a definite climb and scramble for several hundred feet over mist drenched and near freezing rock. As they proceeded in their climb to the south, Campbell the Weasel, with his naturally inquisitive eye, spotted something anomalous to the natural surroundings, hidden between some boulders.

"Looks as if someone else hid their boat a little further along than we did," he said out loud to no-one in particular.

Fenton and Mr. Battfin were the first to respond and leaped and rushed their way over boulders to the boat. They were quick to read the name on the stern.

"The Brazen Manticore," said Fenton to everyone. "Looks as if my friends from the Smugglers Cove made their way straight here. I would suspect we are on the right tracks."

The group joined them in a viewing of the boat which meant that someone maybe viewing them at this moment.

"You mean to say that the thugs you met under Rampart rowed all the way here?" asked Campbell.

"Well this little boat has got a sail as well Campbell so I would doubt it," Fenton replied. "They probably used the same wind we did for most of the way. They couldn't believe their luck when they saw me."

"Like you say though Percy," said Egremont. "This is good news and means that we are on the right tracks. A wolf, who has been in Rampart, heads straight here and therefore must be heading for Kantishna. Let us all be vigilant now. For although we know we are in the homeland of the enemy we now know that we can probably expect that they are expecting us. Be ruthless. This isn't under the jurisdiction of Rampart now. Let's go."

With that the wolfhound led the way up the chasm with a vigour of the hunt in him. The boulders were tricky in places and they often had to help each other with a supportive shoulder to a clambering foot or leaning back over a ridge to grab a wrist in assistance but at length they were up in the main body of land of Kenai and could see the mountains stretching ahead of them and Kantishna looming large over all. After a brief pause to rest after the climb they formed a column of single file with Egremont leading and Is-Is acting as rear guard and they marched towards the mountain.

Y'Bor Kaz found himself behind Egremont and gave a burst of speed to draw level with him.

"I've been meaning to ask you a question Master Wolfhound since I shook your hand at the abbey in the Old City," the warrior asked.

"Yes I rather suspected to have," Egremont replied keeping his head facing firmly forward. "Keep it quiet old chap and I'll answer as best I see fit."

"Well, you said that you are Master Elect of the Nine and well there are ten of us plus you. Aren't there supposed to be nine?"

"Well, Y'Bor this isn't some sort of prophesy, some long written tale that we are seeing rise from the pages of myth and legend to make come true."

"No I don't suppose it is, sorry Egremont," Y'Bor replied.

"But your point is well made. I was made Master Elect of the Nine by Sir Bartle Rourke who did have some power of divination. I am supposed to be leading nine and as you quite rightly point out there is you and nine others behind me."

"So what does that mean?"

"Well it's been playing on my mind as well as it happens. Either Tumbletick does not count because he is so special and he is outside of the whole definition that was attributed in the bestowing of the title on me, or..." and the wolfhound gave a long pause.

"Or?" Y'Bor prompted.

"One of the others is a traitor just waiting to betray us all. But don't worry, I don't think it is you my Perfect Master."

"I will be watchful Egremont and I appreciate your confidence."

"Keep your watch on Tumbletick at all times. He must be protected."

"It will be as you command my Lord."

Chorus Ten

The one white eyed wolf led the way through the well known rocks and ravines of Kenai. The four warriors followed him at his brisk pace, heading for the large mountain of Kantishna. This was their first time to the southern continent but they had been relishing being here for as long as they had known the charismatic wolf and that was about three years ago.

The wolf's name was Ragna and he had brought them enlightenment and a sense and promise of power which they had never felt before as mere brigands condemned to life in the prison that was the Old City of Rampart. Ragna had entered the Old City with a small pack of other wolves and had made their way swiftly to the castle which was then just the dangerous centre of the prison which attracted the tougher adventurers and prisoners drawn by the quality of the buildings. It was also the place that earlier spies of Ahriman had suggested was the most likely place to find converts. Ragna and his pack had entered as adventurers but seemed totally uninterested in the usual pursuits of killing and attaining wealth. The lead wolf was an eloquent and persuasive speaker but only ever to prisoners. Any other adventurers they had come across in the early days of their mission to the Old City had been either shunned or dismissed. Soon Ragna had a coterie of condemned men around him who were constantly attentive to his diatribes about Ahrioch beliefs and his own leader Ahriman. Many had heard before but now many listened. Within the confines of the castle Ragna held sway over attentive and growing audiences. The groups continued to swell and attract more who found Ragna's passion and belief contagious and his view of the world compulsive. The old orders were going to change; the soft and corpulent lands of Umiat were destined to collapse with their moral laxity and absence of belief. The Ahrioch Wars before had been but a test of the strength of Umiat, now plans were in place for a complete and utter regime shift. The men in the castle of the Old City would be the ones who would be saved when Ahriman gained hegemony over the hedonist north. Rampart would no longer be allowed neutrality, all would have to worship in the Ahrioch way and join the Horde in admiration. The men around Ragna would be safe as true believers. So the coterie grew to a large pack of believers within the prison and they defended their ways by building up the walls of the castle again so that they were safe within to await the coming of Ahriman.

Ragna had been pleased with the success of his mission. The men in the Old City were easy to convert and he developed them in readiness to become another element within the army of Ahriman. For when the time came, Ragna would be ready with souls to provide as warriors doomed to fight or as sacrifices doomed to die.

As it turned out his men were to become early combatants in a skirmish before the main war and he found that he led a defence of the castle against an attack from the hedonistic types that he despised. Within their ranks were the very elements of horror he had hoped to defeat, the deformed son of Sir Bartle Rourke and old warriors from the Ahrioch Wars that had stood against them. What made this fight worse was the use of a demon against those who would usually worship its ilk. This battle had gone badly wrong but Ragna was confident that his gods were behind him, as a spy had revealed the plans of the hated enemy and he and four of his most trusted men were able to escape down old and rarely used passages to find a sycophant waiting with a boat. He had escaped by swimming while the tide was still high but they had used the vessel which remained to make their way back to Kenai and were now on the way to Kantishna to join with his fellow followers of faith.

Chapter Eleven

It was cold in Kenai but as long as the wind kept coming from the north it was not the devastating cold that many had expected. With Egremont still leading the way towards the looming bulk of Kantishna, the rest of the party remained in a strict marching order. Behind the wolfhound came Mr. Battfin and Seton Rax, then Campbell and Percy. At the back, Y'Bor Kaz and Is-Is were the rear guard with Beran and Nazar Grant ahead of them. This left Tumbletick walking along with Vixen to his left. His now constant companion was an annoyance to him and at every break in the journey he would instantly seek out another member to talk to.

The landscape was sparse, dark rock with broken scree around the little valleys along which they walked. These ravines often meant that Kantishna was hidden but all were aware of it and its peak would appear and then hide again as they made their way through the rough terrain.

Campbell would often scout ahead, breaking away in a silent and rapid manner. Egremont was concerned that this was a greater risk than usual due to being in enemy territory and knowing that a wolf and some henchmen were ahead of them. Campbell's reply was always consistent that it was for precisely those reasons that he had to scout ahead, at least to know the lye of the land and areas where any ambush might be likely. Egremont's reply to that was also equally consistent, the wolves could not know that they were coming this way, they would have expected a landing in Ende and the group ahead were only five in number and therefore it was more likely that their own group would stumble across the one eyed wolf and his men and surprise them. Campbell had remained insistent and felt that seeing as they were taking a track that had been walked for millennia it was essential that he knew the way ahead with confidence.

The group had come to another rest session during the day long walk. The next one would be to make camp for the night and they would do that when a good location was found for pitching the tent rather than just making camp when the time for marching was at an end. A fire was unlikely for warmth and cooking due to the need for stealth and the poor availability of fuel in the mountains. There were vast forests in Kenai but they were in more sheltered valleys and away to the west. Many realised how tired they now were after the landing in the morning and striving all day over broken ground and rocks. This was much more sapping of their strength than the yomping on the plateau of Rampart had been. Walking on slopes and checking your footing with each step to avoid a trip or a loose rock buckling an ankle was physically and mentally draining. The one main benefit of travelling in Kenai was the vast amount of fresh water about. At almost every turn there would be the noise of rushing water from a steep mountain stream, they would often be walking alongside rivulets making their way to the sea and it was this that made Tumbletick realise that they were actually constantly climbing towards the spine of Kenai and Mount Kantishna. This slow and never ending climb must also be contributing to their fatigue but the strength of the individuals meant stamina quickly recovered during their rests. Tumbletick however felt a degree of pride as he sat next to Is-Is and found that he was coping far better than he had expected he would. He was definitely toughening up, he thought. He grabbed the hilt of his long knife that was within easy reach and he felt a surge in his confidence as he grasped the leather entwined handle, he felt sure he would be able to use it should the need arise. Is-Is noticed the steel in the little man beside him and gave him a mighty blow on the back with his broad paw. Tumbletick slumped with the slap towards his crossed legs and felt his stomach tighten due to the constriction of being forced so far forward but he sat back upright with a wide grin on his face due to the attention from the hare. It was then that they all heard a huge roar that echoed around their current canyon, distorted but sounding very near.

Is-Is leapt up and sliced out two kukris into a position of battle readiness.

"What the hell was that?" exclaimed Percy Fenton.

The others stood and drew weapons and looked around for the source of the roar but it could not be seen.

"One would suspect," said Mr. Battfin calmly. "That 'that', would be a rather large monster."

"Well they are known to inhabit the wildernesses of Kenai," Campbell replied, his head darting this way and that and nose twitching. "But I would agree with our pirate friend that, 'that', does sound like rather a large one."

"One you missed on your scouting trips?" asked Vixen standing close to Tumbletick.

"Quick, let's get moving again," urged Egremont. "Get some distance from it. Whatever it is. Those echoes are disorientating but it sounds close to me."

"And hungry," said Percy, quickly closing up his pack and shouldering it.

Another roar rocked the ravine and inspired movement from the group.

"That is a different animal," shouted Campbell.

"How do you know?" said Percy looking around anxiously.

"Because both of them are climbing over that ridge, let's move!"

Fear or curiosity caused all to look in the direction that Campbell was running away from. Over a precipitous ridge two huge beasts were now climbing clearly into sight. Tumbletick found himself riveted and staring at them. Eblis had been a large and fearsome demon but somehow these creatures caused more fear being in their own environment, wild and not provided for the pleasure of an audience. There was doubt about what they had derived from, maybe a reptile or a bear but they were massive, primeval and elongated, perhaps twenty feet in length and standing a full six at the shoulder. Long legs were protruding more from their sides than belly and they bent at vast bony joints at right angles, like a lizard. At the end of these legs were huge paws with strange gripping fingers ending in individual claws. The creatures carried their bulk well and moved in a stealthy way of controlled, regular movement, over the ridge, gripping with their strange clawed paws. Their heads looked exactly like a bears but their mouths revealed row upon row of fanged teeth. They crawled towards the group and then down a nearly sheer surface of rock, snarling and continuing to make their way in an unrelenting manner, seeking out slight gaps in the rock or enclosing protrusions with the flexible talons.

"What the hell are those things?" asked Fenton again, standing next to Tumbletick.

"I suggest we don't hang around to find out," said Y'Bor then turning and running after Campbell he shouted over his shoulder. "There's no shame in a tactical retreat."

Tumbletick felt himself grabbed around the waist and hoisted above the hip of Is-Is. The hare was still holding kukris in both paws and Tumbletick felt very conscious of the blade near his face as Is-Is bounded up the canyon and was soon ahead of both Y'Bor and the fleeing Campbell.

Seton Rax, Beran and Mr. Battfin retreated backwards keeping an eye on the creatures who continued to slink their way down the cliff-face and towards the floor of the ravine. They moved in a more saurian manner than a bounding bear, their heads keeping constantly still, facing the three men who faced them back.

"I think," said Beran. "That these creatures could quite easily crush my armour and I doubt that my sword could injure them."

"Then aren't we lucky I've got a battle axe?" Seton said.

"We don't engage unless it is absolutely necessary," Mr. Battfin replied. "No risks with beasts of that size unless your life depends on it. Keep moving backwards and do not turn your backs upon them."

"Do you think this might be an occasion where the crossbows should be used?" asked Beran. "I think we might still have time to wind a bolt on each."

"If we decide to fight then fire all three bolts into the same beast," said Mr. Battfin. "Try and slow one down and then deal with the other conventionally."

Then Is-Is returned, having sped Tumbletick away from the immediate danger he was there to stand with his fellow. He already had his bow unslung and an arrow notched. Beran, Mr. Battfin and Seton Rax dropped their weapons and began winding their crossbows. They place their feet in special stirrups near the firing end and cranked handles at the butt to wind the string taut. Is-Is tensed his own bow, selected the beast most vertical on the rock face and fired at its broad back, immediately he drew another arrow before the first struck home. The monster roared in indignance as the point sunk into its body, it paused for a while as its companion kept climbing down towards the warriors. The second arrow from Is-Is also found its mark and the monstrous creature howled in pain again, an awful noise full of wild confusion and rage. Is-Is had already fired the third arrow by the time Beran, Mr. Battfin and Seton Rax had fully wound the crossbows, placed a bolt in its guiding track, levelled the weapons and aimed at the wounded beast. The other creature, uninjured had continued its climb and had now reached the ravine floor.

"Perhaps we should shoot the closer one?" shouted Seton, a touch of nerves in his voice."

"No continue with the wounded one," instructed Mr. Battfin. "Fire!"

The three warriors made final alterations to their aim and unleashed a volley of three stumpy thick bolts at the monster, just as Is-Is fired a fourth arrow. The discharge of the missiles was accurate and with the mechanical power of the crossbows behind them the bolts sunk sickeningly deep into the flesh of the beast. Even the strength of Is-Is and his longbow could not get the metal pointed shaft of his arrow dug as deeply into the monster. The three bolts combined with the final arrow was devastating and the beast convulsed and lost its grip and fell and rolled down the cliff to a crashing slump of pain and then death.

"No time for another volley," shouted Seton Rax as the other behemoth was now scrabbling towards them at a frightening pace, its legs in a frantic crawl like a crocodiles run in a straight line.

As it got nearer in its attack it became plain that any resemblance to a bear was only in its head, this was fundamentally more a dragon with a long body but no tail. The body was brown in colour but of leathery skin not fur yet the warriors found they were focussing purely on its opening mouth.

They dropped their crossbows but Is-Is calmly took the time to reholster his bow on his back, confident that he still had time before the monster reached them. Small rocks were scattering and flying off in all directions as the creature sped towards the group. Is-Is started to move off to the right and up a slight incline. Mr. Battfin with cutlasses drawn stood on one side of Beran in full plate, shield and broadsword. Seton Rax stood to his other side with both hands on his battleaxe.

"Lord protect me with this shield," prayed Beran as he braced himself behind it while placing his broadsword in a levelled pose to accept the charge.

The monster was heading directly towards the paladin, the slobber now visible around its stumpy pink tongue and between its teeth. Seton Rax moved away a bit as did Mr. Battfin, leaving Beran isolated. Is-Is had decided to use the other weapon kept on his back and drew his double handed sword. The beast was nearly upon them and Beran the

Bold, hidden by his visored helm gritted his teeth in anticipation. At the final moment the dragon raised its huge bulk, running on its rear legs only and crashed into the shield of Beran with one claw grabbing the whole of its face. Its other front claw batted away Beran's sword and it smashed the knight down to the ground and then started to swipe and to pound with its taloned paws.

Beran's gritted teeth transformed into a scream of pain as his shield arm was broken under the strength of the onslaught, his forearm snapped in spite of a shield in front of him and an encasing of steel. The other leg was now fixed firmly across the knight's chest and head. Beran heard the metal in the helmet give and felt a huge shock of fear as the side of his helm started to press fearfully against his skull. Beran sensed the terror rise as he felt his head was about to be crushed under the enormous weight of the beast. There was a complete and inconsolable fear for Beran as he heard his own skull fracture and thoughts of an ignoble death took him to near unconsciousness. The breastplate and helmet were just about holding up against the weight of the monster as Mr. Battfin, Seton Rax and Is-Is came to his defence.

Then it was the turn of the warriors to fight back as the giant lizard was mauling away at the mail armour of Beran, the limited intelligence of the beast focused on the man under it. Seton Rax was closest and with his grip positioned on the shaft of his double handed battle axe he swung the hacking blade in a wide arc with all his weight and skill behind a running attack. The axe thwacked into the beast's flank, behind the shoulder of the front right leg that pinned Beran down. The creatures skin was tough; arrows and bolts could penetrate it more easily. With all of Seton's strength and the keenness of the axe blade the attack only dug in a few inches. The power of the blow though was felt by Beran beneath and again the paladin roared in pain as he felt the weight increase on his broken arm. The monster turned towards a dumbfounded Seton, eyes wide in despair at the blow that would have cleaved a horse's head. Beran, with just enough strength remaining in his body took the opportunity to roll away to his right and then attempt to scramble away as Mr. Battfin leapt over him and began his swift and devastating cascade of cutlass swipes as the monster advanced on Seton. Mr. Battfin chose to attack at the underside of the beast with horizontal slashes, only allowing the tips of his blades to give razor thin bites of lizard flesh. He thought this might weaken the monster, to attempt to kill it one go seemed futile after the barbarian barrage. He was ready for a reaction but the dragon kept its attention on Seton Rax, snapping with its maw and being fended away with defensive bats of the battle-axe.

Then Is-Is was in the fray, running from his higher point of vantage he held his broadsword with both paws in an overhand grip, charging, holding the blade directly in front of him like a lance of steel. His arms were still close to his body, tensing and ready to thrust. Is-Is ran fast and at the very moment the tip of his sword touched the beast at it ribs he continued to run and push with all his strength, exploding his arms outwards and with that power the entire sword blade slipped into the monster. Is-Is ended up with his own chest slamming into the beast, blood spurting from the wound around the hilt and over the hare. Mr. Battfin gasped at the realisation of the might of Is-Is in battle, having shoved a full five feet of cold steel into the mountain dwelling dragon; Is-Is would now definitely enter into legendary pirate tales. Seton Rax was soon aware of Is-Is' success as well as the monster coughed up a bubbly red froth of bile and blood, vomiting it onto the barbarian. The monster, fatally wounded, collapsed. Is-Is with a flourish, sliced out his sword and stepped away casually from the plume of blood that shot from the devastating wound. As the beastly lizard gasped a final gurgle of air, Is-Is was beside Beran and lifting him to a standing position with one paw. The knight was trying to hold his badly broken forearm in a position that didn't bring blind pain. Mr. Battfin came over to the two as Seton was still shaking his wrists and hands, trying to flick away globs of blood. His top, donated by Egremont, was soaking up great purple stains.

"Is-Is, that was an astounding strike," exclaimed Mr. Battfin, stirred from his usual coolness by the avenging brilliance of the blow.

The hare checked that Beran was steady on his feet, then simply walked off in the direction of where the rest of the party had headed, guiding Beran who limped along with him. Mr. Battfin re-sheathed his cutlasses and picked up the paladins crushed shield and lost sword. Seton, still dripping, sneered in disgust, kicked the dead dragon in the head and followed the slowly moving trio along the gently sloping rocky ravine.

A circling vulture began to descend to gain an unexpected meal of Kenai mountain dragon, hoping to arrive before other carrion-eating beasts in the area picked up on the scent of death and blood.

Chorus Eleven

The handsome, pale blue eyed wolf, dark grey with flecks of silver, stood at the prow of the boat as his pack sailed from Tetterton to the city of Ende. He had watched the unclean bunch of miscreants he had been tasked to track leave the port and sail underneath the Rampart Portal, earlier that day. The wolf had wished that he had been given freer rein to pick a few of their number off with an ambush but his orders had been clear. 'Watch. Follow. Report, while on Rampart.' Other packs may have had other orders, different orders, but his had been followed. Now with them leaving and with the knowledge of where they were going, he was to sail as if the fiery gusts of hell were chasing him to Ende and make that report.

The tip of the Kenai Peninsular was now in sight; shortly he would be striding through the capital to his master's home, Beth Col. The centre of all that was holy to the wolf and his ilk. He sniffed the sea air to see if he could pick up the familiar scents of Ende.

"Balloch!" the wolf called and another cloaked lupine figure ran across the deck.

"Yes Rok?" the wolf named Balloch said standing behind the blue eyed wolf. Rok did not turn to face his minion. "What can I do for you?"

"Bring me a sacrifice Balloch. A good one. Something our Lord would find...amusing."

"Yes Rok. I've got something in the hold. I'll get it," Balloch dashed off.

Rok continued to look out over the Sea of Kaltag, his cloak blowing in violent ripples of cloth around his rigid and muscled form. He was now certain that he could pick up the aromas of home, the streets of filth, death, decay and bowls of bull's blood burning over many a charcoal brazier. Not pleasant to some he conceded but still home to him.

Balloch returned with a struggling white thing in his claw. Rok turned and looked at the little mammal trying to fight against the grip of the wolf.

"A monkey? Certainly amusing Balloch," Rok took the tiny white marmoset by the scruff of the neck. Spiny fangs showed as the skin round its skull was pulled tight and it's bulging brown eyes skitted around in fear. It's little arms tried to fight against the much larger wolf but to no avail.

Rok sneered in contempt and pulled a dagger from a sheath on his belt. It was a broad blade, with an arrow head shape at the point. It had a serrated edge on one side. He held the monkey over the splitting sea at the bow, spray wetted the little mammal and its fur clumped together in brushed back tufts. Rok took the serrated blade to the throat of the marmoset and drew it deep and slow across it and through the entire neck. As he did so he spoke loud and clear;

"Oh Count Ashtoreth! Be propitious to me and cause that this night the great Demon appear unto me and that he grant me, by means of this sacrifice that I deliver to him, the deliverance of my chance to face my enemies in vengeance."

The body of the monkey fell into the sea and Rock was left holding the head with a gaping jaw, lolling tongue and now still, deceased eyes.

"A good prayer my Lord Rok," said Balloch. "I'm sure your chance will come. The demon Lord Ashtoreth will appreciate noble words and a sacrifice."

Rok turned the monkey head and smiled at its little dead face.

"There is another hairy little beast I have some noble words for Balloch."

He threw the head with disdain into the deep and walked off towards the cabin at the stern of the boat. He stopped and turned towards Balloch.

"Get the pack ready. We land within the hour. Straight to Beth Col to report to Ahriman. Then let us hope for some hunting. We know they are in Kenai! I want to be the one that brings the heart of Tumbletick to Him. I want to be the one that brings the heart of Egremont to Him. I want to be the one that brings the heart of Is-Is to Him. You and the boys can have the others but I want their still beating hearts presented by me to Ahriman."

Rok strode to the cabin leaving Balloch on deck. The wolf felt pride swell in his heart for his pack leader and vowed to follow him always.

Chapter Twelve

Is-Is continued to guide the badly wounded Beran along the ravines. Mr. Battfin scouted ahead now and Seton Rax wearily brought up the rear finding that he smelled very badly of dragon gut blood. Mr. Battfin found whom he suspected, lurking around a corner.

"Campbell, quick, we need Nazar Grant. Beran is badly hurt," the pirate ordered.

Campbell sprinted away in his peculiar gait and within minutes was with the other six whom were standing in a tight, attentive huddle, between some boulders that acted as a good defensive position. The thief came to a skidding stop on the loose scree beneath his feet.

"Quick Nazar. Beran's wounded. They are a few minutes away."

Nazar made a move in the direction the thief had come and the rest of the group followed with concern across all faces. Night was not far off now and Egremont was growing anxious.

"Where we meet them we make camp," the wolfhound said. "Everyone helps to make it in the best place nearby while Nazar sees to Beran."

They met the forlorn looking trio of Is-Is, Beran and blooded Seton Rax in a shallow valley of rock, filled with many large black boulders of basalt. Old spewing remains from ancient volcanic activity. Beran's helmet was obviously buckled and contorted, Seton Rax looked both distraught for his friend and like an abattoir worker. Is-Is was steadfast, calm and still supporting the paladin in his agonising walk.

Nazar Grant was quick to the side of Beran and had his pack off and opened. Is-Is guided the knight to a seated position. Egremont had a word with Y'Bor Kaz to keep a guard on the area and then set about himself selecting a location for the camp.

"Beran, where are you injured?" Nazar asked, feeling he knew the answer but the warriors reply would also indicate state of mind as well as levels of pain.

"My cracking head's cracked and I've broken my arm," came the angry reply.

"Good, good. We'll be able to unhook the armour on your arm," said Nazar looking carefully over the suit of mail. "But I think we are going to have to cut the helmet off somehow. It is badly crushed my friend."

"Fine just get them off and give me something for the pain," Beran replied through gritted teeth. Partly due to the agony and partly because his face was held in place by the damaged headgear and he could not move his jaw well.

Nazar Grant undid the buckles behind the vambrace that protected the left forearm. The leather straps were tight and the pressure applied by the cleric to extract the buckle's pin from the eye of the strap was enough to send flashes of white searing pain within Beran's entire body as his broken bone scraped against the metal casing. The paladin fainted, falling backwards a way to be steadied by Is-Is who still stood by. Nazar took the opportunity of the swoon to rip off the encasing to reveal the snapped bone puncturing Beran's shirt. The cleric took a deep breath.

"I don't think my herbal remedies are going to be very good for this one and we'd better do it while he is asleep. Is-Is hold him tight while I reset this in place. Very tight. Then go and ask Fenton for his whiskey."

Is-Is wrapped his long strong arms around the right arm and torso of Beran. Nazar Grant pulled the left arm to a straight position and then examining the alignment of the revealed bone, pushed it firmly with the palm of his hand, back through the open wound and into a rough, field dressing, fix.

The yell of pain from within the crumpled helmet was extremely loud for a man that couldn't move his constricted jaw much. Then there was silence as the paladin passed out again. Nazar took some of his medicines out of his pack, jars of ointment; leather pouches with herbs and selected a small terracotta pot that contained a white cream beneath a broad cork stopper. He rubbed some of this over the wound, then broke up some large dry leaves from a pouch and crumbled the fragments over the cream. He then took a couple of bolts from his own quiver, placed them side by side on top of the forearm and wrapped yards of bandages around both arm and splint.

"Is-Is, I think you can let him go now. Can you fetch Fenton for the whiskey and Campbell? Tell Campbell to bring his tools please?"

Is-Is nodded and gently laying the unconscious Beran to the floor went off to get the pirate and the thief. Nazar then examined the visored helmet. He hoped that Campbell would have something tough enough to cut through it and be able to release the helm easily. Nazar checked on his bandaging work and waited the short time for Campbell and Percy to arrive.

Percy already had his large silver hipflask in his hand and Campbell quickly kneeled beside the prone paladin and examined the helmet. He unrolled his tools and selected an arcane looking clamp and started pulling at the pins which hinged the visor in an attempt to loosen them.

"If we can get the visor open we can at least get some whiskey into him," Campbell said.

"I have got another bottle in my pack," said Percy seriously. "I was kind of hoping to keep it mostly for myself but needs must and I think Beran will appreciate it. Not for the taste unfortunately. He doesn't drink that much usually does he? I mean if he's not used to it, it won't take as much to numb the pain will it?"

"He held himself well at 'The Grobbling Smith'," said Campbell concentrating on the visor. "Drank at the same rate as all of us. Then he beat Egremont at chess. Easily."

"Oh," said Percy, looking forlornly at his hipflask. "Pity he can't savour it really."

Campbell was holding Beran's head down with the palm of his left hand and was now pulling firmly on the hinges with the clamp in his right. He pulled out a couple of different pointed tools and then started to lever away at the visor as well. Part of the strength of the helmet had gone following the dragon attack and Campbell managed to loosen the buckled visor enough that he was able to lift it open with a slow yawning creak. It revealed Beran's handsome, sleeping face, covered in streaks of dry blood, old trickles from an unseen wound closer to the crown.

Nazar Grant quickly inserted fingers to the open helmet and felt where he could for signs of fracture but he could only reach just short of the knight's temples.

"Bleeding is actually a good sign," the cleric said pulling his hands back out and wiping some of the congealed blood off the end of his fingers. "But I think he is going to have some bruising and I'd be happier if the whole thing came off Campbell."

The thief sucked in air through his gritted teeth, a sign of doubt about the job ahead of him. He looked at his tools, and then at the helmet and then at his tools again.

"That's solid plate mail that is," he said. "Most of my tools are precision instruments for locks and devices intended to keep me out. They are not supposed to get through a quarter inch of hardened steel."

"Beran has got an open wound on his head, possibly a fractured skull as well." Nazar Grant replied. "What the dragon did not kill, a festering wound might. Besides if I do not get him cleaned up he is going to begin to… well, you know. Begin to smell pretty bad as well."

"Okay, okay. Let me have a think about how to get it off," Campbell replied and wandered off in thought.

"Meanwhile, I think some whiskey might be in order Percy," Nazar said. "Try to get him to drink some even if it does wake him up."

Fenton took his turn to kneel next to the Beran and lifting his back and head slightly he placed the neck of the hipflask between the lips of the warrior and slowly poured some of the beautifully burning amber liquid into his mouth. The restorative powers of the well-made whiskey did their job and revived Beran. He eagerly swallowed some more before grabbing the flask with his good arm, snatching it from Percy and cascading the contents into his gullet. Percy sighed deeply and his thoughts turned to his last bottle.

"Beran that was at least a pint in there," Percy protested.

"Sorry, but that's going to feel a whole lot better in a little while," said Beran. He looked down at his bandaged arm. "Your skill is indeed great Nazar. Thank you."

The tent had been quickly erected between a couple of large basalt boulders. Tumbletick decided to creep quickly in and hide from the forbidding landscape and potential attacks from monsters, wolves or fanatics of Ahrioch. Nazar Grant was telling Egremont that he must have a fire tonight on which to boil some water for herbal infusions to aid Beran. Egremont agreed. A fire could well boost all their spirits and he believed that they could hide it reasonably well between the tent and the boulder from all but the most prying eyes. Is-Is went to work constructing the deepest fire pit he could in the loose scree sitting on bedrock, while Mr. Battfin and Seton Rax scoured the wind blasted rock terrain looking for scrag ends of knotty wood that occasionally clung to life in sheltered areas. They returned to Is-Is with embarrassed looks and only handfuls of fuel.

"We'll keep searching," said Seton Rax apologetically, looking at his injured friend. He looked at Vixen and Fenton. "Some help might be good though."

Y'Bor Kaz was keeping up a vigilant perambulation of the perimeter so Vixen and Fenton went off in opposite directions to continue hunting for enough bulk of wood to make a fire that could last long enough to boil some water at least. Time was against them now and the remaining shadows from a pale southern sun, cast from peaks and ridges, began to grow into a wider night. The four fuel hunters returned again with mere handfuls of matter that might hold a flame. Is-Is had lit a couple of lanterns to compete with the enveloping night and had placed them either side of the shallow pit he had constructed. The pieces of wood they had found were placed within the pit and made a small and meagre pile.

"We might be able to get the water warm," said Nazar Grant getting a small cooking pot out of his pack. He filled it with water from a couple of canteens and waited for Is-Is to get the wood lit while the others stood about watching.

The hare decided that the fuel needed a little encouragement and poured some oil from a third lantern onto the bundle. Quickly he took out his fire starting kit and started making sparks by striking flint onto a neat rectangle of metal. The scattering sparks spat onto a ball of dried moss that Is-Is bunched in his paws. He blew lightly upon it and a bright glow grew within. A fine flame suddenly leapt up out of Is-Is' paws and he placed the burning mass down to the base of the fire and watch carefully to ensure the flames took. He picked a couple of stray pieces of wood and placed them more strategically over the flames. With the aid of the lantern oil the fire spluttered and spread within the wood. Is-Is reached over to beside the resting Beran, took his broadsword and laid it over a small boulder near the fire. He then wedged the tip with another boulder so the hilt was above the flames. Then he took Nazar's cooking pot and hung it on the sword hilt.

"That should do nicely, thank you Is-Is," said Nazar Grant and the cleric began to busy himself with the right selection of herbs to aid Beran's pain once the whiskey had worn off. He kept a close eye on the water waiting for the right moment to add the collection of leaves he had picked.

"Campbell," said Nazar as he briefly checked the fire for signs of fading. "Any more thoughts about how to get Beran's helmet off?"

"Well," replied the thief tentatively. "I think we will have to cut it at the narrowest point, near the chin, and then try and pry it open a little so we can pull it off. But, Nazar, and it is a big but. I don't have anything that can cut through plate mail which is designed to actually stop blades. It might be better just to pull the damned thing off. He got it on by putting it on over his head, why can't we just pull it off again?"

"I think it is too crushed to come off easily. You saw it up close when you got the visor open. I've got to check the wounds on his head."

"I haven't got anything that can cut through it though!"

"Fine. Fenton, get your other bottle of whiskey out," said Nazar Grant. "It might be easier if Beran were unconscious again while we pull off the headgear."

"Gentlemen," said Beran with a slight slur. "I appreciate your discussions but I would not wish to deprive Percy of any more of his dwindling supplies. Just get Seton Rax for me. He'll get the cracking thing off."

"You can look for some more wood Campbell if you are not going to be of any use with your tools," said Nazar Grant to Campbell. "The fire is already looking a little low."

Campbell strode into the distance muttering to himself and soon he had disappeared into the murk. Seton Rax moved to stand behind the reclining paladin and began to examine the shape of the damaged helmet. Is-Is turned from his fire tending duties and put all his weight on Beran's thighs. Seton placed his hands either side of the helm and was instantly surprised by a yelp of pain from his friend.

"Percy, perhaps just another swig for courage?" said the injured knight.

Fenton took the bottle out from his pack with a resigned look of loss. He passed it to Beran, who eagerly pulled the cork out with his teeth and slugged down a couple of large mouthfuls.

"Another pint," whispered Fenton and took the bottle back. He decanted some of the remains into his hipflask, took a swig himself and then offered the remaining liquor around the group. Only Beran took him up on the generosity and finished the bottle.

Beran gritted his teeth again as he felt Seton Rax grab the helm. Is-Is reapplied pressure to the knight's thighs to anchor him in place. Seton flexed his arms and began to pull as straight as he could. The helmet was extremely tight and combined with Seton's strength it meant Beran's torso began to lift as well. Is-Is pushed back down and kept him on the ground. The knight's response was growls of rage, fighting against the pain in his head as Seton kept on pulling. The barbarian twisted the helmet a little and a dent in it ripped the wounded scalp a little more and blood began to flow again over the tightly closed eyes of Beran. Seton steeled himself. By looking at the dented helm he felt certain that a little further twist to the left would mean it would come loose. He twisted and pulled at the same time and with a thick slurping sound the helmet came off. Beran was swooning on the edge of awareness as Nazar Grant moved in and started examining the warrior's head. Thick congealed areas of blood had matted his short hair and new blood was flowing through it. The cleric started to clean the wounds after cutting away clumps of hair around them. That done he carefully applied pressure with his fingers to the skull, searching for any sign of give in the bone that would indicate a serious break. There was bruising and blood but no sense of a major disintegration of bone. Probably a fracture though. Nazar took more bandages and wrapped them around Beran's head. That done the cleric checked on the water in the cooking pit and finding it beginning to simmer he opened up the little leather pouch where he kept his herbs. With the right combination already selected he ripped up the leaves and tipped them into the water.

Is-Is had gone to join Y'Bor Kaz, patrolling in the dark. The others sat quietly, talking only a little and looking at the wounded Beran, who now slept, his arm in a sling and his head heavily wrapped. The herbal tea was brewed and Beran was roused from his light and fitful drunken doze to drink it.

"That tastes a hell of a lot worse than the whiskey," said Beran after a couple of sips.

"Drink it all. It will do you good. Combined with the whiskey that collection of herbs will help you fall into a proper deep and restful sleep tonight," Nazar said.

Seton Rax helped his friend into the shelter and the knight got himself into a position where his arm and head did not hurt too much. Tumbletick was sleeping beside him at the end of the tent, curled up under a thin blanket and using his arm as a pillow. Beran finished his drink and watched the sleeping Tumbletick. Inside the tent and feeling the whiskey and herbs taking effect, Beran was surprised to find that the overwhelming emotion he felt was anger with himself for being bested by the dragon. Now with his shield arm broken he was considerably more vulnerable in a fight and he had therefore weakened the strength of the unit. If this meant that harm was more likely to come to Tumbletick now then his own honour was forever shamed. With the others outside preparing some food on the remains of the fire, keeping watch and holding low conversations, Beran and Tumbletick were fundamentally alone in the bare grey tent. The slightest amount of light from the fire and the lanterns made it into the shelter so even if Tumbletick had awoken to look at Beran he would have been unlikely to see the tears in the paladin's eyes, swelling and ready to break onto the top of his cheeks.

Outside the night grew blacker than most had ever known. Thick clouds blanketed the sky, no star or moon to give even hints of light. The small unit of warriors, pirates and thieves was huddled around the dying embers of the tiny fire. Their guards stopped patrolling and took up positions by the boulders flanking the tent. Soon only the lanterns remained to provide light and the group took turns to sleep and keep guard during their first full night in Kenai.

Chorus Twelve

Rok stepped onto one of the quays in the massive port city of Ende. It was a blustery day and he wrapped his cloak a little tighter around his furred frame. Balloch was dealing with the sailors they had hired in Tetterton, paying them with gold pieces for a swift and safe delivery to the wolves' city. The rest of the pack were disembarking as well and they were keen to get to their own homes in the vast and sprawling conurbation.

The sailors were happy with the generous pay from the wolf. It more than recompensed for what would end up being more than a week out of Tetterton. 'Not all wolves are that bad then' ran through several nautical minds as they rolled the coins around swarthy hands. Other thoughts turned to the bars and brothels of Ende.

Rok turned to look at the city he so loved and hated. Built on two huge spurs of land jutting out into the Kenai Sea a full thirty miles apart at the widest point. On many a day one side of Ende could not see the other. The rest of the city sprawled and rose to fill the hinterland to the north. A full fifty miles of hotels, pubs, industry, great old temples. Every form of construction mashed together over the centuries. There were also large areas abandoned, left to decay. With the amount of space offered by the tip of Kenai often it had been easier to leave sections to the elements and the wild. Ende was by far the largest city in the known world. It drew in all the trade, all the activity, all the belief and villainy of Kenai into its throbbing heart. Rok loved it because of the anarchy and the freedom it offered his sect and hated it because it did not fully adopt the ways of the Ahrioch Horde. There was too much freedom, not enough law but the followers of Ahriman were growing again, back nearly to the heights of the last war with Umiat. Therefore Rok still looked on Ende as fundamentally flawed because not all of its minimum of two million inhabitants worshipped the demon lords with the passion and diligence he did. He relished in the desire of getting to Beth Col, his master's home and into the inner sanctum of the substantial mansion where he could sacrifice and pray with a devotional mania he had missed so much due to being on field operations for the last few months.

Balloch was beside him again; they could be off through the streets. The rest of the pack would protect against any footpads or vagabonds who might make a foolhardy attack against them as they made their way to Beth Col. It was about twenty miles from the wharf they had docked at and they would have to do it on foot.

Around the docks, as in any dock of the world, warehouses towered over squat dive pubs, merchant offices and homes competed with shipyards for space. Ende was a sprawl and a vomit of town planning. Where Rampart was neutral and well run with a planned and neat port of Tetterton, Ende was individuals who came together to trade, to pray, to hunt wild beasts or search for gold and mineral wealth in the many miles of mountains and badlands of the Kenai Peninsular. Merchants would trade anything for the gain of gold in Ende. Not just the usual foodstuffs and materials of trades but also pelts of animals, slaves of all breeds, anything that could turn a profit. Then, after a successful day they could retire to their mansions with their private army barricading the doors. Ende was not regimented, not run by any central authority. Groups flocked together and fought for their own space but the Ahrioch Horde were perhaps now the dominant force and still were growing. They had influence; their temples were inviolate, safe from ransacking through fear of religious power. The poor and the wretched masses of Ende, living in the hovels slumped against once great buildings or in the shanty towns to the north, were a recruiter's happy hunting ground for conversion to the faith or as a sacrifice for it. No one noticed the death of a vagrant here and there in Ende. Then there were the vast sections of ruin where nature clawed her way back after buildings fell and people moved away.

Rok thought to himself how glorious it would be for the Ahrioch Horde to be totally dominant and to clear the city away and rebuild great temples, libraries of knowledge in arcane law, great civic works and uniform housing for the faithful. To have a central temple again for the worship of demons as a society and watch the sacrifice of unbelievers in front of a jubilant crowd. Soon it would come, soon. He looked to his side in disgust as he saw a vagrant cut the throat of another and steal a little begged money from the twitching corpse.

His loyal pack closed around him in case there were several cut-throats about looking for treasure. Perhaps they had seen Balloch handing out glinting coins to the sailors. The murderer looked up with his scraggy beard and unkempt greasy hair framing his face. Contempt and a sneer for the wolves, yet no attack, just a retreat into a garbage filled alley, clutching his stolen coins. Within minutes the vagrant would be buying leaf or a mug of putrid ale brewed in some back street joint or paying for a cheap whore who plies her trade on the open alley floor.

Ende was not a pleasant place, unless you had power. Then it offered all you could want. Every luxury, every vice, every sin. All could be within your hands if you had the power. If you had the power you could operate here, thrive and grow. Enclaves existed within the city of Ende for the powerful, areas behind high walls and gates where control did exist. Such an area was around the great house of Beth Col. Within the wide reaching walls all was serene and dedicated to worship. The most dedicated believers living in the buildings closest to Ahriman's home, their braziers always lit in adoration to the demon lords. In the houses further away, the servants and the guards. All believers still but not as pure and full of faith as he. Rok had his home in the second tier of Beth Col. One further away than the rare high priests whose ranks he hoped to be part of soon. If it was he who could deliver Tumbletick to Ahriman then that reward was certain. However, he was painfully aware that Ragna was still abroad and may have found a way to follow them. Then of course there were the other agents in the field who might find a way to get Tumbletick away from his protectors but they had blatantly failed so far. Assassination was forbidden. Tumbletick had to be delivered to Ahriman for ritual sacrifice for revenge for the killing of his general. Sir Bartle Rourke's only son had to have his heart ripped out and burned in Beth Col.

Chapter Thirteen

Day arrived with peace in the wilderness of Kenai. The night had only been haunted by winds rather than by more monstrous things. Those who were last to sleep awoke and stretched out muscles pounded by the hard rocks beneath the floor of the tent. Breakfast was a cold and meagre affair. With the fire long since dead no attempt was made to find more fuel and as such there was not even a chance of one of Nazar Grant's herbal brews to start the day.

Beran had slept full and long despite his wounds. The combination of the whiskey and the right mixture of leaves in his infused tea had, as promised, knocked him into a darkness of bliss and no pain. Upon waking however, he felt his head tight with suffering twinges and his strapped up arm was in a constant pulse of pain.

They started to break the camp down and to readjust kit around their backpacks ensuring that sheathed weapons could still be accessed easily. Is-Is, who carried the tent when packed upon his broad strong back, had to have his broadsword positioned over his left shoulder and tucked neatly behind the bulk of the tent. His longbow and quiver of arrows he merely attached to the side of the camping equipment. Most others had their weapons hanging by their sides, sheaths hanging from broad leather belts. Their backpacks hardly restricted any mobility at all. It was cold and a shimmering of white frost gently touched the rocks around them adding a crisp brightness to the stark land.

"We should make Kantishna by nightfall," said Egremont to the rest of the group. "Keep clear of any dragons today. Or other things that might come our way. We were lucky that Beran was not more frightfully wounded by those creatures. Stay in marching order and we will take a lighter pace today. Night will bring us some answers and I expect them to be asked by the sword."

Tumbletick found himself standing again to the right of Vixen and behind Percy as they sauntered off following Egremont. The winds of Kenai began to rise through the course of the day and sliced around them as they trekked to the south and towards the ever-growing bulk of Kantishna. The mountain did not seem to get closer as they moved, just fill more of the vista in front of them. Tumbletick felt slightly more at ease when a local peak or rocky ridge would hide the view of the mountain but it always re-emerged. It was like a pyramid in shape but climbed to a single rounded peak. Tumbletick realised that it was more of a cone but from the direction they were approaching, pyramid seemed the right description to him. Permanent snow clung to the peak and to about a third of the way down, brutal winds bent and moulded the snow into curved forms and blew a haze of looser crystals off to the west. The lower part of the mountain was black rock and bare of any life like much of the blasted land in this part of Kenai. Tumbletick thought how harsh life would be here without the plentiful streams. He knew from conversations that there were also wild and wicked rivers that thrashed in torrents around deep canyons in Kenai, longer and broader than even the great tidal waterways of Umiat. They were fed by the masses of rivulets and melting ice flats and glaciers to the East, massive and destructive yet found on no map. It was these rivers that meant that life could exist here. Food was plentiful within them and so was the vast mineral wealth that was constantly churned up. So people came to hunt for jewels and gold and set up camps where they believed their luck would see them strike riches. Lonelier types also came to Kenai to hunt for furs from the animals that lived near the rivers and ate the fish. Braver types hunted for the fur of the larger beasts that ate the animals that ate the fish. Then there were those that looked for wealth in the forests that were widespread to the west of Kenai, logs would be cut and dragged or floated to Ende for trade. Life found a way to cling to this mountainous land and Tumbletick suspected that the two dragons that had been killed were now being devoured by scuttling things that would have emerged from under rocks where they waited long in the cold and dark for such a feast to come. Dark hidden things that moved slowly, ate rarely but deeply when they could, gluttonous for the flesh of the recent dead. Bony and hard with grabbing claws and slow ripping teeth that did not chew but just swallow.

The day dragged on walking south and always at a gradual incline. The chasms and corridors of rock they had been marching through since they had arrived on the pebble beach began to flatten out on the older spine of Kenai. Now no other incline or wall of obscuring cliff face would ever hide Kantishna again. The wind on this moulded and undulating plateau of ravished earth was harsh. All in the party felt it brightly biting through their skin and deep into their souls. Those with extra clothing took time in this exposed highland to dress again. Seton Rax looked miserable and dejected with his bloodstained top and he began to shake and shiver with the unrestrained chill.

"Has anybody got anything they could spare to keep me warm?" Seton asked digging around in his own backpack for clothes he knew he didn't have.

"Thought you said you were as 'tough as nails'!" replied Campbell.

Vixen swung off her pack giving a little laugh as she did.

"Well until we are able to acquire some cloaks from our Ahrioch friends, you might find this protects a little," she said as she dug around in her kit and with a flourish whipped out a cerise wrap which spread in the wind with a matador like flair and grace.

Seton's down turned lips took a further dive of despair as he realised his ensemble would be open to much malignant derision. He took the wrap and placed it over his shoulders and around his back, before replacing his own pack over the top of it. Vixen handed him a delightful silver brooch, intricate in the design of a coiled serpent, the pin being the tongue. Seton took it and fastened two corners around his neck just above his sternum. He tried not to notice that Mr. Battfin and Campbell the Weasel had turned their backs on him to hide their giggles of ridicule.

"Bit of a classic look for a mountain that Kantishna, hey?" said Seton Rax attempting to distract attention from his new garment.

"Bit of a classic look for a barbarian," laughed Campbell the Weasel in reply.

"Getting back to our objective," chided Egremont. "One would suspect that Kantishna like all of the eight great peaks of Kenai, is actually an ancient volcano. Now long dead like the souls of the Ahrioch worshippers who flock to its base thinking it an entrance to Hell. Technically one could almost describe it as a monarch like mountain as it stands so high against the land around it."

"A real monarch mountain would be like Kabuk though. In Umiat," said Percy Fenton with authority. "As Kabuk actually rises out of a completely incongruous flat area of land that surrounds it for miles. Kantishna rises out of a plateau of its own creation which is surrounded by mountains."

"Well yes," said Egremont. "I did say you could almost describe it as a monarch. My point was that Kantishna is so vast and so classically shaped like a mountain of myth or imagination that you could describe it as a monarch. Although I bow to your more technically correct description of Kabuk actually being a geographical monarch Percy."

"Well it is a monarch to the Ahrioch Horde," said Vixen. "Such a perfect piece of sculptured rock, true believers feel it could only have been created by the greatest of demon gods as a tomb for their most beloved of followers. In ancient days the lower slopes would have been covered with campfires of the dutiful who would make their way here in religious fervour to worship. I believe that once there were great forests here as well that grew on the fertile slopes but they were removed to make the mountain look cleaner and to provide fuel for the fires of ritual purification."

"Fires of ritual purification," scoffed Egremont. "The Ahrioch Horde was well known to relish in the removal of hearts for the braziers of their hungry demons kings. When they couldn't get enough willing volunteers they used to use their vast donated wealth in the slave markets of Ende to traipse those who were less eager to give their hearts to the braziers. Demons don't really care whose vitals are boiled up for them in bull's blood though. I'm so glad we defeated them before. We can not allow that foul practice to rise again in the vastness that it once did. I will remind you all of how important it is that we complete this quest as one small act of defiance. I wouldn't want to see columns of people from Umiat being transported to that mountain in the future. Not ever."

"Do you really think it would ever come to that Master Wolfhound?" said Y'Bor Kaz.

"If they keep the Umiat Stone, rise again and the will of Umiat is broken. Perhaps," Egremont replied.

"Well let's make sure it doesn't come to that and continue with the quest," said Mr. Battfin. "No mercy. No quarter. No-one left to spread their views of the world."

The group said nothing more but readjusted packs and set off to the south with their solitary goal easily in sight. The going now was easier, despite the chill. The ground underfoot was solid rock picked clean of all life and earth by the harsh, scouring winds. The sounds of warriors could be heard tramping in the group as hobnailed boots clinked with each step. Tumbletick, Vixen and Campbell trod quietly within the group. Fenton's heeled boots making a sharper click than the out and out warriors. Tumbletick suspected that all three of these glamorous reprobates would be devastating in battle without the armour of the others. It struck him that he had not really seen any of them in a truly violent action yet. Campbell though still bore the wound on his face from the battle in the castle in the Old City of Rampart as proof of recent encounters. His thoughts turned to what dangers lay ahead. What chance could a small group possibly have if they were marching towards a huge gathering of the Ahrioch Horde? They knew from what Percy had said that at least a few tough customers were somewhere ahead of them. Who were they joining up with around the majestic mountain that filled the sky in front of them? Was the Umiat Stone even to be found at Kantishna? What was he doing here with them? Then he looked to Egremont at their head, his fur pushed neatly back against the side of his handsome and noble head. Tumbletick knew that he would rather be here than anywhere else in this world that had grown to a terrifying vastness compared to the comfort of his little hut, hidden within a copse, in a land many miles to the north.

"Okay, let's stop here," commanded Egremont. "We are close enough to send out the scout to find where they are holed up. Should be easy enough to spot them amongst this desolation."

The land they stood on was higher than the visible base of Kantishna but its peak was ominously above them. Campbell had already disappeared into the bleak landscape, able to hug contours and to vanish where others could not.

"Rest up. Campbell will not be long I suspect," said Egremont, his eyes squinting either due to the freezing wind or because he could already spot movement on the mountain. His face was now set in a viscous determination to fulfil the quest.

"Might be an idea to leave any non essential kit here," suggested Percy. "You know so we don't even have a hint of extra baggage to hinder the old sword arms."

"Good idea," replied Egremont. "But I think we will leave that type of equipment in a cache when we are a little closer and a little more sure. We will also likely leave a couple of guards, just in case any other type of creature wants to investigate it."

They sat around and rested, eating half-heartedly or taking care of weaponry. Nazar Grant changed Beran's bandages and cleaned up his seeping head wound. Egremont was deep in a private conversation with Is-Is, the giant hare never once looking up from his wide range of blades that he had laid out in front of him. Tumbletick found himself sitting with Percy who had a far off look of resignation in his eyes. The pirate took a swig from his hipflask and passed the ornate silver vessel over to Tumbletick while he continued to gaze at the mountain to the south.

"There's a little left Tumbletick. Finish it. Memories of a better night by the fire hey?"

Tumbletick eagerly drew deeply on the marvellous whiskey from Noatak and handed back the empty flask to Fenton who skewered the lid back on and tucked it away in his jerkin.

"Don't worry Percy," said Tumbletick. "I'm sure we will share some more one day."

"Yes, I'm sure we will Tumbletick," said Fenton despondently. "Here comes Campbell with hopefully better news than 'we are out of whiskey'."

Campbell the Weasel ran straight up to Egremont, the rest of the group responded and got up to stand behind the wolfhound as the thief began his report.

"They are there. Not the huge gathering of worshippers we could have feared but I counted forty-one. Men and wolves combined. They have got a bunch of old huts built around one of many ancient stone temples, on the lower slopes of the northwest side of the mountain. They've also got a large bonfire ready to be lit in the centre of their shanty town but there is smoke already coming from the temple," Campbell reported.

"Let's move out," said Egremont immediately. "If the stone is there it is ours tonight."

They followed Egremont who was off at a run in the direction Campbell had indicated. The thief gave a huge shrug of his slender shoulders, twitched his nose a little and sprinted off to be in front of the wolfhound and ensure they did in fact go the right way. By dusk they would be over looking the enemy.

Kantishna was once ringed with temples of Ahrioch. There were dozens of them to handle the worshippers and the offerings to their demon lords and kings who were believed to live below this entrance to Hell. With the cult of Ahrioch now mainly growing in the urban centre of Ende, this collection of huts around a dilapidated squat stone temple was not filled with masses but fanatics who felt the old ways were best.

Egremont, Is-Is, Percy Fenton, Mr. Battfin, Campbell the Weasel, Vixen, Seton Rax, Beran, Nazar Grant, Y'Bor Kaz and Tumbletick stood on a slope that led down from the plateau to the base of Kantishna. The group watched as this outpost of Ahrioch went about their activities before a night of revelling in demon worship. The bonfire had been lit and a couple of slaves, stripped, had been brought out from one of the huts and each had been chained and manacled to a large wooden stake, one of many in front of the temple.

"Are we planning on launching a rescue mission as well?" asked Percy.

"Sorry but no," replied Egremont stoically. "When they have made their sacrifice I have a feeling we may well see the true side of Ahrioch devoutness and that may well be of benefit to us."

Those with better eyesight saw clearly the fear in the eyes of the naked slaves as they were taken into the temple by a collection of cloaked and hooded figures. All, however, heard the screams in the chill blackness as first one then another was pulled backwards over a granite block and had their hearts ritually removed by whomsoever had the highest rank in the priesthood. The smoke rising above the temple puffed a little thicker a couple of times as the heart was removed and then plumped into bowls of boiling blood.

Soon the group on the hillside was watching a large group of men and wolves make their exit from the temple and in spirits of high revelry start to cavort around the bonfire. Bottles of drink had been fetched from supplies in a hut and were being passed around the worshippers.

"Looks a little stronger than communal wine," said Nazar Grant in disgust.

"Let them imbibe my friend. It will make the mission that much easier," replied Mr. Battfin. "I have never known a drunken man to hold his sword correctly."

They waited, as the night grew darker, secure in the knowledge that the eleven still figures on the hillside would be invisible to the fanatics in ecstasy below. The wolves and men grew steadily drunker into the night and still Egremont decided to wait before giving the order for point five of his plan, that of execution. Eventually, about three hours before midnight, ten of the men below entered one of the huts and came back out quickly with strange, elongated attachments fastened to their arms. They then proceeded to run around on all fours, these devices allowing them to canter like beasts in their drunken religious delight. Egremont let out a growl of disgust and anger at this sight.

"Looks like we have some real ultra zealots down there," the wolfhound said. "Those on all fours believe themselves to be demons when they wear those. They are actually serrated swords under very hard leather scabbards, carved to look like the legs of demons. They whip off the covers in battle, go completely on their rear legs, mouths frothing in rage and religion and wade into battle with slashing swipes of anger and self-righteousness. They are, sorry were, the shock troops of the Ahrioch Horde. A little harder than the usual trooper employed."

"They believe themselves to be demons?" said Tumbletick. "Why would anyone want to be a demon?"

"The important thing is they are just men," replied Egremont. "Slightly less fear than most men because they have belief and faith and that is dangerous in itself. We will though have no issue in cutting them down as well. Okay lets leave the non-essential kit here, to free up those sword arms."

"Is it time to go then Master Wolfhound?" asked Y'Bor Kaz heaving both of his warhammers up to his chest. "I fancy crushing some skulls!"

Mr. Battfin drew both his cutlasses; the rasping sound against the firmly tanned leather of the scabbards like the breath of a man with a sword skewered lung.

"Unleash us Egremont. The time has come for some retribution," said the black first mate.

"Time for me to claim a cloak," said Seton Rax, twitching his pectorals under the bloodstained top he still wore. "Battleaxe rents or not, I will be warm!"

"Religious readjustment shall be my cause," threatened Nazar Grant swinging his mace.

"Oh please," said Vixen. "Come on guys, less of the bravado."

"There have been times when a war-cry would be more pertinent and stir the blood before battle," said Beran.

"Well we're not going to go running in screaming 'Bellomancer' are we," said Campbell, still smarting from the choice of name for the operation. "Some men do often need to steel themselves before a fight.

Or we could all stay quiet and you could send just me and Is-Is to go and do some nifty knifework while they sleep off their revels."

"No. It will be a stand up fight," stated Egremont. "Are you fine to fight Beran?"

"My heart is filled with the spirit of valour and this is a just cause," the paladin replied.

"Excellent. Then they will see us coming, if only briefly and will know their fate before it strikes. However, we will not all fight tonight. Percy and Vixen will remain here with Tumbletick and the rest of the kit. You can come down and warm yourselves by the fire when the work is done. No complaining Vixen?"

"Just wondered why you chose me and Percy to stay and guard Tumbletick," she said.

"I have my reasons. I think you two are best for the task," Egremont replied with his eyes still firmly fixed on the demonic enchantment below. "The rest of us will deal with the particular pleasures that await. About five each, shouldn't be too much of a problem. Make it nasty, brutish and short gentlemen but let's keep some for questioning as well."

Egremont took the first step and with him went Is-Is, Mr. Battfin, Campbell, Seton Rax, Beran, Y'Bor Kaz and Nazar Grant. Fearsome in the dark they approached the small collection of huts and the followers of Ahrioch. Egremont gave a couple of quick gestures and split the group into two quartets, to diverge and then attack together in two punches of destructive vengeance. Egremont moved off to the left with Is-Is, Mr. Battfin and Campbell. They arrived out of the dark in a frenzy of violence at the same time as the other squad attacked from the west. Six kills of shadowed surprise immediately, those on the edge of the firelight. Shock from the victims, scrabbling for weapons or flight from the remnants of revellers around the fire but the death and the violence still came. Tumbletick and his bodyguards watched with nervous interest as their companions treated the fight as butchering work.

Is-Is was fighting with the favoured two kukris, giving him the freedom to move well in close quarter work. Within seconds the hare had bounded beyond the perimeter of light from the fire and now in the bloody red glow he slashed at throats and ripped out guts of the enemy in front of him. In particular the hare headed for the pack of zealots with their peculiar bladed legs. Those ten men had reacted well to the attack and rearing to their own legs, from the imitating four legged devotion before, they slashed their arms in an outward motion. The heavily carved scabbards had weighted metal claws at their tips and the whole cover slipped off to reveal long serrated blades. The zealots had had the blades bound to their forearms with leather straps and their hands held onto purposefully crafted handles that allowed for both combat and support for when they wanted to move about in the animalistic pose. These ten zealots moved into a tight circle with backs to each other and weapons spiking in a defensive wall. Is-Is kept his distance and gauged their potential, distracted only for a moment as an enemy wolf rushed towards him with a frenzied snarl and a sword high above his head, held with two paws. Is-Is ducked as the attack closed upon him and stepped towards the assailant. His mail-covered shoulder hit the wolf in the stomach; Is-Is then stood quickly again and watched the wolf roll in the air and crash to the ground near the fire. Campbell who was a little way behind his companion moved in for the final kill and found an exposed piece of neck where he efficiently inserted a dagger leaving the wolf to die of shock and blood loss.

On the other side of the camp, Seton Rax, Beran and Nazar Grant had assumed their well rehearsed fighting threesome to which Y'Bor Kaz added an additional defence fighting off other assailants. Even with a bandaged arm, Beran fought well with his broadsword, batting off an assault from an oily faced man with stains of drink down the front of his cloak. A couple of parries against the slovenly slashes and Nazar Grant cracked him round the back of the head with his iron mace. With a fatally smashed skull the man died in mid combat pose, still on his feet. Beran shoved his broadsword into the upper stomach for good measure and Seton Rax moaned for the loss of a good cloak as blood sprayed like sparks in front of the fire. Beran kicked the dead man off his blade and watched him collapse straight to the floor.

Mr. Battfin was now fighting alone. Having quickly decapitated a couple of drunks who had been seated in sated happiness of alcohol and post sacrificial bliss. He was now focussed on three wolves protecting a man in purple robes with an elaborate peaked piece of golden cloth on his head.

"Protect your priest! Protect your priest!" the man was gabbling in a high pitched whine but none of the other faithful came to his aid. Just the three wolves remained in front of him, snarling at Mr. Battfin and brandishing a sword and dagger each.

Egremont came to stand beside the pirate, his own rapier wet with blood.

"He's the one we want alive Mr. Battfin," Egremont stated then launched himself against the three wolves with a startling burst of speed. His first lunge caught a wary wolf off guard and following a missed defensive move, Egremont stabbed the lupine foe beneath the sternum.

Mr. Battfin engaged the other two, his cutlasses raining against the four blades of his opponents. They defended well against the pirate's controlled aggression but the one to his right could do nothing against the thrust of the sword that came from the wild-eyed Egremont. With the second wolf despatched the wide eyed and shocked priest, turned and lifting his robes ran towards the ten zealots who were still facing off versus Is-Is who calmly stared back at them.

Mr. Battfin against only one remaining assailant soon had him hacked down with a blade dug deeply between the shoulder and neck and another slash across the midriff that parted cloak, fur and flesh alike. The pirate looked around for other threats, saw none immediately near and so kicked the three dead wolves into the embers at the edge of the bonfire, relishing in the smell of quickly burning fur. Egremont had gone after the priest and came to stand by Is-Is as the ranks of the formidable men opened to allow their religious leader access to the potential safety within.

The trio of Seton Rax, Beran and Nazar were dealing with a final knot of defence. They were facing six men when Y'Bor Kaz came crashing into the enemies at the rear, his heavy warhammers knocking over, killing and smashing in an indiscriminate rage of power and frenzy. Seton Rax with his heavy bladed battleaxe scythed through the defensive blows and Beran and Nazar despatched the men who tried to crawl away from the devastation.

Now all that remained were the ten fanatics and their priest. Campbell was rifling bodies before Mr. Battfin rolled them into the fire, ready to react should the zealots decide to break ranks and fight. Seton Rax and company, now finished with the penultimate encounter went to stand with Egremont and Is-Is in the face off for the final fight to come. The zealots remained around their priest.

"Nasty, brutish and short," said Egremont the Lord Seau du Duvet to the others.

"As requested," said Y'Bor Kaz resting his warhammers on his shoulders. "Now for this bunch."

"Not a problem," said Egremont. "Keep the priest alive. Is-Is if you could start us off please. Let's keep it professional."

Is-Is resheathed his kukris and from over his shoulder took his longbow and an arrow. The ten zealots and priest kept to a tight bristling bunch of swords as the giant hare notched the arrow and levelled the bow pulling the string tight. Aiming slowly and deliberately Is-Is released the taut and straining bow with the simplest of movements and sent the arrow careering through the fire lit air and straight into the forehead of a zealot with a sickening crack as the arrow slotted itself through the skull of the man. He slumped backwards down to a convulsive death. The zealots held their formation as Is-Is reached for another arrow and calmly placed it next to the string. Again he pulled so the bow moved into a straining curve. Again the simple release and the thwack as another zealot died. Still they did not break their rank but just closed into a tighter defensive knot.

"Idiots. Attack!" screamed the priest. "Or that heathen will just pick you off."

With the order from their religious advisor ringing in their ears the men screamed and peeling off into a line charged at Is-Is and his companions. The priest not waiting to see the result darted off into the darkness. Campbell the Weasel seeing this left his own defensive line and slinked off with his tracking gait following the priest, listening for panting panic and heavily falling steps in the dark.

Is-Is let fly a third arrow into the chest of a charging assailant, dropped the bow and decided to draw his broadsword for two handed combat against this wall of enemies. Seven against seven. With the burning bodies of recently defeated foes adding to the sense of carnage. Is-Is leapt forward in a counter strike, not happy to receive a charge. He thrust once to his left, ripping into the ribcage of a zealot and hewing out vital organs as he pulled the sword out with a twist of his body. Turning the sword over in a change of grip he smashed the blade into the stomach of the man to his right, then drew the long, razored edge across the width of the zealot's body, leaving the man almost severed at the waist and very obviously dead. Five fanatics remained as the final fight, drunk but still pumped up with religious mania they died quickly. Mr. Battfin stepped passed one and decapitated him with aplomb; a horizontal slash ending in a pose of statuesque victory for the pirate as the man slumped down. The second received an upward swing from Seton Rax's battleaxe, which bit deeply from the groin and into the chest. Seton used all his strength to continue to lift the man in jerky efforts. The zealot eventually hung about a foot in the air as he continued to split under his own weight and the efforts of the barbarian. The third managed to slice Beran's wounded arm before Nazar Grant landed his mace fully on the top of the man's head. Four and five were dispatched by Egremont and Y'Bor Kaz in quick succession, Egremont's feinted attack finding a way simply by the blades with a drop of his head and a forceful thrust. Y'Bor Kaz received two blows with defensive blocks of his warhammers to either side then smashed the man on the bridge of the nose with a headbutt. Stunned the zealot then died due to an attack from Egremont and a follow up thump to the side of the head from Y'Bor's warhammer.

The group looked at the death around them and felt pleased. The only wound received was by Beran to his already damaged arm. The assault had called for surprise combined with ruthlessness and professionalism and it had been gained. A cry in the darkness hinted that Campbell had caught his quarry and as the group looked carefully around for any hiding Ahrioch followers in the huts and shadows, the thief dragged the priest back from the black and to the feet of Egremont.

"Sorry Egremont," said Campbell. "I had to hamstring him as he wanted to run away. But I'm sure he'll answer your questions as a way of avoiding any other unnecessary medical procedures."

Egremont knelt down on one knee beside the whimpering priest and placed a chipped claw against the man's windpipe.

"If you want to be taken into your temple and leant backwards over your own altar and have another encounter with Campbell and his knifework then all you have to do is not answer my questions." Egremont said calmly and slowly.

"Who are you people?" hissed the priest through gritted teeth of fear and pain.

"Representatives of the Court of Rhyell," Egremont replied.

The priest looked at the faces he could see. They were terrible faces, half lit, half shadowed from the flames. Faces that had just butchered his loyal flock within minutes. Behind this evil looking wolfhound, the twitchy faced man called Campbell, with his scant beard and thin pointy nose was leering at him and turning the blade of a wicked looking knife so that it glinted light from the fire into the priest's eyes. An awful looking barbarian, covered in bloodstains was pulling the cloak from one of his victims. The dead man had been a dutiful servant, now he was dead with half his head caved in. The barbarian was taking care to remove the cloak so that it did not touch the pulpy mash of the skull. The priest turned his head again away from the wolfhound and saw a massive black man, with ritually scarred face easily lift another victim and throw the body onto the fire. It cracked burning charred limbs of wood underneath the weight of the fall and was enveloped in flames. The huge man laughed as the body burned with another muscled man with shocking spiked red hair. He was heavily tattooed on his arms, a disgusting tradition that marked him as a heathen from the north.

"Are you mercenaries? I'll pay you double what you are being paid to leave me be," the priest pleaded in fear.

"As I have already clearly said we are from the Court of Rhyell. You need to answer my questions. That will be payment enough," said Egremont. "Otherwise it is Campbell and the knife."

"And I'll ensure to make it slow and painful," Campbell said leaning into the conversation. "No ripped out heart for you matey!"

"I'm sure you'll be able to exist here, hobbling around with the ghosts of your flock for company. You probably get a supply train coming by every now and then don't you?" said Egremont. "You ready for the questions?"

"Yes anything, just promise you will leave me alone," the priest whimpered back full of fear, devastation and pain from the wound at the back of his knee.

"Question one. Where is the Umiat Stone?" enquired Egremont. Campbell was still close by to add threat and listen to the answers.

"Beth Col, Beth Col," came the quick reply.

"Who or what is Beth Col?"

"It's the home of our glorious master, Ahriman. It is in the heart of Ende."

"So the stone has been taken to your dead leader's home?" Egremont probed.

"Dead? Dead? Ahriman is not dead. He thrives in his victory at Beth Col," the priest replied with a little more vigour than his position would have requested.

"Ahriman died in the Ahrioch Wars a decade ago. I saw him die," Egremont asserted.

"No, that was not 'He'. That was merely a minion, a general sent before to claim your lands and people."

"Yes. We have heard that before," said Egremont. "Go on."

"That man failed. Now Ahriman himself has taken the lead and we await the glory times to come."

"Didn't seem like your troops were up to much just now. Not much chance of glory with soldiers like that," added Campbell.

"You took us by surprise," the priest retorted.

"Hmm. Just as Ahriman took us unawares in Rhyell," said Egremont. "We believe you had some other visitors who would have arrived by surprise as well recently."

"Yes. That was Ragna and some of his bodyguards."

"Ragna?" asked Egremont.

"Ragna is a high ranking wolf in the hierarchy of Ahrioch. He arrived a couple of days ago, maybe three. He took part in a religious ceremony, used up most of our slaves, took some supplies and then headed off across country to Ende. He has trodden the paths of pilgrimage many times before between Kantishna and Ende."

"So to clarify. Ahriman and the Umiat Stone are in Ende in a house called Beth Col?" said Egremont.

"Yes," confirmed the priest.

Egremont turned to look at Campbell.

"Well that was easier that I thought it was going to be," the wolfhound said.

"Yes. You're a very loquacious fellow aren't you?" Campbell said to the supine priest.

"You are going to let me live aren't you?" said the priest trying to crawl away a little with kicks of his good heel.

"Oh yes. You are not going to be able to get very far and raise any alarms," Egremont answered. "Plus if you do get rescued I would like you to explain what happened here. If it is a caravan of traders they may take pity on you. If it is some of the faithful looking for redemption, then I think they will have someone to start the sacrificing with in you."

The priest rolled on to his front and scrabbled away towards one of the huts.

"Right," shouted Egremont. "Do a quick sweep and ensure no other survivors other than the priest. Take what we need and then we head back to the beach and get onto 'The Brazen Manticore' again and head for Ende."

"Bit of a wasted journey then?" said Y'Bor Kaz.

"Not totally," said Seton Rax, wearing his newly acquired cloak with pride.

"And we did learn the name of Ahriman's residence in Ende," said Egremont.

"Sure we could have found that out by spreading a bit of Jackson's cash about in that city of notoriety and rapscallions," countered Campbell.

"Well yes we could have but then we wouldn't have had quite so much fun here, now would we?" said Seton Rax.

"Precisely," said Egremont. "Ah here comes Percy, Vixen and Tumbletick!"

The trio had left their vantage point and the supply dump and ventured down to warm themselves by the fire now the threat was quashed.

"Just admired a pretty tasty bit of battle there Eggers," enthused Percy.

"Well we wanted to provide you guys with a bit of entertainment," replied Egremont. "But I am afraid we have a bit of bad news. As soon as you have warmed yourself by the fire and we have taken anything that will be of use to us we are setting off for Mr. Battfin's cove and heading for Ende and Ahriman's residence which is called Beth Col."

"Well I could have told you that!" said Vixen. Egremont gave her a quizzical look. "Oh come on. I am head of the Secret Service."

"Information that could have come earlier Vixen."

"Well you seemed set on checking out Kantishna first," Vixen protested. "And I did state that this was an older centre of worship for the ways of Ahrioch."

"Okay then let's move out!" said Egremont. "We march through most of the night. We rest up when we get back on board 'The Brazen Manticore'."

Mr. Battfin and Y'Bor Kaz threw the two remaining corpses onto the fire and then scampered to join the rest of the group who were already heading back north. They picked up their kit from where it had been dumped. The only additional supplies that had been requisitioned from the Ahrioch camp were a few neat bundles of wood to make the preparation of a fire easier.

With only a couple of lanterns lit to aid their way they trudged over the easier landscape of the high plateau that surrounded Kantishna, it was probably the result of ancient lava flows moulded smooth over time.

By the time they reached the rougher land of crevices and ravines and the descent towards the coast it was about three hours before dawn. Egremont decided it was time to make camp and to take a rest.

The tent was quickly erected and a fire lit with the carried wood. Vixen and Percy kept watch as the others either found room in the tent or curled up close to the adequate fire.

'At least now we have a name and a location to head for,' thought Tumbletick as he felt the weight of darkness creep around the edges of his mind and sleep take him.

Chorus Thirteen

Rok sat cross-legged in the inner sanctum of Beth Col awaiting an audience with Ahriman. The Umiat Stone sat on a pedestal in the middle of the octagonal room. The pedestal was once part of a column from the original temple to Ahrioch. Rok noted the semicircular indentations that rose from the floor to the surface where the shield boss and set stone rested. Umiat's hope embodied in a stone, set in a design meant to be on the ceiling of a cathedral. 'Pathetic,' he thought. Hope should be in the hearts of the citizens of a country. Four braziers burned around the pedestal and lit the room. On the braziers, raised bowls of bull's blood bubbled and spat. Purple and red drapes hung alternatively on each of the eight walls of the room. No other furniture adorned this space of personal reflection for Ahriman. His personal rooms were off this chamber and no one saw them apart from Ahriman himself. This was as close to perfection as any follower got and Rok felt secure with his performance to have been invited here for the one on one audience with his leader. He continued to sit and meditate, waiting at peace with himself.

Rok heard a door open behind one of the purple drapes. The curtains parted and into the room walked Ahriman. He was dressed in a simple cloak of a believer, no adornment that was favoured by some of the priests. His power derived from his mind and an ability to raise the dead, demons and spirits from arcane plains of power. Dimensions, the underworld, from the earth of an ancient battlefield, Ahriman had sway upon them all. His dark cloak had the hood lowered and Rok looked upon the skeletally thin man with black greased back hair before him. His beard and his teeth were shaped to points and he was as tall as any man Rok had ever met.

"Rok," said the master. "I am pleased with your report."

"Thank you my lord," Rok replied, knowing that Ahriman had merely dipped into his mind to retrieve the information.

"The people you were tracking will be coming here now. I have seen it through the eyes of many in their last moment on this world. They destroyed an enclave at Kantishna. They looked for the stone there first."

Ahriman stood by the pedestal and held his hands above the shield boss and the dull polished stone within its frame. It was as if he was warming his hands over a fire.

"This item has no power within itself Rok. No magic. Not like the magic we have. But yet they will still come for it and me. You are to set about making the Beth Col compound formidable in its defences. Ragna is on his way as well. He may well be here before the others. If you can track them and kill them in the streets of Ende before they come to my home then excellent. Kill them all but Tumbletick. Otherwise work with Ragna to defend me."

"Surely my lord we will do so," said Rok looking down to the feet of his master. "But could we not use your powers to raise a host of demonic bodyguards to patrol as well as loyal men and wolves?"

"You shall have all that I can muster and control. But look to the power of steel and the weakness of flesh before relying on the inconsistency of demons or short minded imps for protection."

"Yes my lord," Rok replied.

"Besides, the deformed bastard son of Rourke leads a charmed life and my powers are weaker versus him. The Lord Egremont and his despised hare also have weapons of power that melt my magic away."

"Really my lord? I did not know that."

"Of course you did not know. But how do you suppose they have been so valiant for so many years? Talent? Nonsense they have magic weapons that guide their arms and kill their foes. Do not doubt me Rok. I read your thoughts and know your deeds of the past and future. Now go and prepare the defences. I can feel they are about to leave Kenai's blessed land. They will approach Ende by sea."

With that Ahriman turned and retreated through the purple drapes to his private quarters.

Rok departed through an opposing door with doubts about the magic weapons and other questions on his mind.

'So Ragna is on his way here too?' he thought. 'I'll do what we need to defend Beth Col but if Ragna and his men could be at the weakest point when Egremont and associates attacked…'

The wolf cleared his mind in case Ahriman was still scrying for a response to his recent commands. Rok went to start to recruit some mercenaries to bolster the defences of Beth Col; he knew someone who knew where to find some good ones.

346

Chapter fourteen

It was towards the end of a daylong trek that they made it to the ravine that led down to the beach where their boat had been hidden. Up a little after dawn to a hot cooked breakfast and plenty of Nazar Grant's herbal tea they had pushed on hard along the same route they had come south on. The carcasses of the Kenai mountain dragons had fascinated Tumbletick. Although not picked clean, huge hunks of flesh had been devoured by creatures now unseen. Bones poked through great rents, eyes had been removed and small, scuttling, crab like creatures were revelling and twisting around, on and in bloated purple and red internal organs.

They started to climb back down the steep cut in the rock towards the beach.

"Shall we drag the original launch back?" said Tumbletick as they clambered down the ravine and passed where the higher boat was.

"Well it would be nice to have 'The Brazen Manticore' with her original launch as you say Tumbletick," said Percy. "The wolf and his cronies pulled it a little further than we did ours and it can sit ten comfortably, plus it has got a sail."

Y'Bor Kaz jumped down the remaining boulders and grabbed onto the stern of the boat Ragna and his men had landed on Kenai in. Mr. Battfin made his way to the original launch as well to check that it had been left seaworthy and with enough oars, giving Seton Rax a sideways glance in memory of the one he had dropped during the landing.

Then Seton Rax, Nazar Grant and Is-Is all went to help Y'Bor and Mr. Battfin and started to heave the launch over the rocks and towards the water at the end of the cove. Pulling, heaving and pushing was easier with the aid of a downward slope and soon the boat was down at the beach. The group stared at the waves lurching down the corridor of water with its rocky walls.

"All we have to do is wait for the tide to change," said Mr. Battfin.

"Wonderful things the tides," stated Percy.

"We'll have to be ready to move quickly though," said Mr. Battfin. "Load up the launch. I reckon it will only be a few minutes until it is absolutely perfect to set off."

"Well that was fortunate," said Campbell. "Turning up just in time like that."

"Not really," replied Mr. Battfin, storing his kit in the ample boat. "We had to turn up at sometime and it just happened to be now. A few minutes before the turning of the tide."

"I would have said it was fortunate if it was a couple of hours before the tide turned," said Seton Rax with a hint of dread. "I expect you are going to ask me and Y'Bor to row again and I would have preferred to have had a bit of a rest."

"I wouldn't worry too much Seton," said Mr. Battfin. "It is likely to be quite a leisurely row when the tides change. And if the wind is right we can raise the sail to get back to 'The Brazen Manticore'."

"So me and Y'Bor again then?" asked Seton Rax.

"Yes," replied Mr. Battfin. "Right everybody in. The launch needs to be just into the water. Is-Is and I will hold it while you get in and then we will give the final push."

The party took their places in the boat. With their kit stowed, Seton Rax and Y'Bor got ready to get the oars into place and row out along the passage and into the Sea of Kaltag. All were watching as the waves died down and the sea suddenly sunk into a flat and tamed body of water.

Mr. Battfin and Is-Is gave a huge shove of might and power and the launch lurched and floated into the water. The hare and pirate then leapt on board. Is-Is clambered to the middle of the boat while Mr. Battfin took his customary command of the tiller.

"Come on boys, row us back to 'The Brazen Manticore'," yelled the pirate.

Seton Rax and Y'Bor Kaz heaved out the oars into the rowlocks and began to pull the blades of wood through the calmed and rippling channel of water. Whirlpools from the oars spun off with other eddies to merge and be swallowed by the depths.

The two warriors made good time and the launch moved swiftly, aided by the deeply powerful tide slurping out of the peculiar inlet. Tumbletick sat with Egremont at the prow again and watched the granite cliffs move alongside them. He noticed birds circling and landing on impossibly small ledges on the cliffs. A couple dived into the water behind them and re-emerged to the surface with beaks full of struggling silver slivers. Food for their brood high above, safe in nests on the high, wind scarred rocks. Tumbletick fought with himself to not envy a bunch of seabirds and their existence of simplicity. He knew he was on an adventure and now he was heading towards its climax in the city of Ende. He had picked up bits of conversation from the others about the sprawling place, vast areas in ruin and desolation, abandoned. Other parts for pirate princes and self proclaimed vagabond kings. The enclaves of merchants rich on minerals or furs, the dens of danger, the mass of people, everything he once so feared and they were heading there. And then, somewhere within all its villainy and threat, there was the compound of Beth Col, Ahriman and the Umiat Stone. Tumbletick wondered if their revenge had been enough with the slaughter in the wilderness at the Ahrioch outpost. Then he thought back to the day at the Court of Rhyell and he remembered the death and panic Ahriman had caused with his demonically possessed baboon skeletons.

The launch passed the point of the protruding spur of land and Mr. Battfin gently turned the boat to head north. All except the two rowers with their backs to the open sea naturally started to strain to see if they could see their anchored yet abandoned ship. If it had broke free of its restraints, or raiders had an inquisitiveness stronger than fear of the flags and aroma of rotten fish, they would be scuppered. Then they would have to face a return to the mainland and a long march through guessed at tracks and passes through the mountains and onto Ende.

So it was with a huge relief, felt by all, when Egremont shouted that he saw 'The Brazen Manticore'. Seton and Y'Bor increased their pace to get to the ship which dipped in and out of sight with the larger waves of the Sea of Kaltag still churning away against the Kenai Peninsular.

"I'd approach from upwind if I was you," shouted Percy Fenton. The wind was blowing directly towards them and as such the sail was not much use. "Those pots we prepared are bound to be pretty nauseating by now."

Laughter bounced around the little boat but it was soon replaced by silence as the beginnings of faint hints of horror tinged the air. Soon many were moved to gagging retches of stomach tightening impulses when the sniffs grew to great whiffs from the pots on the deck.

"Oh my god, that's disgusting," screamed Vixen. "Do what Percy said and get up wind of that smell. Quickly."

Mr. Battfin adjusted the tiller and Seton Rax and Y'Bor managed a frenetic row as they struggled against their own instincts to hurl as well.

"Ah that's from the very guts of Hell's worst demon. After a year of feasting on maggoty meat!" approved Mr. Battfin, breathing deeply. "The old pirate tricks are the best."

Out of the direct emanations from the boat, laughter again rose at the pirate's description and replaced the involuntary spasms of spewing. They swung the boat round to the north of 'The Brazen Manticore' and Fenton and Campbell volunteered to disembark when they were within reach of the hull. The launch rose and fell next to the starboard side of the hull and the two men bravely leapt and caught hold of the bulwarks. Holding their breath they scrambled onto the deck and scampered about lifting the pots and at arm's length dropping them into the sea. Large splashes swallowed the pots and water seeped through the pierced sailcloth covering, they sank to the hidden watery world below.

"Some crabs are going to be happy with that feast," said Campbell. "Most pungent. We should have attached a line to them and fished them back up."

"Aye," replied Percy. "What's done is done and I don't think I could have held my breath long enough to have tied them up. Let's get the launch hooked up and get everyone back on board. Time is an enemy too."

Fenton ran to the stern of 'The Brazen Manticore' and threw ropes off to the starboard side to be caught by Nazar Grant and Is-Is. The warrior priest and the hare attached them to the boat and then Campbell and Percy pulled the launch so that it came tautly next to the rear of the ship. Those who were confident enough clambered on board, pulling themselves up to the ship. Vixen, Tumbletick and Mr. Battfin remained on the launch while it was hoisted up out of the sea. Mr. Battfin ensuring it was all guided properly as Percy and Campbell operated the pulleys to raise it out of the sea.

Once on board, possessions were quickly stowed away and Mr. Battfin and Fenton darted about to get the ship ready to take advantage of the northerly wind that would help their passage to the west and then south. It had been a long day and many opted to find a place to lie down and sleep as the two pirates took control. Soon the breeze was cracking the canvass sails and 'The Brazen Manticore', free from its anchors, thrusted through the waves heading towards the tip of the Kenai Peninsular and the city of Ende.

Egremont, Is-Is, Y'Bor Kaz and Campbell stayed up late into the night in conference about the new plans as Mr. Battfin and Percy Fenton continued to share the duties of sailing around them. The moon was out tonight and was bright, stars filled the rest of the sky. The deeper black coast of Kenai was ever present to the south but Mr. Battfin was confident in his knowledge of these waters as the ship harried along cresting white capped waves.

"So what is the plan now then?" asked Campbell.

"Virtually the same as before. Same as when we thought Kantishna was a good place to head for and to attack," replied Egremont.

"Get in. Cause a lot of damage. Retrieve the artefact and get out," said Y'Bor Kaz.

"Precisely," concurred Egremont. "Except now it will be enclosed combat within a well guarded building of which we do not know the layout."

"Or even its actual location," said Campbell, cleaning his nails with a dagger. "However, money will be very useful in Ende. There'll be plenty of pleasant types who will let us know where Ahriman resides. They'll do virtually anything for a pile of coins or a bit of leaf."

"Well then. I've got something which maybe useful as well in my pack," said Y'Bor with a grin, his red hair dark in the moonlight. "I'll be back soon."

Y'Bor Kaz weaved his way to the cabin and returned swiftly with a large leather pouch. He opened it and showed the small group the contents. Rolled up tight were many wads of the narcotic leaf.

"If you hadn't noticed, I haven't been laughing that much recently," the warrior said. "Been keeping a clear head. You know, remaining focussed. But you never know when something like this will come in useful."

"Tough times or for trade," said Egremont.

"Exactly the reason I brought it with me," Y'Bor replied.

"Well then," said Egremont. "I suggest when we get to Ende we hole up somewhere safe and Y'Bor and Campbell go and work their magic on the streets to find out where Beth Col is."

"Done," said Y'Bor and Campbell in unison.

"Then it is points one to six of 'Operation Bellomancer' again," the wolfhound continued. "We keep Tumbletick with us and he carries the Umiat Stone back all the way to Rhyell and Princess Annabella Blaise. Hopefully we can find a safe dock for 'The Brazen Manticore' and some guards for it. Then we have our way back to Umiat secured. Mr. Battfin will we be able to find some pirate protectors there?"

"Aye. No problem at all Master Egremont. No problem at all," replied the first mate, his biceps and shoulders bulging as he turned the wheel slightly to port.

Chorus fourteen

Rok, pale eyes penetrating, sat across the table from a huge and ugly brute of a man. They were in a dingy back street ale and whorehouse in Ende. The man wore an iron helmet wrapped in two-tone furs. A nose plate covered a large proportion of his face, 'thankfully' thought Rok. His eyes were darkest brown and his cheeks were heavily pockmarked as the result of some childhood disease. He had teeth missing when he spoke and a thick moustache that drooped like a couple of fangs to well beneath his jaw line. He was a powerful man, there was no doubt there but he was rotund in his strength rather than lean or broad and square. He wore chain mail but had again insisted on covering himself with a large fur cloak.

"So you have a contingent of thirty warriors who are prepared and willing to do some mercenary work, Adomai?" said Rok.

"Indeed. Your henchman Balloch was fortunate to know of us," Adomai replied in a thick accent from the east of Kenai. "Thirty veterans of wars, vendettas and brawling on a daily basis."

"But you can command them?" asked Rok.

"When pay is involved they are more disciplined than any army. It is just when they spend the pay that they are a little... raucous."

"Any issues with working for followers of the old faith?"

"We work for one faith and that is gold. As I understand it, this job is some guard duty with the chance of battle against some Umiat types?"

"Correct," replied Rok. "There will be some other 'guards' as well but they will be well briefed not to hurt any of our friends within the confines of Beth Col. What is your rate?"

"Four pieces of gold, per man, per day. Plus meat and lodging."

"Naturally," replied Rok. "Payment to me made when?"

"When we ask for it," said Adomai. "You do have certain guarantees though that we don't just leave after a week. I'll give you a lunar month of protection for half payment now, half at the end of the period. The men will take half a day to round up and sober up. We will be at the gates of Beth Col at sunset."

"Agreed," said Rok. "Payment of half to each man as he steps through the gates. They'll be a little ceremony going on when you arrive which will mean each man will be marked as a 'friend'. Plus there will be a whole bull, freshly slaughtered, blood removed, on a spit for a great welcoming feast."

"Then all seems in order," Adomai said, standing up an extending his mailed glove to Rok.

Rok clasped the hand, gripping it tightly; looking up into the dark eyes of the large man that towered above him.

"As long as you are all exceedingly violent and efficient," said Rok.

"Let me assure you. Me and my men are the most brutish bunch of head cleaving scum you could buy. And we will actually do the job you have paid for. Our reputation and future depends on it. The 'Landsknechts' are yours until you decide you do not want to pay us anymore."

"Excellent," replied Rok. "I look forward to working with you."

Ragna arrived at Beth Col with his contingent of bodyguards. They were weary after their trek through the western arm of Kenai. The trip to Kantishna had not been too arduous but the supplies gained from the religious outpost had been a welcome addition. The information they had received in the Old City had been a blessing indeed. After months of attempting to clear the tunnels to the catacombs the attack from the Monks of Delight had been an inconvenience only. Escape was possible and the enemy had provided it to them in the shape of a fleeing pirate and a left launch.

The route from Kantishna to Ende was well known to Ragna, having been a holy pilgrim many times before in his formulative years. To have made the trip once was an aspiration for many members of the Horde but Ragna had been on many expeditions as a fully entered novice in the religion. His devoutness and willingness to face the hardships of the trek had brought him to the attention of regional priests and so Ragna's career within the ranks of the Ahrioch Horde began. Soon his passion for the sacrificial altar and his natural skill as a demagogue had brought him to the attention of Ahriman himself and so Ragna found himself in the inner circle and picked for duties of other kinds.

They had stayed at Kantishna for less than an hour before heading off through the inspiring mountains and forests of the western arm of Kenai. Ragna pushed his men hard. He had been keen to make it to Beth Col to offer his report of the growth of the Ahrioch Horde within the Old City of Rampart. He also desperately wanted to be present when Ahriman took a further step in his victory over the unbelieving north and began to muster his forces into ever growing numbers before they could launch a true invasion of Umiat.

Ragna had secured an outbuilding within the compound for his men to rest in and had returned to his own home within the complex. He took a short while to remove his travel stained garments and change into a more befitting set of robes for his audience with Ahriman.

When the message came that the Necromancer was ready for him, Ragna felt the wave of elation he had always felt when nearly in the presence of such a great man. He made his way quickly to the large central building of Beth Col and took familiar passageways to the private sacrificial suite of his master's home. He waited, sitting cross legged as many had before him in the sparse room. He already knew the significance of the shield shaped piece of sandstone that stood on the central pedestal and Ragna was in a state of nervous ecstasy when Ahriman appeared.

"Master!" Ragna gushed in adoration and started to crawl towards the leader he had been without for so long.

"Ragna I am pleased with you," Ahriman replied allowing the wolf to kiss his slender hand. "You have shown us a devotion which I could trust to few. Your work at the Old City of Rampart was invaluable to us."

"Thank you master but the faithful were killed in a battle. We lost many a dutiful servant," Ragna replied.

"But my most dutiful escaped and has made his way back to me following holy paths and passing many trials. Ragna I am thankful for your work and the proof that many a northern man can be brought to understand the ways of Ahrioch by one as convincing as you," said Ahriman. He paused for a while and warmed his skeletal hands by a brazier. "I have seen that we are to gain a great gift that travels to us now and Ragna you are to be by my side when we consecrate the cursed Umiat Stone into our own faith."

"Master, how can I thank you?"

"Say prayers with me now and we will offer a sacrifice in the main temple. But later, as I have foreseen, we will be together when I claim that great and valued heart. The bastard son of Rourke will baptise the Umiat Stone into our faith with his death."

Chapter Fifteen

'The Brazen Manticore' headed directly south, the extreme tip of Kenai slipping passed to port in the chilling light of dawn. Tumbletick was on board early, standing at the bulwark with Egremont, Is-Is and Campbell, all were looking towards the vast city of Ende. It clambered over the shape of the land but this close to the coast even Tumbletick and Campbell could pick out details in the city. Collapsed quarters abandoned back to nature sat next to large columned buildings of ancient importance, still maintained by someone. The reports that those who had never seen the city before were right. To the north, on the steeper slopes, buildings were temporary and shanty style, wooden lean-tos and tents, swarming over the highlands. Strings of smoke spiked into the sky from countless household fires to be blown away by the coastal winds. Tumbletick wondered who lived there. Families waiting for fathers off trapping or panning for gold, the disenchanted, the poor workers who cleaned the houses of the wealthy to the south.

Campbell was focussing on these southern buildings. Large and substantial walled enclaves of the rich that you would find in every city. 'When the powerful want their own areas they shut themselves away from the squalor,' he thought.

There were the towers of temples and spires of churches and cathedrals. Ende was nothing if not fair to the faiths of the world. All types came to this city and many wanted to pray. More however wanted to relish in the freedom though, freedom to do as you please in the anarchy that was Ende. This was a tough city, tougher than the wilderness, more random than the Old City of Rampart. They would all have to watch their backs in this place of violence and fear. The only easy certainty would be when they did find Beth Col and penetrated its heart; it would be a violent expedition again.

"Getting out shouldn't be too much of a problem," Campbell said out loud. "Plenty of side streets to disappear into. A veritable labyrinth of despair."

Egremont was looking at the colossal city but planning their first moves rather than taking in the view. He was confirming the thinking of how staying on board 'The Brazen Manticore' may well be the best idea. Campbell and Y'Bor could scout for information as to the location of Beth Col but after Percy and Mr. Battfin had searched the dockyards and found some pirates to guard the boat. Then they could all go ashore once Ahriman's house was found. 'Yes that is the more secure method,' he thought. He now focussed on the decayed splendour of Ende and despaired at the scale of the place. Egremont had studied many a map and he knew that the city was doubled over the horizon with the second spur of land jutting into the Kenai Sea. That piece of land was a peninsular in itself and was also covered in sprawling architectural swarm.

"Probably the population of Umiat gathered onto the tip of this despicable continent," said Egremont.

"Why do they choose to live like that?" asked Tumbletick.

"History. Geography. Politics," Egremont replied.

"The usual reasons," added Campbell. "And we will find our way through it all and succeed in Ahriman's lair."

Percy Fenton and Mr. Battfin had shown considerable stamina over the four days and nights it had taken to sail to Ende. Taking snatches of sleep or adding Nazar Grant to their roster of helmsmen, they were able to get safely to the tip of Kenai. Nazar Grant, it turned out had been on many of the supply vessels that monthly crossed the Porcupine Gulf, having spent much of his time many years ago on the island monastery at Aklavik. This was deemed as experience enough to aid the two pirates when combined with a steady mind and a steadfast hand.

Egremont went to speak of his new plan with Mr. Battfin at the wheel.

"It seems a fine idea Master Wolfhound," Mr. Battfin replied. "I'll take her to the most northern and central dock."

"Why that dock Mr. Battfin?" asked Egremont.

"Well it will be the most central to the city and therefore provide a better chance of being close to Beth Col. Plus there are some places I know round there that are often frequented by pirating types. It means we have to travel further through the enormous docks but I should be able to pick our way through to the top," Mr. Battfin replied.

"Fine idea Mr. Battfin."

"Also the docks to the south are the most expensive to moor at as they are the quickest to be out to sea from and you don't have to navigate so much around the other traders. You'll see a lot of boats in about an hour," the pirate said keeping the ship ripping the waves and heading south.

Within the hour, with the rest of the group briefed on the new plan, were all on deck and awaiting the view of the huge natural harbour of Ende to open up before them. The sight of the city nearly doubling in size and the harbour in a frenzy of trade over such a huge scale was formidable as it filled the whole horizon in front of them. Vessels of all designs and size sat moored or skipped across the waters. Small junks criss-crossed the bay carrying local materials or passengers wanting an easier journey than walking the long way round. Clippers and merchantmen loaded with cargo or delivering much-needed foodstuffs from Umiat and beyond. Although there had been enmity between the lands of Umiat and Kenai many times before and there had always been mistrust, the power and lure of money and the desire and need for goods on both sides meant there was a constant hunger for trade. Huge galleons, converted to slavers plied a profession mostly popular in the massive continents to the south where very few visited unless it was to be worked to death in the mines. The southern continent was reportedly so far away beyond the ice filled seas that the climate grew warm again. Campbell pointed these larger ships out to Tumbletick and how their hulls had been covered with plates of metal for protection against the frozen sea, icebergs and growlers they would have to sail through.

Mr. Battfin was now tacking in a vaguely northerly direction. It was a continuous to and fro complicated by avoiding other boats, both smaller and larger around them. Time slipped by easily with so much to look at after the monotony of mountains for the previous four days.

Tumbletick pointed out a trireme, with three rows of oars heading towards the only island of the bay.

"An affectation of the owner of the isle Tumbletick," said Campbell wistfully. "A very rich and powerful man lives there. He probably doesn't know it but with the death of our friend Jackson, he has become the richest man in the world."

"What's his name Campbell?" Tumbletick asked.

"Oh, no-one really knows. He goes by many names. But I would love to get on that private reserve of his one day and have a good look around at some of his possessions."

The trireme glided easily up to a jetty and with well-rehearsed elegance Tumbletick watched as the oars on the starboard side were withdrawn in unison. Many men on the dock caught lines shot by large crossbows on the deck and then worked hard to pull the beautifully shaped vessel alongside.

With the time it was taking to tack to the north Tumbletick and Campbell were joined by Y'Bor and Beran to watch as a portable ramp was brought up to the trireme and a column of warriors with burnished brass breastplates and helmets with feathery plumes disembarked. They had large round shields, each with individual designs and carried a long spear each.

"Not bad for a private army hey?" said Campbell.

"They are probably into fighting as a phalanx rather than as individual warriors though," scoffed Y'Bor slightly.

Tumbletick scanned the mountainous island. It was heavily wooded with hardy trees. He thought he could catch glimpses of marble buildings hidden within the trees but no large palatial residence could be seen. He watched with the others as a column of the guards marched off up a well-constructed path towards the centre of the island. They were followed by a small group of men in robes, surrounding some slaves, carrying on their shoulders a sedan chair, covered and hiding its occupant. Another column of well equipped guards followed and the procession disappeared into the trees.

"Well I suppose it is one way to travel," said Campbell.

"Stand to," Mr. Battfin suddenly shouted from the helm. "Grab some fenders. We are entering a particularly busy stretch of water."

As 'The Brazen Manticore' entered the waters to the north of the bay the traffic of shipping had less space in which to manoeuvre. Tumbletick, Y'Bor and Campbell left the still injured Beran with his one good arm to grab some ropes with fenders attached to the ends. They took up strategic positions around the ship to lower these between the hulls of any approaching vessel. They came close many times but only once did Tumbletick and Campbell have to place the fenders in a defensive position and watch a squarely built dhow harmlessly bounce away in a sluggish wallow. Tumbletick felt a great deal of accomplishment in his quick work and a connection with the white robed man at the wheel of the other boat. The man smiled, in appreciation of the effort, a full and hearty toothless grin. Tumbletick realised that the man had shown no sign of repugnance at his own form, just openness and thanks for the fending off. 'Perhaps there are good people in Kenai,' he thought to himself. 'Just because it seems all my enemies are from here doesn't mean everyone from here is my enemy.' Tumbletick watched the dhow plough away and he waved to the man on deck. The man waved back, not really paying attention to where the boat was heading.

Mr. Battfin had sailed 'The Brazen Manticore' to the north and the last of the remaining docks. They were constructed of rocky boulders placed in the shallows, with smaller stones elegantly located and then cement had been added to square off the edges and hold the structure together. Mr. Battfin expertly had Percy lower the sails to precise commands and the ship drifted neatly next to the dock. Local men received thrown ropes but Percy jumped down to ensure everything was attached correctly. He handed out a few small coins to the men and they went happily away. Percy then trotted off to the wood cabin at the end of the dock and spoke to the dock master, handing him enough coins for an extended mooring and silence if anyone started to ask questions. Fenton then returned to the secured vessel and leapt aboard with a dash, landing close to the waiting Egremont and Campbell.

"Okay that part's taken care of," said Percy. "I suggest we go and hire some of the extra 'crew' for added security now. Tough, tough place Ende. Mr. Battfin and I are sure to find some fellows we know of and can trust. I think about six sturdy lads should be enough."

"Agreed," said Egremont. "Campbell, give Percy some more cash for incentives and when he returns you and Y'Bor can head off."

Campbell handed over some promissory notes and some more coins. Percy tucked them away in an inside pocket. Then checking he was fully armed he and Mr. Battfin disembarked again and walked as casually as a pirate can, beyond the end of the dock and disappeared into the maze of towering warehouses and grotty dockside taphouses.

The remaining party stayed in the cabin or wandered around in pairs on the deck, taking in the sights and maintaining a lolling attitude of repose. Nothing to attract attention and the business life of Ende went on around them nonchalant and uninterested in another boat among many.

Fenton and Mr. Battfin ensured their weaponry was extremely visible. Mr. Battfin puffed out his enormous chest and Fenton swayed with the confidence of the capable. A little for show but such displays would keep opportunist thugs away. Both pirates had been to the docks of Ende before in their careers and although mile upon mile of coastal harbour confronted them with alehouses, drug dens, brothels, gambling dives and sometimes all four combined, they knew the better places to find some additional crew.

They headed for 'The Queen's Head' first. A favoured tavern in this quarter of the city. The sign hanging at the level of the second storey window was a particularly bloody depiction of a young decapitated sovereign.

"Umiat ports have a little more class, Mr. Battfin," said Fenton.

"Indeed they do Percy. But a little less character," his first mate replied.

Inside, three rooms all on slightly different levels to allow for the gradient had been combined with rough brick archways allowing access to each. A bar ran the length of the pub giving leaning space in all of the three areas. It was dark and smoky inside. There were three grimy, small leaded windows not allowing the late afternoon light in. Flaming lanterns were lit behind the bar, casting shadows of the customers back towards the door.

The landlord was a powerfully built stocky man with a shaven head, thick moustache and tattooed arms. 'Probably extremely dangerous,' thought Percy as he went to the middle bar. Mr. Battfin stood behind his captain and a natural space of caution opened up around him as the men drinking in that part of 'The Queen's Head' moved a modicum away.

"Two pints of your best bitter please landlord," requested Fenton.

The innkeeper said nothing but expertly pulled two ales from a hand pump straight from a cask in the cellar below. Percy was slightly surprised to see that the glasses proffered to him, full with a rich and glinting ruby red beer, were exceptionally clean. The landlord obviously caught Percy staring at the pint.

"Brewed on the premises and I take a great deal of pride in what I do."

"I doubt it not sir!" Percy said. "Please accept this gold coin as payment for me and my friend. Also for anyone else who wants a pint, here's another."

Percy knew what he was doing. Such generosity and displays of wealth would attract attention quickly. The fact that he was backed up by a very threatening looking pirate meant that people were likely to be friendly. Bodies turned around and soon the landlord was pulling several times on the pump to provide ale for many a dock worker and sailor.

"The name is Percy Fenton," he said a little louder than necessary. "This is Mr. Battfin."

The landlord quickly rubbed his hand dry on his apron and reached across to shake both the pirate's hands.

"Your reputation proceeds you sirs!" the landlord said.

"Yes, I rather hoped that it would," Percy replied. Years at sea cultivating their name had paid off several times before and they wanted to take advantage of it quickly now. "Would you happen to know if there are six or so good lads who might be looking for a little guard and sailing duty? Simple job as I say. Just looking after our boat for a couple of days then helping with a little jaunt up to Rhyell with some passengers."

"Sure we could find some for you sir. I'll send the potboy over to 'Hummels' for you. There are some pirates who were drinking here earlier that are staying there. What would the finders fee be sir? Another gold coin?"

"Certainly. If they are good lads known to us and the code," Fenton replied whilst Mr. Battfin looked disparagingly at the quality of the men currently drinking in 'The Queen's Head'.

Percy paid for some more beers for the pub to keep the locals compliant. There wasn't any potential for crew among them. The potboy had scampered off a while back and returned to whisper in the landlord's ear.

"Apparently they are a little busy at the moment but the mistress of the institution says they'll be along about dusk."

"Excellent. More time for ale. A perfectly pleasant diversion when the beer is of this quality," Fenton said lifting his glass to the lantern light and finding himself amazed again by its depth of colour and the perfectly clean glass.

Percy drank a lot quicker than Mr. Battfin who remained silent the whole time. They waited and kept the very happy customers plied with further free drinks. Percy was ebullient with the crowd around him. He told stories, sang a couple of rousing songs and generally let on he was more affected by the ale than he really was. Then as the sun was setting unseen, in walked a group of eight men obviously affected by years of working at sea. Broad hats, with feathers, covered craggy faces in deeper shadow. Long coats covered weather beaten clothes and swords at their sides. They instantly moved to the bar, recognising two of their own ilk among the weaker, drunken men of the pub.

The man of highest rank started talking with Percy in hushed tones. Secret words and knowledge were exchanged and Fenton was soon convinced they were men of honour and followers of the Pirate's Code. It was agreed that they would take up the job that Fenton was offering. Three of the men would bring their own ship, 'The Boreas', which was a sprightly corsair, into the dock next to 'The Brazen Manticore'. The other five would stay on board Percy's boat and guard it while the mission was accomplished. When the passengers returned to 'The Brazen Manticore' both boats would head for Umiat immediately. As soon as Rhyell was reached addition payment would be made which was more than an average years plunder. The three selected to move 'The Boreas' left immediately while a final pint was bought and drunk to secure the deal with the remaining five.

Percy leant across to the landlord as Mr. Battfin left with the remaining pirates.

"I don't suppose you have got a bottle of Noatak whiskey I could purchase off of you have you? Rinkabar if possible," Fenton enquired.

"Rinkabar? Noatak? Not much call for that around these parts sir!"

"Hmm. Yes I suppose my tastes are a little selective. Do you have any whiskeys that I might restock my supplies with?"

"Well I do have this Mr. Fenton," the landlord said and revealed a dusty old brown bottle from below the bar. He brushed the label with the back of his hand. "Something from Kenai I'm afraid though. It is from the slopes of Kuskok."

"Fantastic. And how much is it?"

"Ten gold coins sir!"

"Of course it is," said Percy counting out the money.

"Like I said sir. Not much call for it around these parts. Just the odd rare bottle for our discerning customers."

Percy took the bottle, paid the money and placing it under his jacket he ran out of the door and quickly caught up with Mr. Battfin and the new crew of 'The Brazen Manticore'.

Chorus Fifteen

Adomai and his thirty Landsknechts arrived at the closed double gates of the Beth Col compound. A wall, twenty foot high enclosed all the buildings within. No battlements topped the defences but four wooden towers had been built over the years, jutting up against the perimeter, they offered some vantage point and archers could use them if necessary.

Adomai pounded on the wooden gates with the hilt of his sword. The Landsknechts were a hardened bunch of warriors. Adomai's boast was no idle one. Each of his men had served their apprenticeship in armies from around the globe. From the level of rank and file all had seen combat in wars from large scale battles to smaller, more intimate engagements. Many had been specially selected for shock troops but all had killed as part of their profession. In more peaceful times they had yearned for adventure and passed the recruiting process of the Landsknechts. Now they fought for pay and the prestige of being a mercenary. All were heavily armed with sword and spiked shield as basic weapons. Daggers and throwing knives hung from belts around the waist or over the shoulder of their chain mail armour. All wore furs, not just because it was cold but because the ancestral home of the Landsknecht garrison was near to the Elias Ice Flats and it was part of the traditional attire of the people who lived there. This was a formidable bunch of bodyguards for Ahriman to employ.

The gates opened and Adomai was greeted by Rok and Balloch. Within the walls one great building stood at the centre and was surrounded by squat little bungalows. The large building was three storeys tall and painted white. It had no windows on the first two floors but the third had evenly spaced circular openings. They were fitted with leaded windows running in a criss-cross design. One door faced the double gates and allowed entrance to Ahriman's home.

"It used to be a temple to Ahrioch," said Rok following Adomai's eyes.

"Not many windows," said Adomai observantly.

364

"It adds to the atmosphere for the ceremonies that were, and still are, conducted there," Rok replied. "But come in, you can probably smell the bull roasting already. Just as you enter though Balloch needs to ensure you are all anointed with a little liquid. If you could all remove your helmets it will mean that some of the other 'guards' who will be arriving soon will not mistake you for a potential threat."

Adomai was shrewd enough to understand Rok's rhetoric and removed his helmet first, indicating that his men should do the same. Balloch had a small black bowl in his paws, containing recently boiled blood.

"It's already been blessed," Balloch said dipping his thumb into the blood and then placing it firmly on Adomai's forehead, just between the eyes. "If you could all ensure you are marked. We have had some of the houses to the east cleared for you for use as barracks."

"Adomai," said Rok putting his arm around the large warrior. "Ahriman wants to meet you personally. You know, ensure my decision was a good one. Plus he wants to introduce you to the other guards."

Rok led the way to the converted temple and took the Landsknecht leader through passageways lit by torches to a central room, once the heart of worship in the temple. The room was square but the centre of the space was a lowered white marble circle. Six tiers rose from the circle to the straight walls, seats for the worshippers. Braziers burned around the room and torches flickered, held in their iron brackets on the walls. Within the marble circle of pure white there was permanent design created in black mosaic marble. Two equilateral triangles were at the centre set into a six-pointed star. Their points touched the circumference of a circle. A slightly larger circle was around this one so that it made a ring. Within the ring where each of the points of the star touched the circle there was an elaborate black cross marked into the design. Between each of these six crosses there was a word. Adomai could easily read these larger clearer words, however within the thirteen sections made by the star within the inner circle there were more designs and lettering which the Landsknecht could not make out from his current view. He started to read the words he could see from standing at the upper tier.

"Tetragamaton. Elohim. Messias. Sother. Emanuel. Adonai Jah."

"Woah careful there my friend. Dangerous words," cautioned Rok.

"Indeed," said Ahriman entering the room from behind them. "Dangerous words indeed if spoken with knowledge. I am pleased to meet you Adomai. Your men look dangerous and I appreciate that. But come with me into the circle and I will summon some support for them."

Adomai felt that the introduction to his paymaster was a little strange but he also knew that great men often did not operate in the same way as those who were deemed as normal.

Ahriman, in his dark cloak, stepped down the tiers and walked into the centre of the design. Adomai and Rok followed him. There was easily enough space for all within the permanent mosaic. The Landsknecht looked down at some of the smaller words and designs beneath his feet. He saw the symbol for pi, '=gram=' and the word 'Alpha'. Rok coughed and the warrior looked up again, Ahriman was about to speak.

"There is no doubt," said Ahriman. "That Necromancy is the touchstone of the dark arts. For if, after careful preparation, the adept can carry through a successful issue of raising the dead from the other world, then he had proved the power of his art."

With that Ahriman reached into the sleeve of his cloak and pulled forth a small pouch.

"The device upon which we stand is not really necessary for a Necromancer of my power. But it adds a little theatre," Ahriman said, opening the pouch and scattering the contents on the floor around him. "I trust that all of your men have been marked?"

"Yes Ahriman," said Adomai, struggling to see the little blanched objects sitting on the white marble floor that the Necromancer had just thrown. "I thought you were a Demonologist rather than a Necromancer?"

"Oh I am both my good man. I like to utilise what is best for any event. Demons, Undead. Different creatures for different occasions. I think for this kind of duty," said Ahriman. "Something a bit more silent than I would usually conjure is called for. Something that lurks but when it grabs does not let go."

The Necromancer concentrated and muttered words of power quickly and precisely but inaudible to both Rok and Adomai. Swirls of yellow light tornadoed slowly up from the teeth on the floor. Within the churning maelstrom of lights, figures began to stand from a crouch position. Skeletal at first but then organs and flesh began to appear and wrap and bind themselves around and to the bones. Flesh began to creep over the collection of human matter, teeth punctured through gums, nails sliced through the end of pink skinned fingers. Yet all the formed monsters had an imperfection, half a missing head, a lopped off arm, entrails hanging from a rent gut. Standing naked, dead and on the verge of beginning to rot again the creatures looked blankly towards the circle and the trio within.

"A cohort of fifty zombies for you," said Ahriman. "Taken from an old, old battleground. Rok, take them to the armoury and equip them with some weapons and some rags to cover them. They will hunt the premises for anyone not marked by our blessing."

Ahriman departed to his quarters and Rok was left with the task of outfitting the undead.

Chapter Sixteen

With the additional pirate guards now secured and on board Y'Bor Kaz and Campbell the Weasel jumped down to the quay and headed off into the city. It was now dark but the constant life of Ende meant the area twinkled with hundreds of thousands of lights. Tumbletick was on deck looking at the marvellous sight with Percy and Egremont. Others were sleeping or preparing their thoughts and weapons.

"It is a whole lot prettier at night," said Tumbletick.

"Indeed. It is peculiar that such pretty things can mask such villainy," replied Egremont.

Vixen came out of the cabin to join them on deck.

"Egremont," she said. "Look, I've got contacts too in this city. I could be of use if Y'Bor and Campbell don't get the information we need. I'll only be about an hour and then I'll be back."

"Fine Vixen," said Egremont. "If you think it will help."

"I'm sure of it," she replied and sprung over the side and was soon enveloped by darkness in her black leather gear.

"You sure it's safe to let her go out there alone?" said Percy.

"Oh Vixen can look after herself just fine," replied Egremont. "She's likely to find out where Beth Col is before Campbell and Y'Bor."

"I suppose she does have some marvellous talents," Percy said.

The trio waited mostly in silence out on the deck. They watched shipping continue to move in the night out on the bay. They listened to the sounds of laughter; anger, love and hate come to them from the city. They wondered who would be most persuasive in finding the location of Beth Col and hoped that all three of their group out on the streets would be safe and successful.

Y'Bor and Campbell had stuck together, Vixen was working alone. The men's approach was slower and more random. They entered into conversations with local ruffians on street corners, asked for directions in pubs but Ende was a large place and even though notorious, Beth Col's actual location seemed vague but they thought they were getting closer. Vixen had headed straight to the place she wanted to go, to talk to the people she wanted to talk to and was soon heading back. She had only been gone an hour when she appeared on the quayside again and climbed back on board to find Egremont, Percy and Tumbletick still chatting.

"Any luck Vixen?" asked Egremont.

"Not really. All I could find out is that we are relatively close. Mr. Battfin's hunch to moor here was a good one. I'm sure the boys will have more success," she replied and went to the cabin.

Campbell and Y'Bor did have more luck and shortly after Vixen was asleep in the cabin they returned to 'The Brazen Manticore'.

"Anything to report?" Egremont enquired.

"Yep," said Campbell. "Been there, seen it, know the way there and the way back. Single wall, one gate, lots of activity going on within it.

"Right then," said Egremont. "We rest up now and attack at dawn when the 'activity' is likely to have died down a bit."

They all went back to the cramped cabin space and found a place to rest. Watch had been organised between the new hired pirates and always a couple of the original company.

At midnight, Mr. Battfin woke Tumbletick and Fenton to have their two-hour shift and they found themselves on the deck again listening and looking at Ende. Tumbletick regretted not going to sleep as soon as they had arrived, he had only caught about an hour of less than restful repose before Mr. Battfin had woken him.

"I enjoy my time with you Percy," said Tumbletick.

"And I do too, Tumbletick," the pirate replied. "If only it were under different circumstances hey?"

The first hour flitted by uneventfully. Their boat and 'The Boreas' were the only ones now at the quay. The two other pirates on watch with Percy and Tumbletick were talking to each other quietly at the other end of the ship. It was peaceful out on deck. It was a clear night and the stars of the heavens reflected on the water and it felt like they continued on the land with the fires and lanterns of the city. Tumbletick felt that a million little lights surrounded him.

There was a light footstep on the deck and they turned to see Vixen walking with a tray and four mugs of steaming liquid. She went to the two other pirates first, gave them a mug each and then approached Tumbletick and Percy.

"Courtesy of Nazar Grant," she said. "A little something to boost the spirits and keep you alert on a cold night."

Nazar Grant waved to them from the doorway of the cabin and then disappeared back in.

"Thank you Vixen, most kind of you to bring it to us," said Fenton.

"Well it was my idea that he make you something. I woke him up deliberately to prepare it."

"Do you think he would mind if I poured a little whiskey in then?"

"Not at all. I'm sure it would do even more good," she replied.

Percy took his bottle of expensive Kenai whiskey and opened it. While Vixen was still holding the tray he poured a decent tot into one mug and with an indicating hover of a nearly tipped bottle over the other Tumbletick gave a large nod. Percy poured the whiskey into the second mug until the combined liquids were nearly at the rim.

"Enjoy," said Vixen as Tumbletick and Percy took their mugs off the tray. "I'll see you later."

Tumbletick sipped his drink as Percy still blew on his.

"Tastes bitter," Tumbletick said.

"Drink it boy, it'll do you good," Percy said with mock authority. He took a gulp of his own. "I must admit old Nazar's herbs certainly mask the taste of the whiskey."

They stood on watch and finished the bitter drink. Percy considered filling the mugs both back up with whiskey but knew that that would be irresponsible. So it was back to their duty and keeping a lookout for threats.

Tumbletick barely noticed the fact that the other pirates had stopped their low but constant chatter. He looked at Percy who was standing but struggling to keep his head from falling onto his chest. He kept nodding violently and then standing straight again. His head fell forward another time but the pirate's body fell as well and he collapsed on the deck. Tumbletick realised that he was sitting down and that all the lights in the sky and the city were going out together. He heard soft footsteps and muffled treading approach, quiet voices of unknown men and a familiar female voice. He did not feel himself being lifted off the deck and placed over a saddle on a black horse, with cloth wrapped around its hooves. Tumbletick was completely unaware as he was led silently away on the horse, surrounded by a heavily armed bunch of four men, a cloaked wolf and a woman dressed in black leather. The group moved to the north, leaving the three sleeping pirates still alive aboard 'The Brazen Manticore'.

Fenton felt himself being roughly shaken and water thrown into his face. He opened his eyes but had to force them to focus on the angry looking face of Egremont in front of him. The rest of the group stood behind the wolfhound.

"Where are Tumbletick and Vixen?" the wolfhound snarled.

"I don't know. Vixen must have drugged us," Fenton replied with a struggle.

"Well she must like you very much to have left you alive," said Campbell.

"What are you saying?" Fenton shouted back.

"Exactly what you thought I was," Campbell spat. "She's taken Tumbletick, but don't worry Percy 'old chap' I'm sure you can guess where!"

"Beth Col," replied the pirate getting to his feet and shaking his head as he held onto the bulwark for support.

"You said you were Master of the Nine," Y'Bor whispered into Egremont's ear. "I guess now we know who the traitor was."

"Yes," replied Egremont. Then he was sterner. "Get yourself shipshape Fenton. We move out in two minutes."

Chorus Sixteen

Vixen stood above the sleeping Tumbletick in the antechamber by Ahriman's private rooms. The four braziers burned brightly and Tumbletick was in a heap at the base of the columned pedestal. Ragna and Rok were also both in the room. She was still dressed in her leathers but the wolves had both changed into clean, ceremonial robes.

"Wake up you little crack of nothing," Vixen bent down to whisper in his ear. "I've got a couple of friends here who want to meet you."

Tumbletick felt Vixen's breath on his ear and strained to open his eyes even though he did not want to see who Vixen's friends were.

"What have you done Vixen?" Tumbletick asked looking at the two cloaked wolves as well as the sneering Vixen.

"Something we have been trying to do for a long time. Get you away from the others and to Beth Col! I would have loved to have done it sooner but the time was never quite right, or someone else was always hovering about."

"You swore on your soul that you were going to protect me!"

"You ignorant little crack! I swore on my 'God given soul.' That part of me went along time ago when I was baptised into the Ahrioch faith by Ahriman himself."

"I knew I despised you all along Vixen, now I know why I was so certain of that hatred," Tumbletick said quietly.

"And I you Tumbletick. But before we perform the ritual we have all waited so long for, I want to let you know something else. Something else before he removes your heart as you are held lying on the Umiat Stone. I'd rather like to be able to torture you. Rok really wanted you to be broken before you are sacrificed. But Ragna here says we must not have any blood loss before your heart is cut out. So I suggested we use hot irons from the braziers or maybe just set your hairy little frame on fire. Or maybe we could see how you stood up to boiling for a few minutes. That was my favourite. But no. You are to be safe from all the pleasant things I have been thinking of for as long as I have had to put up with your company."

"I bet you were always leaving messages for the wolves, or meeting with them when you slinked off, weren't you?" said Tumbletick.

"You don't even have the slightest idea of what I was up to."

"Why did you want the wolves to attack us on the plateau of Rampart?"

"I thought it might have been a good time to take you then but Rok was under strict orders just to follow, watch and report."

"More like they were scared of my friends," Tumbletick said boldly.

"We were not scared of your friends," spat Rok. "I told you before in that awful bar in Tetterton that had I wished we would have killed you all there and then but I was under orders."

"What about the wolves that attacked us in the Old City?" asked Tumbletick. "We made pretty quick work of them. They attacked us."

"Different pack. Different orders. Different leader," Rok replied.

"I can not believe that a cult such as yours would not have a unified and coherent strategy. Would not have mattered if you did or not have a single simple plan though, my friend Is-Is had them dead or fleeing within seconds," Tumbletick taunted, determined that he would fight with words if he could not retaliate in other ways. Plus he was gaining time.

"Talking of your friends. That brings me neatly around to what I wanted to tell you before you die," Vixen interrupted and then brought herself just a little bit closer to Tumbletick. "Your friend Jackson was one of us too!"

Tumbletick paused, shocked to take in this information from Vixen who leaned over him leering in delight.

"You lie Vixen! He was not. He was a good man," Tumbletick yelled.

"No Tumbletick he was not," Vixen replied slowly. "He was more faithful than I and if he had not unfortunately died he would be with me now. By my side. Why do you think it was I who ran to his aid when he was shot?"

"To ensure I was safe so that I could eventually be brought here."

"Well partly. But I also wanted to rescue Jackson. Your other friends all ran off and couldn't give a stuff. But I did and I was distraught to see him die. His role was to befriend you. Win your confidence and then get you here."

"You lie to torture my mind Vixen," Tumbletick screamed.

"Not true Tumbletick. If Jackson had been here now he would have been more jubilant than all of us. The Ahrioch faith helped him to grow wealthy. The rise of the Horde would have satisfied his faith and increased his business interests as well. Nothing like a good war to boost the economy and the bank accounts of arms dealers."

"I don't believe you Vixen," Tumbletick cried.

"Look into your weak and emotional heart and your memory. You will know it to be true," she said. "And what of your other friends. They don't care about you either. You were just along for the ride. All they care about is what Egremont thinks of them and this piece of rock set in some carved sandstone. Pathetic."

"They care Vixen. And they'll come for me and the Umiat Stone."

"I doubt it," she replied.

As she paused to think of more things to taunt Tumbletick with there was the sound of a huge crash, muffled in the distance. Tumbletick noticed looks of concern on the faces of the wolves and Vixen as they suddenly became alert. Soon after another wolf came running in.

"What is it Balloch?" said Rok.

"A flaming wagon of lumber had been crashed through the gates. Heathens are rushing into the compound in large numbers," Balloch replied.

"Quick, get back to the compound and ensure the Landsknechts are there to defend the gates," Rok ordered.

Balloch departed as fast as he could run, down the short corridor, a turn to the left, down two flights of stairs and then quickly unbolted the front door, sprinted through, shut the door behind him and was off to the housing set aside for the Landsknechts.

Chapter Seventeen

Y'Bor Kaz sat on top of the wagon of lumber they had bought off a very happy trader. He had walked away with a wad of notes worth ten times the value of the cart and the wood combined and had got to keep his oxen who plodded after him as he counted his money again.

"Left a bit guys," Y'Bor said eyeing up the slope of the road that led to the gates of Beth Col. Seton Rax, Mr. Battfin and Is-Is pulled on the yokes now devoid of bovine strength.

"That's on target," Y'Bor shouted. "Now go."

The warriors ran off into the darkness and round to the other side of the Beth Col compound. Y'Bor Kaz took some flasks of lantern oil from his pack and started pouring them liberally over the lumber. Then he went to the front of the wagon and took down the two lit lanterns that helped guide the way at night. Unhooking them he carried both to the back of the cart and put them on the ground. Y'Bor stood squarely and flexed his muscles. Then he placed his palms at the back of the wagon and leant into a massive shove. The warrior strained and felt the wagon begin to move. Just a couple of feet and it would hit the start of the slope. Y'Bor felt his calves and thighs burn as they added to the effort. The wagon made the peak of the gradient and started to move on its own accord. Y'Bor turned, picked up the lanterns and then threw them onto the back of the wagon. They smashed, spilling flaming oil and wick over the soaked cedar wood. The flames took hold of the oil and began to spread as the wagon picked up speed.

"Wah Hey that baby's gonna do some damage," Y'Bor shouted and then more calmly, apparently to no-one in particular he continued to speak out loud. "Even if it doesn't hit the gate that lot would probably take down the wall."

Y'Bor was to wait to see if the wagon did do the damage it was expected to. If it created a breach in the walls he was to move to the second stage of the hastily put together plan. He watched intently, walking after the speeding wagon as it rushed towards the gates. When it did strike it was fully ablaze. It hit one of the gates squarely and part of the wall. The wagon smashed but the lumber in the back was thick and heavy trunks of cut wood and it was these that crashed through the gates and wall in an explosion of bursting splinters.

Hordes of people spilled out of nearby buildings and hostelries to investigate the noise and saw the broken gates and a red haired, well built man jumping up and down with glee.

"Free leaf," Y'Bor started to shout at the top of his considerable voice. "Free leaf for those that want it. Free leaf. Free leaf."

Y'Bor started to run closer to Beth Col and was soon being chased by a large crowd once they realised what the lunatic was shouting. The red haired warrior started to throw wads of leaf over the walls and into the enclave. The crowd grew and conversation turned to riotous yells in the desire to get at the leaf the man was throwing away.

The crowd rushed to the broken gates and individuals started pouring into the courtyard and beyond looking for the little bundles of narcotic. When they started to be attacked by the men who defended the compound, they fought back. All carried weapons in Ende. Some of the warriors among the defenders seemed to move a little slower than others but any potential threat to the mob and their quest for leaf would be fought with in the dark.

Y'Bor was soon approached by some brighter individuals who realised there was probably less risk if they took on the one man who was throwing the leaf rather than attempting to clamber past a burning wreck and into a riot. Y'Bor faced four men who had already drawn their weapons to confront him.

"Give us the bag," a fat oaf said. "Or I'll slit you up!"

"Oh please," said Y'Bor. He pulled back his arm and with a mighty throw launched the bag over the wall. The four men watched its arced flight, spilling contents as it flew before it disappeared beyond the wall. "Off you go if you want the bag but the leaf is worth more though."

The men turned and ran after the flight of the bag and entered into Beth Col with throngs of other hopefuls.

'They should be in by now', thought Y'Bor. 'Where's Beran?'

Y'Bor Kaz looked around for the injured paladin. He should be about somewhere, waiting to launch their own part of the plan. Y'Bor saw him in the shadows of a nearby pub.

"Beran, time for us to make more of a contribution."

Beran came towards Y'Bor, arm and head still bandaged, his sword already drawn. The red headed warrior took his warhammers in hand too.

"I'm ready Y'Bor Kaz. May we both be valiant," the knight said.

"Then let us go. Our task is clear. Keep the distraction going for as long as we can and keep the exit clear," Y'Bor replied.

Y'Bor Kaz and Beran walked steadily down to the burning wagon, the broken gate and wall and to the edge of a violent riot.

As the wagon crashed into the gate, three grappling hooks were thrown over the wall of Beth Col and pulled tight. Is-Is, Seton Rax and Mr. Battfin climbed up the outer wall and began to stealthily lower themselves down the other side. They held onto the edge of the wall and dropped down the rest of the way onto a conveniently built bungalow right against the wall. Next came Campbell the Weasel, Egremont and Percy Fenton. Nazar Grant followed the agile little thief who was faster than any of his companions up the ropes borrowed from 'The Brazen Manticore'.

"The diversion's working," whispered Egremont. "In and out quickly guys."

They leapt in turn down from the single storey house and crouching and running made their way through the shadows towards the building at the centre of the compound. As they skirted along the walls of the old temple they could hear an uproar at the gates. Heavily armoured men, cloaked wolves and shambling creatures were all moving towards the flaming wagon and rioters who flowed in. However a small group of the slower moving guards somehow spotted them and were shuffling towards them in the shadows. There was five but probably more behind them as well.

"Seton, Nazar, deal with those," said Egremont and then led the rest of his assault team towards the doors of the heart of Beth Col.

Seton Rax and Nazar Grant stood ready against the approaching guards. With disgust and holy awareness the cleric noticed first that these were servants of the Necromancer.

"Undead! Seton do not fear them," he said and then quickly made a prayer. "In all that is holy I abjure thee."

The cleric and the barbarian stepped out towards the creatures. Their revulsion at the zombies was forced to be suppressed as they went about the business of destroying the threat. Seton swung with his axe

377

and decapitated the first and then with a might backswing severed a second through the rib cage. The barbarian noticed with sneering interest that the beheaded undead stopped moving immediately while the one he had hewn in two, pulled itself forward, towards him with its arms in the dirt, mouth still moving and leaving a trail of innards behind it like the tentacles of a squid.

Nazar approached a trio of zombies and swung at the head of the first with his mace. He made a massive contact with the skull but the weapon just mashed into the vacant eyed monster, slamming the head against a shoulder. The zombie did not drop but continued to walk with outstretched arms towards the priest. Nazar panicked a little and was not quick enough in backing away and as Seton was concentrating on hacking up the torso crawling towards him, another zombie grabbed at Nazar's tunic and with a startling burst of final speed locked its teeth into the cleric's exposed throat.

Nazar roared in pain and abhorrence and managed in a controlled move to shake the vile thing off of him with a chunk of flesh still bloodied in its dead mouth. The cleric heaved his mace with adrenalin pumped force into the chewing head and knocked it clean off to roll into the darkness.

Seton moved in and sliced off the head of the zombie Nazar had first hit. It was a difficult strike as the monster's head was still lolling on its side. He then countered the final zombie with a roundhouse kick to the chest, knocking it off balance and to the floor. As it attempted to regain its footing the barbarian brought down his axe in an executioner style hack and finished its cursed existence. He then moved swiftly to Nazar who was clutching at his throat.

"There are some more on the way. Quick let's get into the building," said Seton. Pulling Nazar Grant along in his wounded state they made after the others.

Campbell was at the front doors to Ahriman's residence. He tried the handle and was surprised to find it unlocked or bolted from the inside. The door swung easily inward.

"Not expecting us yet then?" he smirked. "Big mistake."

With the riot behind them attracting most of the attention the five men darted into the corridor lit with burning torches.

Seton Rax and Nazar were quickly in behind them. The others did not notice the wound on the cleric's throat as he pushed the doors back shut.

"No mercy," said Egremont. "Find Tumbletick and the stone."

The group moved off through the corridors of the building, splitting off at intersections and investigating behind doors into smaller rooms. All instinct told them that what they were looking for would either be found on the upper floors or in the largest room of the building, probably at the centre on the ground floor.

Campbell, Is-Is and Egremont found stairs and immediately pounded up them, ignoring a landing to the middle floor and continuing to the top. Mr. Battfin and Fenton headed along the main corridor, obviously constructed to lead towards a ceremonial heart. Seton Rax remained with Nazar Grant who moved slowly, shocked from the vicious bite upon him. They decided to move back towards the entrance and try to ensure that it was kept secure to afford an exit later.

Mr. Battfin and Percy Fenton opened the door to the central chamber with the tiers leading down to the marble floor and the necromantic design. Across the room, sitting on the top tiers, playing with small bone dice were four of the Landsknechts. They were completely ignoring three zombies that milled about the bottom of the chamber who were completely ignoring the Landsknechts. Mr. Battfin was incredibly quick in deciding what to attack first and with two bounds he was down the six tiers and towering above the already maimed undead. With his two cutlasses glinting in the light of the braziers and torches he hacked the zombies to twitching crawling pieces as the Landsknechts, stood, drew their swords and grabbed their shields. Only one of the mercenaries took the time to put on his helmet as well.

Fenton gave a brief look of disgust as the remains on the floor kept moving towards the hacking Mr. Battfin. Fenton felt sure the body parts posed little threat now though.

"Mr. Battfin, I think I need your attentions here," called Fenton as he circled the tiers, attempting to keep in an opposite position to the Landsknechts. Two of the mercenaries decided to step down to the rooms circular floor and take on the black warrior, while the other two moved in differing directions to give the flamboyantly dressed man little chance of further evasion.

Mr. Battfin again took in the threat facing them. He retreated and climbed back up the tiers to be by Percy's side. With the potential of having four heavily armoured men engage them at the same time, Mr. Battfin decided to take a defensive stance and with his arm across Percy's chest he pushed him back out of the room and into the doorway, which was only wide enough to allow two men to attack them at once. Percy threw a dagger at one of the advancing warriors but the mercenary easily deflected it by raising his shield. Then the first two Landsknechts were upon them in the doorway. Mr. Battfin dropped to his knees and thrust a cutlass into the lower stomach of each of the two attackers. The men roared in agony and as Mr. Battfin withdrew the blades they fell away to either side of the door. Percy was left facing the remaining couple of fighters who moved in quickly to take advantage of the momentarily vulnerable warrior they had just seen destroy three zombies and mortally wound two of their companions. The Landsknechts blades came down heavily but Percy moved to counter with a horizontal blade and Mr. Battfin used his cross cutlass technique above his head. The clashing of metal hit with anger and held hard in defence burst down the corridor and was heard by others in Beth Col. Percy reached for another dagger with his free left hand. Rather than attempting to turn the weapon so he could use the blade he hit straight with the butt of the hilt into the mouth of one of the attackers, smashing gums and teeth. Then the pirate captain brought the dagger with a back handed move against the other foe, cutting into the left of the man's neck underneath his helmet. The Landsknecht punched back with his shield, the spike narrowly missing the pirate but Percy was slammed against the corridor wall with great force.

Mr. Battfin stood up now to his full height and glared down at the warrior with his bleeding neck. The smashed mouth mercenary was stumbling around spitting out teeth and blood. Of the other two, one was already dead from the wound the other close to unconsciousness in his agonies. Mr. Battfin punched the remaining man in the face with the hand guard of a cutlass then cut into the other side of his neck with his other blade.

"Helmet didn't do you much good hey?" said Mr. Battfin as the cutlass cut through the spinal cord. The pirate pulled free his blade and stepped into the room and butchered the remaining men as Percy fell away from the wall shaking his head and trying to catch his breath again.

Nazar Grant and Seton Rax remained by the entrance growing increasingly concerned by the scratching and shuffling and low moans of the undead on the other side of the door.

"They're pushing quite hard Nazar," said Seton with his bulk shouldered against the wood of the door. He occasionally showed a slight shudder as the weight of the zombies increased. "I think we are going to have to go out there and clear a few of them."

"I think that would be an extremely bad idea," said Nazar as he finished wrapping a bandage around his neck, blood was already growing in a large dark mark on the white cloth.

"They are getting really quite agitated Nazar," said Seton as his feet started to slip on the stone floor. He pushed back with all he could muster but the doors kept thumping and shifting inwards. "We need to do something now!"

"I know Seton. Though I fear my mace is not the right kind of weaponry for this devilry."

"Then just try and keep them off me. It's axe wielding time. Ready?"

"Ready. We clear what is out there and then come back in here right?"

"Right," said Seton. He indicated that he would allow the door to open on the count of three. He started with a nod of his head. Once, twice and on the third nod he pulled open the doors to be faced by a throng of the undead.

A large body of ragged, deformed zombies suddenly surged forward into the corridor, arms outstretched and mouths hungry for flesh. The weapons that Rok had equipped them with had all been dropped. These monsters wanted to rend and claw to soft, tasty organs beneath. Seton was surprised. He had expected to be able to leap out to the courtyard beyond and be able to move with a little freedom among the slow zombies. To be able to swing with relative ease. Being confronted by a thickness of bodies filling the doorway, blocking each other, with more beyond desperate to fight their way in stunned him for a moment. The lead undead almost grasped at the barbarians still favoured black cloak, before he had time to recover, step back and take a first hack with his battleaxe. A couple of outstretched limbs fell to the floor but still the throng approached. Seton Rax and Nazar retreated along the corridor backing away from the zombies. Seton kept up a rhythmic swing of defence against the unfearing monsters.

"It's me they want," Nazar said. "They can smell the blood. It agitates them."

"I think they want us both," said Seton in strained reply keeping up the strategic withdrawal.

As they moved back along the passageway they came to a junction. Seton Rax was concentrating on defending against the advancing mass of flesh and did not notice that Nazar Grant retreated around the corner rather than keeping straight towards the centre of the building. Seton was horrified after the zombies that had been following him simply turned at the junction and went after the priest. A wall of shambling corpses traipsed by the stunned barbarian before four of the monsters bringing up the rear decided to head towards him instead of following the others. The barbarian could hear the increasing groans of the zombies down the side passage as they advanced on his friend. He could just pick up the dull squishing thump of the mace against flesh as the cleric fought back with all the strength he could find.

"Help!" screamed Seton, no other word seeming applicable as he stopped his retreat and started hacking at the four zombies ahead of him. The width of the corridor restricted his full ability in combat but in desperation to aid his companion he soon had two of the creatures so violently chopped up that their mobility was removed and they just twitched on the floor.

As the screams of Nazar Grant echoed down the corridor the barbarian heard running footsteps behind him. His stomach turned quicker than he could in fear of being trapped but his hope soon surged when he heard Mr. Battfin calling his name.

"Quick," the barbarian yelled. "Nazar's alone against them!"

The large black pirate came to Seton's side, his cutlasses more effective in the enclosed space. The two of them together were able to effectively deal with the threat. With the last zombies now truly dead in this section of the corridor the two men rushed towards the junction as Percy Fenton came groggily up behind them.

The sight they had to take in, within the shadows cast by the torches of the corridor would stay with the men always. A heap of hunched bodies were attacking the defeated cleric after his death. The undead were ravenous in their inhuman lust for flesh and blood. They ripped at his body and his vitals were already spilling on to the floor and being gathered up by the creatures in cupped hand to feast upon. Others that could not get close to the bloodied corpse moaned in resentment and tried to push their way to the body.

"Percy. Ensure the front door is shut and guard it," said Mr. Battfin. "You okay to end this Seton?"

"Yes Mr. Battfin," Seton was grim and stern faced. "I mean to ensure Nazar's sacrifice allows the rest of us safe exit. Let's destroy them while they are…busy."

"Well said Seton," Mr. Battfin replied. "We came here to rescue Tumbletick and the stone who are both still at risk. But let us destroy this threat now."

The barbarian and the pirate simply walked towards the horror in front of them. Seton felt secure next to the first mate, steadfast in his knowledge of combat. Together they approached the zombies and with extreme violence filled that section of the corridor with the remains of decapitated and hewn undead bodies, thankful that the body of Nazar Grant was unrecognisable amongst the carnage.

Vixen, Ragna and Rok remained silent at the news Balloch had brought. They all looked at the form of Tumbletick on the floor and each was willing to despatch him themselves but knew that it was the desire of their master to do so personally.

"Who is going to knock and get him then?" asked Vixen.

"Not me," replied Rok. "He'll come out when he is ready."

"If you hadn't noticed what Balloch said, the heathens are attacking now!" Vixen replied.

"I've been a senior member of the Ahrioch Horde for twenty years and there is no way I'm going to knock on his door and summon him," Ragna said.

"There are enemies in the courtyard and I'm pretty sure that means my erstwhile companions are going to be about as well. Probably in the building right now," Vixen urged. "If we are not careful there's going to be an angry wolfhound and an extremely dangerous hare bursting through the door very soon. Get Ahriman now!"

"No need to 'get' me Vixen," said Ahriman as he entered the room from his private quarters behind the purple drape. He held a large bowl in his hand and he placed it on a nearby brazier. "Prepare the sacrifice immediately please."

Ragna and Rok grabbed Tumbletick as he lay on the ground and lifted his struggling small form so that he lay on top of the Umiat Stone. Ragna pulled hard on Tumbletick's arms, Rok delighted on tugging his legs taut. Tumbletick felt the bulge of the stone in his back as the wolves held him place. The little, deformed man shut his eyes and breathed uneasily as Ahriman stepped forward and brought out a large curved knife from his deep sleeved robes. Tumbletick was resigned to his death after the betrayal of Vixen and her information about Lord Jackson of En'Tuk.

Ahriman started to chant in an arcane language that Tumbletick did not recognise but it sounded seductively melodic and he kept his eyes closed so that he would not see the blow come. His arms were pulled tighter still and he felt that the moment must soon come. His heart would be cut out and probably still beating be placed in the bowl that the Necromancer had nearby to gently boil away as an offering to his demon masters.

Tumbletick heard a door slam open and a scream of rage and pain above him. His arms and legs were released. He opened his eyes to see blood dripping down towards his face and Ahriman, towering above him tugging at an arrow which had penetrated his bare forearm. His hand still clutching the knife, aloft from where he was about to plunge it into Tumbletick's chest. Ragna and Rok had drawn swords and were rushing towards the attack. Tumbletick took his chance and rolled off the pedestal to crash to the floor. He looked up and saw Is-Is notching another arrow. Egremont was advancing on the wolves and Campbell the Weasel was running towards him as he lay on the floor. Tumbletick was struck by the venom in the eyes of Egremont, the calmness of Is-Is and how handsome and yet stern Campbell looked. The thief came to Tumbletick's side and handed him a dagger. From the look in Campbell's eye, Tumbletick could sense that someone was approaching them. He stood beside the man whose quick wit and realistic honesty had always been a relief. Tumbletick turned and saw Vixen advancing on the two of them with daggers drawn.

"You haven't got a chance against me Vixen," Campbell said calmly.

"I'm eager to find out though Weasel," she replied.

Is-Is released the arrow as soon as he entered the room, the door having been kicked open by Campbell. The piercing shaft split the smooth skin of the forearm of Ahriman as he held his knife in a sacrificial pose. Egremont and Campbell were into the room as the arrow struck home. Egremont moved towards the two wolves, Campbell was running to the aid of Tumbletick and intercept Vixen. The hare notched another arrow and aimed at the highest priest of Ahrioch. The man made no attempt to run; he just stood, incredulous in his agony. Is-Is, lowered the bow and fired the second arrow into Ahriman's thigh and leaving the Necromancer wounded he drew his kukris and went to the aid of Egremont.

Egremont was fighting well against the two wolves but the intervention of Is-Is swung the battle quickly. The hare sidestepped a clumsy retaliation, twisted his body and stepped behind Ragna. Is-Is clutched him with one long arm and simply cut the throat of the wolf and let him drop to the floor.

Rok backed away from the two warriors and stood with his back to a red curtained wall. He looked to his wounded master for help but saw none coming as Ahriman just stood still.

"You should never have ventured out of Ende wolf! To have attacked us in Rhyell and taken the Umiat Stone was a grave mistake," said Egremont.

"But we did prove you to be weak. Our faith is strong and we will rise again. I assure you Egremont," Rok replied.

"Your final words? Or do you want to watch me as I cut your master's throat?"

"Your honour does you proud," spat Rok. "Giving me such a choice shows your true worth. But I'll leave you with these utterances. You have not won!"

Egremont stepped forward and thrust his rapier through the wolf and brought his face close to the enemy.

"Funny that. It kind of feels like we have," Egremont said and stepped away as the blue eyed wolf slumped down the wall nearly pulling off the drapes that hung behind him.

Vixen and Campbell were engaged in an epic knife fight. Spinning and turning, clashing blades held in two hands in quick succession. They kicked at each other, blocked blows with arm against arm and tried to trip their opponent with flicks of their feet. Tumbletick backed away from the threat. He watched as Is-Is easily killed Ragna and Egremont had an ominous conversation with Rok. He stared at Ahriman who stood still in the room between two braziers by the pedestal. Two arrows were in his body but the man just remained stationary. His mouth was moving though, muttering again in the arcane mellifluous language that Tumbletick could just make out above the continued fighting of Vixen and Campbell.

Is-Is came to stand with Tumbletick and affectionately put his paw on his friend's shoulder. Tumbletick smiled at the massive hare and then both turned to look at Ahriman again. Egremont walked over having left Rok to die on the floor and embrace his chosen afterlife. The wolfhound showed Tumbletick his love and relief at seeing him still alive by hugging him only briefly as a remaining issue still needed to be dealt with.

"Is-Is if I could borrow your broadsword please? I think that perhaps something a little more theatrical is in order than just cutting his throat," Egremont said.

The hare drew the long blade and handed it to Egremont. Tumbletick turned his back as Egremont walked up to Ahriman and looked him in the eye. The leader of the Ahrioch Horde said nothing directly to Egremont, just finished his mutterings, smiled and lowered his arms. Egremont the Lord Seau du Duvet heaved the double handed weapon through Ahriman's neck, beheading him cleanly.

Vixen screamed as she saw her master standing before Egremont. She kicked out at Campbell catching him in the chest. Egremont swung the blade with his coup de grace of Ahriman and Vixen took the opportunity with Campbell slightly off balance to run behind one of the purple drapes that alternated with the red around the room.

"There's no point trying to hide," shouted Campbell. "It's all over."

"Finish her off," ordered Egremont. "We'll take her head as well for the battlements at Rhyell. Two traitors together, they'll adorn a spike well."

Egremont gathered Ahriman's head up in a piece of the Necromancer's robes that he cut off. Campbell and Is-Is advanced on the purple drape and going to either end of the hanging they grabbed the edge and tore it down to reveal an open door in the centre of the wall.

"Crack!" shouted Campbell.

"After her," shouted Egremont but Is-Is and the thief were already chasing after Vixen into the private quarters of Ahriman.

There were only three rooms and the two adventurers quickly scanned two small chambers leading off a short corridor before moving into the large sitting room at the end of it.

Is-Is and Campbell both came to an abrupt halt. A round window was smashed and a chair placed beneath it. A swift view of the sparse room and they were certain that she had already made her escape. Campbell sprung to the chair and looked out of the window into the night but he could not see Vixen.

Egremont and Tumbletick came into the room behind them and took in the scene. Egremont was clutching his macabre baggage as he spoke.

"Fine. She's gone. We better get back to 'The Brazen Manticore'. Tumbletick you had better go and claim the Umiat Stone."

The four adventurers walked back into the octagonal chamber and after the hectic last few moments they took a little time as Tumbletick approached the pedestal. He paused as he reached out towards the shield boss that recently had nearly been his own personal sacrificial altar.

"Take it Tumbletick. Take your destiny. Take back what you guarded for so long," Egremont said summoning up dignity to his voice for the instant they had all been questing towards had arrived.

Tumbletick grabbed the Umiat Stone and clutched it to his chest.

"Right let's go. That's enough ceremony," commanded Egremont.

The quartet ran back through the corridors and passageways of the upper levels. Is-Is led the way followed by Campbell, Tumbletick following his fellows on paths they knew, Egremont brought up the rear. All speed was now to be spent on escaping Beth Col and making it back to the docks.

Percy Fenton, Seton Rax and Mr. Battfin waited near the front door of the converted temple. Seton was constantly listening at the door, anxious not to hear the approach of shuffling moans. He turned back to look at Fenton and the black pirate in constant silent communication that all was well.

They heard the sound of running from the corridor with the stairs to the upper levels, weapons were readied in case of attack but they were all relieved when Is-Is appeared in the torchlight of the main corridor, instantly followed by Campbell, Tumbletick and Egremont.

"Everything okay?" asked Egremont.

"We lost Nazar Grant to zombies but there are no threats left on the level," said Percy.

"How about you?" asked Mr. Battfin.

"Ahriman dead. Stone retrieved. Vixen escaped," replied Egremont. "We'll grieve for Nazar later. Let's get out now."

Campbell pushed his way to the door and opened it a slight amount to peer with a thief's eye into the compound.

"Right. The plan was to make a quick escape through the main gate," said Campbell. "Beran and Y'Bor Kaz are still there but there's also a bit of a clash going on."

"No time to wait. We dash through the crowd. Cut down anyone who gets in our way. Mr. Battfin and Is-Is will lead. Then me and Tumbletick. Campbell, Seton and Percy act as vanguard," Egremont stated.

The group adjusted their positions in the corridor and took a few breaths to ready themselves before the sprint through a brawling fight in the enclosure. They hoped Beran and Y'Bor Kaz would keep the exit clear of any major challenges. Then Egremont barked the order to move.

Beran and Y'Bor Kaz stepped into the breach made by the crashed wagon and watched the large group of locals searching the ground for the wads of leaf that had been thrown in. Within seconds the two warriors watched as guards inside Beth Col approached and began fighting with the people of Ende. Some of the guards did not use weapons and just latched on to the rioters to bite and rip with their hands. Other guards were cloaked wolves or heavily armed warriors who were fighting in a more professional manner.

"Tactic of throwing stuff over walls has worked well hey?" said Y'Bor.

Beran said nothing in reply but pointed as he noticed their companions appear at the front doors of the main building and quickly gain access. A few moments later Seton Rax and Nazar Grant followed them. The two men at the main gate by the burning wagon were then disturbed to see a large group of the shuffling, slow, wounded looking men begin to congregate by the door of the old temple.

"You think we should clear that bunch back a bit?" asked Y'Bor as the zombies started to hammer on the door.

"No," replied Beran. "Our orders were clear. Protect the gate and ensure the riot continues. It would be too risky to try and circumvent that fight before getting into another with those creatures by the doors. We should move the riot up a gear and add money to the equation."

Y'Bor nodded his agreement to stick to the plan. The two men started shouting again at the large crowd gathered outside of Beth Col. The flames, crashed gate of the mysterious structure and ongoing noise of the rampage inside had attracted quite a large set of spectators.

"Money. Free money," Y'Bor shouted showing large clutches of promissory notes in his hands. Beran joined him after sheathing his sword to carry out the act with his one good arm. The crowd was instantly more attentive and when Y'Bor and Beran let go of the paper money and it blew into the courtyard of Beth Col they both simply stepped aside to allow more people rush into the increasing fight in the quest for wealth or narcotic pleasure within.

Beran and Y'Bor watched intently as the fighting grew. Who was attacking who now was unclear but both were sure most of the guards in Beth Col were being attracted to this part of the complex. Their interest in the distraction though was directed again to the group of strange shambling men by the door to Ahriman's residence. Both warriors grew concerned that these guards were fully intent on gaining entry and all other fighting in the courtyard was ignored by them. They watched a little longer but stayed true to the plan that Campbell had come up with and Egremont had sanctioned. Suddenly the door opened and they briefly saw Seton Rax as he was pushed back by the surge forward of the guards that had been outside. All the men pushed their way in, in a peculiar swaying walk.

"Crack!" shouted Y'Bor and he made his way forward to help but Beran drew his sword and placed the flat of the blade in front of Y'Bor's chest.

"They can deal with it Y'Bor. Stick to the plan. If we do not secure the exit then all may be lost," the paladin said. "Now, look to the left there."

The two men watched as a tight knot of men in chain mail, furs, helmets and shields had fought through the riot and assembled together. A very large bulky man in the same gear was shouting orders to the men that could not be heard this far away over the sound of the raging fight. Understanding their subsequent actions was simple though. The group of men started walking slowly through the riot killing everyone in their way. They simply hacked people down efficiently, shields were held at their sides, protecting all in a linked up wall. Their leader was at the front, alone, immensely capable at dealing with the foolish individuals who came close to him.

"They could be a problem," said Y'Bor. "I think we need to fan the flames again!"

Again Y'Bor used the trick of throwing money into the air to be carried by the breeze. A few more inhabitants of Ende decided to seek a quick gain and found that they were soon fighting for their lives.

Beran and Y'Bor stayed by the gate. No fighting had come their way and they waited and watched happy that the distraction was growing but concerned by the way the band of chain mailed warriors were depleting the ranks and enthusiasm of the rioters. They kept their eyes also on the doors to the old temple. Somewhere along the line the doors had been closed again after the shambling men had entered. They hoped that all was going well inside the building. Here there was enough space to easily escape if their comrades came out at the same time and headed straight to the gate. They waited, weapons drawn and ready to defend their party, continuing to watch both the threatening looking warriors and the doors.

Then the doors were pulled open and out came Is-Is and Mr. Battfin, running towards them. Tumbletick and Egremont behind them, followed by Seton Rax, Campbell the Weasel and Percy Fenton. All except Tumbletick had weapons at hand as they ran. Tumbletick was clutching a shield shaped piece of stone. Success! No Nazar Grant though, a casualty? Y'Bor stepped forward towards the group, Beran slightly behind him. Y'Bor with his two warhammers, Beran, head bandaged and arm in a sling, holding his broadsword. Is-Is and Mr. Battfin cut down a couple of rioters who got in their way, their running party hardly halting in their fleeing strides. Beran pointed with his broadsword at the group of chain mailed warriors in the tight unit. Y'Bor looked and noticed that they were moving to intercept their companions at the gate and a chance of escape to the streets of Ende. They could easily see that if they did not slow them a bit then the tough guards would block the way. Y'Bor and Beran could see the look of concern on all their friend's faces as the other warriors closed on them and the gate. Y'Bor and Beran positioned themselves between the two advancing groups.

"Quick," shouted Y'Bor Kaz towards Tumbletick and company. "Make the gates! Make the gates! We'll hold them up a little."

The red headed warrior and bandaged paladin stood in front of the Landsknechts. Adomai had recognised the diversion as soon as he had managed to muster his men from individual combat. The Landsknecht leader begrudgingly acknowledged the tactic. Now it was about restoring order. He knew not if any of the men feared by his employer were in the riot but the experienced warrior could recognise a violent dash for freedom when he saw one. He could also recognise that the wounded knight and the flame haired barbarian were more than just usual opponents. He looked to the group making the run towards the gates. Yes they must have been the foes Rok had engaged his services for. There was the Umiat Stone being clutched by a deformed dwarf, desperate to keep up with his swifter companions. Adomai had twelve of his men with him. Others were posted in the main building and on the other side of the compound. They had quashed a fair amount of the rioting but it was now time to stop the main threat. Seven opponents in the group running from the heart of Beth Col, two heavily armed warriors, but one wounded in front of his own troops now. He had twelve so what was the split if he sent off some to intercept the running group? Adomai summed up the situation and decided none should break rank. They would all attack the knight and the smiling red head together.

"Quick," shouted Y'Bor Kaz towards Tumbletick and company. "Make the gates! Make the gates! We'll hold them up a little."

Is-Is and Mr. Battfin cut down another couple of obstacles and the rest of the rioting parted in front of the rampaging group. Y'Bor Kaz looked at the group of guards cantering towards him and Beran. If they gave ground then this group of fighters might make the gates first and cause a significant threat.

"Well my brother, are you ready?" Y'Bor asked Beran.

"As I said earlier. May we both be valiant," Beran replied.

Y'Bor Kaz turned his head and caught sight of Egremont and Tumbletick fleeing, he smiled as he saw the Umiat Stone held so tightly by his friend. Lifting his warhammers he strode forward. Beran beside him had a look of peace and contentment on his face, he raised his broadsword. Both men facing thirteen warriors felt calm and they engaged with yells and prowess as a rank of four Landsknechts came crashing against them.

Beran's first strike caught an opponent on the neck and the blade bit deep down and into the man's spine, killing him as he stood. The mercenary to his right thrust out with his spiked shield and punctured the plate mail of Beran with the strength of the blow. Beran felt the metal punch through his body and he stood looking into the face of the man who was about to kill him. The mercenary showed no anger, no fear. His companion had just died beside him but he felt nothing more than professionalism as he shoved the short stabbing sword through the throat of the wounded knight set in brief battle against them. Darkness took Beran and he fell to the ground when the Landsknecht pulled out his sword and shield from the paladin's standing corpse.

Y'Bor Kaz swung his warhammers in terrible frenzy, catching both the mercenaries in front of him with massive pummelling blows. One to the head and another on the shoulder. Both men fell, one dead the other injured but they were immediately replaced by another two. Y'Bor saw Beran kill one warrior but then be swiftly butchered by another. Y'Bor wished to revenge the death of his friend and still protect the fleeing others in the very instant that he saw the blade pass into Beran's throat. He knew he had a major battle to contend with now. Again he swung his weapons and smashed at the spiked shields raised against him. He was nearly surrounded as other Landsknechts moved in around him. He swung again with both warhammers and hit shields but his arms were left raised from the strength of his blows and he felt incredulous as two swords came swiftly stabbing towards him from behind the shields. One missed but the other thrust through his leather armour and into his side. Y'Bor raged in the pain. There came no second stroke to end his life and the agony. He was buying time for his friends now certainly but he could feel the blood gorging out of the wound and filling his own guts, stomach and throat. He wondered how much longer he could hold the threat up. He saw Beran's slumped body briefly and knew that he was to join him soon. 'A glorious death' he thought, 'What I once wished for with all my heart.' Y'Bor dropped to his knees and smashed with his warhammers below the level of the shield in front of him. He caught the shin of a man and took great joy when he saw the leg snap and the mercenary fall to the floor too. He tried to lash out with a strike with the war hammer in his right arm but found there was no strength left to even lift the weapon on that side of his body. He struck out again with the warhammer in his left hand but only managed to make contact with a deftly lowered shield. Y'Bor could feel that the adversary had no issue in defending the strike. He coughed up some blood and spat it on to the body of the one Landsknecht he had killed. He took little pleasure at having only taking one life, at least another two were wounded though and some time had been bought. Y'Bor looked up at the throng of shield baring mercenaries around him. They suddenly took a step back and one stepped forward. He was a large and brutal looking man, with pockmarked skin and a moustached that dropped beneath the level of his jaw. The man smiled and revealed missing teeth. The warrior lifted his sword, angled it correctly and shoved it into Y'Bor, through the collarbone and down through the torso.

Adomai pulled out the sword, Y'Bor Kaz slumped to his right. With his last sight, before darkness enclosed him as well, he saw Tumbletick and Egremont pass the burning wagon and make the streets of Ende. Y'Bor sighed his last sigh with a wry smile.

Is-Is and Mr. Battfin had made the broken gate. Beran was dead. Tumbletick and Egremont made the gate and Y'Bor Kaz died. Percy Fenton, Seton Rax and Campbell the Weasel made the gate. Campbell turned briefly and looked back, he saw the Landsknechts advancing again.

"Time to go guys!" the thief yelled. "Don't look back, just follow me!"

Campbell put on a turn of speed that was astounding and in the darkness of the streets of Ende he raced to the front of the group. Is-Is paused, sheathed a kukri and turned to lift Tumbletick, placing him on a hip and then bounded after Campbell towards the docks.

Adomai and his Landsknechts reached the broken gates and the burning wagon. Hunks of lumber lay around with destroyed masonry. Behind him bodies of rioters and warriors laid strewn in death and lasting agony. Two of his own men lay dead, two others were seriously wounded from the blows of the red headed warrior's warhammers.

The mercenary leader watched the fleeing group as they disappeared beyond the light of the burning wagon. His engagement was completed as agreed. 'Guard the compound.' He felt sure that the four men he had placed within the heart of Beth Col were probably dead, so six men likely lost but all their honour was still intact. The work had been completed as laid out by his more than likely dead employer.

"God speed," said Adomai aloud after the heels of Seton Rax disappeared. He turned back to his remaining men. "Right let's clear out the rest of this scum. When that's done I suspect we will be free to look for other employment."

Chorus Seventeen

They reached 'The Brazen Manticore' and clambered aboard whilst Mr. Battfin untied the mooring ropes before leaping aboard himself and headed straight to the helm. The hired pirates busied themselves and soon the ship was drifting away from the wharf, caught a breeze as a sail was unfurled and started to sail south. 'The Boreas' was soon following with its reduced crew and the two ships left in the dark, across the harbour and towards the Kenai Sea. The tip of the peninsular followed and then it was on into the Sea of Kaltag and the journey to Rhyell and Umiat beyond.

Tumbletick was slumped in the cabin still clutching the shield boss to his chest. All except Mr. Battfin sat in the confines of the covered few rooms with him.

"Was it worth it?" Tumbletick asked Egremont.

"Yes," the wolfhound starkly replied. "I only wish we had killed Vixen as well. But for the death of the Ahriman and the retrieval of the Umiat Stone it was worth it. Whether or not he was the real Ahriman is really unimportant. We have beheaded two men now who claim to be him. I know which one I suspect was the original. I also suspect that their disgusting religion will quake a little and falter now."

"Looks like Vixen left her pack behind," said Campbell pointing out her kit which was still stowed in the cabin.

"I suggest that if you opened it you would find that she took at least one item with her," said Egremont. "Look for her diary in there Campbell."

The thief crawled over and deftly undid the straps to the bag. He rummaged through her possessions as only a thief can, looked up and shook his head.

"Not surprised," said the wolfhound. "I should have known though."

"Egremont," whispered Tumbletick. "When I was alone with Vixen and the others she said something to me about Lord Jackson."

"What did she say?"

"She said he was a traitor too and a believer in Ahrioch."

"And did you believe her?"

"No. Not really Egremont. I thought she was just trying to hurt me."

"I think you were right to think that. Lord Jackson of En'Tuk was well known to me Tumbletick and I doubt that he was what she said he was."

"Thank you Egremont," said Tumbletick. He closed his eyes and with the gentle swaying of the boat he fell asleep with the wolfhound on one side of him and the hare on the other.

Seton Rax found himself looking around the ship with the knowledge that he was the one last remaining member of the party that had entered the Old City on Rampart only a few weeks before. He wondered what the future would bring him now but he felt certain he had gained new adventurous companions should he need them. He thought back to the money Nazar, Beran, Garraday and he had received in notes rather than the coins that remained at the merchant's house in the Old City. Perhaps he would find another group who would be prepared to head back there in search of the chest and the gold. He thought that perhaps someone else had found that trap now and he wished he had taken the two thousand five hundred in promissory notes from Garraday, Beran and Nazar before they had died. With those thoughts of resentment and foolishness in his head he closed his eyes and tried to forget it. His original quest had been all about the search for wealth. Now he had been part of something much greater but he did need to think about his future too. Suddenly his eyes opened and looked towards the packs that Beran and Nazar had left on board the ship when they had set out on the final mission to Beth Col. Perhaps they had left him a final gift with which he could drink to their memory and take reward from the adventure they had originally set off together on.

They all fell asleep in the cabin except for Is-Is who kept a watchful eye on Tumbletick beside him. The hare put his arm around the little man and pulled him close. Tumbletick's head slumped and rested on Is-Is' chest. Is-Is gave a broad smile and thought back to the days when Tumbletick had been a child, all innocent playing in Egremont's castle. Then back to the days when he had moved to his hut and been happy guarding his father's grave and the Umiat Stone in ignorance of what both really meant. Then the hare reflected on Tumbletick's current journey and thought that because of it the two would be closer than ever, more understanding of each other. Is-Is closed his eyes too and relaxed. They had about a week at sea before they arrived at Rhyell and Is-Is looked forward to sleeping for most of it.

Mr. Battfin came into the cabin when they had cleared the vast harbour of Ende. He trod lightly through his sleeping companions and gave Percy Fenton a firm shake of the shoulder. Fenton gave a slight moan, got up and went to stand at the wheel on deck. Mr. Battfin slumped next to Seton Rax, who was hugging the packs of his dead friends and fell asleep.

Chapter Eighteen

Princess Annabella Blaise stood with her new chamberlain in the nave of Rhyell Cathedral. Egremont the Lord Seau du Duvet stood with Is-Is, Campbell the Weasel, Mr. Battfin, Seton Rax, Percy Fenton and Tumbletick. They had been back in Rhyell for a day and messages had been sent to the princess that the quest had been a success and that the Umiat Stone should be set again in its rightful place. There was to be no major ceremony today and the cathedral was empty except for them, a detachment of palace guards and the artisan who was climbing the wooden scaffold towards the ceiling. They all watched as the man at the roof took little scoops of cement from the bag he had carried with him and fixed the Umiat Stone back in the space which had remained vacant for so long. The craftsman held the shield boss in place for a while and then satisfied that it was secure he began to descend, removing the scaffolding as he did so.

"Well that is that then," said the princess turning to leave.

"Your highness," said Egremont. "The Umiat Stone has been returned and I would remind you of your father's pledge."

"We have been through this before my Lord," Princess Annabella Blaise replied. "I will not marry your ward despite the great service he has provided."

"That is fine your highness," replied Egremont giving a great and pronounced bow. He stood again and looked the princess directly in the eye. "It turns out that Tumbletick does not wish to marry you either. I just wanted to remind you of the pledge. That is all."

With that Tumbletick and Egremont walked towards the great doors of the cathedral. The other followed. The princess was left to consider Egremont's words as the artisan continued to throw bits of wood to the floor, the clattering shattering the silence.

Outside the cathedral the remains of the party looked across the city to the nearby castle and at the small round object on the tallest spike. They mused silently for a while in front of the massive granite nave and then shook hands with each other.

Seton Rax was to head to the northwest plains beyond Noatak. His lust for adventure had been well sated. He had admitted his thoughts of taking the money that he had found in Beran's and Nazar's pack and Campbell had been the first to speak up for the barbarian. Egremont had agreed and had insisted that he be paid an additional two thousand five hundred for the money that had been lost when Garraday had been killed by Eblis. Rich now, all ten thousand his, Seton Rax said that he intended to head back home and start a safer business than adventuring.

Mr. Battfin and Percy Fenton were to head back to the docks and take 'The Brazen Manticore' and look for the rest of their fleet and get back to 'The Ardent Panda' as soon as they could. Percy told the rest of the group that Mr. Battfin was to be made up to a captain himself and would take command of 'The Brazen Manticore'. There was a great deal of back slapping and congratulations for the worthy man but all he did was show the slightest of twitches at the corner of his lips in recognition of the adulation. Both pirates intended to search for and find Vixen if they could and bring her to justice. Every ship that approached Umiat in the next few months was extremely likely to be boarded and the traitor looked for.

Egremont and Is-Is were to go with Tumbletick back to his hut in the grounds of the Lord Seau du Duvet's castle. Campbell asked if he could tag along for a while too before he decided what was next for his career. He did consider becoming a pirate again and help find Vixen in order to finish their unfinished fight but the thought of being with Tumbletick, Egremont and Is-Is for a while longer was appealing.

The grouped hugged each other in final farewells. Then they separated and with last looks over shoulders they walked off in differing directions.

Egremont, Is-Is, Tumbletick and Campbell took their time walking towards the north. They stopped at 'The Ram' for an excellent evening meal, Tumbletick was pleased to see the pigtailed waitress again and it struck him that she remembered him too but could have had no concept of what he had been through since she last served him. They could have slept at 'The Ram' but decided to sleep rough over night as they still had the tent with them. They found a campsite away from the main track and lit a roaring fire on the plains of Umiat. Conversation ran late into the night of their adventures and they slept late the next day.

When eventually they did make it to Egremont's home they decided that to take some supplies down to Tumbletick's hut and have a drunken night together, roasting meat on an extremely large fire, would be extremely pleasant indeed. Egremont's servants were surprised to see their master and his companions but they had kept his ancestral home well run and they soon had large trays of thick cut meat and two wooden crates of bottled ale for them to carry down to Tumbletick's copse.

Tumbletick was full of skips and excited agitation as he drew close to his humble home. He pushed his way through the thick trees and into the little clearing. With great joy he opened the door, hanging still on one hinge and threw himself down onto the bed of leaves and bracken.

"Nice place you've got here Tumbletick," said Campbell looking around the door and into the single room. "Ought to get this door fixed though."

The thief got out his roll of tools and went to work on the broken hinge.

"You know," said Egremont. "You ought to take the rest of Jackson's money Tumbletick. You might not have got the reward we wanted for you but surely there is something you could do with our friend Jackson's wealth."

Campbell pulled a slight face as he worked as if he thought that the others might have forgotten about the remaining money now.

Tumbletick stuck his head from out of his bed where he still relished. Leaves and twigs attached themselves to his hair. He looked at his friends crowded around the door. Campbell on his knees, fixing the lower hinge and Egremont and Is-Is standing in the last light within the frame.

"You know Egremont that I would like to stay here but there is something else I would like to do as well."

"And what is that Tumbletick?"

"Well with your permission I'd like upgrade the hut a little. You know, a little more permanence as I am going to stay here to tend the grave of my father."

"Of course. No problem at all. We'll get some proper artisans in though to help this time. Not just me and Is-Is hey?"

"Thanks Egremont. There is something else as well though."

"What is it?"

"Well, I've developed quite a taste for beer on our travels. Really, really enjoyed some of them. I'd like to use the money to build a little brewery and craft my own beers."

"An admirable decision Tumbletick. I think you'll make an excellent brewer. A fine profession. I'm sure you'll have plenty of friends now who will want to drop by and sample the ales you create."

"Great idea," said Campbell, standing up now and testing the door a little. "There is easily enough money for you to build quite a nice little outfit."

"Will you let me build it next to the copse Egremont?" asked Tumbletick.

"Of course," the wolfhound replied. "It will be nice having a brewery on the doorstep. Most convenient indeed, especially when you know the Head Brewer!"

"I'd like to name some of my beers after the friends that we lost."

"I think that they would have liked that Tumbletick," Egremont replied.

By nightfall Is-Is had erected the tent and was constructing a very large fire pit in the soft earth around Tumbletick's hut. Campbell and Egremont had collected vast amounts of dry wood in the easiest expedition for fuel they had had. They had already stacked burgeoning bundles around the fire pit and the blaze they were likely to build looked as if it would dwarf the fire they had fought beside at Kantishna. Tumbletick was spitting steaks with sharp sticks he had whittled with the dagger he still carried with him that Campbell had given to him in the octagonal chamber in Beth Col. Tumbletick kind of wished he had stolen the curved knife from the dead hands of Ahriman as it would have made a very interesting conversation piece and maybe a logo for his brewery.

The fire was started, beers drunk and meat roasted. For the second night in a row they stayed up late talking. This night, however, was more pleasant with the addition of the ale and meat and the further promise of Tumbletick's own bed and a very spacious tent.

"What about Vixen then Egremont?" asked Tumbletick at one point in the evening.

"Well she'll probably be spending a lot of time avoiding pirates and her own people in the secret service. The princess has been advised of her treachery and there will be a substantial price on her head," he replied.

"I'll be looking for her too," said Campbell. "She probably thinks she won that fight with me but I was trying to lull her into a false sense of victory when I faked that stumble. Then she ran away as if possessed."

"I wouldn't worry about her coming here," said Egremont. "Plus you will always have Is-Is or I nearby."

They drifted into a comfortable silence, listening to the fire burn and looking at the stars through the canopy of the copse. They were full of fine meat and relaxed by the beer when Egremont raised a toast to their lost friends Y'Bor, Beran, Nazar Grant and Lord Jackson. Then he set four more bottles, just opened by the fire. They drank deeply in respect and fond remembrance and then just sat in silence with their own thoughts of their recent adventure.

Tumbletick fell asleep very much at peace and did not feel Is-Is gently lift him, place him on the pile of leaves and bracken in his hut and then silently shut the now well hinged door.

THE END